A PROMISE OF LOVE

"It wasn't supposed to happen this way, Sarah. I didn't mean to fall in love with you. I knew better."

Sarah smiled at him, tears welling in her eyes. She knew this was insane, but she didn't care. She wanted to make love with Keller. She wanted to share with him what she knew she would never be able to share with another man. She wanted to give to him the only thing she had to give, before he went way. "You can't hurt me, Keller. Your love never could."

"Sarah . . ."

He seemed so torn between duty and logic and what he felt for her.

"It's all right," she whispered.

"Didn't you hear what I said? They might send me away. They might replace you."

"It's all right," she repeated. She was kissing him; he was kissing her, their kisses growing more urgent with every passing moment. "It doesn't matter."

"I don't want to lose you," Keller whispered desperately.

"So let me give you a part of me." She laid her hand over his, guiding him, urging him to touch her as no man had ever touched her before. "Let me give you a part of me you'll never forget no matter where you go." Their gazes locked. "I need this, Keller. I need to share this with you."

"Oh, Sarah, Sarah, I'll find a way." He was kissing her again. "I'll find a way for us to be together. I swear I will!"

—from "Man of My Dreams," by Colleen Faulkner

To Love And To Honor

**PHOEBE CONN
COLLEEN FAULKNER
DEBRA HAMILTON
VICTORIA THOMPSON**

**ZEBRA BOOKS
KENSINGTON PUBLISHING CORP.**

CONTENTS

A GROOM FOR HOLLY
by Phoebe Conn   7

MAN OF MY DREAMS
by Colleen Faulkner   93

DAISIES
by Debra Hamilton   175

THE WRONG MAN
by Victoria Thompson   263

A Groom for Holly

by
Phoebe Conn

One

John Cochrane got down on one knee. "Please, Holly, I'm begging you. Sam Driscoll is the best friend any man could ever hope to have, and he's desperately lonely. I've tried to help him, but he needs the benefit of a woman's insight. He raises the swiftest horses in all of Virginia, and his father's death last year left him a wealthy man. He lost his mother when he was small, and that's undoubtedly why he lacks all hint of refinement. He wants a wife so badly, but he just can't seem to impress a woman on his own. Please say you'll help him, and I'll be forever in your debt."

Although Holly was touched by her brother's poignant plea, she simply did not feel up to the challenge. She fidgeted nervously with her ivory fan. "You might just as well ask me to turn lead into gold," she replied. "Now get up off your knees. You look ridiculous."

John remained planted at his sister's feet. At twenty-six, he was nine years her senior, but Holly was an enchanting hazel-eyed blonde who had an abundance of beaux and he was positive she was precisely the tutor his friend required. "You offer such sage advice to your female friends when they want to catch a man's eye. I know you can help Sam learn how to please a woman. He's sure to win the races held during Publick Times, and if he could dance the minuet at the Governor's Ball, then—"

"My God!" Holly gasped. "You expect me to teach that lumbering oaf how to dance?"

"He's not clumsy," John argued. "He's just never been taught how a man ought to stand and sit. I don't believe his father ever discussed anything except horses with him; and since he lacked a mother's influence, it's no wonder he's awkward around women. He has such a good heart though, Holly. He would make a fine husband. He just needs a chance to learn how a gentleman ought to behave."

John was a handsome young man with hair a few shades darker than Holly's honey-blonde and eyes of the same golden brown. He was as protective of her as their father was, and she had always trusted his judgment. This was the first time she could recall his coming to her to ask a favor. She was enormously flattered and would have gladly granted him anything else.

Holly shook her head sadly. "Isn't there a pretty wench at the Raleigh or one of the other taverns who would be delighted with Sam's money and overlook his lack of manners?"

John's expression fell. "There are probably dozens, but he deserves better than a serving wench. He has property and a fine home, although I will admit the house also suffers from neglect."

Holly could not accept this new demand any more calmly than she had the others. "You can't possibly expect me to redecorate the man's home as well."

"No, of course not. Just help Sam acquire a little polish, and the woman he chooses can tear down the house and build a new one if she likes. Sam can afford it." John gave Holly's knee a tender squeeze. "Please, Holly. Think of Sam as an orphan who's bereft of love and lend your support as an act of charity. We have three weeks before the Publick Times begin in April. I've already gone with him to our tailor and helped him order new clothes and fine shoes so he won't have to wear buckskins and moccasins."

Most of her brother's friends were from families like theirs who raised tobacco on prosperous plantations. The young men had all been classmates together at the College of William and Mary and were delightful companions who lacked for nothing in either appearance or manners. Sam Driscoll, however, had little to recommend him other than the speed of his magnificent horses. Holly considered that asset a moment and then poked John in the chest with a beautifully manicured nail.

"You're forgetting just how well I know you, John Robert. Now tell me what Sam Driscoll's offered you in exchange for my help."

John's eyes widened in surprise. "He's a good friend. I'd not demand payment for doing him a favor."

Holly regarded her brother's display of stunned innocence with a skeptical frown; and just as she had expected, in mere seconds, his carefully posed expression began to waver. "He's promised you a colt or two, hasn't he?"

John struggled to his feet and, not truly wishing to fool his sister, admitted the truth. "Yes. He has offered me my pick of his stock, but the idea was his, Holly. I told him I'd ask for your help, and he insisted upon paying me."

Holly was wearing a charming muslin gown in a white print sprinkled with delicate bouquets of violets. She adjusted the drape of her skirt before looking up. "Let me see if I understand this correctly. I am to do you this enormous favor and teach your friend, who cannot even walk through a doorway without lurching into the jamb, how to dance the minuet—as well as how to impress women with something other than his horsemanship—and you are the one who's to receive the expensive colt."

John plucked a piece of dark lint from the front of

his white waistcoat and then clasped his hands behind his back. "I didn't mean to give you the impression that I'd not show my gratitude in some meaningful way."

"Really?" Holly rose to face him. He was easily a head taller than she, but she had never been intimidated by his height. As she saw it, she would be wise to secure his expression of gratitude now, before it became obvious to him that he had asked the impossible. Then, her lack of results, rather than her valiant effort, would be the issue.

"I doubt the finest French dancing master could successfully teach Sam Driscoll the graceful moves of the minuet," she declared, "but as an incentive for me to begin what is surely a great folly, I'd like a gown made from the bolt of exquisite lavender satin my dressmaker received only this week."

John was horrified by the extravagance of that demand. "You expect me to pay for one of your gowns!" he exclaimed.

Holly folded her arms across her bosom and tapped her foot lightly. "The expense will be slight compared to the miracle you've asked of me. If Sam Driscoll's friendship isn't worth the price of a gown to you, then forget it. Of course, if I don't tutor him, then you'll not receive the prize colt either, will you?"

John was continually amazed by his sister. From the day Holly had learned how to talk, he feared she had outwitted him. "You are a manipulative little witch," he described darkly.

Holly's smile grew wide. "Precisely, which is why you came to me in the first place. Frankly, I don't believe three weeks is nearly enough time. You ought to have come to me at the beginning of the year."

John readily agreed. "I've been working with Sam myself since then. He's made great progress, too. He still dresses like a frontiersman, but he'll have his new clothes soon and that's sure to be a big improvement."

"It will have to be. When will you see him? We ought to begin the first morning he can come for a lesson."

John's whole face lit with a triumphant grin. "He's here now. I asked him to wait on the steps until I'd talked with you."

"You didn't!" Holly lost all patience with her brother. "What if I'd said no? Didn't you realize how cruel it would have been to get Sam's hopes up and then have to tell him I'd refused?"

"I would have kept begging until midnight," John swore, "but I would never have let you refuse."

Holly rested her hands on her hips. "The new gown is merely the beginning, John. If I have to exhaust myself teaching Sam Driscoll to be a gentleman, then you are going to see that I am well rewarded."

Elated that she had agreed to begin, John grabbed her shoulders and kissed her cheek. "I won't voice another complaint. You have time now, don't you? Let me bring him in."

Holly was afraid she had made an awful mistake, but tried to imagine how beautiful she would look at the Governor's Ball in lavender satin. She thought she probably ought to go into town that morning to order the gown, but could not send Sam away for such a frivolous reason. "Does he still have a beard?"

"No. I convinced him to shave it off last month."

"Well, that's a relief, but I've no idea where to begin. I'm no dancing master, and—"

"You said yes, Holly, and I won't let you go back on your word." John left the parlor at a run, and his footsteps echoed across the highly polished pine as he crossed the entryway.

Holly could hear a low rumbling murmur as John talked to Sam and prayed Sam would have sense enough to bolt rather than put himself through what would surely be a fruitless ordeal; but in the next instant, he followed John into the parlor. Holly thought it could easily have been a year or more since she had last seen Sam Driscoll, but she would have recognized him anywhere.

Slightly above six feet in height, he had a well-muscled build. His buckskins made it easy to appreciate his broad shoulders and narrow hips; but his dark brown hair, while tied at his nape, was too long, lending him as wild an appearance as he had had with a beard. His averted glance made it apparent he was as badly embarrassed as she, and Holly decided to take her brother's advice and regard whatever help she might provide as a charitable act. Gathering her courage, she went forward to greet Sam.

"Good morning, Mr. Driscoll. I can't recall the last time we spoke, but I'm flattered that you've sought my advice."

Sam swore softly under his breath, and John jabbed him in the ribs with his elbow to silence the curse before it reached Holly's ears. Sam's head came up with a jerk, and he fixed Holly with a defiant stare. "A man ought not to have to prance around to music like a damn fool to impress a woman," he declared emphatically.

Sam's eyes were gray and framed with dark expressive brows and thick lashes. Without the full beard to hide his well-shaped mouth and dimpled chin, he was surprisingly handsome. Holly had not expected that; but knowing it would provide a decided advantage in his quest, she began to relax. "You're absolutely right, Mr. Driscoll, and let me assure you that what any woman wants is a man of good character who will provide for her; but first you must attract her attention. Being able to dance well will allow you to do that."

Holly's manner was so warmly inviting that Sam nodded rather than argue. Then he turned to John. "I hope you didn't plan to stay and laugh."

Holly came forward to take Sam's arm. "Of course he's not going to stay. Our lessons will be completely private. Goodbye, John." Holly waited until her brother had given her a cocky grin and left the room to continue. She glanced around the parlor, then drew Sam over to the open area near the harpsichord. She released her hold after giving him a light pat and stepped back.

"The Governor's Ball is a fabulous party. They must light the ballroom with a thousand candles, and the musicians are always inspired to perform their most beautiful music. John told me you're having a suit made; and if you trim your hair, you'll be quite dashing." Sam shot her a darkly menacing glance, and Holly took immediate exception to it.

"Don't you dare look at me like that, Mr. Driscoll, or I'll ask you to leave right now and not return. If I'm going to offer my time and expertise to teach you to dance, you'll have to be a good deal more cooperative."

Sam looked away. The Cochranes' parlor was painted a pale amber and decorated with beautiful fruitwood furniture upholstered in forest greens and golds. It looked like a palace to him, and he felt as out of place there as he knew he would at the governor's mansion. He had not thought John could actually convince Holly to help him and was ashamed both to have had to ask and for needing it.

"I'm sorry," he murmured grudgingly, "but no one's ever going to describe me as dashing, so I'd rather you kept such fanciful thoughts to yourself."

Perplexed by his demand, Holly took a long moment to reply. "I realize this isn't going to be easy for either of us, Mr. Driscoll; but if you follow my instructions carefully, you will indeed impress the woman of your dreams. I don't mean to be presumptuous, but is there someone in particular whose heart you'd like to win? If

I know her, I might be able to offer more specific suggestions to help you succeed."

Sam looked down at the toes of his moccasins and shook his head. "I don't dare hope for anyone in particular," he stressed. "I'm just praying there will be at least one woman in Williamsburg who won't find me too rough-hewn for her tastes." He glanced up then. "All I need is one."

Holly did not think she had ever heard anything sadder in her whole life. Her first impulse was to hug him, but she curbed it as totally improper and relied instead on the sweetness of her smile to convey her optimism. "Yes. We'll hold that thought. Today, let's concentrate on the basics of dancing. First, take my hand."

Sam wiped his right hand on his pant leg and reached out for her. "Wait a minute," Holly implored him. "When did you last wash your hands?"

Insulted, Sam again turned belligerent. "I washed them outside just before I came in. I know enough to do that."

"Yes. Of course you do. I was just afraid you might be worried they were dirty. Well, no matter." She extended her hand, and he grabbed it so tightly she winced. "Please, Mr. Driscoll. You needn't hold me as though you were about to yank me from a rain-swollen creek. You must use a very gentle clasp. Here, let me show you."

Holly pulled her hand from his and then placed her thumb on the back of his hand and her fingers against his palm. His skin was deeply tanned. His fingers were long and slim and not at all unpleasant to touch. "There. You want to exert as gentle a pressure as you would collecting eggs from your henhouse."

Sam responded with a derisive snort. "If women were as fragile as eggs, they'd never survive childbirth."

Taken aback, Holly wondered what could have possessed him to push her innocent advice in such an indelicate direction. "That may very well be true, Mr. Driscoll, but references to childbirth are totally out of place in a polite conversation between you and any young woman you might wish to impress. Now, you're simply going to guide your partner through the steps, but she'll know them and need no more than a feather-light touch to respond."

When Holly released him and gestured for him to again take her hand, Sam tried to be gentle, but his grasp was still far too firm. "A light touch is greatly admired, Mr. Driscoll. I wish there were a way for you to practice. I could stuff one of my gloves so you would have something to hold, but you'd have no way of knowing if you were doing it correctly."

Sam dropped his hands to his sides. "I've got much better things to do with my time than fondle your old gloves, Miss Cochrane."

"Then you think of something," Holly scolded. "I'd like to move on to the steps of the minuet, but how you hold your partner's hand will set the whole tone for the dance."

Sam could not understand how. "Just give me your hand, and I'll try and do better."

Holly was pleased he was at least making an effort and offered her hand, but again he held her much too tightly. "Have you ever returned a baby bird to its nest?" she asked.

Sam nodded and tried to imagine Holly's hand as being that fragile. She felt very soft and warm, and when her fingertips brushed his skin, the erotic image that flashed through his mind had nothing whatsoever to do with dancing. He quickly released her and began to back away. "I can't do this after all," he apologized. "I can't touch you and think at the same time."

That he would be so bashful was another surprise. "That's very sweet, Mr. Driscoll, but other men manage that same feat and I think, with more practice, you'll master it, too. Let's stop for today and begin at the same time tomorrow."

Greatly relieved, Sam was so eager to be on his way he backed into a delicate Queen Anne chair, but turned in time to grab it before it crashed to the floor. He then set it aside with exaggerated care. "I'd just be wasting your time," he complained.

He had just provided a perfect example of the clumsiness her brother had denied, but somehow, it now struck Holly as endearing. He was, after all, a man who spent his time out of doors training horses, and it was no wonder his gestures were too broad for their parlor. She hastened to reassure him. "The fault is undoubtedly mine, Mr. Driscoll. I've never taught anyone to dance before, and obviously I'm doing it poorly. Will you please be a little more patient with me?"

"It's not your fault," Sam insisted, "and we both know it. I'd rather you didn't lie to me, Miss Cochrane. Do all women twist the truth so shamelessly?"

"I'm not lying!" Holly fumed, convinced she had merely been polite. She raised her fingertips to her temple. "Oh, my goodness." She had expected tutoring Sam Driscoll to be difficult, but she had not dreamed it would be this exasperating. "John asked me to help you only this morning, so I had no time to prepare, and I do honestly believe I must be approaching this incorrectly or you'd not be shouting at me. Now I positively insist that you return tomorrow, and I'll endeavor not to disappoint you again."

Sam looked her up and down. From her golden curls to her tiny slippers, she was the most perfect young woman he had ever seen, so he did not understand how she could think he was disappointed. "I'll bet your beaux all know how to dance, don't they?"

"Let's not concern ourselves with what other men

may or may not be able to do, Mr. Driscoll. John and I learned to dance as children, as did a great many of our friends."

Sam's frown deepened. "I can't even remember being a child."

Again, Holly felt an almost overpowering impulse to embrace the solemn young man, but she feared he would misinterpret the gesture as pity and be deeply offended. She contented herself with slipping her arm through his and walking him to the door. "I've seen you with John; and because I knew your name, I felt as though I knew you, but that was my mistake. Tomorrow, let's spend some time getting acquainted before we try dancing again. It may seem unnecessary to you, but the practice will help you speak with other young women more easily."

"I think maybe I'd be better off just to keep my mouth shut."

Holly gave his arm a fond squeeze as she pulled away. "Everyone has something valuable to contribute, Mr. Driscoll; and if you don't speak, a woman will swiftly grow discouraged and think you don't like her. It would be a shame if that happened after you've gone to the trouble of buying new clothes and learning to dance."

Sam opened the door and began inching through it. "I've not learned a single step yet."

"You just keep coming back, and I promise you'll learn to dance." Sam responded with a skeptical glance and walked off toward his horse, but Holly remained at the open door to watch him. When he wasn't so terribly self-conscious, his gait had an agile grace, and Holly hoped she could encourage him to show it on the dance floor.

John tiptoed up behind his sister and whispered. "How did he do?"

Holly took the precaution of closing the door before she replied. She leaned back against it and tried to find a way to describe their first lesson, but she feared it had been a dismal failure. "Sam Driscoll is the saddest individual I've ever met, and I'm afraid all I did was depress him further. Dancing is supposed to be fun, but he acts as though it were some ritual torture he has to endure to impress a woman."

John laughed. "He's not the only man who thinks that way; but all he has to do is walk through a minuet, and surely you can teach him how to do it."

"I can only promise to try."

"That's all I ask."

John winked and walked away, but Holly remained where she stood. She believed Sam Driscoll did indeed have a good heart, and now hers ached for him.

Holly rode into Williamsburg that afternoon with her friends Roger and Caroline Wincott in their carriage. Roger was twenty-four. Fair-haired and slender, he prided himself on his discriminating tastes and kept Holly and his sixteen-year-old sister entertained the whole way with his sly observations on their friends' foibles. Holly's hand lay in Roger's; and as she observed the grace of his elaborate gestures, she realized just how impossible it would be to turn Sam Driscoll into an equally impressive young man in three short weeks.

Roger wore his costly apparel with a casual self-assurance that served to focus everyone's attention on him rather than the well-tailored garments. That day he was wearing a brown suit with a blue satin waistcoat. The lace at his throat and cuffs was as beautiful as any adorning Holly's gowns. Like most young men, he powdered his hair rather than wear a wig, but the effect was equally striking.

Holly had always admired Roger enormously; and as soon as her parents had allowed her to have callers, he had been among the first of her brother's friends to visit her. She enjoyed his attentions and, grateful for his advice, frequently invited him to accompany her to the dressmaker's. Caroline giggled more than she spoke, but Holly preferred having her along to a more conventional chaperon.

The capital of the Virginia colony since it had been relocated from Jamestown in 1699, Williamsburg had been carefully planned by the Royal Governor, Francis Nicholson. Stretching a mile between the College of William and Mary and the Capitol, Duke of Gloucester Street, the main thoroughfare, was lined with shops catering to the needs of plantation owners and townspeople alike. Holly loved to come into town simply to shop and visit with friends and did so often. That Roger preferred her company to that of the young men who whiled away the afternoons playing billiards in the back room of the Raleigh Tavern was one of the many things she liked about him.

The spring day was bright; Roger was in high spirits, and Holly was eager to order the gown her brother had promised to buy. As their driver pulled the team of matched bays to a stop outside Sally Lester's shop, she took note of the other carriage parked nearby. "Please, Roger, tell me that Annette Hemby isn't here."

Roger waited for the footman to open the door and then stepped down from the carriage. He walked over to the dressmaker's window, glanced in, and then came back to report what he had seen. "Miss Hemby is indeed at Mrs. Lester's. Let's go for a stroll until she leaves."

He offered his hand, but Holly was reluctant to leave the carriage. "I despise the bitch," she whispered to Caroline. "She tied my dear brother's heart in a knot and then threw it back to him."

Caroline's pale blue eyes widened in horror. "You don't mean it!"

Caroline was a pretty little thing, but Holly had never

thought her particularly bright and feared she had confused her. "Metaphorically speaking, of course," she added. She placed her hand in Roger's, and his touch provided precisely the correct amount of pressure to ease her from the carriage without making her feel like a recalcitrant child.

"How is it that you never fell under Annette's spell?" Holly inquired of her escort.

Roger raised her hand to his lips. "I am immune to all women's charms except yours, my pet."

While he sounded sincere, Holly had learned never to take anything Roger said too seriously. "I'm flattered, but tell me the truth. You have such a discerning eye, have you found a flaw others miss?"

Roger helped his sister from the carriage and then drew both young women close to respond. "With her sable hair and blue eyes, she is a striking creature; but rather than elegant, I fear her neck is a triffle too long. Have you never noticed that she resembles a goose more closely than a swan?"

"Oh, Roger!" Caroline erupted in a fit of giggles, while Holly merely smiled.

"In truth, I had not made that connection," Holly admitted, "but now that you've brought it to my attention, I most definitely will. Come, let's go in Mrs. Lester's, and I'll look Annette over right now."

Roger hurried to open the door, and Holly led the way inside. The dressmaker's shop was one of her favorites, filled with beautiful fabrics and fine lace. The air was always scented with expensive perfume. Roger Wincott was one of the few men who dared step through the door, but he did so often and without the slightest hesitation.

Rather than the length of Annette's slender neck, what caught Holly's attention was the bolt of lavender satin Sally Lester had spread over the counter. She held her

breath, praying Annette would show no interest in the
fabric, but the brunette had already made it her choice.
She spoke in a low, sultry whisper.

"I must have the gown in time for the Governor's
Ball, Mrs. Lester, and it must be the most beautiful dress
you have ever made."

"You shall have it, my dear. Let's schedule your fit-
tings now." Before consulting her appointment book,
Sally greeted Holly and her friends with a smile. "I'll
be right with you."

"Take all the time you need," Holly replied graciously,
but she turned her back on the counter and made a furious face only Roger and Caroline could see. As could
be expected, Caroline smothered her giggles behind her
fan, while Roger gave Holly's arm a sympathetic
squeeze.

Holly wished she had come into town that morning,
but refused to blame Sam Driscoll for delaying the trip.
He was already so heavily burdened she would never
mention Annette Hemby had just purchased the satin she
was positive had been meant for her. She leaned close
to Roger. "With her milk-white complexion, lavender
won't even be pretty."

Roger cocked a brow. "Shall I tell her that? It might
be amusing to convince her she would look better in
green."

Holly glanced over her shoulder. Annette was bending
over Sally Lester's appointment book, selecting a time;
and now that Roger had planted the image in her mind,
she had to agree the brunette's neck was too long. Perhaps her sloping shoulders contributed to the picture,
but rather than the graceful beauty Holly had seen before, she now saw a goose stretching her neck to snap
up a tasty kernal of corn. She had to turn back to her
companions to hide her laugh.

Her business in the elegant shop concluded, Annette

paused before leaving. "Good afternoon, Roger, Caroline, and Holly. My goodness, I haven't seen you in ever so long, Holly. Have you been ill?"

Holly had simply been avoiding her, but forced a smile. "Not at all. We merely have a different circle of friends now that I choose mine more carefully."

That insult registered in a slight upward twitch of Annette's brows; but too well-mannered to reply in kind, she reached out to caress Roger's sleeve and then left.

Holly opened her fan to stir the air. "It smells better in here already."

"I think the shop always smells like perfume," Caroline remarked innocently.

Roger slipped his arm around his sister's shoulders. "Isn't she a delight?" he asked, but he rolled his eyes to reveal his true feelings.

Holly moved to the counter and ran her hands over the lovely bolt of lavender satin. "I'd thought about ordering a gown made of this, Sally, but I'd sooner go to the Governor's Ball nude than dressed in the same fabric as Annette Hemby."

A model of discretion, Sally refrained from entering her customer's feud and instead gestured toward her other satins. "This bright gold would be glorious with your eyes, or perhaps you'd prefer this lovely apricot."

Holly had had her heart set on the lavender and was sorry she had not had a way to pay for it earlier. Her parents were generous, but she had already ordered several new gowns that spring and had not wanted to abuse their benevolence. Now she felt cheated and was angry she had been too late to have her first choice.

"What do you think, Roger?" she asked.

Roger rubbed the lavender satin between his finger and thumb. "This has a rich feel, but with your tawny coloring the gold will be absolutely magnificent."

Holly brushed his cheek with a light kiss. "Thank you. Please show us your latest designs, Mrs. Lester, and I'd appreciate it if you would delete the one Miss Hemby chose."

"Certainly," Sally agreed; but because Annette had the crystalline beauty of a winter night and Holly, a summery warmth, she knew she could dress them in identical designs and no one would ever notice.

As they rode home later that afternoon, Holly pressed Roger's hand. "You are always a joy to be with, Roger. Was it an effort to acquire the polish you display no matter what the occasion?"

"An effort?" Roger was nonplussed by the question, but provided a lucid response. "Gentlemen are born, Holly, not pieced together like one of your beautiful gowns. Whatever made you ask such a question?"

Holly simply smiled and shook her head rather than reveal she had embarked upon the impossible task of making a gentleman of Sam Driscoll. She knew better than to ask Roger's advice when he would surely dissolve into a giggling fit that would rival his sister's. No, she and John would do their very best for Sam and, if they had to, pay Roger and his kind not to laugh.

Two

Sam Driscoll arrived at the Cochrane home for his second lesson clutching a handful of wilted sweet peas. He thrust them into Holly's hands and stepped back. "I picked these for you this morning, but I guess I should have kept them in water."

Holly inhaled the pastel flowers' delicate fragrance and responded with a delighted smile. "They're beautiful, Mr. Driscoll. I'll just trim their stems, put them in water, and they'll soon look as though they were freshly picked."

She took his arm to guide him into the parlor and then borrowed her mother's tiny sterling silver embroidery shears and worked at the tea table. "I'm surprised you have the time to grow flowers. I assumed tending your horses would keep you, too busy."

Sam frowned slightly, then stammered a halting reply. "I don't actually have a flower garden, Miss Cochrane. On the ride over, I just saw those growing wild and grabbed some."

That it had been a spontaneous rather than a carefully planned gesture didn't diminish the gift's appeal in Holly's mind. "Well, thank you anyway. They're lovely. I'll add these to this bouquet for the moment, but later I'll find a vase for them and take them up to my room." Holly slipped the sweet peas into a bowl of white camellias, where their lacy prettiness added a nice touch of color. She laid the dainty pair of scissors aside and then looked up at her reluctant pupil.

"You trimmed your hair!" she exclaimed, then feared she had been tactless. "What I mean is, you'll now look more sophisticated when you begin wearing your new clothes."

Sam's hair had a slight wave; and now that he had hacked off a good six inches, it not only made it easier to tie at his nape, it curled under like the most expensive wig. He missed the weight of it on his shoulders, though, and hoped it would not take long to grow back. "You're awfully obliging, Miss Cochrane. Do you have some pretty friends who are as easy to please?"

"Yes. I'll introduce you to as many as I can during Publick Times, so, by the ball, you'll know them all. '

Sam looked down and shuffled his feet. "I still don't think I'm ever going to be able to dance."

Holly reached out to lift his chin. "Look at me when you speak," she told him. "You must also gaze directly into your dancing partner's eyes. If you don't stare at your feet, no one else will notice them."

Sam found that impossible to believe. "They will when I step on their toes."

Holly tried not to lose her temper, but it was difficult to instill confidence in a young man who rejected every piece of advice she gave. Growing desperate, she moved close and lowered her voice to a seductive whisper. "You have beautiful eyes, Sam; and if you concentrate your attentions on your partner's face rather than on your own feet, you'll easily enchant her."

Sam's face flooded with a blush that reddened his tan; but before he sent his embarrassed gaze right back to the floor, Holly caught a glimpse of a charming grin. This time she placed her hands on his shoulders. "Oh, Sam. You have such a handsome smile. Why are you hiding it?"

For a moment, Sam didn't know if Holly were pleased or simply making fun of him, but her perfume smelled so good he really didn't care. He looked right into her amber eyes and smiled easily. Then he grew frightened that she might actually teach him how to dance and he would lose his reason to come see her.

Sam had even white teeth that contrasted handsomely with his deep tan. When he smiled at Holly, she stared in rapt wonder, every bit as enchanted as she had promised him his partners would be. She held her breath, waiting for him to slip his arms around her waist and kiss her, but he just smiled. Shocked to have longed for more from him, she quickly lowered her hands and stepped back to create a more discreet distance between them.

"There now," she said in an effort to recover the detachment she had lost. "A smile will put your partner at ease, too. I bet you hadn't realized that women are even more nervous than men. After all, we're expected to be graceful, so if we step on a man's toes, it's an unforgivable blunder."

"You have such tiny feet, I doubt I'd even feel it."

Holly clapped her hands in delight. "That was the perfect thing to say, Sam. Mr. Driscoll, I mean."

Liking the more informal tone, Sam quickly announced his preference and, without the sarcastic edge, his deep voice was as compelling as his smile. "I like having you call me Sam."

"Thank you. Please call me Holly." Thoroughly distracted and all too aware of him, Holly hastened to refocus his attention, as well as her own, on his learning to dance. "Now, let's see about your lesson. The minuet is a simple series of steps, graceful bows, and turns. Take my hand, and we'll work on the first of the figures."

Sam released a poignant sigh, but took Holly's hand with a touch more closely approaching the gentle one she had endeavored to teach him yesterday. She gave his fingers a tender squeeze. "That's perfect, Sam. Balance is a vital part of dancing; and because you ride so well, you must already be adept at keeping your body in balance with your mount. The minuet requires a similar skill, so perhaps if you think of it as being close to riding, it will come more naturally to you."

Sam looked skeptical, but nodded. "At least when I ride a horse, I get somewhere."

"Well, you're trying to get somewhere with dancing, too, aren't you? I do believe your problem may well become one of having too many young ladies interested in you, rather than too few."

Sam laughed out loud at that unlikely prediction. He had a rich, rolling laugh that echoed through the parlor and brought John Cochrane to the door.

"I thought you two were supposed to be dancing," John called to his sister and Sam.

"We are," Holly assured him, "and we're having a good time of it today. Now, go on about your business and leave us to tend to ours."

John remained at the doorway. Holly was a delicate creature and looked very small standing beside his strapping friend. She was dressed in an aqua gown that day and was as pretty as the spring morning. "Be careful, Sam," he advised. "Or rather than teach you how to dance, Holly might make you forget your own name."

Without releasing Holly's hand, Sam took a step forward. "Get out of here," he ordered gruffly. "Holly's having enough trouble without you bothering her."

John laughed and went on his way, but Holly feared her brother might have been right. She had not anticipated the tug Sam exerted on her emotions, but she did not want to encourage him so energetically he got the mistaken impression her interest was in him rather than providing dancing lessons. When Sam turned back toward her, his glance softened and she again had to fight the attraction that had begun with mere sympathy but had swiftly become something far more compelling.

She felt at a loss and wasn't certain how to behave. Sam deserved more than a sterile recitation of the steps, and yet, she did not want to mislead him. There were too many young woman, and Annette Hemby was at the top of the list, who amused themselves endlessly at a man's expense, and Holly had never approved of such unprincipled behavior.

She took a deep breath and tried to think of the stately grace of the minuet rather than her surprisingly appealing partner. She talked Sam through each step; and while they produced only the most basic interpretation of the dance, it was recognizable as the minuet. Not wanting to tax his patience or her own wavering ability to concentrate, she again kept the lesson short and then walked him to the door.

Sam turned toward her as they reached it. "I appreciate what you're trying to do for me, Holly. Please don't think me ungrateful just 'cause I don't learn real fast."

He looked so sincerely troubled, Holly feared that in trying to distance herself from him emotionally, she had become aloof. "I'm enjoying myself, Sam, and I'm actually looking forward to tomorrow. I had more time to plan today's lesson, and I think it went much better as a result."

"Well, until tomorrow then." Sam backed across the porch, then nearly tripped when he reached the steps.

"Be careful," Holly warned. Embarrassed, Sam turned, ran down the steps, and hurried off to his horse. He leapt upon his back with an easy stretch that again confirmed Holly's belief he did indeed possess a natural grace. She closed the door, went into the parlor to remove the sweet peas from the bouquet of camellias, and—as promised—carried them up to her room. She filled a small crystal vase with water from the pitcher on the washstand, added the fragrant flowers, and placed them on her dresser.

She then went to the window seat, sat down, and tried to decide how best to handle her next lesson with Sam. Their plantation bordered the James River and she had a pretty view of the water from her room, but that day it wasn't soothing. Yesterday she had doubted Sam Driscoll could ever learn the minuet, let alone in three-weeks time. Today he had done so much better that she was beginning to hope he could not only learn, but do it passably well.

He had asked about her friends; and while she would keep her promise and introduce him to all of them, she could not think of a single one who would not prefer a more sophisticated man like Roger Wincott. Roger was a delightful companion who could not only dance, but could intelligently discuss any topic from art to tobacco. Of late, Holly had been spending more of her time with him and her mother missed no opportunity to compliment Roger's looks and charm. She did not need to be reminded that the Wincotts' wealth rivaled their own, not when her father remarked on it so often.

She leaned back and wondered if the Wincotts spent an equal amount of time recommending her to their son. The prospect of marrying Roger was not at all unpleasant. He would be a generous husband and dote on their children. He had already hinted at a coming engagement, and she had never given him any reason to doubt what her answer would be to a proposal.

She looked over at the little bunch of sweet peas. Water had restored their charm, and she could not help but smile as she recalled how awkwardly they had been presented. Sam needed a woman who would appreciate the sweetness of the thought behind his halting words and clumsy gestures. Holly wondered if it might not be a good idea to confide her favorable opinion in her friends so that they would treat Sam well even if he only acquired a thin veneer of gentlemanly behavior.

"He would be humiliated if he found out, though," she mused aloud. They still had so much to accomplish; but if Sam succeeded in winning a nice woman's love, his whole life would be transformed. If he failed, well, they would just have to keep working and hope that when the Publick Times came again in November, he would be better prepared.

Although Holly clung to that thought, deep down, she still felt apprehensive as if she had made some terrible mistake; but she knew she had done nothing wrong. When Roger Wincott came to call that afternoon, she found it difficult to concentrate on his conversation. Almost by accident she discovered they could converse at length without her having to do more than offer an appropriately placed nod or approving murmur. It was precisely the technique she had frequently observed her mother using on her father. That was so appalling a thought, she promptly interrupted Roger's wandering description of the party his family planned to host during Publick Times.

"My brother is one of your closest friends, isn't he?"

"You know that he is," Roger exclaimed. "Did you think I'd neglect to invite him?"

Holly waved her fan with languid strokes. "No. I knew you'd include him. I was just wondering if you told amusing stories about him to others, the way you tell me humorous tales of your other friends."

Roger considered her question a long moment. "Frankly, I can't recall the last time John did anything particularly amusing, but I suppose I must have at one time or another. Why? What is your real worry, my pet? That I talk about you?"

Holly had not considered that, but she could not think of anyone else in their circle who had escaped Roger's biting wit. He was a master at ferreting out embarrassing secrets and relating them as entertaining anecdotes. He was also better than Cupid at discovering the first stirrings of romance. He was even adept at matchmaking, and Holly could name three couples who had married after he had pointed out what perfect pairs they would make.

"No," she assured him. "I'm even less amusing than John, and I'm not privy to any delicious secrets. I just wondered if anyone ever consulted you in strict confidence about matters of importance."

"My God, Holly. Do you fear I lack substance?"

He looked horribly offended, and yet Holly found it impossible to care. She rose, turned away, and then glanced at him over her shoulder. "It is something to consider, isn't it?"

Roger left his chair and came after her. "I'm studying law and will someday sit in the General Assembly. Rather than being extravagant, I manage my money well and invest it wisely. I've actually increased my family's fortunes, which damn few of my friends can say. I don't understand what's happened to you. You've always been the most agreeable of companions, and suddenly nothing I do seems to please you."

"You're exaggerating, Roger. Perhaps it's merely the lovely spring weather. Do you find it stuffy in here? Let's go out into the garden."

Roger glared at her. "Are you certain you wouldn't rather that I leave?"

Roger was wearing a black suit with a gold-striped waistcoat and yellow stockings. As always, he looked absolutely splendid, and Holly had not meant to upset him simply because she didn't feel at ease. "Please stay," she replied in an inviting whisper. She came back to take his arm, and his expression immediately relaxed into a smile.

"Now that you mention it, it is a bit warm in here," he agreed. He patted Holly's hand, and they strolled the garden for nearly an hour in their usual amiable fashion.

It wasn't until after Roger had left that Holly realized she could not recall a single thing he had said.

By the end of the week, Holly knew she should never have agreed to teach Sam Driscoll to dance. It was not that he was not learning, he was. The problem was that her inexplicable weakness for him made the rest of her day seem terribly empty. Her chest ached with an unfamiliar longing she had no idea how to assuage. They had agreed to suspend the lessons for the weekend, and Saturday morning she went to Sally Lester's for a fitting. Her friend Mary Beth Parker accompanied her, but even then Holly was uncharacteristically subdued.

"I do wish you'd hold still," Sally complained softly.

"I am," Holly argued.

Mary Beth took Sally's side. "You're fidgeting as though you were draped in a cloud of mosquitos rather than gold satin, Holly. That color is as rich as butter. I wish I looked as pretty in something so bright. I'm wearing blue again to the Governor's Ball. At least it matches my eyes, but blue is such a sleepy color and you'll stand out like a ray of sunshine."

"Not if I do not finish this fitting, she won't," Sally warned.

Holly closed her eyes and took a deep breath to savor the enticing fragrance that filled the shop. She was trying to stand still, but she felt as though her skin itched from the inside and it was an awful chore to affect a calm she didn't feel. "I'll bet Annette Hemby can stand as still as a statue, can't she, Sally?"

Sally had to remove a pin from her mouth before she

replied. "Fortunately, yes, but then perhaps she doesn't have nearly as much on her mind."

Mary Beth's eyes narrowed slightly. "Have you gotten hold of some scandalous secret, Holly? Tell me now before Roger Wincott makes an entire play out of it."

John had not told anyone Holly was teaching Sam Driscoll to dance, and she was loath to do it herself. Not that her lessons constituted an intriguing secret. After all, everyone knew Sam bred horses and he had never excited any interest beyond that. Still, she wished she had someone in whom to confide her growing misgivings about her life. Her mother was a dear, sweet, soul, but she would not even understand Holly's discontent, let alone be able to suggest effective remedies.

"Holly?" Her friend's expression had grown so wistful, Mary Beth became alarmed. "You are preoccupied, aren't you?"

"Who isn't?" Holly responded flippantly. "Here's another spring, another Publick Times that will fill the town with folks from miles around hoping to enjoy themselves, and what does it all mean?"

"It means we're all another year older," Sally interjected darkly. "Now a quarter turn to the left should do it."

Holly took a step to her left. "That's it, I suppose. If nothing significant happens, then we're all just older—and not a bit wiser."

Mary Beth was completely confused. "What do you count as 'significant'?"

Holly rested her palms on the smooth gold satin. "Something that causes a real change. I don't want to simply drift through life, but I fear that's all I'm doing."

"Three-quarters of Virginia would love the opportunity to drift with your family's money," Mary Beth pointed out. "Now stop being so silly. The Wincotts are hosting the first big party of Publick Times. What are you wearing?"

Mary Beth had just provided a perfect example of the frivolous existence Holly had suddenly found far too confining. "I don't know. I hadn't thought about it."

"Well, do. Hasn't it occurred to you that Roger might choose that night to propose?"

Suddenly feeling light-headed, Holly had to grab for the chair at her right. "I'm sorry, Sally. I lost my balance for a moment."

Sally straightened up and smiled. "Sit down if you like. We're finished for today."

Grateful to conclude the fitting, Holly sank down into the chair. "Do you really suppose that he might?" she asked Mary Beth.

After admiring a bolt of lace, Mary Beth turned back toward her friend. "Don't tell me you're shocked. The man adores you. He's been your steady companion the last few months. The party at his family's home would be the perfect time to announce an engagement."

Holly laid her arm across the back of the chair and rested her cheek on her wrist. "Roger would be a fine catch," she remarked absently.

"Indeed he is. Almost as fine as your brother. I'd love for you to give John a gentle hint on the subject of marriage." She came close and bent down to look Holly in the eye. "Will you do it?"

Holly still felt dizzy, but sat up. "I really don't think that would be wise, Mary Beth. John would be sure to suspect you were behind it, and I think you'd be much better off to let the idea occur to him on his own."

"What do you think, Sally?" Mary Beth asked.

Sally gestured toward the silver tray where she displayed delicate bottles of French perfume. "I always recommend a seductive fragrance, Miss Parker. It lingers

in a man's mind and recalls the wearer with most agreeable memories."

Holly had worn the same light floral scent for several
years, but after removing the gold gown and donning
her own pale-green muslin dress, she sampled the shop's
newest perfumes. "What do you think of this one?" she
asked Mary Beth.

Mary Beth placed a drop on her wrist, then frowned.
"Too heavy. It's almost decadent."

"Decadent?" Holly rather liked the spicy fragrance.
She raised the stopper to her nose. "I think it's wonder-
fully seductive. Think of midnight, with a single ray of
moonlight."

Mary Beth couldn't suppress a throaty laugh. "Much
too dangerous for me. Why don't you buy some? Not
that you need to inspire any more devotion from Roger.
You've already stolen his heart."

"What do you recommend, Sally? Is this too dark a
scent for a blonde?"

Sally noted the shape of the crystal bottle and nodded
toward Mary Beth. "That's one I suggest for brunettes,
but if Miss Parker doesn't care for it and you do, then
by all means try a bottle."

Holly debated a long moment, then decided the sultry
fragrance was precisely what she wanted. It reminded
her of something an ancient goddess who might dance
through the forest after a rain would wear. "Yes. I'll take
one today. Please just add it to my bill."

Sally bent down behind the counter to remove a new
bottle from the case and handed it to Holly. "You must
be sure to tell me what effect this has on your beaux.
I have a feeling they will find it very exciting."

"I certainly hope so," Holly revealed with the first
genuine smile of the afternoon. She made another appointment in the coming week for her final fitting, then
left the shop with Mary Beth, who had other errands to

run. They were walking down Duke of Gloucester Street toward the Capitol on their way to the milliner's when Mary Beth took Holly's arm.

"Look who's just leaving Wetherburn's Tavern across the street. It's your darling brother John, and who's the man with him?"

Thinking it odd Mary Beth didn't recognize one of John's friends, Holly raised her hand to shade her eyes. What she saw was John waving to them enthusiastically as Sam Driscoll, dressed in a new dark-gray suit, stood by his side looking painfully self-conscious. She hadn't known John was coming into town, but thought it likely he was merely marching Sam up and down the street to get him accustomed to wearing his new clothes.

"That's Sam Driscoll."

"Not the Sam Driscoll who raises horses," Mary Beth replied.

"The very same. They're crossing the street. I'll introduce you."

Mary Beth sucked in her breath. "Oh, Holly. He's beautiful."

Holly thought so, too. John's tailor had fashioned the gray suit superbly, and it showed off Sam's broad shoulders and narrow hips even more handsomely than his buckskins did. His collar and cuffs were trimmed with lace, his stockings the same creamy shade as his waistcoat, and his shoes adorned with bright silver buckles.

"Flirt with Sam," Holly urged quickly. "Perhaps all John needs is a bit of competition to realize how much he appreciates you."

"Gladly," Mary Beth agreed. She smiled prettily as John reached them and then positively beamed up at Sam. With dark brown hair and pretty blue eyes, she was an extremely attractive young woman. "My father bought a beautiful mare from you last fall," she reminded Sam after they were introduced. "She has been a delight."

"Yes. The little sorrel, I remember her," Sam commented. "I'm glad to learn that you're pleased with her."

"Oh, yes, indeed we are," Mary Beth enthused. "I do believe she's the finest mount I've ever owned."

Sam nodded, then glanced toward Holly. "You've changed your perfume."

Holly's heart caught in her throat for she had not wanted Mary Beth to know she had ever been close enough to Sam Driscoll for the man to recognize her scent. That he could tell the difference on the street convinced her she had put on too much. "We've just come from the dressmaker's," she blurted out nervously, "but I hadn't meant to drench myself in her samples."

Sam leaned a tad closer. "That's only one scent, not several, and I like it."

"Thank you. I thought I'd try something new."

Mary Beth and John exchanged a startled glance, yet neither interrupted the flow of conversation passing between Sam and Holly. They simply stared at the way the pair spoke in hushed whispers—and gawked. When Holly finally realized how closely she and Sam were being observed, she grew even more flustered. She waited for Mary Beth to make another remark or for John to speak, but both had apparently been struck dumb. She gave Sam a regretful smile and tugged on her friend's arm.

"We have to stop by the milliner's before she closes. It was nice to see you, Mr. Driscoll, and I'll see you at home, John."

"Good day to you both," Mary Beth added, but as soon as they entered the milliner's, she began to complain. "Why haven't you ever mentioned Sam Driscoll's name? I would give anything to have John look at me the way Sam looked at you."

Holly was close to collapse and immediately sat down on one of the milliner's padded stools. "I have no idea what you're talking about, Mary Beth. Now what was it you meant to buy, a new hat for riding?"

Thinking it fortunate the milliner was occupied with another customer, Mary Beth drew up another stool. "Frankly, I've completely forgotten why I wanted to come here. If you're not interested in Sam Driscoll, then I am. Will he be at the Wincotts' party?"

Holly was still having trouble catching her breath and knew it wasn't because she had laced her corset too tightly. Sam was a handsome man in buckskins; but in a well-tailored suit, the effect was simply devastating. She was grateful her brother's efforts to turn Sam into a gentleman were bearing fruit. She was so proud of him she could have cried, but she dared not do so here.

She regarded Mary Beth with a shocked gaze. "I would swear that not more than half an hour ago you asked me to drop hints about marriage to John. Did one glimpse of Sam Driscoll make you forget my brother entirely?"

Mary Beth sat back and shrugged. "No. Of course, not. John is definitely the type of man I'd like to marry, but I certainly wouldn't object if Sam Driscoll wanted to call on me."

"Should I ask John to relay that message?" Holly asked innocently.

Mary Beth looked horrified by that suggestion. "Don't you dare. I'll find a way to get a message to Sam myself."

Holly reached for a straw hat topped with a cluster of bright pink ribbons. "This is pretty, don't you think? For John's sake, I'd rather not know what happens between you and Sam Driscoll, but I wish you luck."

Mary Beth took the straw hat from Holly and fussed with the ribbons. "Thank you. This is pretty, but I'll need it with blue ribbons."

Holly didn't care what color ribbons her friend chose, but she could not bear the thought of Sam spending his afternoons with Mary Beth, or any other young woman she knew either.

John found Holly seated alone in the parlor before supper. "Well, what did you think of Sam?" he asked excitedly.

Holly had been reading the same sentence in *Gulliver's Travels* for the last twenty minutes and finally laid the book aside. She had expected a question or two from John and was ready for him. "He looked very handsome; and while he appeared rather nervous when you first waved to us, he talked easily enough with Mary Beth."

"Do you think she was impressed with him?"

Holly wasn't sure how to respond. "She likes you, John, but surely you already knew that."

"Yes. She's very pretty and I like her, too; but what did she think of Sam?"

Holly couldn't understand why every thought of Sam Driscoll made her chest ache. "Do you want her to switch her affections from you to him?" she asked.

"No. Of course not. I just want to know if she thought he was attractive. I realize they only exchanged a few hurried sentences, but I thought he did well enough. I know if I asked Roger to invite Sam to their party, he would. It might be a good chance for Sam to practice being with pretty young women before the Governor's Ball."

The prospect of having to contend with both Roger and Sam at the same time was more than Holly would accept. "It's not our party, John. I really don't believe it would be proper for you to suggest additions to the Wincotts' guest list."

"Perhaps not, but Roger would do it for you if you asked him."

It was all Holly could do not to burst into tears at that request. "I'm afraid if I asked Roger to invite Sam, he'd be jealous; and you know Roger can become positively mean and tease someone unmercifully. I'd not want to subject Sam to that ordeal."

John frowned pensively and rocked back on his heels. "I hadn't thought of that, but you're right. Comments Roger might regard as good-natured fun could wound Sam so badly he'd refuse to attend the Governor's Ball. We can't risk having that happen."

"Not after all the effort Sam's put into learning how to dance."

"It wasn't easy getting him into the new suit today either. It was fortunate that we saw you after I'd poured a couple of pints of ale into him rather than before. You didn't have a chance today; but on Monday, tell him how good you thought he looked, and maybe he won't mind wearing it again."

"I'll do my best," Holly promised, but she felt so torn, she did not even know if she would survive until Monday.

Three

Sunday morning, Holly went to the Bruton Parish Church in Williamsburg with her family, then visited with friends the remainder of the day. She struggled the whole time to pay close attention to everything said to her and yet revealed few of her own thoughts. With the fairs, banquets, and balls of Publick Times fast-approaching, she was thankful there was plenty to discuss, but she found it increasingly difficult to care about the popular amusements she had once eagerly anticipated.

Monday morning, she had difficulty just getting out of bed, but she wasn't really ill and did not want to alarm her mother and say that she was as an excuse to remain in her room. She just felt unsettled, as though her neatly woven life had begun to unravel and she had no idea how to repair the damage. Once she had finally summoned the strength to leave her bed, she dressed in a lovely apricot gown; but the perfection of her appearance failed to lift her spirits.

She sipped tea at breakfast and reduced a corn muffin to a pile of crumbs, but took only a few bites. She had been blessed with so many advantages and she was grateful for them all; but she would soon be expected to make a fine marriage and, rather than the joy she had seen her friends display upon becoming engaged, the thought of receiving a proposal from Roger Wincott filled her with dread. Even more horrifying was the realization that a few months earlier she would have welcomed it. What she had once hoped to have no longer pleased her, and she was appalled to think she might have become as fickle as Annette Hemby.

When Sam Driscoll arrived, again clad in his gray suit, she ushered him into the parlor before beginning the compliments John had asked her to pay. "I had no opportunity to tell you how nice you looked on Saturday, but really, your new clothes make you even more handsome."

Sam tugged at the ruffles brushing his throat and grimaced. "Well, I hate having to wear lace."

What Holly noticed was the sharp contrast between the white lace at his cuffs and his deeply tanned hands. She had never known another man who reminded her so constantly of the simple fact he was male, and it was disconcerting. Because he was there for advice, she promptly provided it.

"Whenever anyone pays you a compliment, the correct response is, thank you, rather than a complaint or argument. You see, when you argue, you're dismissing the other person's opinion as worthless and their feelings will surely be hurt."

Sam looked sincerely pained. "Did I hurt yours just now?"

"Quite honestly, no, but that's only because I know how unhappy you must be to have to wear something other than buckskins. Just be grateful you don't have to lace yourself into a corset each morning. That's far worse torture than having to wear a fine suit. Besides, I don't think there's anything more appealing than the delicacy of fine lace falling across a man's hands. It makes you look more masculine, Sam, not less."

Embarrassed by her comment, Sam quickly hid his hands behind his back. "I'd never thought of that; but then, it's not the type of thing that would occur to a man, is it?"

Holly was positive Roger Wincott would be aware of it, but shook her head. "No. Probably not. Let's try again. You look very handsome in your new suit, Sam."

Sam appeared puzzled for a moment, then grasped her intention. "Thank you, Holly. You look pretty in all your clothes, but I sure hope a corset doesn't truly feel like torture."

Holly leaned close to whisper. "It's never polite to discuss a woman's lingerie in public; but because I started it, I can scarcely complain. Fortunately, I'm slender and don't have to be squeezed into my gowns as some women are."

"Why do they suffer through that?"

"Why are you wearing that suit? Because they hope to impress men, just as you hope to impress women. There's really very little difference between men and women, Sam; truly there isn't."

Completely confused by that surprising opinion, Sam considered it fully, then shook his head. "No. We're nothing alike. Most men would be happy to run through the woods naked, and I've yet to meet a woman who'd prefer her own skin to satin and silk."

Holly had again worn the seductive scent which had called a goddess to mind, although she had not imagined her cavorting through the woods in the nude. "I swear I do not understand how our conversations continually stray into such inappropriate subjects, but let's go back to the beginning. Women are raised to flatter men, but that doesn't mean they aren't sincere; so if someone pays you a compliment, thank her. Pay a compliment of your own; but again, please make it sincere."

"What if she isn't as pretty as you? I can't lie and say that she is."

Inordinately pleased by his flattering remark, Holly felt better than she had all morning. "Beauty isn't the only thing upon which you could comment. Let's say a little dumpling of a woman compliments your appearance. You could still say that you had never seen a more attractive gown, which doesn't mean she looks good in it. Or you could say that her jewelry is exquisite or that she has such pretty eyes, or dainty hands, or perhaps her voice is especially musical."

Sam straightened his shoulders. "What you're saying is that I should look for details, the way a smart man buys a horse."

Holly saw no comparison between buying a horse and complimenting a woman, but nodded as though his comment made perfect sense. "Yes. That's one way to look at it. Then if you wish to continue the conversation, ask her how she's enjoying the party."

"And if I don't care to chat with her?"

Holly licked her lips thoughtfully. "You're tall; pretend you've just seen someone on the opposite side of the room wave a summons. Excuse yourself politely and walk away."

"Like this," Sam focused his gaze above her head. "Oh, I'm sorry, Holly, the governor's trying to catch my attention and I must go and speak with him."

Holly's smile was immediate. "That's perfect. Just make certain the governor isn't standing at your elbow when you use it."

"That will be easy enough."

Delighted with the ease with which Sam had demonstrated her suggestion, Holly thought he had made remarkable progress. Then she remembered to what use he planned to put his newfound confidence and her heart fell. She glanced away and tried to recall what it was she had planned for their lesson.

"Holly?" He sounded fearful. "Did I do something wrong?"

"What? No. Not at all. Let's begin where we left off

on Friday. I want the steps of the minuet to come so easily that you'll actually enjoy dancing them."

Sam greeted that remote possibility with a rude laugh and then reached for her hand. "Sorry. I have some chalk; and I thought if you'd make a diagram for me on paper, I could trace it on my floor and practice again at night."

"What a splendid idea," Holly replied. "Should a friend arrive, you could simply rub it out before you went to the door."

"I don't invite friends to my home," Sam assured her. "I don't share it with my livestock, but it isn't as neat as it should be."

"Then perhaps you ought to begin working on your home as well. After all, you don't want to carry your bride over the threshold and have her race right out the back door."

Highly amused by that colorful image, Sam laughed along with Holly. "The house isn't that bad," he protested, "but I'll start fixing it up." He glanced around the parlor. "It won't ever look this nice, but it could be better."

John walked by the parlor, glanced in, and saw Holly and Sam holding hands and conversing quietly. He waited a moment and, when they still didn't notice him, he spoke up. "Is that some kind of a new dance you're practicing or are you two just holding hands?"

Sam looked angry rather than embarrassed, and Holly hastened to respond before he could. "Don't criticize my methods until you've seen the results. Now please give us the necessary privacy to continue."

"Yes, ma'am," John replied, but he still looked highly skeptical as he turned away.

"Don't mind John," Holly insisted. "We haven't wasted a minute." She coaxed Sam through the first few steps and then gave fewer directions as they moved into the turns. On their second practice, she remained silent and Sam traced the steps flawlessly. When he bowed at the end, she clapped her hands.

"That was perfect, Sam, and I didn't have to help you at all."

"What do you mean? Of course you helped me."

"Say, thank you, first, Sam."

Sam sighed impatiently. "I hate this. Can't we just talk without having to thank each other constantly?"

Holly took a step back. Sam had just done the minuet with admirable precision, and yet he was angry with her for complimenting him. That didn't make a bit of sense to her. "Saying thank you in response to a compliment is merely polite, Sam. I think we've done enough for today. Wait just a minute, and I'll make the diagram for you."

Holly left the parlor and went into her father's study for paper and ink. She had known Sam had a temper, but she did not like having him snap at her. She slipped into her father's chair, drew the graceful figures of the minuet with light flowing strokes, and then waited for the ink to dry. By the time it had, she realized Sam must not feel nearly as confident of his ability to dance as she. She had not meant to give him the impression their lessons were at an end before he was ready and returned to him able to smile.

"Here you are." She went over the diagram briefly to make certain it was correct, then handed it to him. "Dancing will become easier every day, Sam; and once you've learned the minuet, I'll be happy to teach you some other dances, too."

Sam folded the diagram carefully and shoved it down into his coat pocket. "If I learn more than one, I'm sure to get the steps confused; but thank you again for trying so hard. I don't mean to give you so many problems."

Holly slipped her arm through his as they left the

parlor. "I enjoy our lessons, Sam." She looked up at him, hoping he would remember to say thank you, but he didn't; and this time she didn't prompt him. As he opened the front door, she glanced out at his horse. A handsome bay, his reddish-brown coat glowed in the sun.

"John's predicted you'll win the races during Publick Times. Is that the horse you'll ride?"

Sam leaned down to whisper. "No. But you mustn't tell a soul that I own a gray stallion that rivals the wind for speed."

His breath brushed her cheek with a delicious warmth, and Holly couldn't help but be proud he had confided in her. "I've never cared much for races, but this year I'm looking forward to seeing you ride."

"Win," Sam corrected with a cocky grin. He hurried away with a long stride that was very close to a swagger.

Holly closed the door and turned to find John watching her again. "Haven't you got anything better to do than spy on me today?" she asked.

John regarded her with a suspicious gaze. "If I didn't know how devoted you are to Roger Wincott, I'd think you were interested in Sam Driscoll yourself."

Holly refused to dignify that remark with a response, but the tears that burned her eyes as she climbed the stairs were answer enough for her.

After John had provided his unwanted opinion as to her motives, Holly took care to make the mood of Sam's lessons as light as her steps. He was still inclined to push their conversations in improper directions, but he did it with such innocent good humor she could not fault him for it. There were days when they spent more time talking than dancing and others when he seemed to have forgotten everything she had taught him and they had to pay strict attention to rehearsing the steps.

When the day of their final lesson arrived, Holly attempted to be her most charming; but that she was sending Sam off to seek a bride from among the young women he would meet during Publick Times was almost more than she could bear. "I imagine I'll see you in town before the races; but if not, good luck, and I'll look for you at the Governor's Ball."

Sam was more nervous than be had been the first morning he had come there hoping John could talk Holly into giving him lessons. "I wish I were better with words," he finally admitted. "A simple thank you doesn't seem like nearly enough for all the time you've given me."

They were standing by the front door, and for one agonizing moment Holly thought he might lean down and kiss her. She held her breath and waited, remembering the first time he had smiled at her and how she had longed for a kiss, but again he made no such move. She could have risen on her tiptoes and kissed his cheek, but knowing how badly she would embarrass him, she gave his arm a fond squeeze instead.

She couldn't bear to say goodbye, nor to wish him luck with finding love; and before she knew it, he was gone. She hurried up to her room and, after locking her door, curled up on the window seat and cried. She had done a wonderful job and taught Sam how to utter the polite responses every gentleman knew; but like the perfect lady she was, she had never whispered a hint of what was truly in her heart.

Saturday night, Holly and her brother rode to the Wincotts' party with their parents in the family's carriage. Despite having had plenty of time to plan, she had waited until late that afternoon to select a gown and had had to try on several before finally deciding upon a topaz satin that reflected the bright sparkle of her eyes. She had styled her hair atop her head, but left several ringlets brushing her nape. After a touch of pomatum, she had used a light dusting of powder to give her blonde hair a silvery sheen.

As they approached the Wincotts' Georgian mansion, Holly fussed with her fan and prayed Roger would be far too preoccupied with entertaining his other guests to propose to her that evening. She had rehearsed appropriate responses should he be so inspired, but she did not want to have to use any of her carefully crafted remarks. She wished she could simply be spontaneous, but feared that would merely compound her problems and be a grave disservice to him.

John took her hand to help her from the carriage, but Roger was at her side the next instant. He was wearing a heavily embroidered silk suit in a vivid blue that matched his eyes, and he looked as handsome as she had ever seen him. She promptly told him so, and his chest inflated with pride.

"Every time I see you, you are more beautiful," Roger replied. He slipped her arm through his and, leaving his parents to greet the rest of her family, escorted her inside.

Holly knew everyone there and greeted her friends warmly; but as the guests continued to arrive, she feared the only man she really wanted to see would not be among them. She smiled and laughed at Roger's clever ripostes, but did not truly appreciate his scathing sense of humor as she once had. The Wincotts had removed the furniture from their parlor; and as soon as everyone had arrived, the dancing began.

Holly had practiced the minuet so often of late that she could have moved through the graceful figures blindfolded, but it was disconcerting to have Roger as her partner rather than Sam. She had not expected to miss Sam so terribly, but then nothing about him had ever gone as she had anticipated. She felt her smile waver as she and Roger moved through a close turn, but her step did not falter and the dance ended as beautifully as it had begun.

"You have wonderful musicians," Holly complimented sincerely. "The fiddler has an especially fine tone."

"Yes. Doesn't he?" Roger brought her hand to his lips. "I've always liked that gown. I do believe it's almost as lovely as the new gold one I helped you select will be."

Holly was fond of it, too, but sensed a hint of disapproval in Roger's remark. "Are you suggesting I should have worn something new tonight?" she asked.

Taken aback, Roger quickly denied the charge. "Of course not. You have an exquisite wardrobe, and I love all your gowns. What would possess you to twist my compliment into an insult?"

Not having meant to take out her frustrations on Roger, Holly quickly apologized. "I'm sorry, but you have such a discerning eye and I feared I'd displeased you."

"That would be impossible. Ah, they are ready for the next dance. I insist that you be my partner again."

"It will be a pleasure as always," Holly replied smoothly, "but I don't want you to neglect your other guests."

Roger came close to whisper. "It's so crowded, they'll scarcely notice."

This was a country dance and, as the two lines began to form, Holly and Roger moved to opposites sides. She had always loved to dance, especially with Roger, who danced exceedingly well; but as in the minuet, she soon longed for another partner. The music was lively, the steps quick, and Holly lost herself in the excitement rather than give in to the loneliness she had never expected to feel in such a crowded room.

Roger waited until shortly before supper was to be

served to invite Holly on a brief stroll of the garden. The crowded house had grown warm and she was only too glad to accompany him, but she was relieved to find other couples also sauntering along the gently curving walks. "It's been a lovely party," she exclaimed. "I'm tired, but in a rather delicious way."

"I hope you're not too tired," Roger replied and drew her into the shadows beneath a towering magnolia. "Holly, you must know how enormously I admire you."

Holly knew exactly what was coming and immediately tried to distract him. "I admire you, too, Roger. You are easily the most charming man in all of Williamnsburg, and I fear your guests must already miss you. Shall we rejoin them?"

Roger raised his hands to frame her face and gave her a tender kiss. "Stay with me," he begged. "Forever."

His lips were soft and, despite the fervor of his request, his kiss was surprisingly cool. Holly held her breath waiting for the surge of exhilaration she was positive she should feel, but none came. Occasionally John would brush her cheek with a light kiss, and Roger's was no more stirring.

"Roger," she sighed regretfully.

"Please," he implored her. "I had such a pretty speech prepared, but now I can't recall a word of it. I would be so honored if you would become my wife, and you know I can give you whatever your heart desires."

What Holly's heart desired at that moment was to be in another man's embrace. That Roger's kisses did not compare to the thrill of Sam Driscoll's smiles filled her with a sad yearning, but Sam had not offered his love and Roger had. She swallowed hard and was grateful she had not forgotten her pretty speeches even if he had.

"I want what's best for us both, Roger; and while I'm honored you want me for your bride, I'd like to take some time to consider your proposal if I may."

Roger had chosen a shadowed walkway so he could kiss her, but now he was sorry he hadn't proposed in the bright moonlight where her expression might give him more hope than her guarded words. He again pulled her close and placed a sweet kiss on her forehead. "I'll try and be encouraged by the fact you'll at least consider my proposal rather than refuse me outright, but it will be difficult to find the patience to wait for your answer. Please don't keep me waiting long."

Holly leaned into his embrace and thought it at least pleasant, even if it weren't thrilling. "There's so much going on during Publick Times, give me until they're over to respond."

Elated that she had not asked for a month or two, Roger laced his fingers in hers. "Fine, my pet. Now let's go have some supper." They had not taken half-a-dozen steps before he drew her to a halt. "I've been meaning to ask about your new perfume. It's haunting, but I really preferred the more delicate scent you used to wear. If you've run out, I'll glady buy you another bottle."

"No. I still have some. I rather liked this new fragrance, but I guess it doesn't suit me after all."

"No, my pet. It doesn't. You must trust me to know what's best for you."

As they returned to the beautifully appointed home, Holly realized that Roger truly did see her as a pet. In some ways it was comforting, for it meant she would be pampered and spoiled with extravagant gifts; but she doubted generosity was ever an adequate substitute for passion.

During Publick Times, residents of the outlying plantations flooded Williamsburg, nearly doubling the population. With an influx of nearly two thousand people, the inns crowded three men to a bed, while female visitors found lodgings with friends. The General Assembly conducted the colony's business, and court was convened to hold trials of the prisoners who had been languishing in the gaol. Market Square, a wide grassy plaza located midway between the Capitol and the College of William and Mary, was the site of fairs and auctions.

Holly had always enjoyed the festivities, but even with Roger providing colorful commentary and his sister giggling, this year nothing seemed as amusing. The threesome strayed into Market Square one afternoon and found a horse auction underway. Before Holly could stop him, Roger began to bid on a mare Sam Driscoll was leading around the makeshift ring. She was an ebony beauty, with a silken mane and tail and a high prancing step, but Holly saw only Sam. He had removed his gray coat, but was dressed in the shirt, waistcoat, and breeches he had been wearing when she had last seen him. He nodded and smiled when he saw her, then led the horse over to a man who had requested a closer look.

"She'll be too expensive," Holly cautioned her escort.

"Nonsense. I could buy you a dozen like her and not exceed my monthly allowance."

As Roger raised his hand to offer a bid, Holly saw Annette Hemby approach the opposite side of the ring. She was with her father, who took one look at the mare and upped the current bid by five pounds. "Let him have her," Holly begged.

Roger shot her a challenging glance and increased his bid. "Hush. If I want to give you a present, then I will."

"It would be most improper to give me such an expensive gift and you know it. What will people think?"

Roger regarded her with a sly grin. "They'll assume I adore you, which is correct."

Enjoying her brother's romantic games, Caroline peeked over her fan and waited for the young woman to respond; but before Holly could counter Roger's argument with a plea for discretion, Sam brought the mare over to them. Caroline reached out to stroke the mare's velvety soft muzzle, but Holly couldn't find the strength to move.

"Why didn't you tell me you wanted a mare?" Sam asked Holly. "I would have given you one."

Roger watched Holly's cheeks fill with an incriminating blush and promptly drew his own conclusion. "Are you actually acquainted with this man or has he mistaken you for someone else?"

One look at Sam had filled Holly with the same delicious excitement that had made their lessons so enjoyable and, for a long moment, she could not even think above the wild beating of her heart to reply. When at last she found her voice, she sounded breathless, as though she had been the one leading the mare around the ring. She introduced the men and described Sam not simply as a noted horseman, but as her brother's friend. Roger still looked suspicious, but responded politely.

Sam leaned close to Holly and whispered. "This mare's all looks, so let her go; I'll give you another you'll find far more pleasing."

"Miss Cochrane does not accept such expensive gifts," Roger hissed through clenched teeth.

Holly could scarcely believe her ears and spoke crossly. "I swear that is precisely what I told you when you wished to buy me this mare!"

Horrified they were creating a scene in public, Roger quickly dismissed Sam. "We won't keep you." He took Holly by the arm and nearly lifted her off her feet, then grabbed Caroline's hand and strode away with both young women in tow.

Holly looked back over her shoulder, but Sam was already walking toward Annette Hemby and her father. The pretty mare was dancing along by his side, but what Holly noticed was the width of Annette's predatory smile—and she wasn't looking at the horse. Incensed by Roger's rudeness, Holly yanked free of his confining hold.

"What is the matter with you?" she complained. "There was no reason for you to be rude to Sam."

"Sam," Roger mimicked sarcastically. "I have no say in John's choice of friends, but Mr. Driscoll is common and I'll not have you accepting gifts from him."

Holly whacked Roger on the chest with the edge of her closed fan. He was wearing his brown suit with the sky-blue satin waistcoat and she doubted he felt her forceful tap, but it was immensely satisfying to her. "If you are going to be such an insufferable bully, I'll give you my answer right now."

The fire in Holly's amber eyes singed Roger's soul; and knowing that in her present mood her reply could not possibly be favorable, he quickly apologized. "I'm terribly sorry. I fear I've made a fool of myself, but you mustn't think too badly of me for being jealous. Driscoll is a handsome man, and—"

"You just referred to him as common."

Roger clamped his mouth shut and took a deep breath. "He sells horses at country fairs, Holly. That scarcely qualifies him to be included in the ranks of gentlemen."

"It's honest work."

Roger glanced toward his sister who, fascinated by their heated exchange, was staring with mouth agape. "Close your mouth, Caroline. You have pretty teeth, but that just isn't attractive." She obeyed with an audible gulp, and he looked back at Holly. "I wanted to please you with the mare, not upset you so badly. Can you forgive me?"

Holly didn't look back toward Sam, but he had had ample time to call on her after their lessons were finished and she hadn't seen him once. Even now, he had not asked how she had been or said that he had missed her. He had preferred to discuss the mare's attributes rather than offer any heartfelt thoughts of his own. Had she needed proof that he regarded her as a tutor rather than as an available young woman, he had just provided it; but the disappointment hurt—deeply.

Roger looked contrite and, knowing his feelings for her were sincere, she relaxed and smiled. "Yes. You're forgiven. Why don't we find a tea room that isn't too crowded and have something sweet?"

Roger again took both young women's arms, but this time he was laughing. Holly, however, was no happier than she had been before, and she was beginning to get awfully tired of Caroline's incessant giggles.

Four

The morning of the races was clear and bright. They were run on a track located near the Capitol and drew a large crowd where informal wagering was brisk. Holly had arrived with John, but Roger found them almost immediately. Even on a day devoted to sport, he was fashionably dressed and complimented Holly on her gown.

Holly had chosen the white muslin printed with dainty violets for a reason, but it was a very private one. She doubted Sam would recall what she had been wearing when their lessons began, but she had and had worn it for luck. "Thank you. I can't recall if you like to gamble, Roger. Have you bet on today's races?"

"No more than a token amount. Watching the horses run is exciting it itself, don't you agree?"

"Why yes, I do, and there are some magnificent horses running today."

Roger addressed his next question to John. "I suppose your rustic friend plans to ride. Of course, a man of his size will undoubtedly require too sturdy a mount to possess much in the way of speed."

John saw a furious gleam fill Holly's eyes, but defended Sam before she could. "I assume you're referring to Sam Driscoll. He's riding in the last race; and if I were you, I'd bet all I could afford to wager on him. I have."

Roger allowed a look of extreme boredom to settle upon his finely sculpted features. "I'll congratulate you on your foresight if he wins, but I prefer to invest my money in commerical ventures rather than risk it on something so inconsequential as the speed of a horse."

"Do these races strike you as inconsequential?" Holly asked her brother.

"Certainly not. Horse racing is known as the sport of kings for good reason. Breeding fine stock and racing is a commendable pursuit for a gentleman. I'm really surprised you don't engage in it yourself, Roger. Are you afraid you're not strong enough to control a powerful mount?"

Deeply insulted, Roger pulled himself up to his full height, which still didn't match John's. "Riding a high-spirited horse," he replied tersely, "requires as much skill as strength, and I don't lack for either."

John shrugged. "Perhaps not, but you've not entered a horse in any of the races, have you?"

John looked far too pleased with himself to suit Roger, and he glanced toward Holly. She was wearing a wide-brimmed straw hat decorated with trailing purple ribbons; and when she dipped her head, he could not tell if she were laughing at him or merely avoiding the sun. "If it would amuse you to watch me ride in these bucolic contests, Holly, then I'll purchase a swift mount and enter in November."

Holly recognized his defiant tone for the clear challenge it was, but looked up and smiled sweetly. "You ought to please yourself and ride only if you'd enjoy it."

"It looks as though the first race is about to begin," John announced, giving Roger the opportunity to drop the subject of his future participation.

They were standing at the finish line; and with the crowd pressed close around her, Holly had not had a chance to look for Sam. She assumed he would be tending his stallion and imagined the gray horse would be both big and beautiful. It was far too easy to allow her thoughts to drift to Sam; but because thoughts of her obviously never crossed his mind, she looped her arm through Roger's and gave him a delighted smile.

"You're very wise to invest your money rather than to gamble," she assured him. "I imagine you could buy a dozen horses with what some men will lose here today."

Roger patted her hand. "You don't know how thrilled I am to hear you being so sensible once again. You've had me very worried, Holly. You've just not been yourself the last few weeks."

Holly dared not explain why and instead chose to mimic Roger's flippant style. "If not myself, then who could I have been?" she asked.

The first race began with the firing of a pistol; and the volume of the crowd swelled with hoarse shouts and wild whistles, so if Roger had had a reply, Holly could not have heard it. As it was, he got caught up in the frenzy with everyone else; and when the winner tore past them in a cloud of dust and glory, he gave Holly a jubilant hug.

"Everything is more pleasurable with you by my side," he said, as soon as he could be understood.

Holly wished she felt the same way about Roger, and then was flooded with guilt because she didn't. She felt hollow, as though her corset were shaping air rather than her lissome figure. She knew women had once wed men of their parents' choosing. Indeed, some couples had not even met before their wedding and yet many unions had been happy. Roger was the type of man her parents would choose for her; and had they not been introduced until the day they were wed, she knew she would not have been disappointed in his appearance.

She recited Roger's virtues at length; but admiration wasn't the same as love, and none touched her heart.

She knew she ought to give him her answer right then
and there, but he deserved better than to be rejected in
front of the whole town and she kept still. As she had
so often of late, she endeavored to concentrate on the
colorful crowd and the gaiety of the moment rather than
her own sorrow. The beauty of the day encouraged
laughter, but little bubbled from her lips.

The second race was as thrilling as the first, and the
winner greeted with the same wild cheers. Both John
and Roger had won money on it; and after sharing in a
common success, their conversation flowed more easily
between the subsequent contests. As the final race was
announced, John again urged Roger to bet on Sam, but
he refused; and Holly noted the same resentful tightness
to his lips that she had seen at the horse auction. It was
a shame Roger was jealous of a man who cared nothing
for her, but she could not assure him of that without
giving him the hopes she would soon dash. Instead, she
leaned out past John to watch as the riders neared the
starting line.

She located Sam instantly. He was wearing his buckskins to ride; and his stallion, eager to run, was tossing
his glossy mane and prancing nervously. "Have you ever
seen Sam's horse?" she asked John.

"No. But that's because Sam's intentionally kept his
existence a secret."

Roger followed the direction of Holly's glance. "Your
friend's riding the gray? That's a mistake, of course.
Everyone knows not to bet on a gray horse since they
never live up to their promise."

"Really?" Holly replied. "I hadn't heard that. Had
you, John?"

"No. I believe it's a white horse that's always a disappointment."

"Gray," Roger repeated more emphatically. "Perhaps
there's still time for you to change your bet."

John laughed at that advice. "Sam will win. You'll see."

Holly clutched Roger's hand. She was so anxious about the outcome of the race she could scarcely draw a breath. She knew Sam wanted to win; and because he sold fine horses, a victory would enhance his business prospects. He also needed the win simply to be noticed by the young women he hoped to attract, but she thought he could simply have strolled through the crowd and done that.

This was the longest race, and the horses would pass their position as it began and again just prior to the finish. Startled, Holly jumped as the starter fired his pistol, then heard only the thunderous pounding of hooves as the horses streaked past them. Even that close to the beginning, Sam had already drawn ahead. There were eight horses entered in the race, but she had seen only the magnificent gray stallion.

"You see," John shouted over Holly's head to Roger. "I told you he'd win!"

"A horse with early speed usually doesn't last," Roger predicted darkly.

"Sam's will," John assured him.

Holly didn't want to watch, then couldn't bear to look away. When the horses rounded the first curve with Sam still in the lead, she had a most uncharitable thought: Perhaps if he lost, he would be too depressed to attend the Governor's Ball and would throw away whatever chance he had to impress pretty women. She hated herself for being so selfish; but as the race continued, Sam stretched his lead from a single length to three and when he streaked across the finish line in a silvery blur, he was fully four lengths ahead of the horse finishing in second place.

John grabbed Holly with a boisterous whoop. "I knew Sam would win, and I'll buy you another fine gown from my winnings."

As her brother set her back on her feet, Holly saw Sam leap down from his horse and Annette Hemby rush onto the track and dance right into his arms. Holly's heart lodged in her throat as she watched Sam swing Annette around with an exuberant joy. He wore an ecstatic smile and crushed the last of her romantic dreams beneath his feet. Choking on tears, she tried to hide her despair behind her fan, but Roger took a firm hold on her shoulder to turn her toward him.

"What did John mean about buying you *another* gown?" Roger asked. "Why would he be paying for your wardrobe?"

He looked appalled by the idea, but Holly raised her hand to plead for a moment and pretended to be distressed by the dust still swirling up off the track. In a very small way, she was grateful to Roger for providing a distraction and finally gave him an answer. "He owed me a favor is all. Now you mustn't jump to conclusions, and obviously scandalous ones. You have a remarkable talent for extracting the drama from any situation, but I really wish you wouldn't display it with me."

Embarrassed by her criticism, Roger's expression slipped from hostile to apologetic. "You're absolutely right, my pet. I didn't mean to be rude." He draped his arm around her shoulders to protect her from the crowd. "Come, let's find a place where it isn't too crowded to breathe and let John collect his winnings."

"What about yours?"

Roger shrugged. "I'll see to them later."

That he would consider her comfort more important was a point in his favor, but Holly had already known how highly he regarded gentlemanly behavior. Couples learned to love each other in arranged marriages; and she supposed, given time, she would learn to love Roger. For the moment, however, she could not resist needling him.

"It looks as though you were wrong about gray horses. Sam's stallion was the swiftest I've ever seen."

Sorry she had recalled the remark, Roger made her a promise. "I'm definitely going to buy a horse and race in the fall," he declared emphatically, "and then we'll see who the winner is."

"I shall look forward to it," Holly assured him with a playful tap of her fan. As they left the track she did not look back to see how many other young women had rushed forward to congratulate Sam, but she hoped he had attracted so many that Annette Hemby had been rudely shoved aside and quickly forgotten.

The Governor's Palace was a luxurious brick mansion surrounded by formal gardens complete with fishpond, shady arbors thick with entwined vines, and an intriguing holly maze. The stately residence had been completed in 1705, and since then had served as the home of the colony's Royal Governors. The Governor's Ball was one of the highlights of any Publick Times, and tonight's lavish party was no exception. Holly had not even considered skipping it; and wearing her new gold gown, her hair powdered to perfection, she entered the brilliantly lit ballroom on Roger's arm.

For the Governor's Ball, many men wore elegant silk suits in vivid shades of sapphire, amethyst, and burgandy. John wore a rich almond shade that highlighted his tawny eyes, while Roger again wore blue. Sam, however, came in black heavily embroidered with black stitching. He didn't bother with a wig or to powder his own hair, but left it dark and caught at his nape with a velvet ribbon. He looked every bit as dashing as Holly had known he would, but she caught only a glimpse of him every now and then and had no opportunity to speak with him before the dancing began.

She held no hope that Sam might seek her out to dance the minuet and would not have been insulted by the oversight had he not chosen Annette Hemby as his partner. Annette's lavender satin gown was a masterpiece of feminine style and fluid drape, but Holly still found the icy color horribly unattractive on the stunning brunette. She tried not to gloat as Roger remarked upon the same thing.

"Annette looks as pale as a ghost in that luscious lavender, but I'm surprised at her taste in men. I must say I'm also surprised at his choice. I should think John would have warned his friend away from Annette when her affections will last little longer than the length of this first minuet."

John was with Mary Beth Parker, and Holly certainly did not want to ask him what he had told Sam about Annette in her presence, but Holly found it difficult to believe the subject had never come up. She smiled at Roger as the music began, but her thoughts remained with Sam. She wasn't near enough to watch his moves closely, but what she could see made it plain he had remembered everything she had taught him.

Her attention strayed as frequently as the steps changed; and when the music ended, she found Roger staring at her with a surly frown. "What's wrong?" she was quick to ask.

"I was about to ask you the same thing. If you would have preferred another partner, I wish you had just said so rather than ignore me."

All too often Roger reminded Holly of a petulant child; but because she felt his complaint was justified, she did not fault him for the manner in which he had expressed it. "I'm sorry, Roger. I didn't mean to make you feel slighted. I can't remember when I've seen everyone so beautifully dressed, and I'm afraid I was comparing my gown to all the others."

Instantly placated by a mention of fashion, Roger brushed her cheek with a kiss. "You are quite simply the most beautiful creature in all of Williamsburg, my pet. From now on, I'll help you select all your gowns and you will continue to outshine all other women."

He had accepted her lie so readily, Holly was ashamed. She did not want to become an accomplished liar and wished he had seen through her silly fabrication. She had been on the verge of tears while getting dressed, and it was only the heady excitement of the fabulous party that was keeping her eyes dry now. She did not want to spoil the night for Roger and took his hand in a fond clasp.

"I'll continue to trust your judgment. You have such superb taste, I'm surprised you've not become an artist."

"And travel from town to town painting dreary portraits of people with ample money and sallow faces? I think not."

"Roger, nothing you produce could ever be described as dreary," Holly assured him. He positively glowed when she praised him, but she was grateful the next dance required a change of partner and did not miss him as she danced away. The spritely country dances were wonderful entertainment, but Holly never lost sight of where Sam was standing as he moved through the crowd of spectators. She saw a flash of lavender and recognized Annette, but there were other women, too, hordes of them from what she could see, trailing him around the room.

The ballroom was soon too warm, and Holly moved out on the terrace for a breath of air. The fragrant evening breeze had barely caressed her skin before Roger appeared at her side. She thought it most unfortunate that he was watching her so closely, while she remained fascinated by Sam. She promised herself right then that neither man would ever learn that bewildering secret.

"I'm enjoying the coolness of the evening. Would you like to tour the gardens?" she asked.

"Only if I can kiss you again," Roger bargained.

"Roger," Holly cautioned.

Roger sighed dejectedly. "Yes, I know. I ought not to pressure you for your decision, but I love you more with each new day and a June wedding would fulfill my dreams."

Holly could not imagine how he could possibly love her when she was continually so distracted. "Why?" she asked with a coquettish dip of her head.

"Why?" Roger appeared to be shocked that she would have to ask. "You are a rare beauty, my pet; and while I do fear I possess several annoying mannerisms, you seldom complain of them."

"And other women do?"

Roger nodded and sighed. "Indeed they do."

"How terribly rude of them." Holly took his arm as they reached the entrance to the gardens. She wondered which of his faults received the most criticism, but was far too considerate to ask. She felt certain that he spent more on his wardrobe than she did on hers, but he was much too sensible to be described as extravagant.

"You're wearing that peculiar perfume again," Roger noted suddenly. "I would swear that I told you I preferred your usual scent."

Holly had made the choice with another man in mind, but the caustic edge to his voice gave her such a valuable insight she wasn't a bit sorry. "You'd like to make every decision for me, wouldn't you? Not simply clothes and perfume, but the novels I read and the friends I entertain. I suppose if I wanted a kitten, you'd select the color, or if I wished to replant a garden, you'd pick the flowers."

Preferring privacy to the company of others, Roger led Holly into the maze. "You've complimented me on my taste in fashion and my judgment in business, so why would you object to relying on me in other areas of your life? I can assure you my choices will always be made with your best interests in mind."

"If we were to marry, and please note that I said 'if' and not 'when,' just what would my responsibilities be?"

Roger produced a cynical laugh at the obviousness of that question and chose the pathway to his left where he hoped they would not be disturbed. "I would expect you to be devoted to me, and taking care of my needs would be your primary concern. There would be children, of course, but you'd consult with me on their upbringing."

"Consult, Roger? You make it sound as though I'd be more of an employee than wife."

"Nonsense. Women quite naturally defer to their husbands in domestic matters. You must know that."

Holly was beginning to feel they should have had this conversation months ago. She felt smothered, and they weren't even engaged. "Just what decisions would I be expected to make on my own?"

Roger was silent until they had reached the next intersection of paths, and this time he chose the one on the right. "You'd direct the work of the staff and plan the menus, but of course you'd discuss any new recipes with me before the cook tried them to be certain that I approved. I do so want our mealtimes to be agreeable, and nothing hinders conversation like tasteless food."

"God forbid," Holly murmured under her breath. The hedges surrounding them were high, and the pathways only dimly lit from torches placed out in the garden. Not wanting Roger to become amorous, she kept plying him with questions on how he intended to run his household. He had a ready answer for everything, but nothing he said encouraged her to believe she would enjoy becoming Mrs. Roger Wincott.

Before long, they had reached the heart of the maze.

When Roger took her hands and stepped close she wasn't surprised, but that did not mean she wished to return his affection. She turned her head, and his kiss landed on her cheek. She expected him to apologize for his boldness; but instead, he grabbed hold of her waist and yanked her close.

"I've had enough of your teasing, Holly. Kiss me."

His mouth covered hers before she could utter a protest, and there was no tenderness in his approach. He kissed her with a bruising passion, providing a punishing sample of what her life with him would be. He wanted a wife who would pamper him with her every gesture; and while he would undoubtedly be generous, Holly rebelled at the prospect of being no more than his pretty plaything.

She lashed out with both fists and struck him hard enough in the chest to send him reeling into the hedge at his back. She fled before he could catch his balance, but ran only a few yards and then, hoping to elude Roger's pursuit, ducked down a side path and stood still. She was breathing hard, but prayed the music from the ball would muffle the sound. She heard Roger calling her name in frantic whispers, but let his calls go unheeded.

She felt incredibly stupid for having tallied the advantages of marrying a man she didn't love, when the truth was they were a horrible mismatch in everything that mattered. She was shaking with fear for she had simply been hurt because Sam hadn't wanted her and had very nearly made the worst mistake of her life. By the time her breathing slowed, Roger had given up finding her and she marched out of the maze with a long, determined step.

When she returned to the ballroom, she was greatly relieved to learn Roger had told John that he was not feeling well and would have to go home early. Her elation was short-lived, however, when she discovered Sam was also nowhere to be found. For the rest of the evening, she had no shortage of dancing partners, but none gained more for his efforts than a sad, sweet, smile.

Monday morning, John went racing up the stairs and rapped insistently on his sister's door. Holly had just finished getting dressed and answered promptly. "My goodness," she exclaimed. "Is the house on fire?"

"No. I'm sorry to have made such a racket, but Sam's here and again in desperate need of your help."

Holly relaxed against the jamb and tried to find a tactful way to refuse. "Our lessons are over, and he can't depend on me any longer, John. I'm sure you can provide whatever advice he needs. I'd begin with an opinion of Annette Hemby, if it's not already too late to warn him she's merely a delicious sip of poison."

"I'd just sound jealous, Holly. Please. He really needs a woman's advice."

Holly's aqua gown had a pleated bodice and a deeply flounced hem. She knew she looked her best, even if she felt far from happy, but she truly did not want to see Sam. "Tell him I'm deathly ill and can't leave my bed."

"He saw you at the Governor's Ball, and you looked so beautiful he'll never believe you've fallen ill."

Holly sighed dejectedly. "Then just tell him no. I know it will sound rude, but I just don't care."

John was in his shirtsleeves and waistcoat; and astonished Holly was being so uncooperative, he widened his stance and folded his arms across his chest. "Why are you treating him this way? I thought you two had become friends."

Holly and Sam had parted amicably; and because she had hidden her feelings so well, neither John, nor Sam, had any idea that she had wanted far more than Sam had been inclined to give. Sam had seen her with Roger and probably assumed she was content. How would he think otherwise? she asked herself. And why would he care?

"You're right," she agreed reluctantly. "He wouldn't understand my motives and undoubtedly would be insulted or hurt and I don't want that. Have him wait in the parlor, and I'll be down in a minute."

John knew his sister too well to believe she was merely bored with tutoring his friend and then cursed himself for not following up on his earlier suspicions. "I asked you once if you were interested in Sam, and you just tossed your pretty head and gave some flippant reply; but you are fond of him, aren't you?"

Holly couldn't flee from John the way she had Roger, but she was much too proud to reveal the depth of her anguish. "Yes. I like him very much, but he has no interest in me so there's no point in discussing it."

John stuck out his hand to prevent her from closing her door. "Wait. You already know Sam's a fine man, but he's not the most perceptive soul where women are concerned. I think you should tell him how you feel. He's sure to be thrilled."

Holly recalled how shy Sam had been when he had begun his lessons. He might have looked splendid on Saturday night, but that didn't mean the melancholy soul with the enchanting smile was gone. She couldn't confront that dear man with tender words of love. "No. I think he'd be absolutely mortified, turn red as an apple, and run from the house. I'm not going to subject either of us to that embarrassment, John. I'm sure that Sam must know men are the ones who are supposed to declare their affections first; and because he didn't, let's assume that he didn't want to, and pretend this conversation never took place."

Not pleased by her decision when it affected two people he cared about so deeply, John offered another suggestion. "I could drop a broad hint."

Holly had been depressed, but now she was terrified. "Don't you dare! That would just make me look pathetic, and I couldn't abide that." She gestured for him to step back and closed her door. She didn't really have anything to do except gather her thoughts; but when her glance fell upon the small bottle of seductive perfume, she could not resist applying a few drops to her wrists and throat. She then hurried downstairs before her courage failed her and John took things into his own hands and said more than he should.

Sam was dressed in buckskins and pacing the parlor with a restless stride. When Holly appeared at the door, he rushed toward her. "I want to thank you again for being so patient with me, Holly. I doubt you noticed, but I made it through the minuet at the ball without stomping on Annette's toes. In fact, she even complimented me on my grace."

"Did she really?" Holly had been in perfect health that morning, but she was fast becoming sick to her stomach. She longed to reach out and touch Sam, but without the minuet to provide an excuse, she dared not. Instead, she clutched her fan with both hands, walked over to the settee, and sat down.

"You were too busy dancing to glance my way, but I did see how well you did and I was very proud of you, Sam. I can't imagine what more you need of me."

Eager to win her help, Sam took a place at her side. "This is my fault because I failed to think things through. I just wanted a woman to notice me, but I didn't stop to think about what I'd do next."

Holly recognized the way he furrowed his brow when he was troubled; but she knew no matter how upset he was, his anguish could not possibly approach hers. "That's not true, Sam. We went over several ways to begin a conversation. Didn't you remember any of them?"

Sam nodded. "Yes. Your ideas worked well. All I had

to do was ask a woman what she thought of the ball and she would begin telling me all kinds of interesting things. That made having a conversation a lot easier than I had feared; but then later, I realized I didn't know what more to do."

Holly toyed with her fan. "Oh, Sam. You're going to have to learn on your own. I can't give you questions and responses to memorize for every occasion. You're bright. You'll do fine on your own."

Sam reached out to take Holly's hand. His touch was very light, just the way she had taught him. "You don't understand. I've never kissed a girl; and if you would just let me practice a few times with you, then I'd be sure I wouldn't be a disappointment."

Holly had not even imagined he could be so cruel. She yanked her hand from his and left the settee. He leapt to his feet, but she backed away. "I have feelings, Sam. I can't just be used for practice and then tossed aside. Besides, if you want a truly expert tutor, you ought to consult Annette Hemby. She's kissed every man in Williamsburg under the age of thirty-five."

"So what? Is kissing all that different from dancing the minuet?" Sam asked.

That he didn't understand the difference between moving to music with carefully measured steps and a spontaneous expression of love ripped away Holly's tenuous hold on composure. She turned her back on him to hide her tears. "Yes! I can't help you. Please go."

Holly felt thoroughly humiliated. She had just announced quite plainly that she had feelings for Sam, and he had not cared in the slightest. She had taught him all the wrong things she realized now, and she had no one but herself to blame. That did not make his indifference any less heartbreaking, however, and she held her breath and waited for him to leave.

Five

Sam was wearing moccasins, so Holly couldn't hear him move, but she felt the heat of his body as he stepped close. "I asked you to go," she stated as firmly as her trembling chin would allow.

Rather than obey, Sam walked around to face her and saw the tears rolling down her cheeks. He raised his hand to her throat, curled his fingers around her nape, and laid his thumb over her wildly throbbing pulse. He leaned down and, with feather-light kisses across her eyelids, began to dry her tears.

Astonished and yet unsure of what was happening, Holly held her breath until she had to reach out for Sam's waist just to remain on her feet. His hand was warm, the pressure against her skin exquisitely gentle, and—as the sweetness of his adoring kisses strayed down her cheek—she drew closer still. The parlor was filled with the bright morning sunshine, but being with Sam made the familiar setting far more romantic than the moonlit maze at the Governor's Palace had ever been.

Holly slid her hands under Sam's fringed shirt to caress his bare skin and felt him shiver with the same joy that coursed through her. She didn't want anything to break the magical spell he had spun around her; and as his kisses edged closer to her mouth, she lifted her head to welcome his kiss and return it. Roger had not been the first of her beaux to kiss her, but none had ever made her long for more the way Sam's tender kisses did.

Sam removed Holly's cap with a careless tug and ran his fingers through her fair curls, sending them cascading over her shoulders. He slid his hands down her back, then enveloped her in a loving embrace. He flicked his tongue across her lips; and when she gasped in delighted surprise, he deepened his kiss and savored her delicious taste until they were both so dizzy he had to move back to the settee and pull her down across his lap.

Once the initial opportunities had been missed, Holly had not allowed herself to dream of kissing Sam; but now that he was showering her with affection, she could not imagine anything more glorious than being in his arms. She welcomed each of his fervent kisses with grateful moans and doubted she would ever have enough. When he broke away to nuzzle her throat, she clung to him, now unwilling to ever see him leave.

"I love your perfume," Sam murmured in a husky whisper, "almost as much as I love you."

Holly was so thrilled she began to cry again; then feeling very foolish, she leaned back and wiped away her tears. "Do you mean it? Do you really love me?"

Sam answered with a devouring kiss and then with words. "I've loved you for years. You might have been no more than twelve the first time I saw you. You were dressed in yellow and looked as pretty as a buttercup. John and I were out at your stable talking when you came to give him a message from your father. I don't know what it was. I don't even think I heard it. I just saw you and thought I'd surely die with longing before you grew up."

"Oh, Sam." Holly framed his face between her hands and gave him a lavish kiss. She didn't recall the day he remembered so fondly, but wished that she did. Then she thought it was probably a good thing that she didn't when she had always regarded him as an awkward young man with a forbidding beard.

"I want you to promise me something," she said with a serious frown.

Sam brought her hands to his lips and kissed her palms. "Anything."

"You are so handsome. Please don't ever grow another beard."

Sam chuckled and pulled her back into a fond embrace. "I'd never thought of myself as handsome until you swore that I was. I want you to keep right on thinking that, too, so the beard is gone for good."

Holly lost herself in another of Sam's marvelous kisses; but when John came to the doorway and cleared his throat noisily, they both jumped. Holly turned toward her brother, but left her arms looped around Sam's neck. She was surprised by the width of John's smile, but not at all embarrassed to have been caught perched on Sam's lap kissing him.

"You needn't gloat," she said, but John just laughed.

"I'm entitled to it," John boasted. "I told Sam if he'd beg you for dancing lessons, you'd fall in love with him for sure."

Holly searched Sam's face, expecting a firm denial, but he was laughing, too. He had just sworn that he had loved her for years and she had been so thrilled by that astounding revelation that she had not realized what it truly meant. "Wait a minute. Did you two have this all planned?"

"Well, we couldn't be certain it would work," Sam explained.

Holly stared into his warm smokey gaze and was shocked by how badly she had been duped. "You let me think you wanted another girl, any girl, and all the while you wanted me?" she asked fearfully.

Sam gave her a quick kiss and then nodded. "John

and I had a bargain. He'd help me court you, and I'd give Annette Hemby a dose of her own medicine. We managed to succeed on both counts."

Sam had a devastating smile, but Holly couldn't abide what he had done and slid off his lap. She quickly retrieved her cap from the floor. "So that's why you haven't called on me?" she inquired. "You wanted to play a trick on Annette Hemby first and then return to me?"

Growing uneasy, Sam rose to defend himself. "I wanted you to be proud of me, Holly. That's why I wanted to look good at the Governor's Ball. It was all for you, not Annette. I don't give a damn about her, but it was about time a man caught her eye and then dropped her as fast as she's discarded her other beaux. Forget her. I want to spend the rest of my life with you."

Holly raised her hand to her temple and tried to shut out this fresh new surge of pain. "You and John hatched a neat little plot, but you didn't once consider my feelings. You wanted me to love you, and so you arranged for us to be together every day for dancing lessons. When they were over, you went off to impress Annette and expected me to be waiting when you got around to seeing me again. Dear God. How could you have been so cruel?"

"Oh, come on, Holly," John cajoled. "Annette Hemby deserved what she got, and Roger Wincott's done his best to keep you from getting bored."

"And that was all right with you?" Holly asked Sam. "You didn't care if I spent my time with Roger?"

Sam responded with a derisive snort. "I knew you couldn't really be interested in a dandy like him."

Sam caught John's eye; but despite their deep chuckles, Holly did not see a bit of humor in the situation. "Well, not only were you fools too stupid to consider my feelings, you forgot that Roger has feelings as well. He proposed to me the night of his family's party. Rather than give him my answer, I've been stalling for time; but because I thought I had no chance with you, Sam, I very nearly said yes."

Sam blanched as though she had struck him. "You didn't."

"No, but I came very close to settling for what he was so eager to provide. There have been mornings when I've been so miserably unhappy I could barely get out of bed, and the whole time you two must have been laughing at how clever you were. Well, Annette isn't the only one who got hurt here. You've hurt me very badly, and poor Roger as well. I'll have to send him a letter immediately and apologize for not being more forthright, but I don't know what to tell you, Sam.

"If you didn't even consider how badly your indifference would hurt me, then I think you'd make a very poor husband. I deserve a whole lot better."

Holly ran from the room before either man could catch her, and Sam erupted in a furious fit of curses. "I did everything you told me to, John, so this is your fault rather than mine. Don't even try to give me any more advice, when what you've already done has probably cost me the love of the only woman I've ever wanted."

"Calm down," John urged. "We can change her mind."

Sam's response was crude, and he stomped out of the house without listening to another of John's ridiculous plans.

Positive Sam was no better than Roger, Holly threw herself across her bed and sobbed. Roger was the spoiled scion of a prominent family, so she could excuse his chauvinistic point of view, but she was obviously no more than a pretty plaything to Sam as well. Didn't men ever understand that a woman possessed a heart as well as a lovely face or attractive figure? They had eyes, but saw only the most superficial of attributes rather than the truth.

She fell asleep before she had sorted out the wretched mess Sam had made of her life, but at noon, her mother came to call her for dinner. Holly sat up slowly and pushed her tangled curls out of her eyes. "I'm not hungry," she said.

Grace Cochrane was well named and crossed to her daughter's bed with a languid stride. "You left for the Governor's Ball with Roger Wincott, but came home with John. Is Roger the cause of your tears?"

Holly had completely forgotten that she owed poor Roger an apology. "No. He's a fine man, but—"

Grace was also a slender blonde and as perceptive as her daughter. "But you don't love him."

"No. I don't love him. Did you love Father when you married him?"

"As desperately as I do today," Grace assured her. "I thought I caught a glimpse of Sam Driscoll this morning. Did he come by to say hello to you?"

Holly left her bed to fetch a handkerchief from her dresser. "He said a good deal more than hello." After a moment's hesitation, Holly described the trick Sam and her brother had played on her. "It didn't occur to either of them how much I might miss Sam. He wanted me to love him, but only when it conveniently fit into their plan."

As disgusted as Holly, Grace moved toward the door. "You'll have to deal with Sam, but I'll speak with John. It was very wrong of him to involve Sam in a plot to hurt Annette. I really thought we had raised him to be more responsible."

"I don't know what to do."

"Wash your face and come down for dinner. When

Sam comes back, and he will, accept his apology and begin anew."

"I'm afraid that's all there will ever be," Holly revealed, "nothing but insensitive blunders and heartfelt apologies that won't change anything."

Grace had never seen her daughter so distraught. "Don't sit up here and brood. Go outside this afternoon and walk in the garden or down by the river. In a few hours, things won't look nearly as bleak."

Unconvinced, Holly slumped down on the side of her bed. "I tried so hard to be respectful of Sam's feelings while we worked on the minuet, and it was all a joke to him. I bet he rode home every day laughing at his own cleverness."

"You're being much too hard on Sam, dear. You must remember that he had no mother to advise him, and you do. Don't let your pride get in the way of your heart. If you love Sam, forgive him."

For a brief interlude that morning, Holly had felt loved and it had been glorious. Now she felt badly betrayed. "I don't want a husband who doesn't regard my feelings as important as his own."

"Then you'll simply have to teach Sam how to behave, even more tenderly than you did the steps of the minuet."

Grace left before Holly saw the wisdom in that suggestion, but she did take her mother's advice and go out for a walk along the river. She had often played along the riverbank as a child, but the James River's bubbling current now called to mind a flood of tears. She paused on a bluff and sought the shade of a stand of flowering redbud trees. She sat down and tried not to think of how desperately sad her life had become.

She might have stayed there the whole lazy afternoon had Sam not come to find her. Her eyes were still bright with tears, and as she looked up at him, she couldn't think of a single thing to say. She simply stared and wondered why he could not have been as splendid on the inside as his fine looks made him appear.

"Your mother said I might find you here. I'm very sorry about this morning. I blamed John the whole way home, then realized I was the one who'd done everything wrong. I was afraid if I just presented myself on your doorstep and asked for your hand you'd simply be shocked and turn me down. That didn't give me any right to play tricks on you, though, and I should have known that."

Holly looked down at her hands. They were trembling slightly, and she laced her fingers together so he wouldn't see. "I really thought I knew you, Sam. I thought you were kind, gentle, and sweet."

She wasn't yelling at him, and taking that as a good sign, Sam sat down across from her on the grass. "I like to think that I am, but I thought what women liked best was strength."

"Yes. I suppose."

Sam waited for Holly to say more, but she didn't and he didn't know what to do. "I played another trick on you this morning," he blurted out. "I've kissed other girls."

His kisses had been so enticing that his confession didn't surprise her. "Yes. I thought that you must have."

Sam gave a rueful laugh. "I've done a lot more than that actually."

"Sam, really. When are you going to learn that there are some subjects that ought not to be discussed?"

Sam grabbed up a handful of grass and tossed it out into the river where the ragged clump was swiftly swept away. "I'm trying to be honest, the way I should have been from the beginning."

Holly put her hands over her ears and shuddered. "I don't want to hear what you did with other women," she implored him. She hoped they had been ones he had paid for their favors rather than innocent beauties who had fallen in love with him as swiftly as she had. She dropped her hands. "I don't want to know their names or where you met them or what you think of them now, and I'll never tell another man about you."

Because Sam didn't want there to be any other men, that promise stung. "Was what I did really so awful that you don't want to see me anymore?"

Holly's chest ached with longing but that did not mean her memory wasn't keen. "That day at the auction, you barely said hello. When you won the race, it was Annette you grabbed to celebrate; and at the Governor's Ball, you didn't even speak to me. You can't love a woman just when it suits you, Sam. It has to be always, and forever."

Sam had been hoping to make her jealous. He opened his mouth to say so, then realized just how heartless it would sound. That he had deliberately neglected her in the hope she would miss him had been cruel. He understood that now.

"I'm not going to give up," he announced suddenly. "I may have wasted my first chance to impress you, but I won't squander another." He rose in an agile stretch and extended his hand.

"Come on. I'll walk you home."

Holly didn't want his company, but the ground was growing awfully hard and she knew she ought to be getting back home. She took his hand, then dropped it as soon as she had stood. She didn't speak as they made their way back to her house; but when it came into view, she saw the Wincotts' carriage parked out front.

"Oh no. Roger's here."

"I'll send him away," Sam offered eagerly.

"Yes. I'm sure you would, but I need to talk with him. What I did to him wasn't nearly as bad as what you did to me, but it was close and I owe him an apology." Not looking forward to the conversation, Holly slowed her step; but as they approached the front of her house, Roger came down the steps. He took one look at Sam and then swept her with an accusing glance.

"Have you decided to purchase a mare?" he asked coolly.

"Well, no," Holly replied. "Not that it's any business of yours."

Sam moved close to her. "Horses aren't the only thing I know," he avowed with a taunting grin meant to inspire the very worst scenario in Roger's mind.

Roger's mouth fell agape, but he quickly recovered and came forward. "I want to apologize for my behavior at the Governor's Ball. It was unforgivable, but you know my feelings were sincere. Please say that you'll forgive me."

"You just said it was unforgivable," Sam pointed out.

"I wasn't speaking to you!"

"Please," Holly begged. She raised her hand to wave Sam back, but he went right by her, grabbed Roger by the lapels of his velvet coat, and lifted him clear off his feet. His right shoe fell off, making him look all the more pathetic as he dangled in the air. "Sam!"

Roger was squirming frantically, but Sam yanked him close and looked him in the eye. "Just what is it you did, Wincott?"

"He just kissed me," Holly swore, "and you said yourself that's no different from dancing. Now put him down."

Rather than set Roger down gently, Sam relaxed his hold on him and let him drop to the ground like a sack of beans. Roger grabbed for the front of Sam's buckskin shirt to catch himself, but he landed awkwardly and nearly fell. Sam stepped back; and as Roger crammed his foot into his shoe, he eyed him with open disgust.

A look of cold fury filled Roger's eyes; and terrified

he would call Sam out for manhandling him, Holly rushed forward and took his arm. "I need to speak with you, Roger," she said in a soothing murmur and, with a forceful shove, propelled him toward the garden. "In fact, I meant to send you a letter this morning, but I really would prefer to talk with you in person." She looked back over her shoulder, but Sam hadn't moved. She couldn't tell if his scowl was meant for Roger or her, but he was clearly angry.

She couldn't deal with both men and continued down the path with Roger. "I've been flattered by the attention you've paid me, Roger, and your proposal was overwhelming. You're bright and handsome."

"And wealthy," he added. "Don't forget that."

"Yes. You're a man of means," she readily conceded. "Anyone would describe you as a splendid catch."

When they reached a wooden bench, Roger drew Holly down beside him. He studied her expression with a narrowed gaze and then spoke his mind. "I didn't mean to frighten you with my ardor and push you into Sam Driscoll's arms. If that's what happened, then the fault is entirely mine. Many women marry at seventeen; but if you aren't ready, then I'm prepared to announce our engagement and set a wedding date in the fall, or even during the holidays if you like. It will be difficult for me, but you are well worth the wait."

Holly was certain he could discuss the price of tobacco with more emotion and she did not understand why she had ever thought him an agreeable companion. "Roger, you have so many fine qualities, but we just aren't a match."

Roger was shocked by her opinion. "Nonsense." He reached for her hand and pressed it between his. "You must trust me to know what a splendid pair we are. I can give you so much, Holly. Please say you'll marry me."

Holly looked down at their hands. When Sam touched

her, she felt the thrill all over; but now she recoiled from Roger's confining hold and withdrew her hand. "I'm trying to be as tactful as I know how," she assured him, "but you just don't seem to hear what I'm saying, which is another reason we'd not be happy together. I can't marry you, Roger. Now I'd like for you to go."

Growing sullen, Roger remained where he sat. "You can't really be interested in Sam Driscoll."

Holly glanced away rather than reply. This had easily been one of the worst days of her life, and she didn't want to vent her frustration on Roger. She knew he had a right to be bitter, and she didn't fault him for it. She just wanted him to go home.

"He dresses in hides like a savage!" Roger exclaimed.

Holly turned back toward him. "If you can't see more of a man than his clothes, then I feel very sorry for you."

"My God!" Roger rose and began to back away. "You're wearing that vile perfume again," he remarked with obvious disgust. "I suppose someone with Driscoll's earthy tastes would actually like it."

"He loves it," Holly replied, and pride lit her smile. She watched Roger walk away with a brisk, angry stride, his velvet coattails flapping, and muffled her laughter behind her hands. She remained in the garden for a while, then in surprisingly high spirits, she went back to the front of the house; but to her utter dismay, Sam had already gone home.

She had expected him to be waiting for her, then realized that was a ridiculous assumption when she had given him no reason to stay. She did not care if she ever saw Roger again, but she prayed Sam would keep his promise and not give up his efforts to win her heart.

The Cochranes had just finished their noon meal the next day when Sam arrived with a present for Holly.

Not certain she was ready to accept gifts, she was reluctant to go to the door, but John wheedled and coaxed until their parents urged her to at least go and speak with her caller. After looking into three pairs of laughing eyes, she knew she wasn't fooling anyone but herself by feigning an indifference she did not feel.

"Fine. I'll talk with him, but I still don't believe it would be proper for me to accept a present."

"Just wait until you see what it is," John teased.

Her curiosity piqued, Holly went to the door. Sam was standing out front with his beautiful gray stallion. He had braided pink satin ribbons in the horse's mane, and when Holly came down the steps, he offered her the reins.

"I said that I'd give you a horse at the auction," he told her. "It hadn't slipped my mind. I want you to have Shadow. He's a gentle soul despite his size, and he'll make a good horse for you."

Holly searched Sam's expression for any clue that this was another of his sly tricks, but there was no hint of laughter in his eyes. "Oh, Sam. I can't take your stallion. He must be the finest horse you own and—"

"Not anymore," Sam insisted. "Come on. Let's go for a ride."

Before Holly could object, Sam pulled himself up on Shadow's back and reached down for her. He moved back in his saddle so there was room for her to sit in front of him as neatly as she would have been perched upon a sidesaddle. Holly sent a frantic glance toward her parents, who had followed her out on the porch, but they smiled and waved along with John; and before she knew it, Sam nudged his heels into Shadow's flanks and they were riding away.

Holly slid one arm around Sam's waist and hung on to Shadow's beribboned mane with her other hand. Even carrying two, the stallion was swift, and the ride was the most exhilarating Holly had ever taken.

"Where are we going?" Holly asked when she caught her breath.

"I'm taking you home."

Holly didn't even know where Sam lived, but relaxed against him. The skirt of her violet-sprinkled gown billowed up around her ankles, and she was glad she had chosen it that morning. She relaxed against Sam's chest and remembered very proper rides in Roger's carriage which had been not nearly as much fun.

Sam's two-story house was off a side road on the way into Williamsburg. Built of wood, it was faced with weatherboards freshly painted white, and the windows were framed with bright green shutters. The front door of the charming residence had also been painted green as the final touch on the job Sam had worked so hard to complete.

He leapt off Shadow's back, then carefully set Holly on her feet. "The very same day that you told me my bride might run right out my back door, I bought the paint and started cleaning up my house. I didn't spend any time with Annette that you didn't see. I've been here the whole time trying to make a home you'd be proud to share."

Holly was near tears again, but tried to blink them away. "Why didn't you tell me?"

Sam took her hand to lead her to the front door. "That would have spoiled the surprise. If there's anything you don't like, just say so and I'll repaint the room. As for the furniture, we can get rid of it all and buy whatever you want. I want you to be happy here, Holly."

Holly didn't know what to expect; but as they toured the rooms, she thought the house as attractive as its owner. Sam had painted the master bedroom a pale apricot shade, and the bed was covered in a bright quilt in a Log Cabin Star design made of gorgeous French calicos. "I've never seen such a pretty quilt. Where did you find it?"

"It was my mother's. My father had it locked away all these years, so it's like new. It's really all I have that was hers and I'd hoped that you'd like it."

Holly ran her fingertips down a line of intricate stitches. Sam was a man who had given her his stallion, which had to be his most cherished possession, and covered their bed with a precious heirloom. This time, moved to tears by the love that filled his every gesture, tears spilled over her lashes.

"Holly?" Certain he had offended her again, Sam sat down on the bed and pulled her down across his lap. "It's all right," he assured her. "It's just an old quilt, and I'll put it away and buy you whatever you'd like to have."

Holly threaded her fingers through the long fringe on his sleeve. "No. It's a beautiful quilt. I love it, and you."

In Sam's view, she was making absolutely no sense. "Then why are you crying?"

"I'm crying because you should have told me years ago that you loved me, and I would have hurried and grown up a lot faster." She reached up to untie the ribbon at his nape and freed his thick, wavy hair. Sam had such a good heart, and her mother had been right: She would simply have to teach him how to please her even more tenderly than she had taught him how to dance.

"I can't wait to dance the minuet with you at the wedding," she whispered against his lips.

Sam put his hands on her shoulders to force her back where he could see her clearly. "You're not just teasing me? Your answer's yes; you'll marry me?"

Holly nodded. "Of course, you'll have to ask my father's permission first."

"I already did," Sam announced proudly, "yesterday while you were telling Roger goodbye."

"You didn't!" Sam flashed the wide grin that had always melted her heart, and Holly no longer doubted that he had. "What made you so certain that's what I was telling him?"

"The way you'd kissed me in the morning. I've waited so long for that, but it was well worth it."

He was definitely presumptuous, but Holly didn't want to fight with him again. "Other than to keep you entertained, what will you expect me to do after we're married?"

Surprised by her question, Sam needed a moment to consider a reply. "Run the house, raise the children, whatever it is women do with their time."

"Would you expect to select my clothes, or my friends?"

Sam's expression filled with disbelief. "Of course not."

"Good. You're exactly what I want in a husband." Holly raised her arms to encircle his neck and invited another of his delicious kisses. In an instant, she was lost in him again, and the few days he had made her wait seemed a trivial offense compared to the lifetime of love he was now offering. This time when she slid her hands under his shirt, he leaned back to rip it off over his head and threw it aside. His chest was covered with dark curls that were a delight to comb, and Holly drew him down on the bed where they had more room to explore each other with touch and taste.

Slow and sweet, Sam let Holly set the pace, but she led him beyond his wildest dreams and the whole afternoon blurred into a passionate feast that left them both fully sated. The sun was nearing the treetops before Sam rose on his elbow. "I'm going to have to take you home and convince your parents to set an early wedding date.

I don't want anyone counting on his fingers when our first baby's born."

Holly caught his hand and brought it to her lips. "You walk around grinning like that, and they'll surely do it. Frankly, I don't even care."

"Holly!"

He looked as aghast as she had been at some of his all-too-spontaneous comments, and she pulled his head down on her breast and combed her fingers through his hair. "I love you, Sam Driscoll, and I don't care who knows it. In fact, I think I'll give you my prize stallion as a wedding present."

Sam rose to look her in the eye. "I would have insisted you keep Shadow even if you'd turned me down, Holly. Of course, he is trained to come home to me."

"Oh, Sam, so am I." Holly kissed him with a sense of wonder she doubted would ever dim, for although she had never seen his house before that day, she knew this was precisely where she belonged.

Holly Cochrane and Sam Driscoll were married in the Bruton Parish Church on the first Saturday in June. The ceremony was fragrant with the scent of gardenias and roses, and no one recalled seeing a more beautiful bride, or more handsome groom. Roger Wincott sat in a back pew between his sister Caroline and Annette Hemby. Both young women giggled continuously at his amusing commentary and, rather than nurse a broken heart, Roger was grateful he had escaped taking such a willful young woman as his bride.

As for Sam Driscoll, he had the woman of his dreams and slid a gold band on Holly's finger with the heartfelt promise *Always, and Forever* engraved inside.

Man of My Dreams

by
Colleen Faulkner

One

"Molly! Molly Commages, come here." Sarah crooked her finger angrily. This was the third time this week Cook had complained to Sarah about her daughter.

"Yes, Mama?" Molly appeared from behind the punched-tin pie safe, her hands tucked mischievously behind her. The cozy, winter kitchen smelled of fresh-baked gingerbread, stewing apples, and roast pork. It was a perfect place for a little girl to hide on a blistering-cold February afternoon.

"Did you take Cook's plate of gingerbread?"

Molly, a tall girl for nine, pushed back one silky blonde braid. "No, Mama."

Sarah stood in the doorway, an ash bucket in one hand, a short twig broom in the other. She was behind on her day's chores and if she didn't complete her work to her mistress's satisfaction in due time, there'd be hell to pay.

Sarah pushed her mob cap further onto the back of her head with her forearm and sighed. It was difficult being the mother of a child when there was no father, no family to support her. It was difficult to know when to loosen the reins and when to pull back hard on them.

"Molly, how can you stand there and lie to me with the gingerbread still on your breath!"

The little girl brushed the incriminating crumbs from the corners of her mouth with the back of her hand.

"Well, Miss?" Sarah knew this was bound to be a good one. She could tell by sparkle in her daughter's honey-gold eyes.

Cook said it was Sarah's fault the child was such a liar. She said that if Sarah didn't constantly fill the girl's mind with fanciful tales, the child would have a better understanding of truth and falsehood. Sarah thought Cook to be a shriveled, sour-faced prune, but she kept her thoughts to herself and only nodded when she ranted. Molly had so little enjoyment in her life, being born into servitude, that Sarah felt that if she could give her daughter a little pleasure with her stories, then they were well worth an occasional berating.

Sarah tapped the toe of her worn leather shoe on the brick floor. "Yes? I'm still waiting for an explanation."

"Well, you see, Mama—" Molly began to wind up, obviously fabricating the story as she went along. "It's true, I must admit, I did take Cook's plate of gingercakes." She held up her index finger. "But only because we had an important guest in the garden this morning, a guest worthy of the best gingerbread in all Williamsburg."

"Is that right?" Sarah lifted her eyebrow. "Do tell. Who came to visit?"

Molly looked this way and that as if someone might be listening. Then she cupped her hand around her mouth and whispered. "The Prince of Wales . . ."

Sarah opened her jaw in feigned shock. Last week it had been German George himself. "The Prince of Wales came to visit the Birminghams? And no one knew? Not even nosy Mistress Tam at the millinery shop?"

Molly nodded, throwing back her shoulders with self-importance. "Indeed, he did come. It was a secret, of course. He was on a peace mission."

"Of course." Sarah didn't smile with amusement, though she was sorely tempted. "So just how is it that *you* came to entertain the prince in the garden behind the *necessary?* Weren't the master and mistress wondering where he was?"

Molly threw up her hand in immediate response. "They were busy. Master Birmingham was having his morning sit-down and the mistress was trying to fit her bosom into her blue brocade gown. You know, the one with the hem the spit dog chewed."

"I see." Sarah set down the ash bucket, dropping her broom into it. "And out of curiosity, what else did you serve the Prince of Wales behind the necessary whilst the Birminghams were occupied? Surely he was thirsty after that long trip across the ocean."

Molly grinned. "Chocolate! Chocolate mixed in hot milk with lots of white sugar!"

"Molly!" Sarah was aghast. "Please tell me you didn't steal Mistress Birmingham's chocolate! Cook will have your head and mine! You know how scarce chocolate's become since the war."

The little girl folded her hands over her soiled apron with indignation. "What was I supposed to do, Mama? I couldn't very well give 'im naught but bitter colonial tea, him being the prince and all!"

Sarah shook her head in frustration. "I want you to apologize to Cook and offer to do extra chores for her to make up for your thievery."

Molly dropped her hands to her sides. "Oh, Mama! She'll make me dump slop pails!"

"Serves you right." Sarah picked up the ash bucket and broom. "Now get your tail out to the herb garden where Cook's digging tubbers and apologize to her. Then I want you to join me in the front parlor *with* a broom."

"Mama . . ."

"Now, miss, before I lose my temper and fan your bottom. You're not too old for me to do that, you know."

"Yes, Mama." She rolled her eyes as she shuffled toward the back door.

Shaking her head, Sarah started down the rear hallway. She had two more fireplaces to clean, and there were still the carpets to be beaten on the clothes line before it grew dark. From dawn until dusk she worked for her mistress and worked hard. But it hadn't always been this way; Sarah hadn't always been an indentured servant.

The years turned in her mind like pages in one of the leather-bound books in the master's library. She'd been no older than Molly was now the year her mother, father, and little brother had died in a London house fire. She'd gone to Uncle Morton and Aunt Peg's to live because she had no other family. Sarah had worked hard in their Fleet Street tavern, cooking, cleaning, and trying to dodge her aunt's brutal fist.

Sarah bit down on the soft inner lining of her upper lip. She still remembered that night her uncle had slipped into the kitchen behind her and put his hands on her budding breasts. She'd been barely fifteen years old. She remembered his slobbering kisses and crude words. It wasn't until he dropped his drawers that she had realized what he was about to do. Even after all these years, Sarah still recalled clearly picking up the fire log and raising it over her head. She had warned Uncle Morton to back off else she'd strike him. He'd laughed and taken a step toward her, tugging on his veined, swollen member. That was when she'd struck him. Uncle Morton fell on the kitchen floor, dead before he hit the warped floorboards. She hadn't meant to kill him, only drive him off. Sarah hadn't known a man's skull could be so soft.

The constable had come at once and dragged her

away. But even the filthy, rat-infested cells of Newgate Prison had seemed a respite from her aunt's shrieking. The English court's trial and punishment had come quickly. The penalty for her guilt in her uncle's murder was death. She was sentenced to hang at Tyburn. But then, by a stroke of God's mercy, she was offered clemency. If she would indenture herself for twenty-one years in the American Colonies, her life would be spared.

Shortly thereafter, Sarah found herself below the deck of a fetid ship bound for America. Two days at sea, a drunken bosun's mate had raped her and by the time she had arrived in the Virginia Colony to stand on the sale block, she was sixteen years old and three-months pregnant. It was a sad enough tale, she knew, but no sadder than others she'd heard.

Sarah smiled as she turned the corner into the parlor, her bucket and broom in hand. Sweet Molly was the one thing she'd gotten for her troubles; and her daughter was worth every tear, every stroke of hard work, every scornful word flung at her for giving birth to a bastard. Molly was her beam of sunlight in an otherwise dark world.

In the fading afternoon light, Sarah dropped the bucket onto the cold brick hearth with a bang and knelt to begin sweeping ashes. The air was so cold in the front parlor that she could see her own breath before her face as she shoveled soot into the bucket. Once the fireplace was clean, she'd light a fire with wood the kitchen boy had already brought in.

The mistress liked a warm room to feed her guests in. Behind Sarah, the square mahogany table was already set for the evening's meal. Since the signing of the Declaration of Independence in a place north of Virginia called Philadelphia, the Birminghams' parlor was often filled with guests all talking excitedly of the war. The Birminghams called themselves loyal English citizens, but Sarah suspected otherwise. There were too many late visitors passing through the garden; there was too much whispering. Despite their claims, Sarah guessed that the husband and wife who held her indenture were rebels.

Not that it mattered much to her. Sarah was in no position to be for or against one side or the other. It was hard for an indentured woman to understand talk of the Crown's oppression or freedom for all. What was important to Sarah was that her daughter be safe, with a roof that didn't leak over her head and food in her belly. If being English would supply that, Sarah would remain an English woman; if the rebels could offer her daughter a better future, than Sarah would be a rebel. For now, she took no side, but only stood in the shadows and watched and listened, realizing that at some point she might be forced to make the choice.

Sarah heard the sound of Molly's leather shoes clunking beneath her as she came down the hall. "Pick up your feet," she instructed her daughter as the little girl appeared in the parlor doorway. "Those shoes have to last a long time."

Molly lifted her worn, striped petticoat and came to kneel beside her mother on the cold, brick hearth, a broom tucked beneath her arm. "I'm sorry I told a fibber," she said, staring into the blackened fireplace dejectedly. "I meant to just snitch a crumb of the gingerbread. But I couldn't help myself." She peered into her mother's face. "It tasted so good, Mama."

Sarah looked away, her tone softening. "It's a wonder you haven't a belly pain eating all that sweet."

"Oh, no," Molly corrected. "I didn't eat it all myself. I gave the stable boy, Jack, two whole cakes, one for his grandmama with the blind eye, and I gave the laundress's little girl one, too."

Sarah scooped up a shovel of ashes and dumped it

into the bucket. "You're generous with someone else's gingerbread."

Molly took the shovel from her mother. "Let me do this. You rest a minute, Mama."

"No." She reached for the shovel. "We've got to hurry along. I've still the fireplace in the master's library and the rugs and it's getting dark."

"Mama, please." Sarah began to shovel the ashes with great efficiency for a child. "Just rest and tell me a story while I work. Will you?"

Sarah sat back on her knees, thankful for a moment's respite. "All right. Which one shall it be? The fish-tailed mergirl?"

Molly shook her head and wrinkled her nose.

"How about the boy that became a radish?"

Molly giggled. "A boy can't turn into a radish!"

"Hm . . . tell that to that little radish in the garden," Sarah teased. "I believe his name is Joshua."

"Oh, Mama. I don't want to hear that one!" She laughed. "You know which one I like best. Tell me my favorite."

"Not that story again! I'm bored to death with it." She reached out to finger one of her daughter's silky braids. Molly's favorite story was hers, too. It was her favorite because secretly it was her dream, her dream for her daughter's future.

"Please, Mama. I swear I'll be good." She pressed her hand to her heart. "No more snitching and no more fibbers."

"Oh, all right," Sarah sighed, hugging herself for warmth in the cold, dim parlor. "But only the short version. I've too much to do to while away the day telling stories."

As Molly swept the charred brick hearth rhythmically, Sarah began to weave a tale. It was the same story she had been telling Molly since she was a babe, embellished over the years. She told her daughter of the young man that would come to the doorstep one sunny afternoon and beg for a young serving woman's hand in marriage. The young woman's name in the story was Molly. She told her daughter how handsome the gentleman was, how well-mannered, how smart and educated, how utterly kind.

"And wealthy, Mama, don't forget the wealthy part," Molly chimed in, dragging the shovel along the bricks.

"And wealthy, with a house in town and a plantation along the James River," she told her daughter.

"And servants," Molly added.

"Servants," Sarah echoed, shaking her head. "More servants than a woman would know what to do with. So many servants that each must take a full day off every week just so there's work for the others."

Molly giggled behind a sooty hand as she dropped the shovel into the full ash bucket. "And they'll love their mistress, won't they, Mama? They won't call her names behind her back or snitch her sweets, because they love her."

"Because their mistress is so good to them," Sarah assured her. "So fair, and giving."

Moll threw her arms around her mother. "Oh, Mama, it's a wonderful story, isn't it?" She lifted her head from her mother's shoulder, her face full of hope and youth.

Sarah smiled sadly. Molly had been born into indenture. She'd not be free until her twenty-first birthday, and then where would she go? What would she do with no education, no skills? She'd end up a scullery maid the remainder of her life. If she were fortunate she would work for decent people like the Birminghams; if she weren't so lucky, she'd work for a man and woman like Sarah's aunt and uncle.

Sarah gave her daughter's loose braid a tug. There was no sense dwelling on what the future would bring.

She knew she needed to be hopeful, just like Molly. "Grab the bucket and let's go," she directed, getting to her feet. "You dump the ashes and meet me in the—"

The sound of male voices came suddenly from the hall and, before Sarah could hurry her daughter from the room, the master and a guest appeared in the shadows of the parlor doorway, deep in conversation.

Molly looked up at her mother wide-eyed with trepidation. Mistress Birmingham wanted her servants to do their tasks efficiently, without being seen or heard. She didn't want her servants or slaves present before her husband unless specifically ordered.

Sarah dropped her hand to her daughter's shoulder. Master Birmingham and his visitor hadn't noticed them in the fading winter light, but there was no way for them to slip out. The men were blocking the doorway.

"Impossible," Algood Birmingham declared, red-faced. "My daughter is visiting in Richmond. I'd not risk it if she were here, anyway."

"But there must be someone," the thin man with the curly, black wig insisted.

Sarah thought she recognized him from Bruton Parish Church services, but she didn't know his name.

"I'd not ask you, Algood, if I weren't desperate."

Sarah felt her palms grown warm and damp. This was obviously a conversation not meant for her ears, but there was no tactful way to get Molly and herself out of the room. The men still hadn't noticed them.

"What of Martha?" the wigged man pleaded. "Would she do it if you asked her?"

"Martha?" Master Birmingham chuckled, the ample middle that hung over his breeches jiggling. "She'd be so frightened she'd faint before she crossed the tavern doorstep. It would take a mule to drag her out if she went down!"

The visitor laughed with him as he pulled a lace handkerchief from his sleeve and mopped his sweaty forehead. Then he grew serious again. "You've got to help me, Algood. We're desperate. Our army's depending on receiving this information through the specified contact. I—"

The sound of a bucket hitting the plank floor resounded through the parlor, silencing the visitor.

Molly stared up at her mother with wide-eyes and a gaping mouth as she scooped the bucket up off the floor, trying to push ashes over the rim with her shoe.

The visitor's gaze searched the room for the source of the commotion and Sarah and Molly were caught.

Master Birmingham turned his head to see them. "What the hell are you doing in here?" he shouted, his ruddy face paling.

Molly gave a squeak.

Sarah linked her arm through her daughter's and hurried toward the door and the two men, her head lowered subserviently. "Cleaning, sir."

He came toward her. "What did you hear? Tell me!"

She shook her head, focusing on the polished silver buckle of his heeled shoes. "Nothing, sir. I wasn't paying attention. I never heard you come into the room until you were here." She stopped in front of him holding tightly to Molly's trembling hand. There was no place to go. "I'm sorry."

"You don't belong here, listening in on words not meant for your ears, woman! Are you dim witted? Don't you understand the seriousness of your error?"

Sarah lifted her head slowly, trying to control the burning anger that rose in a lump in her throat. It was true she was this man's indentured servant, but she was still a person with rights. She had a right not to be called stupid. If there was one thing she would teach her daughter, it would be to demand fair treatment for herself, from anyone from the lowest stable boy to the king himself.

"I said I was sorry, sir," she said, looking him straight in the eyes. "But you didn't see me when you and your guest stepped into the room and began your conversation. I was supposed to be here cleaning. The mistress sent me."

The man in the wig chuckled. "She's got a point, Algood. We didn't look to see that the room was unoccupied."

Sarah refused to look away. "Are we dismissed, sir?" she asked.

Before the master could nod, the man in the black wig spoke again. "What about her, Algood? She's got enough backbone to stand up against you. Why not send her?"

Two

Sarah looked up at the visitor, wishing she'd paid closer attention to the men's conversation. She had no idea what they were talking about. Send her where?

Algood Birmingham tucked his hand thoughtfully into the waistband of his mahogany breeches. "Send *her?*"

"Yes. Why not? The task is simple. Carry the message, meet the contact, dine with him, and return home."

Master Birmingham plucked at his dimpled chin. "She's inappropriately dressed."

"So, dress her appropriately."

"She's a servant for sweet Christ's sake. It's likely she has the manners of a Turk."

"She doesn't have to say anything. Our contact is expecting a woman. Nothing more."

Master Birmingham glanced at Sarah.

Sarah still didn't understand exactly what the men were talking about, except that she guessed it was a mission, a secret mission. And though a part of her was afraid for her own safety, deep inside, she was trembling with nervous excitement. Sarah had spent her entire life living vicariously through her own stories. Through the tales she told, she lived romance, she lived adventure, she dressed in fancy gowns, she ate the finest food, she experienced all the pleasures life had to offer a few chosen people, knowing she would never be one of the chosen.

Now suddenly she had the chance to actually live a little of that adventure and the thought intrigued her.

"What's your name? Mary, is it?" Master Birmingham asked.

Sarah shook her head. "No, sir, Mary is the slave who works in the kitchen. She serves your meals, sir. I'm Sarah, Sarah Commages. And this is my daughter, Molly."

Molly bobbed a curtsy.

He ignored Molly, squinting at Sarah as if seeing her for the very first time. "You've been here with us a long time, haven't you?"

"Ten years, sir. The mistress bought my indenture when I was sent from London."

He nodded, as if recalling when she'd arrived, though Sarah knew he didn't. Ten years she'd been in the household and the man didn't know her name. The thought made her feel very small, that her life was insignificant.

"You say this is your daughter. No husband?"

Sarah refused to lower her head. She refused to accept blame for what had happened on that ship so long ago. "No, sir. No husband."

Then the master slapped his ample thigh. "That's right, I remember Martha speaking of your situation." He glanced up at the visitor. "Convicted felon, Roger."

"Thievery?"

"Murder."

Both men stared at Sarah.

"Were you innocent of the charges?" the visitor asked.

Sarah lifted her chin, meeting his gaze. "No, sir. I killed him sure enough, a blood relative. He sought to take what wasn't his. I hit him with a piece of firewood. I didn't mean to kill him, only defend myself; but he died just the same."

He chuckled. "I like this woman." He studied Sarah's

clean-scrubbed face. "Send the child away," he said softly. "She need not hear what I have to say to you."

Molly immediately gripped her mother's hand, staring at the man called Roger as if he were an ogre from one of her mother's fairy tales.

Sarah took the ash bucket and broom from her daughter's clenched fingers. She knew she could tell the man no. She was certain he couldn't make her deliver the message if she didn't want to, but she wanted to do it. Heavens, she was only twenty-five years old. She still felt so young inside. She wanted this moment of excitement, of danger. Just this one time in her life she wanted to live through her actions rather than through her stories.

"Go," Sarah ordered her daughter. "Go to the kitchen and help Cook prepare the evening's supper. Stay with Cook until I come for you."

"But, Mama—"

Sarah gave her daughter a look that bid her be silent, and thankfully, for once, the girl listened.

Sarah stood between the two men and waited until the sound of her daughter's footsteps died down the hallway. Only then did she turn to address the man called Roger. She was exactly the same height as he, so she could look him straight in the eyes. She didn't take the time to set the bucket and broom down. "You want me to carry a message? Where?"

Roger looked to Master Birmingham as if for consent. The master nodded ever so slightly and Roger turned his gaze back to Sarah. "You would be but a courier. There's no danger. You'll simply carry the message to the Crook and Crown Tavern off Gloucester, sup with the contact, and return home. I'm afraid I can't tell you what the message concerns—"

She lifted her palm, knowing it had to be soiled with the soot of the fireplace, and shook her head. "I don't need to know. I don't want to. I'll do it."

"You will?" Roger, perhaps only ten years her senior, broke into a boyish grin. "You'll do it?"

She looked to Master Birmingham. "If my master so bids me, yes sir."

Roger clasped his hands, then reached out, around Sarah, to slap Birmingham on the shoulder. "I knew you'd come through, Algood. I knew I could count on your support. I told the men we could count on you."

Master Birmingham nodded, obviously pleased with himself. "Glad to be of service."

"Now," Roger went on, directing the conversation to Sarah again, "it will be necessary for you to change clothes."

Self-consciously, Sarah ran a hand over her sooty apron. "I've nothing else, sir, but a Sunday frock, and I fear that's patched, too."

Algood lifted a meaty hand. "So send her as a lady's maid."

Roger shook his head. "No. The orders were specific. The agreement is that the *lady* will meet with our contact and dine with him. We have to follow orders, even when we don't understand them, Algood. After that scare last month, I would trust that's become obvious to us all." He crossed his arms in thought, then after a moment, spoke excitedly. "I have it! Sarah's nearly the same size as my wife. Let me take her home with me; Eliza can dress her and I'll send her on her way." He extracted a gold watch from his waistcoat to check the time. "But we'll have to hurry. If she's late, the contact won't wait. That's a direct order from Morristown."

Before Master Birmingham could speak again, Roger took the ash bucket and broom from Sarah's hands and pushed it into her master's. "I'm sorry I won't make it back for supper, Algood, but give my regrets to Martha, will you?" He was already ushering Sarah out the door.

She halted in the dark parlor doorway. "Wait, sir. My

daughter. I have to tell her I'm leaving, else she'll be frightened. Someone needs to keep an eye on her whilst I'm gone."

"Algood can take care of that, can't you, Algood?"

Master Birmingham made a sound in his throat. "I . . . I suspect so, Roger."

Roger rested a hand on her shoulder. "Who would care for the girl if you had gone to the market or the millinery?"

"Mary. Mary could put her to bed." She glanced at her master. "Could you see to it, sir?"

After a second of hesitation, he gave a swipe with the broom. "Hell, yes. I'll see to it, Sarah. You just do as Roger asks and return home when you've completed the task."

"Yes, sir." Sarah bobbed a quick curtsy, then followed Roger out of the dark parlor and down the hallway to the rear entrance to the house, her heart pounding. Minutes later, she was taking her very first ride in a covered carriage.

Sarah spun around in front of the floor-length, gilded cherub mirror, unable to suppress a sigh of delight. In less than an hour's time, Roger's wife, Eliza, had miraculously transformed Sarah from a simple housemaid into a lady of quality.

Eliza, a woman no older than Sarah herself, smiled, a row of dress pins in her mouth. "Wait, wait." She laughed. "Let me nip the waist in just a bit here, and then you'll be ready."

Sarah couldn't believe the reflection in the mirror. She couldn't believe that the woman with the silky strawberry-blonde hair and powdered cheeks was really Sarah Commages.

The gown Eliza chose for her on the cold February

evening was what Eliza called a sensible traveling habit, something that would not draw attention to her, but was of obvious good taste. It was the most gorgeous bit of cloth Sarah had ever laid eyes on.

Sarah's forest-green skirts hung without hoops, a black wool petticoat beneath for warmth. She wore a wool caracul jacket of the same forest green, and beneath the jacket was a black-velvet girdle with a gold pocket watch that hung from a green ribbon. Her black stockings were heavily clocked, her shoes a supple black leather.

Eliza had allowed Sarah to take a bath of hot water and sweet-smelling soap in her own bedchamber; then, while Sarah sat wrapped in a warm cotton sheet, Eliza combed the serving girl's hair out, drying it near the fire until it hung in a sheet of pale red down her back. Eliza had twisted Sarah's hair this way and that, securing it to her head with a handful of shiny gold bobkins. Then, she had heated a metal rod and careful pulled down wisps of hair to curl. Eliza crowned her masterpiece with a tiny Irish-lace mobcap. Sarah felt like a princess, like a queen. She knew it was foolish to be so vain, but she didn't care as she spun before the mirror. This was her one night of adventure in an otherwise dull life, and she was going to enjoy every moment of it.

The kind, sweet Eliza gave Sarah a pair of dyed-black doeskin gloves, and a black wool cloak that smelled of lavender. Only then did she escort her down the back staircase to a hired carriage. Roger waited there in the dark doorway.

"Take this." He pressed a velvet lady's bag into her hand. "It contains the message," he whispered. "The driver has the order to take you to the Crook and Crown. You will go inside and instruct the innkeeper that you wait for a gentleman. She will take you to a table between the rear door and the fireplace in the public room. Wait there for the gentleman. Dine with him when he comes. He will accept the reticule, and then take your leave."

Sarah looked into Roger's grey eyes. She felt stiff with the tight stays, the heavy clothing, and powdered face. "How will I know the gentleman?"

Roger smiled. "He'll know you, dear. Now, the important thing is that you not reveal anything about yourself or ask the gentleman any questions. You could risk not just your life and his, but many others' lives as well. Do you understand?"

She nodded.

"Good luck, then." He dropped Eliza's cloak over her shoulders. "The driver will return you to the Birminghams' after you have completed the task."

"Godspeed," Eliza whispered, lifting the hood over Sarah's head and tying it beneath her chin. Then she gave Sarah's trembling hand a squeeze, and Sarah was pushed gently out into the frigid darkness.

The carriage driver met her halfway across the snowy yard and helped her inside, saying nothing. A moment later she was alone in the coach, clutching the reticule for dear life, her chest filled with nervous excitement.

Only a few minutes passed before the carriage rolled to a halt. Sarah felt the weight of the driver lift off his seat and she heard his footsteps outside in the snow. They had arrived at the Crook and Crown Tavern. Sarah had passed it many times just off Duke of Gloucester Street on her way to the market, but she'd never been inside. She'd never been inside any tavern but her aunt and uncle's.

When the driver swung open the door, Sarah took a deep breath. She could do this; she knew she could do it. Then, she lifted her chin and alighted from the carriage just as the women in her stories did.

The driver said nothing. Sarah said nothing. She walked across the snowy brick walk, directly beneath the creaking wooden tavern sign, and opened the front door as if she did so every evening.

The entryway opened into a warm, noisy public room. Sarah closed the door behind her, trying to keep in mind she was a lady tonight. She was not Sarah Commages the house maid, Sarah Commages the indentured servant. She was a woman without a name come to meet a gentleman friend, a secret lover, perhaps. She was a woman of mystery, of intrigue.

A short, bosomy woman in a crisp white apron, carrying a tray, spotted Sarah and immediately pushed the tray into a passing tavern-maid's hands. "Good even' to you," the bosomy woman called, hustling across the sanded, plank floor. "I'm Mistress Gordon, innkeeper here."

Sarah had to make a conscious effort not to curtsy. Mistress Gordon was above Sarah's station. Practically everyone in the town of Williamsburg was above Sarah's station, except the slaves.

"Good even' to you," Sarah said, trying to imitate the sound of Eliza's voice.

Mistress Gordon stood before Sarah, her hands buried in the folds of her pristine apron. "How can I assist you?"

So far, she didn't seem to suspect the truth. She didn't realize who or what Sarah really was. The thought gave Sarah confidence. Her gaze strayed as she pushed back the hood of her cloak. She was looking for the contact.

Was he here already? Was he that tall man with sparse hair or the short bewigged fellow with the rosy cheeks? Would he be as old as Papa John, the white-haired slave who carried firewood for the Birmingham house? Or would the contact be a young boy, barely into breeches?

"I . . ." Sarah met the innkeeper's gaze with an air of mystery in her voice. "I'm here to meet a gentleman."

She pointed to an empty table. "There. Nine o'clock on the hour."

The innkeeper's fuzzy eyebrows lifted with understanding. "Yes, yes, I see." She stepped smoothly to one side. "We are always discreet here at the Crook and Crown, I can promise you that. Let me show you to your table. Will you be ordering before the gentleman arrives?"

Sarah followed the innkeeper to the table between the door and the fireplace. "No. I'll wait." She slid onto the bench seat, giving a nod of dismissal.

Mistress Gordon hung by the trestle table's edge for a moment, then backed away. "I'll send a girl for your order once the gentleman has arrived."

"Thank you," Sarah said gracefully. Then she looked away, just as her own mistress did whenever she was dismissing one of her servants.

Sarah made an event of folding her cloak, attempting to cover her nervousness, as she studied the busy public room. It was filled mostly with men, men of the same caliber as her master and Roger. They were talking at once, of the war and politics no doubt, eating and drinking. Glasses clinked. She heard the sound of ivory dice rolling behind her. There was masculine laughter interspersed with the occasional sound of women's voices. There was so much to see that Sarah was beside herself. She wanted to take in everything: the smell of the Roanoke tobacco, the sound of the pewter plates being stacked by the serving girl, the taste of excitement in the dim, smoky public room. She wanted to remember it all so that later she could go back and tell Molly what it had been like.

Sarah was so caught up in watching two men argue over a hand of cards that she never saw the redcoat approach her table. Suddenly there was a pair of shiny boots at her feet. A soldier! She'd not expected him to be an English soldier. Now she was really confused. Was her master truly a loyal English subject or was this merely a ruse? Slowly she looked up.

He was smiling, and he was the finest man she had ever laid eyes on.

Sarah could do nothing but smile back at the face as he took her hand and brushed his lips across the palm of her glove. He was a tall gentleman with a striking jawline and laughing brown eyes. He had the eyes of the man in Molly's favorite story.

"My apologies for being late," he said, sliding onto the bench across from her. "Have you ordered yet?" He spoke to Sarah as if he knew her . . . as he'd known her a lifetime.

"No," she managed to answer. "I . . . waited for you." He removed his uniform hat and slid it across the scarred wooden table. He was an officer; she could tell by the insignia across his broad shoulders.

"Girl, here." He snapped his fingers, and a maid with a tray of sloshing ale tankards hustled to the table-side.

"Sir?"

"Supper for us both, an ale for myself, and for the lady . . ."

He glanced at her and for a moment Sarah felt a wave of panic. She didn't know what to order. She'd never had anything to drink in her life but water, tea, and a little sweet cider in the summertime.

Her soldier turned his gaze back to the barmaid with the ease that must be born of a gentleman. "The lady will have a glass of verdelho." He lifted an eyebrow, waiting for Sarah's consent.

"Yes." She glanced at the barmaid, then back at him. He was grinning with a lazy smile that set her at ease. "That would be . . . perfect," she finished sweetly.

Then the barmaid was gone and they were left alone. Sarah didn't know what to say or what to do. All she could do was stare at the man seated before her and wonder when she would wake up from this wonderful dream.

"Trouble getting here?" he asked, seeming to sense her nervousness.

She lowered her gaze, fiddling with the black-velvet reticule. "No, no trouble."

He nodded. "Good."

Sarah felt suddenly so inept. "And you? Trouble?"

"I came by horseback. The roads are easier to manage."

She nodded. "Of course." Of course she didn't know. She'd never ridden anywhere on horseback, neither here nor in London.

He chuckled after a moment of silence and reached for her hand. Sarah knew she shouldn't allow a stranger to touch her with such familiarity, but it was all part of the game, wasn't it? She was perfectly safe here among a roomful of ladies and gentleman. So why not pretend he was her lover? What harm was there in that?

Her soldier turned her hand in his as she watched him. She was glad she'd left her gloves on. If she hadn't, he'd have known she wasn't the lady she pretended to be. He would have known by the red, callused flesh and short, broken nails.

He was smiling so that she wondered what he was thinking. How many hands had he kissed in this tavern or the next? Whom was he thinking of? Who was he wishing, or even pretending, she was? A wife? A betrothed? A lover? For some reason it was important for her to know.

She smiled at him, studying his laughing eyes. "Have you someone?" she asked softly.

He lifted an eyebrow and then released her hand with another lazy grin.

She lowered her gaze to study the table. "I'm sorry.

I . . . I'm not very good at this," she whispered. "I know I shouldn't be asking personal questions."

He shook his head, pausing for a moment, waiting for the barmaid to set down their ale and wine and walk away before speaking. "I've met many a contact," he said, his words obviously meant for no one but her. "But I have to admit, you're the most intriguing." He lifted the tankard of ale to his sensual mouth. "No," he said then. "I've no one. You, I suppose, have a husband?"

"No." She sipped the wine, liking the fruity taste as it tingled going down her throat. "No husband."

"A betrothed, certainly."

She shook her head.

"Then I'm even more intrigued."

She glanced over the rim of her glass to see him watching her intently. He was flirting with her. This handsome man with the gentle laughter was actually flirting with her!

She took another sip of her wine. No one had ever made her feel like this before, with a simple word or gesture. Sarah was giddy inside.

"Tell me something about yourself," he murmured, sipping his ale.

She stared into the glass of wine. It was already half empty. She wanted to savor the taste, the smell of it. She wanted to forever imprint it on her mind. "That's not a good idea, do you think?" She looked up at him, across the table from her, so close she could see the tiny laugh lines at the corners of his mouth.

Suddenly his voice was serious. "No, I don't suppose it is. I wouldn't want any harm to come to you. You're very brave to do this."

"I don't feel brave." She ran her index finger along the rim of her glass. "So what do we talk about, if not you or me?"

He leaned back, pushing his empty ale tankard to the

table's edge to be refilled by the next passing maid. "It's not necessary that we talk at all." He reached out with one strong hand as if he were going to touch her face, but then withdrew midway between them. "I . . . I've never seen hair quite the color of yours. I could just sit here and look at your beautiful face the rest of the evening."

She frowned. "Boring, don't you think?"

Then they laughed . . . and talked. They never spoke of themselves, never shared names or places, but somehow they found things to speak of, things close to their hearts.

The evening passed so quickly that Sarah was shocked by the lateness of the hour when she finally peered down at the pocket watch that hung on the green ribbon at her waist. It was nearly midnight!

"I must go."

He tossed his linen napkin on the table littered with nutshells. "I, too."

Then he helped her with her cloak, left coin on the table, and escorted her through the thinning crowd of the public room. Outside it was beginning to snow again.

Pulling her cloak hood over her head, Sarah reached out to catch a white snowflake on her black glove. The carriage was waiting in the alley, but she didn't want to see the night end, not ever. Out of the corner of her eye, she spotted the driver waiting patiently.

Her soldier leaned close to her, holding her with one arm. To a passing stranger they would have appeared to be a couple. "I believe you have something for me?" he said gently.

Flustered, she let her hand and the captured snowflakes fall. The feel of him so close made her skin tingle, her cheeks grow warm. "Yes, yes I guess I do." Then she pressed the small velvet reticule into his hand. Even through her leather glove, she could feel the heat of his touch. "Good night," she whispered.

He leaned closer until his warm breath was faint on her lips. "Good night, sweet."

Then he kissed her. It was an innocent-enough kiss. His lips barely touched hers, like the glide of a moth's wings. But it was her very first kiss.

Her soldier brushed the back of his hand against her cheek, his gaze meeting hers for the briefest moment, then he was gone . . . gone into the snowy night, the reticule containing the secret message tucked safely into his uniform coat.

As Sarah made the brief journey back to the Birmingham town house, she found she couldn't recall what she'd eaten this night or how many glasses of the sweet golden wine she'd drunk. All she could think of was her soldier and the magic of the night.

Three

Sarah lifted her rag over her head to dust the oval mirror hanging above her mistress's clothespress. As she wiped away the winter grime, she couldn't resist peering at her own image. The face that looked back at her was smiling.

It had been nearly a week since the night she had gone to the Crook and Crown Tavern, nearly a week since she had met her soldier, and she was still smiling.

Sarah chuckled to herself as she dragged her dusting rag along the mahogany chair rail that framed her mistress's bedchamber. Though it had been six days since she'd carried the secret message for her master, she could still remember every word her soldier had spoken to her, every touch of his hand. She could still recall the heady masculine scent, the feel of his lips brushing hers as he kissed her goodnight.

Sarah knew that she would never see her soldier again, her soldier whose name she would never know, but she wasn't sad. How could she be, when she had experienced such a magical night, one she would remember the rest of her days? How could she be sad knowing most women lived their entire lives never being as happy as Sarah had been that night. Every time she thought of her soldier—a hundred, a thousand times a day—rather than feeling cheated or bitter for what she would never have, her heart swelled with happiness for what she had possessed for that very short time. For the rest of her life, no matter what happened, she would always have those secret hours to treasure. Those memories in her mind couldn't be stolen or bought or cheapened over time. They were hers forever.

"Mama . . . Mama."

Sarah turned around, startled. She hadn't heard Molly come into the room.

Molly chuckled, snatching the dust rag from her mother's hand. She began to dust the chair rail with smooth, efficient strokes. "Caught you dreamin' again." She giggled. "You're always tellin' me I'd best put my mind to my work and not fanciful thoughts."

Sarah had to smile at her daughter. "Caught me with crumbs still on my face, didn't you?"

Molly wrinkled her nose, taking a closer look at her mother. "I don't see any crumbs on your mouth. Did you snitch some of Cook's gingerbread, too?"

Sarah laughed, leaning over the four-poster bed to fluff the pillows. "I meant you caught me daydreaming and I couldn't deny it."

"I see." Molly took another swipe at the chair rail. "Oh, Master Birmingham's going to send for you."

The hair rose on the back of Sarah's neck. She turned away from the bed to face Molly. The master had never called for her, never in ten years. He could want but one thing. . . . "What do you mean, the master's going to send for me? Did he tell you to fetch me, Molly?"

Molly leaned over a sidetable to reach another strip of chair rail, taking care not to knock over a lavender-colored glass perfume bottle. "No."

"Then how do you know he's going to send for me?"

The little girl turned her back to her mother, shrugging. "Just heard."

"Heard? Heard where? The kitchen?" Any gossip in the household worth knowing came from the kitchen.

Molly's blonde braids swung as she shook her head no.

"Then where did you hear such a thing?"

Molly walked past her mother, ducking before Sarah could catch her. "The master's office."

"The master's office? What were you doing in the master's office? You know you're not permitted in there." Sarah followed her daughter across the room, bringing her finger to Molly's nose. "Were you spying again?"

"No, ma'am."

"Eavesdropping?"

Molly shook her head emphatically. "You told me no more listening in on what wasn't meant for my ears. It could get me into trouble."

Sarah dropped her hands to her hips in exasperation. This conversation was getting her nowhere. "Then when did you hear that the master was going to send for me?"

"I heard when he was whispering to the mistress in his office."

Sarah's eyes widened. It took great effort not to raise her voice. "You were in the office?" She could see by the look on the child's face that her mind was churning.

"I . . . I was, but . . ."

"But what, Molly? You know the rules. No children in the master's office, not even to clean. And certainly no one goes in there in his presence."

Molly stood in the doorway twisting the dusty rag in her hands. "It was an accident, really."

"Yes?"

"How I got in there."

Sarah crossed her arms over her chest. "Go on."

"See. . . . See I was supposed to be helping the laundress with the wet sheets, but Charlie got away."

"Charlie? Who's Charlie, Molly? I'm losing my patience."

"Bonnie Prince Charlie, the cat, of course. You know,

the black-and-white one with the crook in its paw. We don't know how he broke his leg. He just—"

"Molly!" Sarah snapped. "You were telling how you came to eavesdrop on the master and mistress."

"Oh." She looked up at her mother with a sweet smile. "That's right."

Sarah didn't fall for it. "Go on. How did you end up in the master's office?"

"Well, as I said, Charlie got away and I had to chase him. He went right through the office door and under that big chest where the master keeps the jars of dead frogs and such."

Sarah tapped one foot. "You were helping the laundress with the sheets outside; the cat got away, and you ended up in the master's office?"

Molly beamed. "Yes, ma'am."

"But how did the cat get in the house to begin with? The cat is not allowed in the house. No animals in the house but for the master's speckled hound."

Molly pointed. "Exactly why I had to get Charlie out, because the master's hound would take a bite out of his ear for certain."

Sarah rolled her eyes, gesturing. "Let's get to the eavesdropping part, Molly. Tonight, before it gets to be your bedtime."

The little girl screwed up her mouth. "So that's it. Charlie ran under the chest; I crawled in after him, and the master and mistress just happened to be talkin' in whispers." She shrugged. "I just happened to hear him tell her to go find you directly."

Sarah laid her hand on her pounding heart. He wanted her for another mission. What else could it be? She didn't think about the danger. Selfishly, she didn't even think about Molly and having to leave her behind while she went out into the night. All she could think of was her soldier. Would he be the one to receive the message again? Was that too much to hope for?

"Sarah! Sarah, where are you?" Sarah heard her mistress's voice echo in the stairwell.

"Here, here, mistress." Sarah gave Molly a gentle push out of the doorway and stuck her head into the hall. "Here, mistress. Just finishing up the dusting in your bedchamber."

Her mistress, a plump woman with hair dyed the color of eggplant, reached the stair landing and stopped to catch her breath. She pressed her hand to the cleavage of her rising and falling bosom. "I must speak with you. At once."

Sarah hurried down the hallway. "Certainly, mistress."

"Without the child." She eyed Molly meaningfully.

Sarah could still feel her heart pounding as she turned to Molly. "Go finish helping the laundress."

"Mama . . ."

Sarah plucked the dust rag from her daughter's hand. "Now," she added sharply.

Molly came down the hall, but as she passed her mother, she stopped to whisper. "Are you going to see *him* again?"

"Hush," Sarah hissed. Of course she hadn't told her daughter the circumstances of her trip to the tavern last week. All she had said was that she had run an errand in town for the master and met a wonderful man with laughing brown eyes. Molly had tried to pry more from her mother, but that was all Sarah had been willing to say. Anything more and she feared she might put her daughter in danger. "Go!" she ordered Molly, pointing to the staircase.

Molly hustled past Sarah and bobbed a curtsy to the mistress as she went down the steps.

Mistress Birmingham waited for Molly to disappear down the staircase before she turned her attention to

Sarah. "Master Birmingham has need of you in his office."

"Yes, ma'am." She lifted her skirts, her dust rag in hand. "I'll go now."

"No. Wait." The mistress touched Sarah's sleeve, but then withdrew it as if realizing what she'd done. "I . . . I want to tell you." She lifted her gaze to meet Sarah's. Sarah couldn't recall her mistress ever looking her in the eyes, not even the morning she'd been purchased on the sale block in Richmond. "I want you to know that you don't have to do this."

Sarah feared her voice would tremble. "He wants me to take another message?"

Mistress Birmingham glanced down at her own polished slippers. "Yes. But it's not part of your duty. I . . . I don't expect my household servants to be a part of my politics."

"I want to do it," Sarah said softly. The truth was, she didn't care about the politics. She couldn't even say for sure at this moment which side the Birminghams or her soldier were on. She didn't care. All that she cared about was the chance to see *him* again.

"It could be dangerous," her mistress went on. "I believe there's more than one outing involved. Do you understand?"

Sarah hesitated for only a moment. What she had done the other night really hadn't been dangerous, or hadn't seemed so. But she understood the warning. It could get dangerous. Slowly she lifted her gaze to meet Mistress Birmingham's. "I would only ask that if . . . if something were to go wrong, my daughter would be cared for."

Her mistress smiled a smile only women could share. "I would see to it personally."

"Her indenture is only until her twenty-first birthday."

"She'd be welcome to remain here employed or I

would give her a small dowry to catch herself a nice stable groom."

Of course Sarah had higher hopes for her daughter, but she couldn't be ungrateful. Nor could she be unrealistic. She offered her mistress her hands. "Thank you."

Mistress Birmingham walked away and Sarah went down the staircase headed for the master's office, taking the polished wooden steps two at a time.

At the door to the master's office, Sarah stopped. She pressed her hand to her pounding heart and made herself take a deep breath. "I can do this," she whispered. "I'll do it for him." Then she rapped on the paneled door with her knuckles.

"In," boomed Master Birmingham's voice.

Tucking her dust rag into the waistband of her muslin apron, Sarah turned the doorknob and stepped into the shadows of the office.

"Close the door behind you," Master Birmingham ordered. He was seated at his desk, the top littered with sheets of paper and books left open, face down.

The click of the door closing echoed ominously in Sarah's ears.

"The mistress told you why I called for you?"

She clasped her hands so he wouldn't see them tremble with a mixture of excitement and trepidation. "Yes." She lifted her gaze. "She did."

"And you're in agreement?"

She studied his heavy jowls. "I think so. She didn't give me details. She only said that you needed me, perhaps more than once."

He dropped his quill into a wooden inkwell. "It's more than likely. We've lost the other contact permanently."

He emphasized the word *permanently,* making her wonder just what had happened to the person, but she didn't dare ask. "Just tell me what you want me to do, sir. I'll do it if I'm able."

He chuckled. "Roger said you were an excellent choice, perhaps one of the best he's made. He may be right."

She smiled, looking down at her worn shoes. "Have I an assignment tonight?"

"You do. The same. Clothing will be delivered. I'll have you and your daughter moved to quarters at the other end of the house. Your own room, so the other slaves and servants won't know when you come and go." He began stacking the sheets of paper that littered the desktop. "You understand that you'll still be expected to perform your same duties during the day. We must keep up appearances."

"I . . . I understand." She looked up anxiously. She wanted to ask if the same gentleman would be meeting her, but she knew she shouldn't. Chances were, he didn't know. "I don't mind the hard work. I don't."

"The reticule will be among the clothing. Meet at the same time, pass it to the gentleman."

"Yes, sir."

"The same coachman will take you and return you here safely. If there's ever trouble, you must tell him immediately."

She nodded her head, barely able to contain her excitement. She was going to the Crook and Crown again tonight! She was going to dress up and go by carriage. Her soldier might, just might, be there!"

"I want you to know that this is a very important job you've agreed to do. Men's lives depend on you." He reached for an open book. "Now, have you any questions?"

She thought for a moment, then looked up at him. "Just one, sir."

"Yes?"

"I understand that it's better that I don't ask questions, but . . ."

"Yes?"

She clasped her hands. "Might I ask which side we're on, sir?"

Master Birmingham burst into hearty laughter, slapping the desk with both hands. "Which side . . . which side . . ." Tears welled in his eyes. "I'm sorry, Sarah; I'm not laughing at you." He came up out of his chair and around the desk, wiping his face with a lace handkerchief. "I'm laughing at myself. It took me too damned many years to know." He stood before her, tucking his kerchief into his sleeve. "We, the mistress and myself, are on the side of freedom, freedom from oppression, freedom to speak, freedom to tax ourselves as we see fit. We are Patriots of The Cause."

Sarah nodded. She didn't completely understand these freedoms, having grown up in her uncle's tavern and having served so many years indenture in the Birmingham household. But freedom for Molly sounded good. It sounded right.

Sarah smiled at her master, feeling more like an equal than a servant for the first time in her life. "For freedom, then, sir."

He walked her to the door. "Now, you understand, of course, that I would deny such a statement. We've been chosen as a family to appear British so that we might help our brother rebels."

"I understand."

He put his hand on the doorknob, suddenly serious. "Do you? Do you understand that if you're caught, we could both be hanged, you and I?"

"I understand." Of course she didn't really. All she could think of was the meeting tonight. Would he be there? She prayed he would, bargaining with God even as the master spoke.

"Go on with you now. Finish your duties. See that your daughter is looked after, and make your appointment on time."

"I will, sir." Sarah bobbed a curtsy and hurried down the hall wondering how she would possibly manage her own hair tonight.

It was a quarter hour before nine when the hired carriage rolled up to the Crook and Crown Tavern. The same driver once again accompanied Sarah and once again remained silent. When the carriage door opened and she stepped out into the dim street light, she was greeted by a dark figure that emerged from the shadows.

"You're early," her soldier said, taking her arm.

Sarah was breathless with relief. What if he hadn't been her contact this time? If this had been one of her fanciful stories, it would have been. But life wasn't like her stories.

"You're early yourself," she managed.

He took her hand, and through the kidskin brown leather, she could feel the warmth of his touch. "I had hoped it would be you," he murmured in her ear, escorting her through the open tavern door. "They couldn't tell me, but I hoped."

She knew she blushed, even through Eliza's rice powder that she'd dusted her cheeks with. "I'd hoped the same."

Their gazes met, and Sarah was lost to the warmth of his cinnamon-brown eyes. "A drink?" he asked her as he took the hunter-green cloak from her shoulders and seated her at their table.

How had it become their table? Sarah wondered. How had this bond between them grown so quickly?

"Yes, a drink would be nice. She smiled, falling easily into her role. Dressed in Eliza's green-and-fawn brocade gown with the Irish lace and matching cap, it was so easy. "You decide for me."

He slid onto the wooden bench across from her, tossing his red hat on top of their cloaks beside him. For a few moments they could only stare at each other, but it wasn't a stare that made Sarah uncomfortable. It was a stare of longing, one she'd never experienced before, but understood.

"Tell me your name," he whispered, when the serving girl had come, taken their order, and left the table again.

"Do you think it's wise?" Her hand naturally stretched to touch his and he entwined his fingers with hers.

"Just your first name, please. I've been trying to guess for a week."

She looked down at their clasped hands. Should she make up a name? A noble name, a lady's name? But she couldn't. She couldn't do that to him. "Sarah."

"Sarah, Sary," he murmured. "Of course. I should have known—a woman so beautiful, such a beautiful name."

She looked at him through her veil of painted lashes. No one had ever called her beautiful. It was the paint and powder, of course. The expensive gown and sweet lavender water she wore. "Are you real?" she asked.

"Flesh and blood." He squeezed her hand. Then he laughed. "What do you mean?"

She sighed. "You don't seem real."

He sat back to take his ale from the barmaid. When she was gone, he leaned forward across the table, sipping his drink. "How do I not seem real to you?"

"None of this seems real. But you, you're very similar to a man in a story I know."

"A story?" He laughed, his rich tenor voice echoing above the sounds of the tavern patrons. "What story is that?"

She shook her head, sipping the sweet red wine the girl had brought her. "Just a story I made up a very long time ago." She glanced over the rim of the glass. "To amuse myself."

He took a long drink of his ale, stretching his long legs beneath the table, brushing her skirts with his boots. "I think I understand what you mean," he said, softly enough so that no one could hear him, but her. "You dream a whole lifetime of someone, and when finally she appears, it's the wrong time . . ."

"The wrong place . . ." she offered, only a little sad.

"Exactly." Then he scooted forward on the bench again and leaned to whisper. "Tell me why you're doing this."

She looked away, not wanting to admit to him that she didn't know much of this cause. She didn't understand why the colonies were at war with their mother country, but she didn't want to tell him that. "The truth?" she asked.

"The truth."

"For you."

"For me?" He touched the breast of his scarlet uniform with his hand. "I understand that's why you came this week, but why last?"

Her mouth twitched in a mysterious smile. "Maybe I knew you would be here."

His gentle laughter mingled with hers and they shared a toast to dreams.

And so the evening went. A supper of roasted pork, sugared sweet potatoes, stewed squash, and thick slabs of bread was served. Sarah and her soldier laughed and talked, knowing nothing could ever come of this tender, forbidden relationship they had fallen into, savoring every moment together, knowing each might be the last.

Finally, midnight drew near and, again, her soldier walked Sarah to the waiting carriage outside. Again, she passed a reticule to him, this one of dyed green-leather. And again he kissed her.

This time Sarah was ready for his kiss, her lips slightly parted, her eyes drifting shut. And when his mouth touched hers, she lifted her arms to rest them on his broad shoulders. She savored his heavenly masculine scent, the sound of his breathing.

His kiss was a gentle kiss at first, their lips meeting tentatively. But then Sarah felt him tighten his grip around her waist and his kiss deepened. She tasted the ale he had drunk and shared the desperation of their plight.

When Sarah pulled away, breathless, giddy, she brushed her hand across his shaven cheek.

I'm sorry," he apologized, his breath frosty in the night air, his breathing irregular. "I . . . I didn't mean to take advantage of you, Sary."

Out of the corner of her eye, she saw the carriage driver. He made no attempt to come toward them, but she saw he watched, poised to come running should she call for him.

Sarah smiled a bittersweet smile at her soldier. She wondered if he were a turncoat, a British soldier betraying his Mother England or if, like her employers, he were simply portraying a part. Not that she cared.

"Nonsense," she whispered. "I'm no blossoming girl. I'm old enough to share a kiss with a man. Don't fear to mar my innocence, that was gone so long a time ago."

"Ah, Sarah, Sarah, I wish I knew you better. I wish I knew who had hurt you, who took that innocence from you. I wish—"

She pressed her gloved fingers to his lips, thinking to herself that it was better this way, really. After all, if he knew who she was, he wouldn't want her as she knew he wanted her now. If he knew who she was, this would never have come about—not this night, not the kiss they had just shared.

"Enough of could have been," she told him, wishing she could see him without his wig, wanting to ask the color of his hair. "Take the reticule and go. I'm expected back. There'll be worry if I don't return soon."

She had to pull on his hand to make him let her go. "Good night," she whispered.

She was only halfway to the carriage when she heard his footsteps in the snow behind her. "Wait," he called.

She turned back.

"My name," he whispered in the darkness. "You never asked me my name."

She smiled up into his handsome face. "Tell me then, if you must, but let me go." She was laughing now, perhaps to keep from crying, suddenly greedy, suddenly wishing the world were a different place, that she were a different person.

"Keller."

"Keller," she whispered. "Good night, then, Keller."

This time he let her go.

Four

The days, the weeks, slipped through Sarah's fingers like the silk hair ribbons Eliza lent to her. The chill of the winter gave way to the warmth of spring as Sarah and Keller met regularly, sometimes even twice in the same week, to pass information on to the rebel army.

In the hours Sarah spent with Keller they never shared more than a few fevered kisses, a touch here, a touch there; but these were the most wonderful moments of Sarah's life. She and her soldier sat by the flickering fire of the busy tavern public room by the hour, eating, talking, playing cards.

Often Sarah would go home to the lonely attic room she shared with Molly wondering how she and Keller could speak by the hour the way they did, yet never exchange personal information as they'd been instructed. But that didn't seem to matter. Keller told her of his dreams for his country. He told her what he fought for, what she fought for, and slowly Sarah began to understand the meaning of Independence.

Sarah spoke to Keller of simple pleasures, new sprouts in the garden, the book she had borrowed from Master Birmingham's office. She told him about the robin's nest outside her window, even the laundress's new baby, but she never revealed to him the truth of her situation.

To Sarah's amazement, Keller didn't guess that she was not the woman she pretended to be. He never knew of the murder she'd committed or the price she still paid each day. He didn't seem to recognize that she was uneducated, untutored in music, lady's manners, and fine embroidery. He wasn't aware that the only reason she could read was because an old tutor had often supped in her uncle's tavern and had taught Sarah to read on a whim.

Perhaps it was deception, not to tell Keller who she really was, what she was, but that had been the agreement from the beginning. They had met realizing they would never know the other truly. For all Sarah knew, Keller could have been a convicted felon as well; but if he had been, she'd not have cared. Her only regret was that she couldn't share Molly with him—her laughter, her smiles, her bright outlook on the world.

But with her gloves covering her chapped, red hands, Sarah felt transformed each time she alighted from the carriage. She told herself this magic couldn't last forever. At some point her services would no longer be needed or Keller would be transferred elsewhere. But she didn't allow herself to dwell on those possibilities. She lived for the present. By the daylight hours she scrubbed her mistress's front staircase on her hands and knees with lye soap; but by night, she became a lady of *The Cause.*

One afternoon late in April, Master Birmingham passed Sarah in the hallway. She was arranging a Chinese vase of dogwood blooms on a sidetable.

"Tonight," he said, as he passed her.

Sarah turned her head, wondering if she had imagined his voice. She so prayed each night that she'd be called, that she feared she was beginning to conjure her master's orders. But the look on his face told her she had indeed been summoned.

She gave the slightest nod of her head. This was the third time this week. She wondered what was up and about, but of course there was no one to ask. Not even Keller would give her details of the messages she carried, details that might put her life in danger.

So, when darkness fell, Sarah gave Molly a good-night kiss and tucked the little girl into bed with her horn book. Molly protested at the idea of her mother leaving again and begged to know what she was up to dressed in those fancy clothes; but Sarah bade her hush, and the child seemed to instinctively know when not to press her mother. She seemed to accept the idea of the secrecy and enjoy being a part of it.

Dressed in rustling taffeta of apple green, Sarah slipped out the back of the house and into the night. The smell of spring was sweet in the air. On a side street, close to the summer kitchens, her carriage waited.

Sarah smiled to the driver as he opened the door for her. Though they had never exchanged a word, she felt that he was her friend, her protector.

"Good evening," Sarah said pleasantly, accepting her driver's hand as he helped her into the carriage. She'd played the part of a lady so long, she had almost convinced herself she was one.

He was cloaked in black, and his hood obscured his face. Of course he didn't respond but to nod.

Sarah arrived at the Crook and Crown promptly and walked in, headed straight for the table she and Keller shared. This was not the only place they now met. Sometimes it was in the William Tavern down the street, other times in the open market. Once she had paused with Keller in broad daylight on the steps of Bruton Parish Church to pass an urgent message. It was the first time she had ever seen him in the light of day; he'd been even more handsome, more charming. What an adventure that had been!

Sarah spotted Keller seated at their table, his back to her. She smiled as she hurried over, breathless with excitement to see him. "Ke—" But when he turned his head, it was not her Keller. It was another man. Another redcoat.

Sarah froze. Was this a trap? Where was Keller? Her pulse skipped a beat, her palms growing damp inside her leather gloves.

She contemplated running.

Roger had said that if there were ever anything out of the ordinary, she was to leave and ask questions later. He made it clear that she was never to pass a message if she did not feel the climate was right. But she couldn't leave not knowing if Keller were safe. She just couldn't do it.

"Good evening, darling. I feared you might not make it," said the Englishman.

She smiled stiffly as he rose to help her with her cloak. *So, he was expecting her.* Sarah allowed him to remove the light wool from her shoulders and then she slipped onto the wooden bench, glancing around the smoky public room. Nothing seemed different or out of place. No one seemed to notice her or that it was not the same man she was meeting that she'd met for weeks.

That was one of the reasons she guessed the Crook and Crown had been chosen as a rendezvous point to begin with. Built on the edge of town, off the main street, it was a tavern patronized mostly by travelers, men and women not likely to stay more than a night. Only the tavern keeper and her staff remained constant, and Sarah had come to the conclusion weeks ago that the mistress was probably a rebel, too.

Clutching her reticule, Sarah settled on the bench across from the stranger. Her heart was beating so loudly that she feared he could hear it. She forced herself to smile her best lady's smile. She had understood from the beginning that Keller might not always be the contact; but after all this time, why would he not be sent? Something was wrong, Sarah just knew it. "Where is he?" she whispered, hoping she appeared calm and lady-like.

"Madame?"

"The gentleman I usually meet. Where is he? Not ill, I hope?"

The soldier glanced up, eyeing the patrons of the public room. He looked back at her. "He sent me in his place."

"Why?" she whispered.

"Just pass the reticule, madame, and I'll be on my way."

Sarah wound her fingers around the ribbons of the lady's purse and tied it around her wrist. "Where is he? I demand to know. Is he all right?"

The soldier broke into a grin and for the first time, she realized his smile was very similar to Keller's. "You're her, aren't you?" he asked.

"Her?"

"The redhead my brother spoke of. It has to be you."

Sarah looked up to see if anyone were paying attention to their hushed conversation. "Take care what you say. I could well be the enemy."

"Nah." He folded his hands. "Redhead with a perfect smile and dancing eyes of emerald. There could only be one Sarah, Sarah."

He had to know Keller. How else would he have known what he said about her? Still, she wanted to be cautious. She'd not be fooled into compliancy with a man's honeyed words, not even those supposedly coming from her Keller. "Tell me who you are and where Keller is."

"Look, sweetheart." The redcoat slid forward on the hewn bench. "He sent me in his place. Just pass the message." He glanced around. "It's gotten hot around here. We shouldn't tarry."

Hot. Dangerous, he meant. Dangerous for Keller. Her heart leapt in her breast. Roger warned her that the pass was always up to her. She didn't have to relay the message if she felt it wasn't safe. If he weren't going to tell her where Keller was, she wasn't going to give him the message. Or at least she was going to make him think so. "I must be going," she said firmly.

He grabbed her gloved hand before she had a chance to slide off the bench. "Sarah, we must have that message. It contains vital information concerning British troop movement," he hissed beneath his breath.

She set her jaw with determination. "Keller. Where is he?"

The redcoat looked toward the wall, then after a moment, back at her. "He didn't want me to say, but . . ."

"But?" she breathed.

He exhaled. "He's been injured, Sarah. I'm his brother. He sent me to retrieve the reticule because it's vastly important."

Sarah had to cover her mouth with her hand to keep from crying out. Keller injured? She had known there was the possibility, but the thought made her blood run cold. "Shot?"

"Just a flesh wound."

She stood up, reaching for her cloak, the reticule still wrapped tightly around her wrist. "I have to see him."

Keller's brother leaped up. "That's impossible!"

Sarah tossed her cloak over her arm and started for the door. "Then I'll take it home with me!"

"Sarah!"

He spoke her name so loudly that a man and a woman looked up from their sausage dumplings to stare.

Sarah hurried out the door with Keller's brother on her heels.

"Sarah! Wait!"

Outside on the brick walk, she halted. She could see her coach and driver in the shadows of the alley. If she needed him, she knew she need only call to him and he would come running.

The brother took her arm. "Please. I can't take you to him. It's not safe. It's not smart. Christ, he'll kill me!"

"I don't care if it's not safe. I don't care!" she said through clenched teeth. "I've been doing this for *The Cause* all these weeks; I damned well think *The Cause* can do something for me."

"You shouldn't become emotionally involved with contacts. It's not a good idea. I told Kell that."

She raised a painted eyebrow, dangling the reticule from her wrist. Of course, he could grab the message and run, but she was guessing he wouldn't dare make a scene on the street. "Well, what shall it be? It would be a shame to return without completing your assignment."

He stared at her with angry eyes for a moment, then broke into that familiar grin again. He lowered his head, shaking it emphatically. "He said you were tough." He gave a low whistle. "Damned if you don't strike a hard bargain."

Sarah couldn't help but smile. He was going to take her to Keller! Her bluff had worked! She lowered her voice. "I have a carriage waiting."

He shook his head. "No. Too dangerous. The driver stays here." He looked down the street. "It's not far." He offered his arm. "Will you walk with me?"

"Yes, but let me tell my driver."

The brother gave a nod, calling after her in a hushed voice. "Just hurry. I don't like standing here in the open with my tail hung out." He tugged at the stiff collar of the redcoat uniform. "Besides, this damned coat of Kell's is too tight."

Sarah went to her driver and bent her head to speak to him. "I have to go elsewhere. I want you to wait here."

His hand snaked out to grab her. She couldn't see his

face obscured by his cloak, but she knew he stared at her. He shook his head "no."

"I have to go," she repeated firmly. "But I won't be long. Wait for me here." Then she pulled her arm from his grasp and hurried back to where Keller's brother waited. "Let's go," she whispered, linking her arm through his.

He turned on the brick walk and headed for the center of town. The dark street was empty. "How do you know I am who I say I am?" he asked her with amusement. "What if I'm the enemy set to take you to my superiors and torture you for information?"

She frowned. "I don't know any information."

"How do they know that?"

"Besides," she added tartly, "you look like him."

"Do I?" He plucked his chin. "I, myself, think I'm more comely."

She smiled at his antics. "How far?" She looked over her shoulder, then back at him. "My driver is concerned for my safety."

"Not far." He looked ahead, then turned quickly down an alley. He was walking so fast now that Sarah had to trot beside him to keep up.

Despite Sarah's familiarity with the town by day, by night, she was quickly lost, which she guessed was his intention. Down dark streets they ran, through yards, past closed shops. They darted through a boxwood garden, and somewhere a dog howled.

"This way," he called. They were approaching a large brick house similar to the Birminghams'. Disoriented in the darkness, Sarah couldn't recognize the home; but it was well lit by candlelight, and music wafted through the windows. As she and Keller's brother cut across the garden, she saw men and women pass by the windows. The men were dressed in red uniforms.

Startled, Sarah turned to the brother.

He put a finger to his lips. "What better place to hide than beneath their noses?"

So she followed in silence, trying not to be afraid.

The brother took her through the garden, around a smokehouse, then into a side door of a large frame structure.

Once she stepped into the pitch darkness, she knew she was in a barn. She could smell the sweet hay and the pungent scent of warm livestock. Horses neighed and shifted in their stalls.

"Up," the brother whispered in her ear.

So she followed him up the steep wooden staircase, brushing the rough wall with her hand to guide her.

He pushed through another door at the top of the steps, and suddenly there was pale lantern light.

"Paul, is that you?"

She heard the ominous click of a rifle hammer.

"Kell, it's me. Christ, don't shoot us!"

At the top of the stairs, Sarah pushed the brother aside to see Keller stretched out on a crude canvas field cot. He'd pushed himself up, a flintlock rifle cradled in one hand. He wore a pair of simple breeches and a shirt thrown over his bare shoulders. His left arm and shoulder were bandaged with fresh, white, cotton strips.

"Keller!" she cried.

"What the hell is she doing here?" he asked. But even as he cursed her, he sat up, setting aside the weapon to put his good arm out to her.

"It's not his fault," she insisted, rushing to the bed. She lifted her rustling taffeta to kneel on the hayloft floor. They were surrounded by a wall of insulating hay that blocked the sound and light, preventing them from being detected below. "Are you all right?" She hugged him gently, trying not to disturb his bandaged arm and shoulder.

"I'm fine." He kissed her cheek, peering into her face

with honest concern. "But you shouldn't have come here." He looked over her shoulder. "You shouldn't have brought her here. Damn it, Paul! You know better."

Paul stood at the top of the stairs. "What was I supposed to do? We needed the blessed message and she wouldn't hand it over. Should I have wrestled her for it?"

Keller pushed back a lock of shiny blonde hair.

He was blond, with silky yellow-blond hair that fell loose to his shoulders. He looked younger to Sarah without his wig and uniform. He couldn't have been much older than she was.

"Paul's right, Keller. I wouldn't give him the message. I told him he had to bring me to you."

Keller frowned. "I should have known." Then he took the reticule from her, gently untying the ribbons at her wrist. He tossed the little bag over her head, through the air, to his brother. "Make the delivery and then come back for her."

Paul caught the bag and stuffed his uniform hat back on his head. "This may take me awhile. You don't want to go back now, Sarah?"

She shook her head, almost scared to look Keller in the eyes. She had been so afraid for him, so scared he'd been injured more severely. "I'll stay here. It'll be all right if I'm late. My driver will wait."

So Paul tipped his hat and disappeared back down the staircase, closing the doors, leaving Keller and Sarah alone for the very first time since they'd met.

For a moment all Sarah could do was kneel on the floor and stare at him. The idea that he could have been killed instead of injured hit her hard. All these weeks of passing messages had seemed so safe, almost a game. Now suddenly Keller was proof of the real danger beyond the barn walls.

"I'm so glad you're going to be all right," she whispered at last. The lamp, set on an old crate beside his bed, illuminated his handsome face. Despite his anger with her, he was smiling.

"You shouldn't have come."

"If *I'd* been shot, would you have come?"

"That's not the same thing, Sarah, and you well know it." He took her hands and drew her up to sit beside him on the narrow camp cot.

"It is the same, Keller," she answered softly, her hands in his.

"Oh, Sarah, my sweet Sarah." He brought her gloved hands to his lips and kissed them. "You don't understand how deadly this venture of ours is. You really shouldn't be here."

She reached up tentatively to brush a stray lock of golden hair off his cheek. She had been so afraid for him; and now that she was here and knew he was safe, at least for the moment, she couldn't take her eyes off him. "I don't care. I had to see you. I had to see for myself that you were all right."

"Ah, Sarah." He caught her hand and stroked his own cheek with it. "I can't stop thinking about you," he whispered. "I try to concentrate on my work, on my missions, but it's so difficult. I feel guilty because I know our army needs me, all of me, but I can't do it, Sary. I can't give them all of me because a part of me belongs to you now."

She smiled a bittersweet smile, knowing she loved him, knowing he loved her, knowing their love was impossible. The sad thing was that Keller didn't really understand just how hopeless it all was because he didn't know the truth about her.

Their gazes met and Sarah felt her heart flutter. That familiar warmth she felt when he was near was spreading through her veins, coursing through her body. He brushed his hand down her arm and she shivered, craving his touch.

"Keller," she whispered, not knowing what made her speak. "I need you."

He knew what she meant. She knew he knew.

He kissed her cheek, the tip of her chin, her earlobe. "Sary, I can't. We shouldn't."

"Why? Because we may never see each other again? Because any day one of us could be gone? Dead or transferred?"

"No, no. Don't say it." He shook his head, but then, after a moment, acknowledged the truth in her words. "Yes. Now that I've been seen, I may have to go. I could be transferred at any time, anywhere."

She caught his face between her palms and forced him to look into her eyes. So, he was leaving her. She had known it would come someday, but why so soon? *Sweet Jesus, why so soon.* "That's why we should, because we love each other," she managed. "I know we've never spoken of this, but you do love me, don't you?"

"Yes, Sary. I do. I haven't told you before because I didn't want to hurt you or make this more complicated. It wasn't supposed to happen this way. I didn't mean to fall in love with you. I knew better."

She smiled at him, tears welling in her eyes. She knew this was insane, but she didn't care. She wanted to make love with Keller. She wanted to share with him what she knew she would never be able to share with another man. She wanted to give to him the only thing she had to give, before he went away. "You can't hurt me, Keller. Your love never could."

"Sarah . . ."

He seemed so torn between duty and logic and what he felt for her.

"It's all right," she whispered.

"Didn't you hear what I said? They might send me away. They might replace you."

"It's all right," she repeated. She was kissing him; he

was kissing her, their kisses growing more urgent with every passing moment. "It doesn't matter."

He brought his hand up beneath her breast, and she heard herself moan. She had no experience, no knowledge of making love. What had happened to her on board the ship had nothing to do with what was happening here. But as inexperienced as she was, she didn't care. She wanted to touch Keller and she wanted to be touched.

"I don't want to lose you," Keller whispered desperately, his breath hot in her ear.

"So let me give you a part of me." She laid her hand over his, guiding him, urging him to touch her as no man had ever touched her with her permission. "Let me give you a part of me you'll never forget no matter where you go." Their gazes locked. "I need this, Keller. I need to share this with you."

"Oh, Sary, Sary, I'll find a way." He was kissing her again, his mouth hot and damp on the swell of her aching breasts. "I'll find a way for us to be together. I swear to God Almighty, I will!"

"Shhh," she hushed, straddling him so that she sat on his lap on the cot. ". . . No promises we can't keep. Just love me, Keller. Will you?"

He groaned, tugging at the bodice of her gown, pulling it down off her shoulders. Sarah pulled at the neckline of her shift, needing to feel his mouth on her bare flesh.

When finally her breasts were free of the confines of her clothing, she gave a sigh of relief. His mouth touched the rosy bud of her nipple, and she moaned. She was hot and tingling all over, a sense of urgency pulsing through her veins.

Keller tugged at her swollen nipple with his mouth, and she arched her back. The walls of the dimly lit barn faded; the smell of the hay and the stacks of drying piles that surrounded them faded from her mind. There was no fear of being caught, no fear of what would happen tomorrow. All that mattered was the two of them and their desperate love, here and now.

Keller eased her onto the mattress.

"Be careful of your shoulder," she warned, her voice sounding strangely husky in her own ears. "Don't hurt yourself."

His muslin shirt had fallen to the floor so that she could stroke his bare, sinewy shoulder and chest. "I'm fine. Fine," he whispered.

So she helped him remove her apple-green gown and tossed it onto the hay-littered floor. Next came her corset, shoes, and stockings.

"I shouldn't take everything off," she said when she lay back on the camp cot wearing nothing but her shift. "Your brother might come back."

"No," he whispered. "It'll be an hour or two. We have time. I want to see you. I want to see all of you. I want to see what I've dreamed of all those nights alone in my bed."

She watched him through a veil of lashes. "All right. But first you, then me."

She watched as he disrobed for her, their gazes never straying. *What a magnificent creation a man's body is,* Sarah thought as he slowly stripped off his clothing until he was nothing but hard muscle and bare flesh.

Once he was naked for her to see, she lay back on the rough wool blanket that covered the cot and let him remove the last bit of filmy cotton between them.

"Now your gloves." He laughed, his voice deep and sensual. "You can't make love with your gloves on, Sary. I want to feel your hands, my love. I want to feel you touch me."

Sarah shrank back. She wanted to keep the gloves on. She wanted to keep her secret. What if he noticed her rough, red palms? But as he lowered his head to meet her lips, she tugged off the gloves and let them fall to the floor. What did it matter, now? She stroked his bare shoulders with her hands, hearing the sounds of his pleasure. *This might be the last time I ever see Keller,* she thought.

The last time . . .

The last time . . .

Five

Sometime later Sarah lay in Keller's arms on the cot, curled on her side, her head resting on his good shoulder. He was stroking her bare back, kissing the hollow of her neck.

"I love you, Sary," he whispered, his voice still husky from their lovemaking. "I love you and I'm going to marry you. I've decided . . . if you'll have me, that is."

She opened her eyes, basking in the warmth of his touch. "You can't marry me," she said drowsily. She wouldn't allow herself to even dream of such an impossibility. "You know that."

"You don't believe me?" He stroked her cheek, brushing the locks of fiery hair that tumbled over her shoulders. "How can you doubt my sincerity?"

She sat up with a sigh, drawing her bare legs up beneath her. She knew she needed to get dressed. Paul would be back soon. Paul would come, and he would take her back to her carriage. She would return to the Birmingham household, to her duties as a house maid, and the spell would be broken. The spell was already broken. Reality was setting in.

"I don't doubt your love for me, but you and I both know we cannot marry," she said, as gently as she could. "You know nothing of me, who I am, what I am—"

"I don't care," he declared fiercely. He pushed up on

the bed, favoring his uninjured arm and shoulder. "All I care about is you."

She smiled, a lump rising in her throat. *If only you knew the truth,* she thought. *You'd not be so free with your words.* But of course she said nothing. She didn't want to hurt him. She wanted to protect this innocent love of theirs. "I need to get dressed," she said, reaching for her shift on the hay on the floor. "Your brother will be back for me soon."

He dropped his legs over the side of the cot, watching her dress. "Are you saying you wouldn't marry me, Sary? Even if I could figure out a way to keep us both safe and my commander happy?"

She smiled a bittersweet smile. "It's enough that you asked me, Keller. But we both know we have a job to do. You need to concentrate on your missions and staying alive."

"And what of you, Sarah? What do you need to concentrate on? he questioned passionately. "Have you a husband? Is that what you're afraid to tell me? Because if you do, I'll fight him for you. Christ, I'll kill him if you want me to." He caught her hand, but she pulled away. "Sarah, do you hear what I'm saying? I can't live without you."

She tugged on the strings of her stays, knowing what was between them was truly over now. Even if Keller weren't transferred, she would tell Roger she could no longer carry messages. A lump rose in her throat, and she fought the tears that stung her eyes. Keller was getting too close. He was prying now. If he knew the truth, it would kill her.

She sat on the edge of the cot beside him to roll up her stockings. He was watching her, saying nothing. She could tell he was hurt, but better now than later, she thought.

"Sarah, I don't understand. Say something, please . . ."

She stood to drop her taffeta gown over her head. "Ask for a transfer," she said softly. "Before you get yourself killed."

The sound of footsteps echoed on the staircase below, and she quickly fastened the pearl buttons of her gown. Her hair was hopelessly mussed, but she didn't care. She would never see Paul again. So what if he thought her a whore?

"Knock knock," came Paul's voice through the plank door.

Keller caught Sarah's hand. "I don't understand," he whispered.

Sarah couldn't bear to look at him. Her heart was breaking. "Keller, please, just let me go."

"Knock, knock," came Paul's cheery voice again.

"Just a minute, damn you!" Keller shouted at the door.

His eyes returned to Sarah. "Just tell me what's wrong, Sary."

"Isn't this enough?" She opened her palms to him, silent tears slipping down her cheeks.

"No. No, it isn't." He stood up, pulling on his breeches. "It's not enough for me."

She hung her head, squeezing her eyes shut, fighting the tears. What had ever made her think this could work, even for a little while? What had made her think she had a right to love a man like Keller? "I'm sorry." Then she turned away from him and walked to the door. She opened it, and Paul stepped into the attic.

He looked first at her, then at Keller.

She stared at the floorboards, barely trusting herself to speak. "Please take me back to my carriage, Paul."

Paul looked to his brother. "Kell?"

"Do as the lady bids," came Keller's voice, cold and distant.

Paul shook his head in confusion and turned back

down the dark stairwell. "Whatever your pleasure. I can have you to your carriage in ten minutes time."

Sarah didn't say a word. She didn't turn back. She stepped into the darkness of the stairwell and closed the door softly behind her.

The following day Sarah met with Roger in the rear garden. She made herself busy clipping spring posies. He pretended to observe the Birminghams' garden while waiting for his host. No one took notice of their brief conversation.

Sarah told Roger she thought it was no longer safe for her to carry messages to the Crook and Crown, and he was in complete agreement. He knew Keller had been shot. They agreed Sarah would no longer be a messenger, not for a while at least. But if he needed her, she promised him he could call on her. The idea of Independence from the Crown had gotten under her skin. She saw herself as a true rebel now, and she knew she'd be willing to fight for Molly's freedom even if not her own.

So, the days slipped by. Sarah returned to the life she had known before her adventure, before Keller. She swept the hardwood floors of the Birmingham house; she polished pewter and ran errands in the market. And she thought of Keller. She remembered every caress, every word spoken. She had no regrets for what had happened, only that she'd hurt him.

Sarah tried to convince herself that the short time that she had been loved by Keller would be enough to last her a lifetime. She tried not to be greedy; after all, these last few months had been more than she'd expected from her entire life. But there was a strange thing about love; once you sampled it, you just couldn't get enough. You just couldn't forget.

Early one evening less than a fortnight after Sarah

had told Keller goodbye, she stood in the front hallway lighting tallow candles. The sound of laughter came through the crack beneath the front-parlor door. The Birminghams had guests. Roger and Eliza were there, and many other well-known figures in the town. Sarah yearned to be one of the women inside the closed parlor. She yearned to be a part of The Cause. Now that she'd had a taste of their life, she wanted it not just for Molly, but for herself as well.

A banging on the front door startled Sarah out of her reverie. A late guest? she wondered as she hurried down the hallway.

The banging came again, even before she could reach the doorknob.

She swung open the door.

Redcoats . . . nearly a dozen of them.

"May . . . may I help you?" she asked, her heart giving an unsteady leap.

"We're here for Algood Birmingham."

"Master Birmingham?" she asked the tall, slender officer.

"Are you addlepated, wench? Yes, Algood Birmingham. This is his residence, is it not?"

"Yes, it is. I . . . I'll get him." Sarah meant to close the door on the soldiers; but before it could swing shut, the officer crossed the threshold.

"I'll wait here," he told her, not bothering to close the door behind him.

Trembling with fear for her master, Sarah ran down the hallway. Without knocking, she burst into the parlor.

The laughter and voices died away suddenly. "Soldiers, sir," she announced to Master Birmingham, who stood on the far side of the room. She tried not to sound alarmed; after all, her master was supposed to be a loyal British citizen, wasn't he? He had no need to fear the soldiers. "An officer with a dozen soldiers here to speak with you."

Sarah heard Roger swear. Mistress Birmingham gave an involuntary squeak.

"I didn't know what to do, sir," Sarah said softly to Roger, who had come to stand at her side. "They pushed their way into the front hall. They wait there now."

Roger looked to her master, whose jolly face had gone pale. "You'd best go, Algood, and see what this is about." He turned to the dozen or so supper guests. Please, no need to be alarmed. Have a seat, and I'll be back to serve as host if Mistress Birmingham would allow me."

The mistress gave a nod as she mopped her brow with a lace handkerchief. The ladies and gentlemen all began to talk at once in hushed voices.

Sarah followed her master and Roger out of the parlor, closing the sliding door behind them.

"It will be all right," Roger whispered to her, placing a comforting hand on her shoulder. "But I want you to wait here. I may need you."

So Sarah stood in the shadows of the hallway, listening to her master and Roger speak with the soldiers. From here she couldn't make out their words, only detect the anger and accusations in their voices.

Perhaps five minutes passed, and then she heard the sound of boots in the front hall again. The door swung shut, followed by footsteps coming back down the hall. Only one man returned.

Sarah stood in the shadow of the grand staircase, her hand over her mouth. Roger appeared.

"They took him?" she asked.

"Yes." He grasped her arm. "They just want to question him. I think he's safe enough, but I need you to deliver a message."

"To the same man?" she asked, knowing her voice trembled.

"I know we agreed you wouldn't, but this is important. He's got to get the hell out of here until we straighten this matter out."

"What matter? Tell me, Roger."

He shook his head. "No. The most important thing to remember is that the messenger should never know the content of the message. Can you do it, Sarah? Will you do it for me?"

She didn't have to consider. Master Birmingham had been carried off. Keller was in danger. She had to go.

"I'll do it."

"Good. He's at a ball at the Lockwood's place. You'll have to go there."

"The Lockwood Mansion? I can't—"

"You can." He checked the pocket watch that dangled from his waist. "But we'll have to hurry so that you arrive on time; others will take less notice of you that way."

"I don't have any clothes. I returned them to your wife."

"I'll send you home with Eliza to dress immediately."

Sarah hung her head, frightened for herself, for Molly. Sarah couldn't go getting herself shot. "I . . . I don't know—"

"You have to do it, Sarah. I haven't time to seek another contact. It will be easy enough. Just enter with other guests, find the gentleman, pass the message, and go."

She twisted her hands in her blue-tick petticoat, her mind racing. "All right, I'll do it. I can do it."

He squeezed her hand. "I know you can. We're depending on you. We all are."

* * *

An hour later, Sarah found herself transformed once again to the lady she had been for so many weeks. Dear Roger had managed to find her an invitation, and Eliza had taken Sarah home and dressed her in her own clothing.

The gown was a rich jewel-blue brocade with a matching busk and beading in jet black and sparkling blue. Thick Irish lace fell from her sleeves; and, concealing her hands, she wore matching blue gloves, beaded at the forearms in dazzling blue and black. Eliza placed sapphire ear bobs in Sarah's ears and hung a glimmering sapphire necklace at her throat. Sarah was primped and prodded, dusted with powder, and sprayed with toilet water until she was once again transformed into the mysterious Lady of The Cause.

The driver, who met her in the rear garden of Roger and Eliza's home, took Sarah directly to the Lockwood Mansion. The Mansion was bustling with activity and bright with white light. Before Sarah had time to think, time to be afraid, she was being escorted into the ballroom of the most magnificent home she'd ever dreamed of.

To Sarah's relief, no one asked her to identify herself or even asked for the invitation. As she moved through the crowd, she curtsied and smiled, trying not to speak, trying to avoid eye contact with the many redcoats that filled the Lockwood Mansion to bursting. Ladies in sparkling gowns floated by, as ornate as the gold woodwork and crystal chandeliers that surrounded them, and Sarah tried not to gawk.

She made her way through the crowd slowly, watching the face of every British officer she spotted. Keller was here somewhere. But where?

Heavenly music filled the grand ballroom. Someone pushed a glass of French champagne into her gloved hands. She was caught in a whirl of confusion and fear.

Where was he? Where was Keller? She had to reach him before they found him first.

Then suddenly, it was as if her prayers were answered. A group of gentlemen parted, and there was Keller standing near a marble fireplace mantel, laughing and drinking with another gentleman. He was dressed in his officer's scarlet uniform, sporting a sword and pistol.

The moment he spotted her, his face lit up in a genuine smile. Sarah was so relieved, she feared her sigh was audible. She had been afraid he hated her for the way she had left him. She had been afraid he wouldn't understand.

"Excuse me, sir," he said with the air of a prince.

Instantly he was standing before her, and she had no eyes but for him. "I have to speak with you."

"I'd hoped you'd be here. I'd prayed," he whispered in her ear. "I tried to find you, but no one would give me any information. No one seemed to know anything about you."

She tapped his shoulder with the Chinese painted fan Eliza had given her. "Keller, this is important." She looked to see if anyone were close enough to hear her. "There's a problem. I have a message in my glove."

He swore under his breath. "Let's step out onto the balcony for a little air, shall we?"

Then he escorted her on his arm through the crowd of dancers. Several gentlemen spoke to him as they passed. Even a striking young woman with hair like spun taffy called to him.

Outside on the balcony they retreated to a corner. Overhead, the stars hung low in the sky, illuminating the night.

"Tell me," he whispered.

"I don't know the particulars. I have the message here in my glove." Her gaze met his. She had meant only to pass the message and go without speaking, without thinking of him in a personal way. It would hurt too much. It would hurt them both; but now that she was here, she could feel her heart breaking again.

"Sarah—"

She slipped the glove off her hand and pressed it into his. Tears welled in her eyes. "I have to go," she whispered. "And so must you. There's grave danger. Arrests are being made."

"Sarah . . ." He clasped her bare hand. "I need to talk to you. I need to know where to find you when it's safe . . . when this is all over."

"Good night," she whispered, forcing herself to pull away. "I love you, Kell. I'll always love you . . ."

She heard Keller call her name as she slipped back into the grand house and through the crowd of dancers. They were playing a minuet. But she ignored his plea, hurrying for the door as if she were suffocating. It was not until Sarah was safely in her carriage that she finally broke down in tears.

Six

"Tell me a story, Mama," Molly begged. They were washing kitchen windows this early June morning.

Sarah stood on a small ladder leaned against the brick wall of the summer kitchen, wet rag in hand. Molly waited in the grass below, handing up rinsed rags to her mother. A blue jay cackled overhead, diving at one of the new kittens hiding in the herb garden. Sweet, warm, sunshine fell on the shoulders of all who welcomed summer.

"I don't feel like a story." Sarah handed her daughter the dirty rag and accepted a clean one. She stretched to scrub the winter's grime from the window pane.

"You always say that. Why don't you feel like stories anymore, Mama? You used to tell me such good ones."

Sarah sighed, rubbing her chin to her shoulder where it itched, then returning to the scrubbing. Molly was right. She didn't feel like telling tales these days. She guessed she just didn't have the same heart or hope anymore. "It's nonsense," she told her daughter. "You're getting too old for nonsense."

Sarah saw Molly's reflection in the glass as the child scrunched up her pretty face. "It's *him*, isn't it? It's because you don't see *him* anymore. The man you told me about with the laughing brown eyes."

"Molly!" Sarah shot her a silencing stare. "They'll hear you." She nodded to the open kitchen window. Inside, pots banged and Cook shouted for more shallots.

Molly thrust out her lower lip, dipping her fingers into the water bucket. "You used to tell me stories. You used to laugh and play with me. When you were dressing in those pretty gowns and sneaking out at night, you sang to yourself when you worked." She twirled her finger in the soapsuds. "It's all right if you don't want to tell me any more stories, but why don't you sing anymore, Mama?"

Sarah sighed, scrubbing harder, putting her elbow into her work. There hadn't been much to sing about lately. Master Birmingham had been released after only two days of questioning, but the house had been very quiet since. No guests came to sup and the master rarely left the property. Nothing was said again about Sarah's carrying any more messages.

Once, Sarah had seen Roger and Eliza on the street at the open market. They'd smiled politely, nodded, and walked on as if she were nothing but a friend's indentured servant. *Nothing but a servant . . .*

Sarah assumed that after Master Birmingham's arrest and subsequent release, the rebel army had ordered him to stay low, at least for a while. She did't dare ask, but she assumed Keller had made it safely out of the city and had been transferred to a place where no one would recognize him. All Sarah could do was pray that he was all right.

She tried not to think about him or remember what they had shared, because rather than being a comfort, the memories stung. Sarah had been greatly relieved when her woman's flux had come and gone as it always had, but a part of her was disappointed. A selfish part of her had wanted another child to give her joy and hope—Keller's child.

"Mama." Molly tugged on her mother's petticoat. "You didn't answer me. Why are you so sad? You miss your friend, don't you?"

Sarah came down the ladder and dropped the wet rag into the bucket with a splash. She pushed her mobcap back on her head and turned to study the blossoming flower bed nearby. "I do miss him."

"Then why don't you go see him again?"

Sarah sighed. Of course she couldn't explain to Molly what had happened. "Because I can't," she said softly.

"Because it was a secret?"

"Yes, because it was a secret." She caught her daughter's blonde pigtail and gave it a playful tug. "Now move the ladder over to the next window and perhaps I'll tell you a very short story."

Molly's face lit up, and Sarah couldn't help but reach out and touch her soft cheek. Here was her happiness now. This young girl was the one Sarah needed to concentrate her efforts on. Sarah knew she would never have the love she and Keller had shared again, but Molly would have a lifetime of love and laughter. Sarah was determined. Somehow, some way, she would make it so.

"A story! You'll tell me a story?" Molly bobbed up and down like a cork in an ale keg. "The one about Molly and the prince? It's been so long since you've told me that one!"

Sarah smiled sadly. "No. Not that one. How about I tell you about the boy who became a radish or maybe the one about the fox and the baker. You like that one."

Molly dragged the ladder along the wall, propping it up next to the closet window. "Oh, all right. I'd rather hear my favorite, but you choose."

Lugging the heavy wooden bucket that splashed water on her patched stockings, Sarah started for the ladder. "There once was a sly gray fox . . ."

As she spun her tale, she watched Molly's face light up with laughter and she knew that though she felt hopelessly lost without Keller, all was not lost. As long as she had Molly, the world would never be hopeless.

* * *

Later that afternoon when Molly's mother sent her to the well to draw water, the child cut through the kitchen, leaving the bucket on the step, and slipped into the big house through the dark back hallway. She went to the attic room she and her mother slept in and knelt at the foot of the cot they shared. In a battered wooden crate, beneath the two Sunday petticoats, an old brush, and a patched blanket, she found the glove she knew her mother had hidden.

The glove was the most beautiful thing Molly had ever seen. Sewn of a soft blue cloth, it was decorated with tiny black and blue beads that glimmered when she held the glove up to the sunlight that spilled through the window high in the eaves. It was Mama's secret.

Molly slipped her own hand inside the glove, trying it on for size. Someday she would wear a glove like this one, only she was going to have two! Molly didn't know exactly what she intended to do with her mother's glove, but she suspected she might need it. It would prove that she was who she said she was.

So, she tucked the beautiful glove inside the folds of the stained green-tick kerchief she wore over her shoulders, then pushed the corners of the kerchief down into the waistband of her threadbare petticoat. That way no one could see the glove, and she would not lose it.

Grabbing her straw bonnet off the nail in the wall, she raced out of the tiny attic room. At the bottom of the steps, she ran down the shadowy front hall. Mama was polishing silver and pewter in the front parlor. She'd be there for hours. Unnoticed, Molly slipped out the back door, cut through the vegetable garden, behind the summer kitchen, and out the back gate. Tugging on the ribbons of her straw bonnet, she hurried along the street, heading straight for the Crook and Crown Tavern. She knew where it was because she'd followed her mother in a carriage there one night.

It took Molly not ten minutes to reach the tavern. There, she walked around the rear to the garden where the back kitchen door was ajar. There an old woman perched on a stump in the yard, plucking a red hen.

"What ye want?" the chicken woman called. She spat a stream of brown tobacco juice on the ground. "We ain't hirin', girlie."

Molly drew herself up, raising an eyebrow. "I'm here to see the mistress," she said in the voice of the Molly in her mama's story. "Is she about?"

The old woman took another handful of the hot, wet red feathers, chuckling to herself. *"Is she about,* you say?" She clucked like the hen must have just before her untimely death. "Aye, she's about, she is, Miss High and Mighty." Then she nodded with her pointed chin. "Inside. Overseeing the evening supper, I'll warrant."

"Thank you." Molly nodded with an air of elegance and went up the back steps. Inside the swinging door she found a kitchen filled with bustling cooks and serving girls. "Excuse me," she called to the young woman in a starched white, drooping mobcap. "Your Mistress, is she about? I've important business with her."

The girl pointed through a set of heavily paneled doors.

Molly smiled sweetly. "My thanks."

Through the doors and down a narrow hallway, Molly found herself in what appeared to be a great dining hall. *The public room, no doubt,* she reasoned. That was what Mama called it, and this was precisely how she'd described it.

A woman with great mounded breasts looked up from where she sorted pewter dinnerware. The room was empty of guests. "Can I help you, moppet?"

She was a cheery sort of woman with a friendly smile.

Molly bobbed a polite curtsy. "Yes, yes I hope you can," she said, trying to sound like Mistress Birmingham. "I pray you can. I'm looking for a gentleman."

The tavern keeper chuckled, her breasts jiggling above her laced corset. "Aren't we all, luv?"

"A . . . a certain gentleman."

"Yes?"

"I . . . I have a very important . . . an important message for him."

"Is that right?" She frowned. "What's the gentleman's name?"

"I . . . I don't know," Molly conceded, her mind racing. "We . . . we're not told, you know." She smiled and whispered. "It's a secret, of course."

"Of course." The tavern keeper nodded as if she understood, but she was smiling in that silly way adults smiled when they didn't believe children. Then she put out her hand. "Why don't you just give Mistress Gordon the message and I'll see he gets it?"

"No. No . . ." Molly took a step back. "It's very important. I have to deliver it to the gentleman myself. A . . . a message from General Washington!" She didn't know what made her tell such a fibber; it just came out of her mouth as smooth as custard pudding went in.

The tavern keeper suddenly put down the spoons in her hand and came across the room toward Molly. "What nonsense are you talking about, child? Hush your mouth. General Washington, indeed!"

Molly could tell the woman didn't believe her for sure, but at least she had her attention. "It's the truth, odd as it may sound." She lifted one eyebrow. "Obviously I am not whom I appear to be."

"Are you serious, child?" She looked her over. "You need the gentleman? Heavens," she muttered. "Now they're sending babes."

"Yes, I do need him. A particular gentleman. The one

I'm looking for would have met a woman with red hair some months ago. She came all the time, at night, but then she didn't come anymore."

Molly saw a light of recognition in the woman's eyes.

"It's really important," Molly went on in a hushed voice. "Vi—vital, I'm told."

"Are ye really carrying a message from the general?" She studied Molly intently. "Ye dress like a maid, but you speak well."

"This is a disguise, of course." Molly looked this way and that. "We must be quite careful, you know. One never knows who might be watching or listening." Then she produced her mother's glove from inside her dress. "You . . . you can give him this. He'll come. I know he will."

The woman took the glove, fingering the pretty beads for a moment. Finally, when Molly was beginning to fear she would turn her away, she pointed to a stool. "Can you wait? This might take some time. They ain't at my beck and call, you know."

"I can wait. I'll fold the napkins if you like." She pointed to the tall pile of snowy linens on the table with the pewter utensils and dishes.

"Ye fold linen, do ye?" she questioned suspiciously.

Molly smiled. "My mother always said that it was important a lady be well versed in the duties of a household. How else will she run her husband's home efficiently?"

The woman gave Molly a queer look and then turned away, shaking her head. "You wait right here, missy."

So Molly climbed up on the stool and made herself busy folding the linen napkins.

An entire hour must have passed before the innkeeper finally returned. She nodded with surprise at the stack of neatly folded napkins Molly had produced in her absence and murmured a thank-you. "This way, ye'll have to see him in the garden." She waved her down the hall.

"Customers will be coming in shortly. He don't want to be seen, your friend."

Molly broke into a smile. He was here, Mama's friend! He would know what to do! He would know how to make her laugh and smile again.

A week later, on a breathtakingly bright day in mid-June, Sarah stood on the back lawn behind the icehouse with a bundle of wet sheets in her arms. The laundress had fallen and broken her leg, so Sarah had agreed to help her friend out until she was back on her feet.

Molly was racing up and down the long hallways of sheets, laughing and ducking beneath them. "She's going to catch me," she squealed, ducking beneath the closest clothes line, nearly knocking the wet sheets from her mother's hands.

Sarah couldn't resist a chuckle. "Who's going to catch you? There's no one there, Molly."

But the little girl only ran faster, laughing louder.

Sarah threw a cotton sheet over the line and began to smooth it out. She couldn't help but smile at her daughter's antics. The child had been like this for days, laughing and saucy. It was as if she was bursting with some secret; yet when Sarah questioned her, she was silent for once.

Perhaps it was the coming of summer, Sarah reasoned as she reached into the tall basket of wet linens for another sheet. What child wasn't excited by the thought of painted butterflies and soft, sweet grass.

Molly circled her mother again; but then, just as she turned, she drew back one of the wet sheets.

"Molly! You're mussing the one I just hung. What are you gawking at?"

"Oh, God, he's here," her daughter murmured in honest shock. "He's really here . . ."

"Who?" Sarah tugged the wet sheet aside with curiosity. "I don't see any—" Her words were lost in her throat. All she could do was stare.

It was Keller. He was here. Here to see the Birminghams.

Sarah immediately dropped the wet sheet to shield herself. Self-consciously she ran a hand over her hair, which tumbled haphazardly from her mobcap. The entire front of her patched tick petticoat and bodice were wet from the laundry. Her bare toes thrust out from beneath the jagged hem, soiled from the garden.

"No," she murmured beneath her cupped hand. "He can't see me like this . . ."

Molly was giggling now, hanging on the sheet that served as a curtain to shield Sarah.

Sarah grabbed her daughter by the back of her cotton dress and pulled her back. The sheet fell into place. "What did you mean when you said it was him?" Sarah demanded, shaken. She had thought she would never see him again. She had resigned herself to the fact that Keller was gone. Why was he here to see the master? Why hadn't he gone to a place where he was safe? "Do you know that gentleman?" Sarah demanded of her daughter, still holding the back of her dress.

"Of course, Mama," Molly beamed. She was hopping up and down excitedly. "He's the man in your story. The one with the laughing brown eyes."

Against all reason, Sarah couldn't help but pull back the corner of the sheet again and take another peek. Her last, she told herself. Just one look and then she'd run for the cover of the kitchen until he was gone.

Of course even if he saw her, she knew he'd not recognize her. Not dressed like this, not here in the Birminghams' garden with a load of wet sheets and a ten-year-old daughter.

But what if he did? She had to hope he would, not

that she wanted him to. She didn't want him to know the truth. She didn't want to hurt him like that . . . or hurt herself.

Sarah stole a quick glimpse. Both the mistress and master were there speaking to him now. He was dressed in rich civilian clothes, without a wig, a handsome cocked hat with a feather cockade on his blond head. He and the mistress were deep in conversation.

Sarah dropped the sheet and grabbed Molly's hand, that familiar ache swelling in her heart. "We have to go in."

Molly pulled from her mother's hand, still hopping up and down. "Not yet. We're not done with the sheets."

Sarah reached for her daughter again. What had gotten into the child? She wasn't normally so disobedient. "Molly, now," she repeated sternly, hoping her daughter didn't hear the tremble in her voice.

Sarah caught Molly's hand, but once again the child pulled away. "Not yet, I said!"

Then, before Sarah could catch her, Molly dove under the sheet and came up on the other side waving her hand toward Keller and the master and mistress. "Here! We're here!" she cried.

Sarah was mortified. What could she do now, but go after her daughter and pray he didn't recognize her. "Molly," she shouted through clenched teeth, ducking under the sheet.

"Sarah? Sarah, is that you?" Keller called.

Sarah thought she would die with embarrassment. He had seen her! All the way across the garden he'd recognized her.

"Sarah!"

Suddenly he was running toward her, leaving the master and mistress behind.

"Oh, Sarah," he called, holding his arms out to her. "It's you; it's truly you."

Tears ran down Sarah's cheeks. She was trapped. She

couldn't move. She was so happy to see him again, so ashamed for him to see her like this.

"I found you," he cried, leaping over a hedge of low boxwood to reach her.

He put his arms around her, and Sarah found herself unable to resist the warmth of his touch. She threw her arms around his neck, hugging him tightly, burying her face in his coat. "How . . . how did you find me here?"

He was grinning as he produced the beaded gloves she'd worn that night to the governor's mansion. "It took a young lady called Molly carrying one of these and telling a hell of a lie to get me out of hiding."

"Molly?" She looked to her daughter, who remained beside the laundry basket, still hopping like a rabbit. "Oh, Keller, she shouldn't have told you where I was. You shouldn't have come."

"Shouldn't have come?" He drew back so that he could look at her with those brown eyes she had lost her heart to. "Does that mean you've changed your mind? You're no longer in love with me?

"No, no, of course not." She rested her head on his shoulder again, dizzy. "It's just that . . . didn't Molly tell you? Look at me, Keller; look at what I am."

"Just what are you?"

"I'm indentured."

"No, actually you're not. I just purchased your indenture papers as well as those of a Miss Molly Commages for a very reasonable price."

Sarah blanched. "You did what?"

"Bought your indenture from the Birminghams. Now what's the problem?"

"I . . . I'm a felon. A murderess. I killed my uncle."

He stared at her blankly. "Do you intend to kill me?"

"Of course not."

He shrugged. "Next problem?"

She dropped one hand limply to her side. What was

he saying? What did he mean? She lifted her hand in a weak gesture. "I have a daughter whom you've obviously met. She's a bastard, Keller."

"There's been more than one fine lady born on the wrong side of the sheets." He winked at Molly as if they were the best of friends. "A good education and a substantial dowry, and that should be of little concern."

Sarah just stood there, still wrapped in Keller's arms, staring at his handsome face. "I . . . I don't understand. You were supposed to be transferred. Why are you here?"

"I *was* transferred. That clever young lady of yours caught me just in time. I've a post in Philadelphia. I'm headed that way. And as for what I'm doing here, I told you I would marry you."

"M . . . marry me?" Was this some joke, Sarah wondered. A dream she would soon wake from?

"So will you?"

Out of the corner of her eye, Sarah could see the master and mistress approaching, both smiling. *He was serious. For God's sake, he was serious.*

"Will you, Sarah? Come, come, I haven't all day. I told you, I'm headed for Philadelphia."

Her gaze met his. "Will I marry you? But, but why would you want me, knowing—"

"Why would I want you?" He lifted her red, raw hand and brought it to his lips. "I want you because I can't live without you. Molly told me everything, and it doesn't matter. It never would have mattered to me."

She looked into his eyes, trying to grasp what he was saying. "But . . . the carriage, your clothes; you're very rich, Keller."

He shrugged. "I may not be after this damned war is over. I may have to sell myself into indenture just to put food in our bellies. Now tell me once and for all, are you up to it? Will you marry a rebel not knowing what his name will be next week or where you'll sleep? Will you and Molly come to Philadelphia with me?"

It was funny, but Sarah couldn't help but think of the tale she had told Molly all these years. This was just how it happened.

"Yes," she whispered.

"What did you say?" He leaned in, teasing her. "A little louder. I want the Birminghams to witness your words."

"I said, yes," she repeated with more confidence. "I'll marry you, Keller." She smiled. "Or whatever your name is."

"It is Keller, truly it is," he whispered, his voice suddenly husky. "And I do love you, Sarah."

Then his lips met hers in a kiss that sealed their fate. His mouth brushed hers with all the tenderness and fire of a love most women only ever dreamed of.

"I love you," she whispered against his lips. "And they lived happily ever more . . ."

About the Author

Colleen Faulkner lives with her family in Southern Delaware. She is the author of over twelve Zebra historical romances, including *Captive, Forever His, Flames of Love, Sweet Deception,* and *Savage Surrender.* Her most recent Zebra historical romance, *O'Brian's Bride,* was published in April 1995 and is available at bookstores everywhere. Colleen has also had short stories published in Zebra's Halloween anthology, *Spellbound Kisses,* and Zebra's Christmas anthology, *A Christmas Caress.* Colleen is currently working on her fifteenth Zebra historical romance, *Destined To Be Mine,* which will be published in February 1996. Colleen loves hearing from her readers, and you may write to her c/o Zebra Books. Please include a self-addressed stamped envelope if you wish a response.

Daisies

by
Debra Hamilton

One

She sat in the garden of the house by the sea, a sheltered place gowned in English daisies and veiled in wrinkled, half-furled leaves. The daisies seemed to have sprung up from the ground and climbed over her lap, their petals a textured pattern of folds which, with a flashing needle, she sewed together. Stitch after perfect stitch she rendered into the masterpiece, finishing a seam, then snapping thread with her teeth and changing it for floss, embroidering yet another daisy at the hem.

The sun raked her bare arms and slowly she felt herself becoming a part of the garden while she stitched, being woven into its golden, bee-sprinkled air. On such clear days, when she grew very still, she could imagine herself kindred with the earth, a part of all that had gone before and all that would come after. A curious notion. She had voiced it once, a long time ago. *He* had understood. He had understood, too, the secret self that no one else dreamed was there.

"Elizabeth! Elizabeth *Honey*bridge!"

The gown automatically vanished into an old carpetbag, every thread and ribbon crammed out of sight and hidden in the tapestry depths with her thimble and scissors. The clasp was sturdy, and she snapped it tight.

It was a wedding gown Elizabeth Honeybridge hid, her own, she who had no bridegroom.

With the bag clutched against her old print dress, she

hurried across the lawn, giving one last glance to the white sails scattered over the sea. Pausing at the stoop, she straightened her apron before ducking beneath the awning and entering the flagstone kitchen with its hissing kettle and herb smells. The bag she shoved behind the collie's basket where it would have to stay until she could whisk it upstairs and out of sight.

"Young Mr. Spencer is coming home this afternoon," announced her mother fretfully, as if Elizabeth didn't already know. "We must have everything just right."

Like a small, off-balance whirlwind, Bertha Honey-bridge bustled from the enormous old Kitchener range—of which she was half-afraid—to the table, a dessert soufflé carried perilously in her hands.

Elizabeth sighed. The soufflé appeared overdone and would surely have to be salvaged by one of her thick fruit sauces.

"I should think you'd be eager to see him after nearly four whole years," continued her mother, who had been housekeeper at Maples House for three decades. "I should think you'd want his homecoming dinner to be grand. Instead, heaven only knows where you've been all morning, leaving me here to do everything. You know I'm quite lost without you. I give thanks to the Lord every day that you're a spinster with no prospects, a plain practical girl, for I don't know how I should manage alone now I'm nearing my dotage. It's as if my mind just slips away from me every now and then."

Calmly, in her capable way, Elizabeth went to the work table and began to julienne the carrots, her knife flashing as neatly as had her needle. "I was only outside an hour, Mother. I needed a breath of air." *I needed, God forgive me, to be away from your clinging, frazzled presence. I needed to forget that I am plain and practical. I needed to savor the news of Spencer's homecoming alone.*

With a flustered lift of her hands, Bertha abandoned the soufflé and flew to the window, throwing up the sash, which tended to stick with its new sloppy coat of paint. "There, dear! Air! Plenty of it coming off the Channel. Breathe deeply, for we'll only have it to ourselves another month or two, you know. Until the tourists invade. They'll be climbing up here with their paintboxes and picnic baskets, crowding the esplanade, poking about the curiosity shops hunting for bargains. And we'll have those dreadful bathing machines starting up!" She clicked her tongue and put a hand to her heat-flushed cheek. "Now, where did I put the strawberries? I *did* get them at the market yesterday, didn't I? Yes, just after Mrs. Maples told me Spencer was coming. How proud she is that her grandson has made such a success of himself in London. What is it he does, dear?"

Elizabeth lowered her head, her knife slicing very carefully through the orange heart of a carrot. "He manages his father's mill, Mother, as he was raised to do." Then, as an afterthought, as if it needed to be said aloud, she added, "It isn't what he wanted to do. He wanted to build bridges and roads, to be an engineer."

"Oh, yes," Bertha replied, half listening, pondering the array of shuddering pots upon the stove. "Well, I'm not surprised he grew up to build things. Always trowelling canals in the flower beds when he wasn't behind the shed with a hammer and saw. Wood shavings falling out of his pockets when I laundered his trousers. And remember that elaborate castle he fashioned on the beach one summer? Rather unconventional, I must say, but he won first prize for it."

Elizabeth's steady hands made a slightly irregular slice. "I remember." *I remember.*

Bertha disappeared into the pantry, the sounds of her frantic search for the strawberries clashing with the rattling lids of the hot saucepans. "Strange how he's scarcely

posted a word to his grandmother these last two months.
Always wrote so faithfully before that, every week. He
hasn't written you lately, either, has he, dear? I always
thought it gallant that he bothered to drop you a line now
and then. But he has the manners of a gentleman. And so
splendid *looking*. I don't care what some of these high-
nosed old cats say about families in trade. One couldn't
distinguish Spencer Kenton from a real lord if they tried."

The carrots, now thoroughly mauled into little slivers,
were swept into a cooking pot. "No, Mother. One
couldn't distinguish."

"Of course, he was irresponsible from time to time
as a boy. A bit too sporting. And that perfectly wicked,
perfectly divine grin of his. Well!" Bertha gave a twitter
of laughter and, having abandoned the strawberry search,
attacked the potatoes with a peeler. "But then, you remember, dear."

I remember. I remember everything.

Here, in this cream stucco house with its picture-view
of the sea, they had grown up together—Elizabeth the
housekeeper's daughter, Spencer the grandson of Mrs.
Maples, who was the lady of the middle-class residence.
Every summer he had come down from London. Every
summer he had made the golden days more golden, his
cricket bats and damp bathing costumes—and later,
shaving kits and riding boots—lending a delightful masculine clutter to the staid feminine household. When
Spencer was in residence, the three women felt as if the
house on the cliffs were in full sail instead of slightly
listing. He had spread his easy charm unstintingly, an
athletic, loosely-put-together young man who stood out
on both the playing fields and the promenade. In child-
hood, when he wasn't attending birthday parties or so-
cials, Elizabeth was his frequent playmate. Indeed, when
he had faced a dilemma at Folkestone, when his own
quick mind had deliberated too long, he would say,

"Where's Elizabeth? I'll ask her. She'll have a different perspective." And so she had.

Spencer had been Elizabeth's *only* playmate. And how exuberant she had been when he had deigned to take her exploring, climbing, shell-searching. How privileged she had felt when, after an hour or so of a private, quiet inwardness, he had hurled a rock out to sea and clenched his teeth, then poured out—always to her alone—the anger he had kept concealed from everyone else. She was the only one who knew the other side of Spencer Kenton, the angry, bruised side who quarreled incessantly with his father at home and was thrashed for it. The side who yearned to go its own way and was not allowed.

As they grew older, the middle-class boy and the housekeeper's daughter became more circumspect and, acquiring the tight-lipped pride of manhood, Spencer voiced his disappointments less often. Also, in the way of a gentleman, he insisted they meet clandestinely to save Bertha and Mrs. Maples worry, for even though Victoria no longer reigned and Edwardians enjoyed their loosened stays, class boundaries had not relaxed completely. Spencer had made a game of their innocent rendezvous. "Tell your mother you're going to the vegetable market. I'll meet you there in a half hour and take you fishing. Bet you a shilling my catch is bigger than yours."

He had never feared discovery or consequences at Maples House, for no matter what the misdemeanor, no matter what the indiscretion, Spencer Kenton was unconditionally, lavishly forgiven everything.

That, however, was not the case in London. After he left at the end of every summer, when young Elizabeth's shoes would crunch upon a sprinkling of beach sand in his abandoned room, she endured an ache unshared with anyone, knowing that he had exchanged the uncritical freedom of Folkestone for his father's unforbearance, knowing he would have the iron rod of Duty relentlessly drilled into him when he returned home.

Later he had gone to Oxford, grown into manhood, and come less often to the house by the sea. But still, when he did stroll into the vestibule carrying his sporting equipment and wearing his golden smile, his relationship with Elizabeth remained an easy, special one.

Now she put the carrots on the stove and crossed the green-painted kitchen to the spice cabinet, pretending to sort through the jars while, with her back turned, she fished a letter from her pocket.

It was Spencer's last to her, filled with the usual news of London, the anecdotes of royalty, the enlargement of the mill. But more importantly, his scrawled lines seemed underscored with a peculiar restlessness that disturbed Elizabeth. In the middle of the letter, he had penned what was surely a cryptic personal message: "I find it tedious to sit alone by the hearth at night. A man knows when it's time to marry." *A man knows when it's time to marry.*

"Elizabeth!"

The letter quickly vanished.

"The soufflé is falling! Sinking right before my eyes! Do something." Bertha stood over the failed dessert with her hand over her chest in a frozen genuflection, her pewter hair sticking out of its bun, color spotting her cheeks. "We'll have no dessert now! And you know how Spencer loves dessert."

Elizabeth leaned to pick up the crate of strawberries misplaced beside the umbrella stand. "Never mind, Mother. Instead of compote I'll make a strawberry trifle. You saved the cake left over from Mrs. Maples's tea yesterday, I hope?"

"Tea?" Bertha echoed. "Oh, my! What time is it? Have we forgotten Mrs. Maples's tea?"

"The kettle is already on, Mother. If you could just

manage to slice the bread and spread butter on it, I'll carry the tray in."

Ten minutes later, as Elizabeth punctually entered the mellow, sunlit parlor with its high ceilings and striped chintz, its Victorian fringes and tassels, its breathtaking view of the sea, Mrs. Maples snaked out a tentative hand to waylay her.

"Fetch your mother and join me, won't you, dear Elizabeth? We must have a . . . a discussion. A rather unpleasant one, I fear."

Bertha ventured in nervously at the summons, afraid of life as always, her feet shifting on the cabbage-rose carpet while Elizabeth leaned automatically to wipe dust from a Sheraton table. Mrs. Maples, as was her habit, hummed a piece from *Faust* and mentally drifted in and out of the room in order to procrastinate her unpleasant news.

She's wisteria, thought Elizabeth, who always compared people to flowers. Ensconced in her old green chair wearing blue-purple, Spencer's grandmother was a drooping, fragrant wisteria. Glancing at her mother with exasperated fondness, Elizabeth thought sadly that Bertha had become a trumpet vine, apt to be found wandering anywhere these days.

"Well, I see no reason to put off my announcement any longer," Mrs. Maples finally said with reluctance. "Since the sea wind has become too bracing for my aging bones, I shall sell the house at summer's end, just as soon as Spencer leaves, and go live with my sister in Bath."

She cleared her throat and kept her eyes away from the two staring women, finding her duty more difficult than her indigestion. "It's quite likely that Maples House will go to summer residents, people who may only need servants a few months out of the year. You *do* understand, dears . . ."

It was a blow, but in the way of blows caused only

a startled silence at first, a kind of impenetrable disbelief followed by numbness. Elizabeth sat staring at the drop-leaf table she had polished a thousand times while visions of the garden, of the sea view, of Spencer's room and all the things in it whirled around her head. They were the only joyful pieces of her quiet, unvarying life. And now, with a few regretfully uttered words, they had been neatly swept away.

Yet, wasn't it silly to panic? She slid a hand into her pocket, assuring herself that Spencer's letter was still in place. Her heart calmed.

"But Mrs. Maples," Bertha exclaimed, "where shall we *go?* There's mostly only summer employment here in Folkestone as you mentioned. Does that mean we'll have to traipse all over some *city* looking for a place to work?"

Mrs. Maples seemed to shrink in her chair. A Victorian relic, she was beyond coping with problems of any sort and avoided them by listening nostalgically to arias on her gramophone. "Well, you must go to a *good* family, of course," she advised sagely. "Not to one of these *nouveau riche* with their shockingly modern ideas. I declare, what was wrong fifty years ago is now right and what was right is wrong. Societal deterioration. I predicted it to my Edmond even before he died." She shook her pin-curled head. "At any rate, Elizabeth will know what to do."

"Will you, dear?" Bertha asked with a quivering chin.

"Of course, Mother."

"Perhaps Spencer will be able to suggest something," Mrs. Maples went on, busily spreading blackberry jam on a scone. "My sister says he has connections in London. She also says he's quite popular. Of course, he was always a favorite here. Succeeded at everything." She smiled mistily, reminiscing. "A good winner. A bit naughty at times, charmingly so, and oh my, too easily *dazzled.* Just let someone trot by on a showy thorough-bred or sail into harbor on a yacht, and off he'd go to charm a ride without a word to anyone." She waved a brown-spotted hand. "But who could stay vexed at him long?"

Elizabeth gazed beyond the old woman's head to the cliffs, remembering how, at fifteen, Spencer had hailed the driver of a motorcar—a rare sight among the Folkestone carriage traffic—and begged a ride. When Elizabeth had refused to go with him, he had doffed his cap at her in mock salute and left her standing on the road. Later, they had quarreled over it until, in typical Spencerian fashion, he had cajoled her out of her mood. It had remained their only serious argument.

Elizabeth rose, feeling unaccountably anxious. "May I be dismissed, Mrs. Maples? There's dinner to see to—"

"Certainly. Oh, and put on my gramophone, will you? Poor Bertha's hands are growing too unsteady to be trusted."

"Yes, of course."

The afternoon progressed slowly as Elizabeth awaited Spencer's homecoming with an anxious impatience. Risking disaster in the kitchen, she abandoned Bertha in order to tidy the upstairs rooms yet again, her efficient hands refolding towels, smoothing coverlets, sweeping the grates to perfection. She went constantly to the window, peering down at the winding road, searching, waiting, then running out to the garden on impulse to cut a bouquet of wild daisies for Spencer's room. *Would he remember?*

A bark, then a few sharply cursed words disturbed her as she snipped, and from around the privet hedge stumped her neighbor Mr. Whistlebury, a bent old stick of a man in coveralls with a dried-apple face. His fingers were hooked in the collar of an elderly collie, and he dragged the poor beast along as if it were a bad child, which, Elizabeth supposed, it was.

"He's been in my vegetable beds again," the old man groused, wagging a crooked finger. "Dug up a whole row of new peas this time and tore the netting down. Second time this week. If you don't keep him tied up, young woman, I'll not be responsible for my actions."

"Yes, Mr. Whistlebury. I'm sorry. I'll not allow him to do it again." Taking the collar of the gray-muzzled collie, she glanced expectantly at the road again while the disgruntled neighbor continued his querulous tirade.

"Ought to have him put down, you know. Too old to be anything but a blasted nuisance. I don't believe in having animals unless they can work and earn their keep. You just see to it he's kept out of my way."

Elizabeth nodded, squinting at the sun-splashed road yet again while hauling the collie irritably toward the kitchen. His muddy paws would track her newly mopped floor. She agreed with Mr. Whistlebury. He *was* a nuisance, always scratching up the back door, shedding, forgetting to hold his water. Blasted dog. Spencer's dog.

She recalled the summer he had brought the pup on the train, hidden it in a basket after it had soiled the rug in the London town house and been thrown out on the street by his father. How angry Spencer had been, his eyes stormy with the strong will of budding manhood, his voice full of the resentment that caused continual strife between him and his sire. When he had asked her with a fierce gaze to care for the dog, Elizabeth had promised solemnly. And she had kept that promise now for sixteen years.

Her heart suddenly softened toward the doddering old dog with its rheumy eyes and arthritic legs, and she led him more compassionately into the kitchen where, after kneeling to wipe his paws on a towel, she settled him in his basket.

"Everyone is growing so old here," she reflected aloud, suddenly struck by the frightening truth. "Everyone. Collie, Mrs. Maples, Mother. *Me . . .*"

As if to rid herself of the disquieting thought, she jumped up and ran out into the sunshine again; and, as she retrieved the abandoned daisies, she heard the slow clop of hooves, which always heralded the approach of one of the rented carriages and its wheezing nag from the village.

Spencer had come!

Rushing to the side of the house with her heart pounding and daisies dropping from her nervous hands, Elizabeth pushed through the lilacs and strained to see.

There, struggling up the steep hill, with the windsong as its fanfare, trundled an old carriage. In a moment it would draw up in front of the house, and before the driver had even had time to brake, its door would swing open and Spencer would vault down, hallooing loudly for his grandmother.

Elizabeth held her breath and touched the letter in her pocket. She felt she had been waiting for him, like this, for twenty-seven years.

She hung back in the shade of a chestnut to savor the moment, feeling a confidence that all would be well now that Spencer had arrived. The tedious routine, the loneliness, the *oldness* would be dispelled. The two of them would be together always.

The carriage creaked. An athletic man dressed in light-colored summer clothes ducked through the opening wearing a straw boater over thick brown hair burnished gold by the sun. At thirty, he was taller and more square-shouldered than before—and so handsome that no woman could resist glancing at him at least twice.

Spencer regarded the house, his eyes scanning the steep patched roof, the inexpertly applied paint, the hydrangeas which had not been trimmed all spring. Had he been a stranger, one might have thought that he found the place lacking, not smart enough for a city gentleman on holiday. But Elizabeth knew better.

With her breath held, she watched him, expecting him to stroll up to the house and announce his arrival in his usual deliberately loud, teasing shout, which Mrs. Maples always insisted hurt her ears even while she trotted toward her beloved grandson with outstretched arms.

But Spencer did not go to the house, turning instead toward the carriage again and reaching in to clasp someone's hand.

It was a slender, daintily poised hand that he drew out, its long, white fingers sparkling with gold rings.

Elizabeth frowned.

The owner of the pretty appendage, surely no more than eighteen, stepped down dressed in a creation of blue satin and a frothy hat. Standing in the sunshine she might have been a girl stolen from the canvas of a Monet, classically featured, pastel colored, her lacy parasol in hand. How well she complemented the man who escorted her up the path, the man whose head was bent solicitously to catch her every word. How tenderly, possessively, her hand rode upon his sleeve. Anyone could see that he belonged to her.

Elizabeth stood still beneath the tree, her feet rooted, her chest suddenly feeling as tightly ringed as the chestnut's core. Her heart was constricting so painfully, in fact, that she doubled over, willing it to stop hurting, to stop screaming, to stop beating altogether.

She had thought . . .

No. It wouldn't do to think. Not now. They would all be waiting inside, her mother flustered, the kettle shrilling, Mrs. Maples jerking the bellpull while the splendid, oil-painted couple declared themselves parched and ready for lemonade.

"God help me . . . don't let me cry." *Just a few min-*

utes, just a few minutes more here in the shade to compose myself.

She looked down. Three or four daisies still drooped in her hand, poor mangled things squeezed too tightly, unfit for a vase now, unfit for much of anything.

With effort, she forced herself to shuffle forward, rounding the house on numb legs, passing the rented carriage and the ancient driver, who had lingered to let his horse breathe.

"Anything the matter, miss?" he inquired.

"No." *Had she spoken aloud?*

As she passed it, Elizabeth regarded the carriage nag with its sagging lower lip, flabby neck, and shabby blinders. Smiling bitterly, she leaned forward and threaded the wilted daisies through its bridle with a quivering hand.

"Wear them well," she muttered, the words tasting sour upon her tongue. "Or better yet, eat them."

Two

As she arranged the tea trolley in the kitchen, she could hear their voices drifting from the parlor, Mrs. Maples's cooing trill, Spencer's deep-pitched remarks, and the musically soft tones of the Impressionist model he had brought.

"Can you believe it?" Bertha exclaimed, trotting across the kitchen with a pitcher of lemonade. "Spencer bringing a young lady home! Have you seen her, Elizabeth? I took a peek. She's a veritable *vision*. Just the sort of girl I always knew he would choose. He was naughty not to tell us in advance, of course, and how like him to pull such a surprise. No matter, Mrs. Maples will forgive him as usual. Er—where's the sugar for the lemonade, dear?"

Elizabeth was amazed that her hands were so steady, so deft at arranging the little iced cakes upon the platter, the silver spoons and forks, the delicate china cups upon their delicate china saucers. She was even able to fold the linen napkins with perfectly aligned corners and angle them beside the platter of grapes.

"Shall I roll the trolley in and serve, dear?" Bertha asked, her hands so tremulant she had to clasp them together like flighty birds.

"No, Mother. If you could stay and glaze the ham, I'll serve." She had decided to get it over with, grit her teeth and look into his eyes, speak with him as if nothing

untoward, nothing shatteringly unexpected had occurred.
She would even discipline herself to look directly at *her*.
It would be a penance of sorts, a reminder of how foolish a housekeeper's daughter could be when she let her
head drift too long in the clouds.

She pushed the trolley over the hardwood floors, her
heels tapping briskly as she progressed toward the sunny,
fern-filled parlor and its occupants. She wore her plain
black dress and starched apron, the one saved for company. Her brown hair was clasped in its practical coil;
her brown eyes were downcast and her spine properly
straight, as befitted a good servant.

When she entered, conversation lulled; and even
though she willed them not to, her eyes sought and
found the face, eyes, nose, mouth, she had been starved
to see.

He stood at the row of seaward windows, one hand
resting atop the chair upon which his lady sat, his left
foot touching the hem of her skirts in an implied inti-
macy, his hair ruffled by the breeze that thrust itself
through the open sash.

The sight of him, so handsome, so dear, robbed the
breath from Elizabeth's body.

Upon seeing her, Spencer stilled, his eyes direct and
alertly interested, remaining so as he crossed the room
in his long, easy stride. Although Elizabeth made no
welcoming move, he took one of her hands in his and
squeezed it.

"Elizabeth," he said warmly, his half-teasing manner
testing the boundaries of propriety. He inspected her in
what proved to be an excruciating examination, his eyes
sweeping her face and hands, taking note of their tense-
ness. He frowned and, in a low, peculiarly wondering
tone, said, "It's been too long since I was here, hasn't
it? Three years. It seems like ten."

He waited for her to answer, staring at her in a hard,

quizzical manner when she remained mute, then grinning in the old way to try and break the strain.

Elizabeth wanted to throw her arms round his neck as she had often done when they were children. How well she remembered the warmth of his body, its solidness, how it had seemed to carry with it the sun and wind of Folkestone, and how it caused her to view life, or living it, with an exuberant perspective.

Now she looked at Spencer Kenton's white smile and tried to understand why the sight of it made her eyes smart so painfully and yet want to go on looking at it while shutting out everybody else in the room, especially the beautiful girl. Did Spencer feel no guilt? She searched his eyes, looking to see if they silently said, "I misled you, Elizabeth, gave you hope when there was none. I'm terribly sorry. But you understand. You'll forgive me."

Yet, no matter how closely she looked, she saw no apology in his gaze, or anywhere in the clean-shaven, golden perfection of his face. He didn't know, Elizabeth thought. He hadn't the barest inkling of what he'd done to her. It had never occurred to him that she might love him or that she might imagine that he loved her. His smile was genuine, recklessly happy, urging her to be happy, too.

"Elizabeth, allow me to introduce Miss Sara Worth," he said. "I'm pleased to say we're soon to be married."

Elizabeth's fingers tightened around the handle of the trolley. She had known, of course, known the moment he had handed the lady out of the carriage. But the voicing of the words, which made them irrevocably real, knifed through her so sharply she nearly gasped.

Then, because there was nothing else to do, she raised her eyes and focused them upon the delicate, incredibly lovely face of his fiancée.

An orchid, Elizabeth thought. Miss Worth was a most rare, showy breed of orchid, the type that grew in secret woods and caused men to search for it, pluck it, and bring it out of its protected gloom for all the world to admire. She was the sort of woman who would excite a man at first glance and keep him excited every time he saw a curl escape from her picture hat or an ankle peek from her lace-edged hem. Sara Worth was a woman who could bring a man to his knees.

And had, by all appearances.

"Sara," Spencer was saying, completing the introduction, "this is Elizabeth."

Much to Elizabeth's dismay, the young woman arose and crossed the room in a fragrant swish of petticoats, her figure a combination of tiny waist and trailing skirts, her hands so soft and white they had likely never done anything more arduous than ply a fan in summer.

"At last we meet," she said charmingly. "Spencer has spoken of you with such affection. He told me that you used to play together. If I were prone to jealousy, I could resent you quite easily, I'm afraid. Is it terribly gauche of me to admit it?"

"I'm sure it isn't," Elizabeth muttered, finding her composure further unbalanced by Sara's airy frankness.

"I was just telling Spencer how wicked it was of him not to have informed us of his engagement," Mrs. Maples interjected. "My old heart can scarcely endure such joyous surprises. But, of course, he only proposed two weeks ago and couldn't wait to bring Sara to Folkestone for his Granny to pamper and purr over. But Spencer . . ." She leaned forward and whispered as if no one else in the room could hear. "Shouldn't you have brought Miss Worth's maid to chaperone? In my day a young woman's reputation would be in shreds before she stepped off the porch steps without a maid. Oh, my, I do hope Sadie Tipple didn't see you get off the train together . . ."

The subject had evolved into a problem, and since

problems must be avoided at all costs, Mrs. Maples turned her mind to food, which was always safe to ponder. "Elizabeth, roll the trolley over here, for heaven's sake! I'm anxious to sample one of those cakes."

"My generation is not quite so strict about chaperonage, Mrs. Maples." Sara commented soothingly. "But you can be assured that Spencer behaved with decorum on the train. He told me all about Folkestone and its amusements, and I can scarcely wait to go down to the esplanade to enjoy the concerts. There seems so much to do here, and manners are refreshingly casual. Spencer tells me there are always hordes of people strolling along the promenade. I'm glad, for I detest being alone, and dear old London can be dreadfully stuffy and dull. I was never one for quiet nooks and embroidery frames. I adore company and gaiety. Indeed, Spencer rescued me from a career that I imagined to be terribly exciting, but I suppose it really would have been scandalous had I taken it up. Didn't you rescue me, dear?" She turned long sky-blue eyes upon her fiancé.

Spencer stole a grape from the trolley, his eyes pinning her for a second or two. "In the nick of time."

"The stage, of course," Sara confided to Mrs. Maples, smiling so radiantly that the old lady's gasp of disapproval died. "He rescued me from notions of the stage."

"Thank goodness!"

Sara smiled and returned to her chair, the manner in which she seated herself an exercise in coquetry, a languid rearrangement of skirts, a tilting of the head so that her picture hat accented the blue allure of her eyes.

Miss Worth needed to be admired and fed upon compliments, Elizabeth thought, eyeing her shrewdly. She needed to show herself off and be shown off. And who better to squire her across her personal stage than Spencer Kenton? He was good-looking, dynamic, never dull or beyond suggesting an adventure. And he was

probably unreservedly passionate as well. A most atten-
tive lover, Elizabeth speculated with an aching heart.

Positioning the trolley between Sara and Mrs. Maples,
she inquired if she might pour tea or lemonade and, after
serving, stepped back to await requests for seconds
while Spencer helped himself, waving her away with a
wink when she would have assisted him.

He lounged about the trolley and ate fruit, attempting
to make her smile by tossing a grape in the air when
no one was looking and catching it in his mouth.

Elizabeth kept her own lips stubbornly clamped, and
he contemplated her seriousness speculatively, noting the
change in her attitude and disliking it. No doubt he
would keep staring at her in that discerning, penetrating
way of his, thinking he could eventually discover the
reason for her grimness.

Well, Elizabeth determined, she would give him no
clue. She would keep her eyes downcast, focus upon
something innocuous, like the lemonade pitcher. Out of
the corner of her eye she saw Spencer toss another
grape, fail to catch it, and lean to retrieve it unabashedly
from beneath his grandmother's old-fashioned skirts.

"Forgive me, Granny," he said when she looked out-
raged. "But I believe you dropped a grape."

Elizabeth turned away, hiding a smile. The rogue did
not deserve one, and besides, if she smiled she would
surely cry as well; tears still threatened dangerously.

Think of something else, she ordered herself. Had
Bertha added sugar to the lemonade?

"You must tell me how you met Miss Worth," Mrs.
Maples said to her grandson. "Was it a terribly romantic
first encounter? Do say yes. It has always been my opinion that a young couple should know immediately that
they are suited for one another. Otherwise, how should
one know whether or not it is all right to fall in love?"

"We were introduced at my father's house," Spencer

answered, taking a sip of the lemonade, shuddering slightly but recovering well. "At dinner."

"Spencer wasn't supposed to notice me, you see," Sara elaborated. "His father meant for him to be enraptured by a Miss Giles—an earl's daughter whose family coffers could have expanded the Kenton mills twice over. How it would have pleased his father if Spencer would have cooperated and done as he should." She flashed her fiancé a radiant look. "But I was at dinner that night, too, and quite by accident wandered into the library where he had gone for a newspaper." She lowered her lashes, a picture of modest womanhood. "He didn't notice Miss Giles the rest of the evening, did you, Spencer?"

"Should I have, Sara?"

Detecting an odd note in the voice she knew so well, Elizabeth glanced at the couple and saw that Spencer observed his fiancée not with tenderness but with admonishment. A faintly discernible tension seemed to stretch between them, as if some issue remained unresolved. Elizabeth surmised that they used words against each other like the arrows of two seasoned archers.

"So it really will be a marriage of fascination in the way of Victoria and Albert, then?" Mrs. Maples sighed, sensing no unpleasant undertones. "Not at all arranged as so many matches still were in my day. But when is this delightful wedding to be?"

Spencer turned his eyes to watch a pair of horsemen gallop past the house. "August," he said. "If it can be managed upon such short notice. Sara would like to spend the summer here. I shall take some time off from the mills, of course, but business will require that I shuttle back and forth by train." He turned to face his grandmother again, the earlier strain forced from his expression as he smiled. "You won't mind your lawn trampled by wedding guests, will you, Granny?"

"Dearest Spencer!" The piece of cake en route to her

mouth stayed suspended. "Do you, mean hold the wedding *here*—in this house?"

"You aren't going to swoon, are you, Granny?"

"Oh, I may indeed!" The pin curls bobbed.

"Shall I fetch the smelling salts?" he asked calmly, before picking up his glass of lemonade and holding it under her nose. "On second thought, a hearty swig of this should do."

But Mrs. Maples had forgotten her faintness as quickly as she had invented it, visions of the grand celebration she was to host filling her head. "We must have musicians, and a reception in the garden following the *dejeune*—the wedding breakfast. Oh, and a cake, the most elaborate Folkestone has ever seen. Ribbons and greenery festooning the entire house, and favors for everyone to take home."

She broke off, waving her hands again. "Oh my! I don't believe I could cope with such a feat of organization. It would take such *energy* to deal with tradesmen and florists and engravers. But," she threw up her hands, "why am I in such a tizzy when I have a most capable organizer right beneath my nose?"

With confidence and a touching dependence, Mrs. Maples turned to the young woman who had been the mainstay of her house for ten years, the woman who was undaunted by sparrows in the chimneys, moths in the wardrobes, or spiders under the sofa. The same young woman who had, unbeknownst to anyone, secretly stitched a wedding gown in the garden just this morning.

"Elizabeth, dear," she cooed. "You can arrange it, can't you? Of course! You will be able to manage the most *spectacular* wedding for my darling Spencer."

Later that evening Elizabeth moved about the kitchen wiping up spills, scraping plates, choosing morsels of leftover meat for the collie, and cutting them into smaller bits to aid his bad teeth. She was weary to the bone, as heartsick as a woman could be, working alone because her mother's chatter and clumsy hands annoyed her own unstrung nerves. She had sent Bertha to attend Sara, to bring her clean towels and peel her out of her dinner gown, which had been a confection of pink tulle complemented by a coiffure in the voluptuous Gibson style.

Only by a determined will had Elizabeth managed to serve dinner, to watch and listen. She had been prepared to dislike Sara Worth, hate her even, but astoundingly, she had not—could not. Anyone must be charmed by Miss Worth's vivacity, her pink-and-white-orchid beauty, her touching, constant need for attention, which—instead of irritating—enchanted.

Elizabeth frowned, disgruntled. She could dislike Sara Worth no more easily than she could dislike a winsome child or blame it for its clamor to be loved.

Taking up a scouring pad, she began to scrub the work table, finding solace in the act. It was something she did every day, after all, and—God help her!—would likely be doing the rest of her life until, like Bertha, she grew too old to manage.

"Have I become such a stranger?"

The voice came from beyond the kitchen door, but Elizabeth did not turn or stop in her scrubbing even though her heart thumped uncomfortably.

Spencer strolled across the room and, finding a clean glass, wielded the old pump to fill it. His hands, she noticed out of the corner of her eye, were just as she remembered them when they had mended fishing line or swung cricket bats. They were just the same as she had imagined them in her recent daydreams—such shameful, foolish daydreams they seemed now.

Unable to bring herself to look at his face, to permit

him to see hers in case he should read it, Elizabeth asked awkwardly, "Do you have plenty of towels?"

"Towels?"

"Yes." She scrubbed more vigorously. "For your ablutions."

He grinned, ran a hand over his jaw, and forced his face into serious lines. "Ah, yes. Well, I haven't counted them yet, but when I do, I promise to let you know if the number is adequate."

The scouring pad whirled in tighter circles. "You have only to ask for whatever you need. As always. If mother doesn't see to it, I will. You have only to tell me."

"That's very good of you," Spencer said gravely.

"You're most welcome."

His hand came down upon hers. "I believe you are beginning to sand the table, Elizabeth."

Color rose to her neck, and she turned away to dry the dishes.

"Am I not to be forgiven?" he asked bluntly, refusing to be put off.

"Forgiven? Whatever for?" Elizabeth brandished the cup towel with as much energy as she had the scouring pad.

"For failing to tell you about my marriage plans ahead of time. A lot of bother, Sara and I are. And your mother is not coping as well as she might. I'm sorry. I didn't know. It must be difficult for you to manage."

The years fell away all at once. Spencer's voice was just as familiar, just as companionable as always, and suddenly Elizabeth yearned to abandon pretense. Above all, now that all her illusions had been shattered and she knew precisely where she stood, she wanted to remind Spencer of her place, and his.

Facing him, controlling her emotions, she said succinctly, "I'm a servant here, Spencer, and you are the man of the house. I'm supposed to manage. Just as you're supposed to be forgiven."

He laughed, unoffended by her starchiness. "I see I have indeed been away too long. You've grown prickly without me to drag you out to the shore or along the cliffs. What do you do all day, Elizabeth? Cook and scrub? That would do very well in London, I suppose, but not here in Folkestone. Look out there through the window; look at the sails in the harbor, at the sunset. It's a sin to waste it. I can't count the times I've thought of our fishing expeditions, of the cliffs and the Roman ruins. They were the best times of my life." His voice lowered. "I get none of that in London."

A silence ensued as a cloudy mood seemed to overtake his usual cheer, but he quickly banished it with a laugh. "If memory serves, you have yet to bring home a bigger catch than I. Shall I give you another chance while I'm here?"

Elizabeth took up another dish, murmuring tightly, "It wouldn't be proper anymore—the two of us alone. You know that, Spencer."

"When was it ever proper beyond the age of ten? Elizabeth." He took the plate out of her hands and put it down. "Good God, don't tell me you've grown priggish?"

"You should take Sara if you want to go fishing," she replied rigidly, keeping her eyes averted.

"Sara? She's afraid of fish unless they're swimming in lemon juice and butter."

"Then escort her to the places she enjoys. Places full of people and music. I should think a man would be proud to have a girl like Sara on his arm." The words were genuine if grudged, and Spencer remained so quiet she feared he had heard the break in her voice. "She's lovely, beautiful," Elizabeth went on, forcing herself to say the words.

"Yes, she is."

When a second silence stretched between them, Elizabeth asked, "What of her family?"

"Her father was a French dancing master who danced out of her life when she was five. Luckily, her mother was the daughter of some obscure baronet and entitled to a small inheritance which, together with a generous income from a series of well-to-do lovers, kept groceries on the table and pretty hats on Sara's head."

Taken aback, Elizabeth stared at him.

"Surprised? Did you assume a girl as fashionable as Sara would have come from quality? Ah, well," Spencer said, smiling ruefully. "We must be thankful to her mother, who, in spite of adversity, taught her well."

He examined the plate he had just put on the cupboard shelf and, finding it not quite clean, tossed it toward her, his action as negligently skillful as always.

"Spencer! For heaven's sake!" With difficulty Elizabeth managed to save Mrs. Maples's best china from the floor. "I've had no practice at it for three years. Give fair warning next time."

"I have faith as always in your reflexes, Elizabeth. Besides, without taking risks, half the fun is ruined."

"Or your grandmother's plates," she said dryly. Dipping a cup into a bin to measure flour for the next morning's breakfast buns, she needled him, testing the waters, watching him closely through her lashes. "I'll wager Sara won't appreciate your tossing her wedding china."

Spencer took the sifter from her hand and idly examined it, leaving puffs of flour on the cuff of his black dinner jacket. "I'm afraid I don't throw plates in London, or get down to the kitchens. In fact, you would scarcely know me in my house across from St. James Park. Quite stuffily settled, I am. No doubt you'd be impressed."

Elizabeth didn't believe so. She wouldn't want to see him any other way than as he was in Folkestone. Of

course, she had always known he had another side, one
molded by responsibility to his father, and she wondered
if after he married, after Maples House was sold, his
more sober persona would prevail and smother the smiling, mischievously irresponsible Spencer Kenton she
loved.

"I always thought as long as there was Maples
House—" he began, as if his thoughts were parallel to
hers. He broke off, uncomfortable voicing whatever sentiment had nudged him. When the collie bestirred itself
from the basket and limped stiffly to his master's side,
Spencer patted it, regaining his lighter tone again.

"Collie, old boy. Elizabeth has been taking good care
of you, I see. How is it we never got around to giving
you a proper name?"

"Because we disagreed on it," Elizabeth put in, crack-
ing an egg on the lip of a mixing bowl.

"That's right. I remember. You wanted to call him
something embarrassing like Sugar or Apple Tart. What
was wrong with King Edward?"

"Don't you think he would have been offended?"

"Collie? No."

Spencer began to roam about the kitchen, rummaging
through the cupboards, helping himself to a tin of bis-
cuits while watching Elizabeth with the kind of thought-
ful frown she found unsettling.

She slapped the dough against the table with more
force than necessary, digging the heels of her hands into
it, taking refuge in the everyday rhythm, unable to look
at the elegant man in evening clothes who filled the
emptiness of her kitchen.

"You don't mind organizing the wedding, do you?"
he asked all at once, his voice brutally direct. "Sara and
I can marry in London if it puts too much work upon
your shoulders. I thought—"

Again, the unfinished sentence, the incomplete expression.

Elizabeth's fingers closed about the ball of dough. She wanted to say, "No! I can't bear to plan your wedding, the wedding I thought would be my own! I can't bear to watch you with *her,* hear you recite vows, and know, once it's over, that I have lost you irrevocably."

Her hands stilled upon the dough and she looked up at him, suddenly wanting to give him—if she could, if it were possible—an equal stab of pain. "Shouldn't I want to do it, Spencer?" she asked intently, looking at him with a pointed gaze. "Since it's the very last thing I'll ever be able to do for you?"

"Elizabeth—"

"Can you let Collie out, please?" she interrupted, refusing to allow him a chance to explain, to apologize. She began battering the dough again. "And please stay out with him for a while. He digs up Mr. Whistlebury's vegetables if left unwatched."

Hesitating, Spencer observed her for several long seconds, but Elizabeth kept her back rigid and her lips clamped and, at last, as if realizing it useless to pursue the subject—or knowing he had no right—Spencer pivoted on his heel. Snapping irritably at the dog to follow, he went out, letting the screen door bang behind him.

Elizabeth left the dough, left the dirty pans, abandoned her kitchen to disorder—something she had never done before—and fled to her room.

She had endured quite enough for one day,

Three

"A Victorian wedding," Mrs. Maples announced with a romantic sigh. "It will be just the thing, don't you think, Elizabeth? Weddings in my day were so much more dignified than these loose, anything-goes ceremonies today. One cannot be too proper, if you ask me. Of course, Sara, if you insist upon not wearing a veil, we can consult Mr. Jeaffreson's book of etiquette here, which I used religiously as a bride."

The old lady reverently opened the tome in her lap. "Ah, yes. He states that a veil isn't necessary, that one can substitute a headdress of white blossoms—although he believes orange blossoms have been overrated. Roses, perhaps, dear. And it goes without saying that one must wear *only* white if one wishes to avoid . . . whispers."

The three women sat in the wicker garden chairs, Mrs. Maples declaring herself up to it since the day's calm would disturb neither pin curl nor bursitis. The wedding, it had already been decided, would be a large affair, with invitations sent to Folkestone acquaintances as well as to friends and family in London. Sara had insisted upon a sizable gathering, doubtless wanting to be admired by as many pairs of eyes as possible.

"I've decided to wear Mama's wedding gown," she announced as if it were a momentous decision. "It's made of Brussels lace, which my father brought from

France. It was given to him by a comptesse he had taught to waltz."

Elizabeth, who was keeping a vigilant watch over the honey-brushed scones by shooing away circulating bees, found the dreamy excitement of the two women scarcely endurable. She sat stiffly, her back not touching the wicker chair, her envious eyes too aware of the strand of pearls circling Sara's neck, the moire-lined hat that could have been plucked straight from the garden, the fingers that were as pale as the almond slivers sprinkled over the iced cakes. She found herself tucking her own chafed hands in her lap out of sight.

"Oh, and the bride cake!" Mrs. Maples exclaimed, wielding her heirloom fan industriously. "It must have three tiers, of course, with cornucopias decorating the first layer, lovebirds the second, and curly-haired angels dancing 'round the figures of the bride and groom. Can't you just picture it!"

"Champagne and *foie gras,*" Sara put in. "Everything done in style. Eight bridesmaids. I shall ask Spencer to give them each a cameo from Harrod's—his groom's gift. I won't have it said the Kentons are close-fisted." She colored slightly, a sugar-pink blush on porcelain-white skin. "Spencer and his father are footing all the bills, of course, since Mama isn't able."

Mrs. Maples frowned, vaguely troubled. "But shouldn't we consult Spencer, Sara? About the expenses, you know. Gentlemen are contrary from time to time when it comes to expenditures. One has to explain the importance of sentiment and propriety every now and then. My Edmond, for example, couldn't understand that *he* must pay for the bridesmaids' gowns until I told him it would look boorish if I asked them to provide their own. I couldn't bear to have anyone whisper that I was marrying a skinflint."

"I believe it's a man's obligation to spend lavishly on a woman," Sara disclosed. "How else does she know she's loved? His spending must be equal to his attentions, Mama says. Don't you agree, Spencer?"

He had strolled up behind them in his summer jacket and trousers, his eyes fixed, not upon his bride-to-be, Elizabeth noted, but upon the rough green cliffs overlooking the Channel.

"Of course," he replied, his smile hardly altering when he added, "Does it follow then, that if a man has a poor year in the stock market, his wife should not be loved at all?"

His grandmother appeared confused by the remark, but Sara, always percipient, reached a languid arm behind her chair to find his hand and clasp it. "You're so droll, darling. But you haven't told me how well my pearls look." She tilted her head, providing a glimpse of her bared throat and, if he chose to enjoy it, a downward, intensely private view provided by her low décolletage.

Elizabeth flushed and turned around, pricked by an overwhelming envy, realizing that before summer's end Spencer would have leave not only to look at, but to slide his hands beneath the lace-edged neckline and caress what lay beneath.

"The pearls are beautiful," he murmured.

"More beautiful than the amber I wore the first evening we met, Spencer?"

"Equally beautiful."

Sara laid his hand against her cheek and almost purred. "Where have you been all morning? You know I like to have you with me."

He took his hand away. "The house needs repainting. The last crew botched the job, and I went to the village to demand that they return tomorrow and do it properly."

"Oh, Spencer," Mrs. Maples said, "what would I do without you? Elizabeth does the best she can with the workmen and tradesmen, but even she cannot always get results when they're surly or difficult. It's this new breed of moneygrubbers with their poor workmanship. No pride in anything, no *conscience,* one is forced to think sometimes." Hauling herself up out of the straining wicker, she fussily positioned her parasol so not a ray of sun touched her withered complexion. "Just thinking of it taxes me, so I'm off to enjoy my arias. Elizabeth, can I trust you to gather up the wedding books and bring them in, dear? Their bindings are rather fragile, you know."

Without waiting for a reply, she waddled off, her absence leaving a hush behind which Elizabeth found so uncomfortable that she stacked the books hurriedly, wanting to escape the two lovers and their little intimacies.

Noting her fumbling haste, Spencer bent down to help, amusement in his voice. "Have they worn you out talking about their plans?"

"Not at all," she mumbled uncommunicatively.

"She's been as quiet as a mouse," Sara put in. "And so patient to sit and take notes on every detail we've suggested. I'm surprised her head's not throbbing from it all. By the way, Spencer, do you think we can afford a new house when we're married? Yours is nice, of course, but so cramped. I had in mind a more spacious dining room. We haven't enough seating for large gatherings."

"If we haven't enough chairs in the dining room, let the guests eat in the kitchen."

"Stop teasing, Spencer. I'm trying to increase our social status, not destroy it."

"Sara," he said all at once, pulling her up from her chair. "Come with me for a walk along the cliffs. Come now." He touched her face, ran his knuckles down the soft line of her dimpled chin. "I'll show you a spectacular view."

Sara laughed beneath his attentiveness, her face radiant, her voice vixenish. "But my shoes will be ruined and my parasol turned inside out in the wind, darling. Men never

think of such things. Forget the cliffs and come back inside with me. We'll sit together over the wedding books
and decide what you should wear—striped waistcoat or
white."

"Come, Sara." Beneath the jocularity, Spencer's voice
held the edge of a flinty impatience.

But she declined again with a pat of her fan on his
sleeve. "Not today. Anyway, you'll have to stop climbing
cliffs and walking in the wind when we're married.
There's hearth and home, you know. And social occa-
sions which will claim us almost every weekend."

Knowing she shouldn't, Elizabeth glanced over her
shoulder to look at them, her eyes fastening upon
Spencer's face. His gaze was upon the cliffs again, his
mouth tight, every line in his athletic, adventurous body
yearning toward the freedom of Folkestone, toward re-
capturing, even for an hour, all the escapes of boyhood.
She pitied him in that moment. And blamed him. She
knew that the reckless, laughing boy of Folkestone she
had known and loved would be, within a few years if
he allowed it, entirely smothered by the needful, persis-
tent charm of Sara Worth.

Perhaps Sara sensed his dissatisfaction, too, and remembered that she did not yet have him bound by a wedding ring. Like quicksilver she changed tactics, smiling
at him brilliantly, lifting her face so that the sun highlighted the perfection of her features. One cleverly placed
hand slipped beneath the lapel of his jacket and moved
in a caress. "Better yet," she compromised, shrewd for
all her airiness, "take me down to the village, to the Leas
you've talked so much about. We'll enjoy a day in the
fresh air. Wasn't that what you wanted, after all, dear?"

Elizabeth herself had shopping to do in the village,
but—hardly caring to risk meeting Sara and Spencer—

waited until they had gone out the door, watching until the tip of the lady's parasol disappeared down the hill. Then, with a wicker basket hooked over one arm, she started out in her dove-grey skirt and straw hat, winding down the road, breathing in the scent of the flowering shrubs on the one side, studying the panoramic view of the Channel on the other.

The sea was a wrinkled blue dotted with white sails and, farther out, strewn with tubby steamers trailing ribbons of smoke. Rimming it, the long strip of brown beach was sprinkled with strolling couples, most of whom would not dip a toe in the creamy surf until August, when the water warmed and the bathing machines started up.

Along the cliffs ahead, called the Leas, chimney pots huddled close, rising above quaint stucco homes with mansard roofs. Leafy trees bordered postage-stamp gardens, and farther down, gulls veered over the long pier and the pavilion where musicians performed.

Usually the walk gave Elizabeth pleasure, but today she could think only of Spencer, of losing him—of his losing himself—and, almost as devastating, of losing Folkestone when Mrs. Maples closed the house at summer's end.

Preoccupied, she did not immediately notice the man and woman sitting to the side of the road, the lady bending over her shoe while the gentleman pushed the straw boater off his brow in a rueful gesture.

"Well, Sara," Spencer drawled, resting his elbows on his knees as if prepared for a lengthy wait, "I have lost a wager with myself. I thought your feet in those flimsy slippers would last two miles, but we have not quite made three-quarters of one, by my reckoning."

"You didn't tell me the road would be so rocky, Spencer," she complained.

"I advised you to change shoes."

"Oh, just give me a moment more to rest, and then we'll proceed. I shall manage somehow."

"Carried all the way in my arms, by the looks of it. Not that I'm unwilling, my love, if it pleases you to be treated as an invalid."

Elizabeth hid a smile, experiencing the first real surge of amusement since the previous disastrous day, and with unashamed maliciousness she decided that Spencer Kenton—who had allowed himself to be dazzled by a beautiful face—was duly receiving his just deserts.

She sauntered briskly past in her sensible black shoes, nodding with a straight face at the pair. "Miss Worth. Mr. Kenton. Good day."

"Elizabeth," Spencer called out. "Slow down that galloping pace of yours and walk with us."

"You don't appear to be walking, Mr. Kenton."

"I assure you, we *will* be walking, one way or another."

"I really must see to the marketing—"

"I insist."

"I decline."

"I insist." And rising, he took her arm and drew her back while Sara, with a wince of pain that managed to look enchantingly forlorn, limped a step or two.

"Yes, *do* come with us, Elizabeth," she said a little too sharply, "since Spencer seems so determined to have you."

"How astute of you to notice, Sara," he replied, taking her elbow in one hand and Elizabeth's basket in the other.

By the time the three of them arrived in the village, Sara was pouting. She didn't spare a glance for the bow-fronted curiosity shops with their silver tea sets or for the ice cream sellers who wandered through the old inns and down crooked streets too narrow for the passage of a Bath chair. Instead, she asked to be taken directly to the esplanade, for her restless eyes had immediately spied the crowds there, the hatted and bonneted young people laughing or sitting in groups, chatting and reading novels in the sun.

"We'll escort Elizabeth to the fish market first," Spencer stated, directing them that way, ignoring the dissatisfied glance aimed at him from beneath a flowered hat brim.

Keeping pace with his athletic step, they proceeded to the seafaring quarter of town with its weathered buildings, its old men mending nets, its mackintoshes hung out to dry along the dock where fishermen hauled catches ashore. The fish were dumped upon the wharf in a gleaming pile, gathered in baskets and carried to the market sheds, then beheaded, disemboweled, and sold by red-complected sailors.

Sara, whose nose wrinkled at the sight and stench, threaded her gloved hand around Spencer's elbow possessively, her eyes glittering, flitting about the market, uninterested in the boats or the busy fishermen. She was seeking, Elizabeth thought, a deserving audience.

While Spencer roamed about with her on his arm, speaking amiably with everyone, shaking his head when Elizabeth would select a fish he judged inferior, Sara clung to him, demanding his attention in a thousand ways but, apparently failing to receive it to her satisfaction. When a group of fashionable young ladies appeared escorted by an elegant gentleman, Sara fastened her gaze upon them. The women were chatting in French, the handsome gentleman buying them ice creams and entertaining them with some amusing story.

Suddenly Sara's hat took flight in the wind and sailed in his direction with unerring aim.

Elizabeth frowned, certain that the hat had been aided by the push of a delicate hand.

With a little cry, Sara hailed the Frenchman, who had

gallantly gone chasing after the wayward hat and, having saved it from the Channel, looked about in bewilderment for its owner.

"Sir! Sir!" she called out, approaching him. "How dashing of you to bother saving the silly thing. Did I hear you speaking French? How delightful. My father is French."

And so it went. Sara Worth had found her audience and performed before them, graciously accepting the compliments of the young ladies who admired her gown, adroitly conversing in their language, her eyes straying every now and then to the gentleman's enraptured face.

"Spencer," Elizabeth said, vexed. She glanced at him, but he seemed either unaware or unconcerned with Sara's antics, continuing to stroll through the stalls and select fresh fillets with an easy wave of his hand, asking to have them wrapped.

"Aren't you going to retrieve Sara?" Elizabeth asked, astonished that he had not glanced twice at his fiancée.

He dug a few shillings from his pocket and paid a fisherman. "Do you believe she needs to be retrieved, Elizabeth?"

Taken aback, she answered, "I think she wants to be."

"I beg to differ. And knowing Sara better than you do, I fear you must concede to my judgment."

"But isn't it your responsibility to make her behave properly?"

He laughed. "Perhaps. But then, I've been known to act irresponsibly from time to time. If you judge me unfit company, I'll not take it badly if you grab your fish and march away." He grinned, and suddenly the grin was one from other years, mischievous, irresistible, affecting Elizabeth's senses in such a way that all the layers of awkwardness and resentment were peeled away.

"I should go home," she murmured.

"I know. But I'd rather you stay, go for a ride with me on the Channel."

"Go riding? In a boat, you mean?"

"We should get wet any other way, don't you think?"

Elizabeth glanced in Sara's direction, noting that the bride-to-be ambled leisurely up the hill toward the esplanade with her newfound knot of spectators, her parasol twirling coquettishly, her eyes darting, once or twice, toward Spencer.

But her fiancé was not the sort of man to suffer a woman's manipulations. He understood Sara Worth well, it seemed; and refusing to establish a pattern for the future and fall prey to her stratagems, he allowed her to go her own way.

"Keep the fish on ice for us, will you?" he asked the fisherman, returning the wrapped parcel and generously offering a pound note. "For an hour or two?"

Turning, he then waylaid a sunburnt lad and, producing ten pounds as if it were tuppence, pointed to a rowboat moored among the fleet. The boy accepted the lavish exchange and with a whoop galloped off in the direction of a confectionery.

"Well?" Spencer asked when Elizabeth hesitated.

Giving him a serious look from beneath her hat brim, she said, "You're very wicked, Spencer."

"But you won't let me go alone. Will you, Elizabeth?"

"I should."

"But you won't."

And because this would be the last time that a piece of their past could be snatched back and sweetly enjoyed and because she had never done anything wicked in her life before today, Elizabeth agreed.

Spencer sat across from her in the boat, balancing easily in the rocky craft while mounting the oars. He put his weight into the rowing effort and soon they were gliding effortlessly past graceful sloops and sleek American yachts.

"Here, take the oars," he said, doffing his jacket and yanking loose his tie before resuming the chore.

The exhilaration of the wind, of the escape, brightened his handsomeness and made it fiercely male. When he grinned at Elizabeth, she couldn't help but smile in return, holding on to her hat, tensing when he veered dangerously close to a pair of yachts. With consummate skill, he wound his way through the traffic. Remembering other similar rides, she laughed.

"Frightened, Elizabeth?"

"A bit."

"Shall I thread us through that fishing fleet to test your nerves?"

"I think not, Spencer."

"I believe I will."

"Use a little restraint, please. Oh, Spencer! For heaven's sake!"

He maneuvered the boat on a zigzagging journey through every sort of peril, making her laugh wildly and grab her sides. Finally, flushed from the high adventure, she begged him to stop so she could catch her breath.

Spencer slackened the pace, taking them on a pleasure route parallel to the Leas, breathing deep from his efforts, leaning back a little to savor the sheer delight of physical exertion and sunshine.

After a while, wanting to know about his business at the mills, his life in London, and recalling the casual way he had tipped the people on the pier, Elizabeth asked quietly, "Have you become very prosperous, Spencer? Should I feel awed?"

He stopped rowing and looked first at her, then out to sea. Taking his time to answer, he laced his hands behind his head and leaned back, closing his eyes against the glare of the sun. "I'm wealthy enough to be extravagant every now and then."

"Do you enjoy it? The wealth, I mean?"

Waves lapped at the sides of the boat, a loud beating sound blending with the wind's rush. After considering, he admitted, "Not particularly. But, more and more, I find that I enjoy simply making the money. I can't explain why, except that it's the only sort of challenge I can find in London." He grew reflective, and when a piece of driftwood floated past, a sinewy, beautiful specimen, he pointed it out. "Do you still have your collection?"

"Yes." She smiled. "Even the very first piece you gave me—that summer you took the mumps, remember?"

"Ah, yes. Inconvenient, those mumps. Caused me to miss two weeks of swimming."

She smiled. "But little else."

"Granny was quite put out, wasn't she?"

"Came as near to scolding you as she ever did, I recall."

The driftwood undulated away, and Spencer reversed the direction of the boat, using one of the paddles to try and snatch the prize, which proved frustratingly slippery. "It's out of reach now," he said. "Shall I jump in and get it for you?"

"Spencer! Of course not. It's freezing."

But he had already pulled off his shoes, and before Elizabeth could grab his sleeve, he dived out of the boat.

"Undaunted as always," she murmured to herself, watching him with the sort of heartsick longing that came from loving without hope. It was the first time in her life, she realized, that she hadn't felt hopeful. In the past there had always been next summer, or the summer after.

Spencer resurfaced several yards away and, after locating the driftwood, stroked strongly, finally snagging the last piece of the collection they had begun twenty years ago and would finish in their borrowed boat today.

In another minute he had hauled himself back into

the bobbing little vessel, soaking wet, his shirt molded to his muscled torso, his hair sleekly plastered over his well-shaped head. Water beads danced off of his body, splattering Elizabeth's skirt. There was something intimate, she thought, in seeing a man in wet clothes.

Without a word he sat down opposite her, reached out to offer her the glistening white gift.

Not meeting his eyes, she clutched it, smoothed it with her fingers, the sound of his breathing, which was still slightly labored from his swim, filling her ears. She glanced at his sprawled legs, the tautness of drenched trousers over hard thighs, but could not raise her eyes to his face, afraid suddenly of what she might find there.

"Elizabeth."

The quietness in his voice caused her stomach to twist, her eyes to close against a pang of emotion. It wasn't fair, she thought, for him to speak in such a tone, to touch the sore heartstrings she had managed to keep securely bandaged until now.

He raised a hand to touch her face.

She leaned into it, keeping her eyes shut, the wetness of his fingers cooling her cheek. She heard him shift, move toward her, and held her breath. When he put his lips against the corner of her mouth, she stiffened, stunned by the forceful thrill of it.

Never had he kissed her, never had she felt his lips. Still motionless with his mouth pressed to the corner of hers, Elizabeth breathed in the damp scent of the man she loved, experiencing for the first time the texture of his flesh and the excitement it brought, the need to know it intimately.

"I stayed away too long . . ." he whispered, almost wonderingly. "Didn't I, Elizabeth?"

And because his voice contained such surprise, such a sudden unguarded spill of regret, she threw her arms about him, embracing his chilled body. When his own strong arms tightened and held her fast, she shuddered with the sorrow of it.

Undirected, the boat drifted and rocked in the breezy sunshine, but neither of its passengers cared, nor did they notice the passing sailboats or racing skiffs. They simply held on to each other. And although Spencer tried to kiss her again, deeply this time, Elizabeth turned her head and would not allow it, refusing to tempt the demon-angel that seemed to be hovering just above their heads offering dangerous tastes of forbidden pleasure.

But she permitted him to stroke her hair, to loosen it, to touch her face, even knowing that the tender liberty was arousing him terribly. He drew her close once more, running urgent hands over her back, pressing the sun-warmed length of it, touching the velvety places beneath her ears with his fingertips.

Both of them grew physically ready for the other, imagining impossible possibilities.

And yet, the time for fulfillment had come too late. Elizabeth denied Spencer what he would have taken, what she would willingly have given him only the day before yesterday,

Pushing away his hands and averting her lips, she cried out for him to stop.

He did and, taking up the oars with his jaw clenched and his eyes hard, rowed the little boat wordlessly back to shore.

Four

"We must host some tea parties so that your trousseau can be marveled over, Sara," Mrs. Maples decreed. "Invite your bridesmaids to come down from London, and I shall have my Folkestone friends in to meet you. We shall give out netted mittens as favors."

The elderly lady and Sara drifted about the garden cutting bouquets, pausing here and there like bonneted butterflies to enjoy the sweet scent of a lilac or carnation, Elizabeth trailing behind with a notebook and pen.

"And Sara," Mrs. Maples advised as she snipped a yellow iris and laid it in a basket. "The week before the wedding you must send the bridesmaids their gloves wrapped in silver paper. Elizabeth, make a note of that, please, so we don't forget—oh, and a note to find a band that can manage a decent rendition of Mendelssohn's *Wedding March*. Or possibly Handel's *Occasional Overture,* which was played at Princess Beatrice's wedding."

Elizabeth jotted down notes and glanced at Sara, who cared not at all that Mrs. Maples made plans on her behalf, just as long as those plans were as grandiose as Spencer's income would allow.

Indeed, she was behaving quite biddably, all things considered. Elizabeth had been surprised that Sara had not even quarreled with Spencer the previous day when, after his boating excursion with the housekeeper's daughter, he had arrived to retrieve her from the crowd on the promenade. In fact, Sara had acted happy to see him, clamping her possessive hand upon his sleeve, making no mention of his sun-dried clothes or asking how he had kept himself occupied in Elizabeth's company. Miss Worth did not even pout over his lapse in attention, and even though she seemed regretful to leave her newfound friends—especially the Frenchman—she was equally content to be on her lover's arm again. She teased Spencer and chatted happily, showing no chagrin when, tense with his own self-discovery, he seemed not to be listening at all.

As they had all walked home together, Elizabeth could scarcely look at Sara, summoning up again, mentally, the feel of Spencer's rough, damp cheek against hers, smelling again in her imagination the sea scent on his skin. When he had held her in the boat, her body had understood completely, for the first time, exactly what it meant to be unfulfilled, to quiver on the edge of both dishonor and ecstasy.

Now, in Mrs. Maples's back yard, Elizabeth followed Spencer's bride-to-be over the emerald grass and thought that Sara's sumptuous, orchid beauty was more vivid than anything the English garden had to offer. It wounded her to admit it, but she instinctively understood that Spencer would never let Sara go. She was the sort of woman to get under a man's skin, the ultimate compliment to his pride. As Elizabeth watched her silk gown slither over the grass, she also knew that if Sara Worth ever believed her place beside Spencer threatened, she would find a way to bring him snappily to heel again. Hadn't he even admitted that Sara's mother, mistress to countless wealthy men, had taught her daughter well?

In contrast, while they had sat alone in the boat, Elizabeth had not offered Spencer anything, She had used no wiles, had not tempted him beyond his own temptation; and when that had proven urgent, she had stopped him.

She had no right to hope for more than those few hard kisses, was mad to imagine more. Even if his gentleman's code would permit it, Spencer, like any other virile man, would never give up an intoxicating orchid for a common English daisy.

"Elizabeth," Mrs. Maples said, "pull that chair into the shade for me, please." Easing her satin-draped bulk into the seat, she leaned her head back and loosened the lavender net that kept her hat moored. "Oh, my! I'm out of breath in this warmth. Elizabeth, have you explained to Sara about the threading of the rings?"

"Yes, do tell me," Sara insisted. She put a white carnation to her nose and, from the shade of her hat, slanted a glance at the housekeeper's daughter. Her eyes seemed to say "I know that you're envious of me and I'm sorry for you. But I like your envy. It reassures me."

Elizabeth explained tightly. "The day before the wedding, the bridesmaids cut strips of cake in the shape of ladyfingers and pass them through the wedding ring. The strips are then wrapped in paper and given out to the unmarried wedding guests. Dreaming emoluments, they're called."

"Dreaming emoluments?" Sara prompted, eyeing Elizabeth calculatingly and moving just out of Mrs. Maples's hearing. "Whatever for?"

"A woman puts them under her pillow and dreams of a lover. Or so it is said."

"Really? Well then, perhaps you'd do better not to put a piece of cake under your pillow, Elizabeth. Love can be quite heartless, can it not? But I'll tell you a secret. Men enjoy it—the heartlessness, I mean—even if women do not."

There was no spite, no cruelty in her remark, merely a philosophy of life.

Elizabeth did not respond, noticing that Sara's ever-skittish gaze had already wandered toward the house

where a member of the painting crew, a dark young man
with a Greek profile and plenty of black hair, had paused
upon the second step of his ladder to admire her. Without a backward glance for Elizabeth, Sara strolled away,
her skirts swaying like the ruffled petals of a flower, her
head tilted to show to its best advantage the willowy
line of her neck beneath the parasol's shade.

She meandered toward the back door, attempted to
fold her parasol, and when the catch proved stubborn
and would not slide, glanced about helplessly. The young
painter noticed her plight, of course, as he was intended
to do, and came swiftly to the rescue.

Disgusted, Elizabeth turned away, spotting Spencer as
he crossed the lawn.

She knew he had been in the coach house inspecting
the dogcart Mrs. Maples sometimes used; and now, wiping his hands on a cloth, he came to stand quietly beside
Elizabeth. "Do you think I should feel wounded?" he
asked quietly.

Unwillingly, she glanced over her shoulder again to
watch Sara's flirtation. Then after a brief hesitation, she
met the gray-green eyes she loved and, because she was
accustomed to telling Spencer the truth, answered
bluntly. "Yes."

"You believe I should admonish her, rein her in with
a heavy hand, punch the fellow in the nose?"

"Yes."

Spencer's eyes locked with hers. "And do you believe
that I'm any less unfaithful in my own thoughts than
Sara?"

Quickly lowering her lashes, Elizabeth stared down at
the undulating summer grass, remembering his rough,
insistent hands as he had touched her in the boat. "I'm
afraid to answer," she breathed.

"Why?"

"Because I should hate to be . . . mistaken."

He nodded, looking toward the sea at the distant blue smudge—so faint it might have been imagined—that formed the shores of France. "There are worse things than being mistaken."

"Are there?"

"Yes."

"Then tell me, Spencer. What is worse than this?"

He turned away slightly, so she could see only his well-sculpted profile, firm mouth, and taut shaven cheeks. He seemed to want to speak of their moments together in the boat, to declare himself somehow, to talk of Sara. But knowing declarations to be pointless, perhaps, knowing that cynicism and even self-mockery would serve better under the circumstances, he laughed and said shortly, "You could be a house painter who has just gotten paint on the parasol handle of the lady you had hoped to seduce."

Elizabeth glanced toward the house at Sara and her red-faced admirer. But she did not smile. Instead, she looked into Spencer's eyes, thinking to find them wounded, jealous, enraged. They were none of those things. Only indifferent.

"One would think you find it all amusing," she remarked in a wondering voice, disturbed that he could exhibit such dispassion toward the woman he was soon to wed.

His eyes changed to a darker shade of agate. "I do."

As she bustled about the kitchen preparing a lemon cake and two kinds of sweet breads for the evening meal, Elizabeth glanced at the watch pinned to her blouse, needing to get to the confectioner's before closing time to pick up the chocolate bonbons Mrs. Maples had specially ordered for Sara's tea party tomorrow. She paused a moment and put a hand to her perspiring brow, her usually steady nerves frazzled. Finding time to do every chore asked of her this warm July was becoming increasingly difficult.

Spencer had departed three weeks earlier for his London business, leaving his bride-to-be to enjoy her lavish parties and brunches, which were overtaxing Elizabeth, who was already overburdened with the wedding preparations.

"Elizabeth, did you see the bride cup Mrs. Maples brought down to be polished?" Bertha asked, showing her the curious silver piece fashioned in the shape of a lady. "See how it works? It's hinged so that the bride and groom can drink from it simultaneously."

Elizabeth refused to touch the novelty. She wanted nothing so much as to get through the summer, endure the wedding, so that her heartache would end and her life could find another path upon which to start.

Bertha sighed and took up an iron to press one of Sara's lace blouses. "Queen Victoria and her Albert were such a loving model for us all. Your father was my Albert, of course. Being a schoolmaster, he always had a primer in his hand and chalk dust on his fingers. What could be more endearing? He wasn't handsome, mind you, but he had your deep-brown eyes. Such a shame you never knew him beyond the first six months of your life. Do you remember him, dear, even the tiniest bit?"

"No, Mother. I'm afraid I don't. I wish I did."

Bertha sighed again. "Do you think Spencer and Sara will have many children? Have you heard her speak of it? Oh, I know it's an indelicate subject, but women usually drop a hint or two regarding the number of babies they'd like."

"I haven't heard her say," Elizabeth muttered, stirring the cake batter.

"Well, I don't imagine she'll have boys," Bertha went on, as if one had the power to choose such things. "Little girls in frills seem more appropriate to Sara's taste. Can't you see them on an Easter morning gathered about her, all in matching sprigged muslins and beribboned bonnets? Do you think Sara and Spencer will be happy together, Elizabeth?"

"No."

"Elizabeth!"

"Well, I don't, Mother. And you needn't repeat it to Mrs. Maples."

"But they're so perfectly suited, one has only to *look* at them to—" She threw up her hands. "Oh, my! I've gone and scorched Miss Sara's blouse."

Abandoning the cake, Elizabeth rushed to investigate and, finding a faint but discernible brown vee on the collar, snatched up the garment, grabbed a lemon and scurried out the screen door.

"I'll wet it with lemon juice," she told her mother through the open window, "and leave it in the sun to fade. If you could just finish the cake, please. And check on the bread in the oven. Lord, it's four o'clock. I have to get to the confectioner's before they close." Untying her apron, she thrust it through the window at her mother, who handed out her pocketbook.

"But, dear," Bertha said anxiously, *"why* do you say Spencer and Sara won't be happy together? I find myself confused . . ."

"Remember to check the bread in the oven, Mother. Please."

By the time she arrived in the village Elizabeth was breathless and, passing the Pleasure Gardens, took a moment to observe the croquet tournament taking place there and the genteel crowd who had paid sixpence to watch it. She remembered playing croquet with Spencer on that smooth green lawn, never besting him, cheering when, summer after summer, he won the championship trophy. The memories were sharp, poignant ones, and

suddenly she missed seeing his tall, wide-shouldered figure moving among the players on the green. She missed
him in every way, and an emptiness began to harrow
her so that she turned away and walked hurriedly down
the boulevard with her eyelids prickling.

Sara had not been languishing over her fiancé's de-
parture. Each morning she asked Elizabeth to hitch up
the old white pony to the dogcart and, after climbing
aboard, slapped the lines and trundled down to the Leas.
More often than not, she would stay all afternoon, and
when Mrs. Maples—vaguely scandalized by her un-
chaperoned wanderings—asked what she had done all
day, Sara would say she had visited the lending library
and sat on the esplanade reading.

And yet, despite the fact that she never failed to come
home with an armload of books, Elizabeth guessed there
had been no reading done at all. How cheerful she was
when she returned each afternoon, windblown, her
cheeks pink with sun, the hem of her pastel skirts soiled,
her eyes sparkling. And every evening after dinner, with
her delicately-boned feet propped upon a footstool, her
peignoir floating about her like a multi-hued cloud, she
would faithfully pen a letter on scented paper to Spencer.

Thinking of her, Elizabeth clenched her fists, wending
through the curiosity shops thronged with families on
holiday, hearing the military band in the pavilion playing
"God Save the King" as she slipped into the caramel-
scented confectionery and paid for Mrs. Maples's bonbons.

When she exited a moment later to the sound of the
tinkling shop bell, she had to stop and wait for the carriage traffic to clear, and her eyes curiously strayed toward the corner where a young man and woman stood
together eating ice cream.

The lady was laughing and, having got a drop of the
treat on the tip of her up-tilted nose, leaned forward to

allow the gentleman—if he could be so termed—to dab it with his handkerchief.

Elizabeth's mouth opened.

It seemed as if the fickle Miss Worth, quite unabashedly, was enjoying the more than casual company of the house painter.

Five

He returned to Folkestone a fortnight later, unannounced, strolling into the house without rapping first, playfully tossing his hat at Elizabeth when she gasped at the unexpected sight of him.

He looked exceedingly well, still dressed as he must have been when he had left his mill office, his dark grey suit and starched white shirt soberly handsome, a ready smile coming to his lips the minute his eyes searched the room and found her.

And Elizabeth knew, without a doubt, that Spencer Kenton had missed her, that he had been eager to return and confirm his memories of that day on the boat, to determine if they were as real as he had imagined them to be while walking the damp streets of London alone.

She wanted to fling down her feather duster and run to him, wanted to hold out her arms and be drawn into the circle of his. Instead, she was forced to watch Sara fly down the stairs in a sprigged muslin gown and rush into his embrace with a husky greeting on her lips.

His maleness, his sexuality instinctively responded, appreciating her beauty, the intoxicating allure of her physical demonstrativeness. But as she tightened her arms about his neck and his chin came to rest atop her spun-gold hair, it was Elizabeth's face Spencer's eyes sought again.

"Spencer," Sara said, drawing back a little, placing

her soft, treacherous hands on either side of his tense jaws. "Thank heaven you're back! It's been so tedious here without you. I've been unendurably lonely—*bereft*, in fact, hardly going anywhere but to the lending library, and doing so much reading I fear my eyes have grown weak. But how well you look—the elegant London gentleman, Grey suits you. Kiss me, Spencer."

And he did, thoroughly, roughly, in front of Elizabeth—not intending to wound her, she knew, but telling her that he had made his commitment, his choice, and regardless of whether or not it had been a poor one, he was honorable enough to see it through, to become one in a long line of men who had chosen beauty for beauty's sake and suffered disillusionment when it was too late.

Carefully, Elizabeth set down the china souvenir of Queen Victoria's spaniel she had been cleaning and, with her feather duster clutched like a dagger in one cold hand, quietly left the room to the sound of Sara's sighs.

She walked through the kitchen like a sleepwalker, not responding to her mother's plaintive calls for help with the overdone roast, letting the screen door bang behind her, having no idea where she went, knowing only that she must have a moment alone to compose herself, to wallow—thoroughly and agonizingly—in the throes of self-pity.

She slipped behind the coach house, her skirts catching on the high, unmown thistles, then leaned against the old planked wall with her eyes closed and her chest heaving, her fingers still gripping the duster. If there had been any place on earth to which she could have escaped, she would have gone that instant, run down the road without baggage or goodbyes and boarded a train. No one in her position, with her feelings, could be expected to carry on under the circumstances, to plan the wedding of the man she loved and watch him hold his bride.

She had no notion of time, only vaguely felt the weak sun on her face, heard the wind rattle the leaves, then the sound of footsteps. Even with closed eyes, she knew Spencer was there regarding her, waiting until she could swallow her tears, blink them off her lashes, and look at him.

The moments passed, and he pressed something to her hand. She saw that it was a braided circlet of daisies, the common English variety that sprouted everywhere in springtime.

He had remembered.

Long ago, when she had invented her game of describing people as flowers, young Spencer had grinned, tilted his head to the side and, after contemplating carefully, declared her a daisy. Elizabeth had been offended at first, having wanted to be a rose or a gardenia; but he had explained his choice, reminding her that only daisies grew on the cliffs, resisting the winds, the rains, the sometimes-turbulent storms that blew off the Channel in summer.

He had laughed at her scowl and, while she decided whether or not to be flattered, jogged about picking handfuls of the white flowers, which he had deftly braided into a crown and settled atop her head.

Now she held another such crown, one freshly woven by square, manly hands, one that told her she was special to him still. And on dreary evenings in London, when he sat at a long polished table across from a sparkling wife, tickets to the opera in his tuxedo pocket, two daughters—replicas of the mother—asleep upstairs, she knew that he would remember still.

She leaned her brow against the weathered coach house, swallowed, then turned to look into his eyes.

He remained silent a moment, propped a foot upon the old stone mounting block half-hidden in the purple thistle, and gazed out toward the hills with his eyes narrowed. "I've never done a single thing I wanted to do in my life," he said quietly, as if uttering the words aloud were suddenly of vital importance to him. "Except for the summers I've been here, which are only escapes, too quickly over and borrowed from my father."

Elizabeth stared at him, struck by the depth of his words, by the sharp edge of bitterness in them, which she had not heard since the troubled days of his adolescence.

"Have I ever told you about my father?" he asked. "I daresay I have, but I'll tell you again. He's Tom Kenton, eighth son of a drunken weaver. He gambled money to buy his first weaving shed, married a girl with a dowry of a hundred pounds to buy his first loom, and since then has employed every means, ruthless or not—but strictly legal if anyone were to investigate—to build his empire. He moves on the fringes of high society and has ambitions toward Parliament. He's managed to get almost everything he ever wanted, except, of course, a suitable son. His dream is not his son's dream, and that's unacceptable. I've always been a thorn in his side, a rebellious ingrate, taking his thrashings without so much as a whimper and sneering at his insults."

His voice lowered. "But, by God, I've been at the mill every day since I was out of school, learning every tedious operation, the names of the employees and how many children they have, how to repair every cog and wheel of the machinery. I've increased profits twofold—done it more to show him I'm capable, when I want to be, than because I give a damn for any of it. I loathe it, as a matter of fact, just as I always have. How ungrateful of me. How spoiled. The mill paid for my fashionable clothes, after all, for my thoroughbreds, for my gentleman's club dues. And," he looked at her intently, "it paid for this house in Folkestone. Ah, yes, Granny would have been out long ago—and you—without my father's money. He reminded me of it religiously whenever I grew stubborn. And so I endured it. Now I'm a man about to inherit half of Father's little empire next year, the rest upon his death. As long as I'm dutifully at the mill at six every morning, I'll get the fruits of his labor, and mine. And I enjoy making money—spending it—don't mistake me. It gets to be a habit after a while, the more merciless and calculating, the better for my sense of adventure."

He leaned to pick up a rusty nail from the ground, contemplated it, then cast it down like a spear. "But I never wanted to be a millmaster."

"You wanted to build bridges."

"Yes. And the odd thing is, I love my father in spite of the prison he has made for me. I respect him. I've never wanted to let him down."

"And you haven't."

He continued to look out over the hills, all the way to the cliffs, his eyes narrowed as if gauging the distance, as if it were important for him to know the number of miles there. "And now that I've told you about my father and the mill," he said slowly, shifting hard eyes to her, "shall I tell you about Sara?"

"No, Spencer," Elizabeth said, suddenly frightened. "I'd rather you didn't."

What purpose could it possibly serve, after all? she asked herself. It could neither alleviate the pain, nor cushion the disappointment, nor change the circumstances. Indeed, if he were to admit his infatuation with Sara, or even confess his regret or his hasty judgment over asking her to be his bride, Elizabeth feared she would cry again.

"It's best to say nothing," she breathed. "To leave it all unsaid. I understand. At least, I believe I do—"

"But you don't," he argued curtly. "And you'll hear me out. My father, as Sara mentioned once, intended me to marry a Miss Giles. Her money could have done much for the mills, and she would even have made a pleasant-enough wife, had I been inclined to take her. Father made no secret of his designs; and even though I told him in no uncertain language that I would chose my own wife, he set about making arrangements for me. At his invitation Miss Giles came to dinner one evening, bringing her friend Miss Worth along."

"And Sara was enchanted with you."

Spencer gave her a tolerant look. "You needn't flatter me, or Sara. As you've doubtless perceived, she has no intention of following in her mother's footsteps. She prefers the security of a good marriage to the insecurity of a series of good lovers. Unfortunately, I didn't realize that at the time."

Elizabeth looked at him, bemused. "I find myself more and more baffled by it all, Spencer."

He ran his fingers through his hair. "I made my interest in Sara known that evening in order to spite my father and to make certain that Miss Giles would decline further invitations. Determined to be as boorish as possible for good measure, I drank too much after dinner and closeted myself in the library. Truthfully, when Sara followed me I wasn't even averse to her company. I didn't even behave nobly when she began to seduce me. By the time I took matters in hand and began to seduce her—too drunk to think of the consequences—she had undressed herself. I don't mean to shock you, Elizabeth," he said, giving her the ghost of a smile, "but most young gentlemen make a habit of dalliances."

Elizabeth bowed her head, wishing he would say no more.

"At any rate," he went on unsparingly, "just as I was finishing what Sara had begun, the door swung open and the entire dinner party walked in, still carrying their after-dinner drinks, Miss Giles in the lead."

"Oh, Spencer—"

His mouth curved wryly. "Sara had set it up, of course. She had been an invited guest, the grand-daughter of a baronet. There was no decent way out of it for me, not without ruining all my father's ambitions, all he'd worked to build. I was irresponsible. It was right that I should suffer for it."

Honorable herself, Elizabeth understood his predicament painfully well.

Spencer shrugged. "At first, I thought to make the best of it. She was beautiful, and by all indications willing enough to accommodate a husband very creatively in bed, but—"

"Spencer, please!" Elizabeth cried, stricken. "I would never have asked you about such things, I don't want to know—"

"But I want you to know," he countered through his teeth, taking her by the arm. "I *want* you to know."

"Why?"

"So you can suffer with me, by God."

She jerked away from his hands. "And I have! I *am.*"

They stood facing each other, their swift fury soaring, then deflating. Blossoms from the fruit trees floated between them on the golden air, and the wind from the cliffs ruffled the daisy braid Elizabeth still clutched tightly.

"She knows I don't love her," he said, giving Elizabeth an intent, significant look. "And seeks to punish me for it in every way her ingenious mind can calculate."

Unable to bear knowing more, Elizabeth thrust the daisy braid at his hands and hissed, "We won't speak of it again. And we'll stay away from each other."

Spencer left again the following Sunday, giving no specific date of return, kissing Sara at the front door, tipping his hat at her in a way most would have described as gallant, but which Elizabeth, glimpsing it from an upper window, found bitterly mocking.

She had avoided him all week, resisting his attempts to speak with her, yanking her arm away from him when he waylaid her in the kitchen, making it known that there would be no more boat rides, no more confessions behind the coach house, no more temptations to steal a few gasping moments away from Sara Worth's summer.

He left without saying farewell.

July passed, crept into August, the warmest month, which brought with it the hoards of weekend bathers, the picnickers and sailor-hatted children who roamed the beaches and the Roman ruins and occasionally came puffing up the cliff road lost and asking for directions.

Sara's bridesmaids were due to arrive the following day, half of them staying at an inn in Folkestone, the other half crowding into the three guest bedrooms at Maples House.

With the wedding date only four days away, Elizabeth felt weighed down with responsibility. Bertha was little help at all, and every morning Mrs. Maples thought of one more task, one more tiny detail that would determine whether or not the wedding was spectacular or only grand. Sara, in the meantime, did nothing but enjoy herself.

She took the dogcart one morning when it could have been used for the shopping. Disgruntled over Sara's thoughtlessness, Elizabeth trudged homeward, a basket on each arm full of satin ribbon and tasselled braid which the bridesmaids would use as decorative garlands.

As she puffed up the hill, Elizabeth suddenly heard the white pony whinny and, glancing over a shoulder, saw him some distance away on the side of the hill where the laurel grew thickest.

Frowning, she set down her baskets, wondering if the pony had gotten loose from the cart in Folkestone and wandered homeward. She pushed through the underbrush toward him, seeing that he was still in the traces, the lines slack enough so he could snatch mouthfuls of the sweet grass.

Muttering beneath her breath, assuming that Sara had not tied him well in the village and he had roamed away, Elizabeth stooped to catch the reins. And then she saw, fluttering like wings in the tall grass, an ivory lace shawl. Beside it lay a feathered bonnet, one long silk stocking, and a man's white cotton shirt.

She paused and looked around.

Nearby, oblivious to the rest of the world, intent only upon the assuagement of what appeared to be a life-or-death need, their whimpers and grunts shockingly loud, Spencer's fiancée and the house painter passionately writhed. Entrenched between her legs, his trousers pushed down to his knees and one hand in her unclasped hair, the young man pleasured himself.

He was so near ecstasy that he failed to hear Elizabeth's stunned gasp or to notice that his not-quite-equally-ecstatic lover raised her head up to determine the identity of the intruder and, after finding it to be only the housekeeper's daughter, relaxed again while he continued his rhythmic strainings.

Not quite knowing how she got there, Elizabeth found herself on the road, so blinded by outrage she could think of nothing but retribution. Sara's flirtations, which she had thought to be naughty but innocent, had proved to be much, much more. Ultimately, they were a betrayal of Spencer Kenton's trust, of his own sacrifice to make a similar sordid situation honorable.

If she had been a man, just a little stronger physically, Elizabeth would have yanked the rutting Greek god off the ground and bashed in his face, then slapped Sara until her head lolled. That's what Spencer would have done, surely, had he discovered them. Or would he?

Elizabeth considered, remembering him as he had watched Sara and the painter flirt together in the garden. He would not have been surprised by the scene in the grass, might even have expected to see it. Might, just possibly, not care? But he must be *told,* mustn't he? If a man were to be cuckolded, especially a man as proud as Spencer, he must at the very least *know.* Being unaware was too ignoble.

Elizabeth was halfway home when she realized she had left the baskets behind and, cursing, backtracked down the hill to retrieve them. She saw Sara in the dogcart whipping up the pony, attempting to prod it into a faster trot. The house painter, likely exhausted and still sprawled in the grass with glazed eyes, was not in evidence.

"Elizabeth!" Sara called with a wave of the whip, repeating the cry more loudly. "Elizabeth! Wait!"

But the housekeeper's daughter marched on with her face set and her spine poker-stiff, her bearing a message to the faithless girl that her flagrant promiscuity was beneath contempt and therefore beneath the slightest discussion.

But Sara was not to be put off, scrambling out of the cart and pursuing Elizabeth on foot when she cut across the dandelion-sprinkled yard. Almost simultaneously, the two young women reached the kitchen door, both nearly tripping over the sprawled collie who lay dozing in the patch of sun across the threshold.

"Elizabeth," Sara cried, catching hold of her sleeve and clutching it with all the tenacity of a bulldog. "I know there's no use explaining, but if you could perhaps be made to understand—"

She broke off abruptly, her startled blue gaze causing Elizabeth to look up, to stare in the direction of the kitchen table where, with a bowl of whipped cream and a glass of milk set before him, Spencer sat enjoying the last of the rhubarb pie.

"Sara. Elizabeth," he said calmly, flashing a smile. "Bertha told me you were both out. I didn't realize you were out together— or did you only happen to time your arrivals to coincide?"

Nothing in his voice indicated that he saw anything amiss in their rigid, speechless poses.

But Elizabeth remained frozen, mesmerized as always by the undeceivable sharpness of his eyes, by his firm square-jawed face, by the contrasting loose-limbed elegance of his body as he rose in gentlemanly deference to the entrance of the two ladies. She feared he would be able to read the expression on her face, to know what she had seen—*whom* she had seen lying in the grass not more than a half hour ago. Suddenly, without understanding why, she realized that she could never speak to him of the treachery she had witnessed—even if he were to directly ask.

Sara, always able to think quickly on her feet, recovered first, although Elizabeth did not miss the second or two of instinctive alarm that darkened her eyes, brought on by the sheer physical presence of her fiancé. "Spencer, dearest, what a wonderful surprise!" she exclaimed. "But you really should make it a habit to wire us and let us know when you're coming so we can be here to greet you properly. So we can be prepared."

"But, Sara," he returned softly, dabbing his mouth with a napkin, his smile in place, "I find it so much more delightful to drop in and see you as you are. Now, for example, you are in such—" he raised a brow, "intriguing disarray."

She glanced down, having been unaware of the extent of her dishabille, of the bedraggled state of the hat she held in her hand, of the lacy shawl crammed inside it, of the grass stains on the back of her white lawn gown.

"Oh," she said glibly, her mind never slow, her inventiveness quick. "The most frightful thing happened. The dogcart turned over as I was coming home. Threw me right out—but I'm not hurt, darling, as you can see. So don't be alarmed. And how fortunate Elizabeth happened along. Wasn't it, Elizabeth?" she asked, turning vivid eyes in her direction, asking, *demanding,* collaboration.

Much more aware of the gray-green gaze than of the deceitful blue one, Elizabeth hesitated, her mind churning while the tension in the room stretched. Finally, with a voice that did not quaver at all and with eyes that were able to look steadily into the keen pair across the room, she said, "Yes. Very fortunate it was, my walking that way."

"She helped me push the cart aright," Sara went on. "She and a gentleman who happened also to be passing. What was his name, Elizabeth? Did you inquire?"

"No, Sara, I didn't." Her reply, again, was collected and cool.

"Too bad. I should like to have thanked him. Well, I really am disgracefully mussed. I'll just go up and change. Wait for me, Spencer, so I can greet you properly." Sara waved a graceful hand, smiled in such a way that promised much, that could, just with a parting of pale moist lips, stir the senses of a virile man. Up the steps she went, an exquisite, very poisonous orchid.

Elizabeth was left behind to deal with the remains of the ordeal, to sweep it up neatly with Spencer Kenton's eyes upon her.

She met them levelly.

For a moment he said nothing, only contemplated her, his gaze sweeping her face, her erect figure, the burrs clinging to the edge of her neat black hem. Then, quite charmingly, but with a sharpness that suggested anger, he said, "Well done, Elizabeth. Very well done. I commend you. You're almost as smooth as Sara."

Six

Two days before the wedding Elizabeth felt as frazzled as her mother—or more frazzled, for she knew that whatever went awry on that glorious day of Spencer's marriage, whatever was not just as succulent, just as polished and as perfect as Mrs. Maples had planned, would be her fault.

There were plenty of troubles. The grocer in Folkestone had no Spanish olives, which Mrs. Maples insisted should go with the chicken. The band leader took cold and sent a message that his son—who was only seventeen—would have to lead. The hothouse fruit for the compote had not arrived; and, most disastrous of all, one of the bridesmaids contracted hives and did not know how they were to be concealed in her off-the-shoulder gown. Elizabeth could scarcely keep all the giggling girls fed, equipped with clean towels, provided with extra hair pins or curl papers, and at the same time devote herself to the hundred other details requiring her attention.

Mrs. Maples scuttled in and out of the kitchen pretending to supervise before the threat of 'problems' forced her back to her gramophone, which blared so loudly Elizabeth's head ached. Spencer, with a sardonic tip of his hat and a remote smile, had abandoned ship, booking a hotel room in the village. Elizabeth was grateful that he spared her his presence, grateful that her frenzied busyness kept her from thinking of him with too much concentrated yearning.

However, the day before the wedding eve, he rode up the drive on a tall chestnut thoroughbred. Folding squares of pastry, Elizabeth watched him through the open kitchen window, admiring him as completely as any woman could, mentally freezing his image in polished riding boots, tan breeches, and top hat so she could remember it later—next week, next year when she was very lonely and recalling with a dim but vivid pain the days of their youth.

Intent upon her own mission, Sara rushed out the back door, grabbing a pair of shears to further deplete the garden blooms, letting Collie slip out, who, with the zest of a younger dog, barked at the postman, then sneaked under the privet into Mr. Whistlebury's vegetable garden.

Waylaying the postman, Sara found a letter for herself and, tearing it open as Spencer tethered the thoroughbred, let out a long, horrified shriek. "She *hasn't!*"

"What is it?"

"Oh, Spencer! Mother has gone off to Italy with some *man*. She's not coming to the wedding." Her voice crescendoed. "She's not coming here to bring me her wedding gown—*my wedding gown!*"

Could any greater disaster occur at the eleventh hour? The world's most beautiful bride-to-be had just found herself without a suitable gown. It was too late, of course, to have one fitted and sewn, too late to travel to London and attempt to find some fashionable couturier—any couturier—who would have one ravishing enough and ready-made for Sara Worth.

"How unfortunate," Spencer said. "Perhaps one of the shops in Folkestone . . ."

"Oh, how ridiculous! They're such poky little places." Sara despaired. The picture of herself as a bride, young yet timelessly old draped in Brussels lace, was now irretrievably spoiled. Even her husband-to-be, who was surely not as sympathetic as he ought to be, turned his attention from her tragedy to the sudden commotion in Mr. Whistlebury's yard.

Collie, yelping sharply, was crawling on his belly beneath the privet, dragging one hind leg, which was gripped in the steel jaws of a trap.

"Good God." Spencer sprinted across the lawn and, after kneeling beside the dog, scooped him up and jogged toward the house. Shouldering his way through the back door he called for water and antiseptic while easing Collie in his basket. With a strong, steady hand he then pried loose the trap and extricated the dog's mangled leg.

"Mr. Whistlebury," Elizabeth muttered, busily uncorking salve, wetting a cup towel with hot water poured from the kettle. "He threatened to do something."

"I'll deal with him later." Spencer cleansed the wound and examined the bone, which fortunately appeared to be unfractured. After applying the salve, he bound up the jagged flesh with strips of a clean cup towel and soothed Collie when he whined. "It's a rabbit trap. I'll need to ask the veterinarian to drop in and be certain of the bone."

Sara had wandered in with her letter in hand, too devastated to be particularly interested in the dog, but knowing she would have to hover near to reclaim Spencer's attention. When she peered into the basket, her toe bumped against an old tapestry bag pushed behind it.

Annoyed, she bent to move the bag out of the way, but her magpie eyes, always alert and acquisitive, caught sight of a white strand of embroidery floss.

Before Elizabeth could stop her, Sara had unclasped the bag and, with an exclamation, drawn out the yards and yards of muslin. Stepping back, she let its trailing length unfold and tumble down, so that the sunlight picked out every flawless stitch of embroidery.

"It's magnificent!" she breathed wonderingly, holding it against her full but willow-limbed body. "So simple but divine. I've never seen embroidery so finely done. Look, it's covered in a pattern of daisies. There must be hundreds and hundreds of them stitched on the skirt, a few not quite finished. The floss and needle are still attached."

Spencer, who had scarcely spared a glance at first, stilled, his hands upon the collie, his eyes riveted to the design of flowers worked so painstakingly, so meaningfully, into the fabric of the dress.

"It's a wedding gown, surely," Sara marveled, touching the simple train and the puffed sleeves, her face radiant with the realization that, in the most miraculous fashion, her awful problem had been solved. "But who does it belong to? Of course, it doesn't really matter, because I must have it. I *will* have it."

Elizabeth said nothing. She could not. She felt as if every drop of blood in her body had rushed up into her face, pumped there by a heart that lay exposed. She was choking with the final humiliation, watching the last shred of what belonged to her being taken now, *claimed,* by the woman who had also claimed the bridegroom.

She rose slowly to her feet, a pair of grey-green eyes following her, mercilessly probing the naked heart and seeing everything inside it, down to its last mortifying, pathetically kept secret.

Despite the fact that her composure was shattered, Elizabeth's legs carried her calmly out the door and across the yard. She walked on, outwardly dignified should anyone see, her head held high. It was only when she reached the road that she began to run, untying her apron and flinging it down, stumbling over the upward path, then veering toward the cliffs.

When she reached the flat, treeless pinnacle, she stood leaning into the wind, her fists closed into balls while she gazed with swimming eyes at the azure and jade and violet panorama below. She could almost believe that the sea surrounded her—wished it did, wished she were alone on an island whose shores could not be breached. She wanted only to stand here alone and let the rest of the world go on without her, to leave her in peace, to make no more demands.

But Maples House lay behind her, its steep gabled roof giving it the look of a sailing ship marooned on a hill. Over the years it had been a safe, predictable, often delightful vessel, one that strangers would occupy at summer's end, one that would not be captained by the golden Spencer Kenton anymore.

From her distant vantage point, she saw him stalk out of the house and vault atop the chestnut thoroughbred, spur it across the lawn and over the privet, its iron-shod hooves churning through Mr. Whistlebury's vegetable garden, snagging his nets and dragging them down as he cantered toward the road.

He would find her. He knew every inch of Folkestone, the hills, the ruins, the cliffs where she now stood buffeted by the wind and her own rough, wild emotion. He would come and she would say goodbye to him, a friend not to be forgotten, a most special man, her past.

When he arrived Elizabeth was waiting, coolheaded, or so it seemed, but with all her nerves tingling, their ends raw and ragged. He walked toward her steadily, the wind catching in his hair and tugging at the wedding dress with its garden of daisies that he had so carefully folded over one arm.

He shouldn't have brought it. How cruel of him to make her look at it, explain it, accept it again. She had no need of the gown now and would give it to Sara. It would be the ultimate irony, she thought, to see Spencer

Kenton's bride standing at the altar draped in Elizabeth Honeybridge's gown. There was something maliciously fitting about such a picture in this topsy-turvy world of unpredictable catastrophes.

Spencer stood before her, unspeaking, searching her eyes intently. He did not hand the gown to her, but held it up and pressed the collar against her throat.

Then, slowly, he draped the sleeves over her shoulders, scrutinizing the length of it from neckline to hem as its folds fell against her body.

She let him observe, let him see how it might have looked, how *she* might have looked as a bride awaiting a groom. Awaiting him.

He moved so near that his feet brushed the daisy hem, then closer so that his body, pressed to hers, held the gown in place between them. His eyes continued to explore her face, to memorize it, to see it clearly for the first time.

And then he reached up and with a gentle hand touched her waist, the full undercurve of her breast, her breast itself, molding the gown to its tautness, possessing her through the fabric.

His mouth descended to her lips, possessing her mouth, too, covering it as if to consume the entirety of Elizabeth Honeybridge. She opened to him, clung, drew his hips to hers, scarcely able to breathe between the tightness of his grip and the force of her own desire to know him.

Without easing his hold an inch, Spencer trailed his mouth over her cheeks, her throat, still shaping the gown against her body. He stroked her with experienced hands that were slightly unsteady with their need to touch the woman who, until now, he had known intimately only in a companionable way.

When she responded, her palms and fingers roaming over the expanse of his shoulders, he grew uncontrolled and Elizabeth knew he was not to be stopped. Joyfully, she cried out for him.

"Just once," he said against her ear, groaning as he thrust a hand through the buttons of her blouse and found her naked flesh. "Just once."

She sank to the ground with him, smelling the scents of sea and salt and his own clean skin, the gown tangled like a long white rope between her legs, his body astride it.

He parted her blouse while she pushed the shirt off his shoulders and drew it down. She clutched the hardness of his back, then ran her fingers over his ribs, following their ridges to his chest. She felt cool air skim over her thighs and waist as her garments were pulled away, then felt the unfamiliar heat of a man's breath.

Every movement, every gasp was frenzied between them, a catching up, a stolen pleasure. Her body belonged to his and she let him know it, encouraging him to tear at her stockings, guiding his hand hectically when her fear of discovery, of unfulfillment, grew too strong.

Spencer poised his own body. Painfully roused, he robbed her of her innocence then, calling her name into the wind. It was an unrestrained, exalted shout.

Clawing his shoulders, Elizabeth drew the dark golden head against her breast.

The sounds of their straining died away and they lay together in the damp matted grass, saying nothing, knowing the last few moments and the savage, tender ones that had come just before would be significant in their lives, coloring everything that would follow.

Spencer tenderly cradled her head in the crook of his arm while she stroked the rise of his hip with infinite care, learning its flesh-and-bone texture until her body stirred again. He kissed the point of her shoulder, then stilled, denying his own need.

They knew, without voicing it, that now that the forbidden had been fully tasted, guilt would prevent a second sampling.

Twisting a strand of her soft brown hair around his hand, Spencer spoke against her brow, his voice hard, troubled, full of a remorse so sharp-pronged it grated upon the edge of Elizabeth's already fleeing bliss.

"And now," he said hoarsely, looking directly into her eyes, "you see that I am no better than Sara."

Elizabeth touched his face, then slowly uncurled herself from his protecting body. She left the warm nest of his love, the illicit heat of his limbs, and feeling very old, very worn, went about collecting her clothes, which had scattered over the cliffs like flitting birds.

When she had dressed, she reluctantly retrieved the daisy gown. She did not bother to fold it, but simply wadded it in her arms, crumpling it just as her spirit had been crumpled.

Spencer had scarcely moved.

For a long while Elizabeth regarded the man who had filled her with himself as he sat naked and pagan in the wind-raked grass. When he bowed his head, the curve of his back was as sculptured as the cliff stone.

She turned away, leaving him to his thoughts, leaving him to the torment he had made for himself.

Seven

"Good heavens!" Mrs. Maples exclaimed, staring in horrified wonder at the three-tiered wedding cake Bertha had just decorated. "Look there! There are little devils dancing all around the bride and groom!"

"Those are *angels!*" Bertha shrilled, highly offended, nearly in tears.

"But they have *horns.*"

"Those are *curls,* the curls you insisted they have!"

Elizabeth intervened. Despite the fact that she was doing ten tasks at once on that impossible morning, three hours from the wedding ceremony, she managed to keep herself steel-nerved. Taking up a butter knife, she meticulously, and with a remarkably steady hand, carved the curly horns made of icing off the sugar angels.

"Now, Mrs. Maples," she said, "if you could just carry those vases of roses out to the marquee and set them on the buffet table. . . . And then ask two of the bridesmaids who are not still abed or primping to roll out the white carpet through the vestibule and into the parlor. Your gown has been pressed and is hanging in your wardrobe. Your corsage is on your dressing table, and the prayer book you want Sara to carry with her bouquet is in the top drawer of the huntboard."

Having dismissed one problem and aiming for the next, Elizabeth went on, her hands busy with a boutonniere while she delegated. "Mother, you have yet to find

the cognac and curacao for the champagne punch. And
if you could stir the oyster sauce before it scalds, I'll
finish chopping the pickles for the chicken loaf. Have
you set out the butter mints yet?"

Bertha was twirling about, befuddled and drooping in
the August heat, so overwhelmed by the amount of work
and the number of people in the usually tranquil household that she was almost beyond doing anything successfully.

Almost single-handedly, Elizabeth had done it all, em-
ploying help from the village, directing, seeing to every
last detail herself. She had seen to the green-and-white-
striped marquee stretched across the lawn, the damask-
draped tables ready to accommodate a variety of
delicately-spiced dishes, the centerpiece of fern and tea
roses that awaited the spiralling white cake and the
smaller groom's cake full of fruit. She had festooned
with white rosettes the chairs lined up for the band mem-
bers. She had entwined ribbons in clever knots through
the garden hedges.

In the parlor an altar brought up in the dogcart from
the Methodist church throned, magnificently dressed in
white satin, flanked by sentinels of roses in iron stands,
canopied by garlands of ivy, overlooked by the stairs
whose clusters of white net would whisper when the
bride floated down. Portable tables standing in lace
awaited the wedding gifts. There were basketsful of favors in the vestibule to pin on carriage horses. There
were lavender-colored mints, lavender-colored ribbons
on the waiters' boutonnieres, lavender-colored menus
boasting a breakfast fare of stewed terrapin, mushrooms
in red wine, cheese rarebit, escalloped oysters, cutlets à
la Provençale, asparagus tips, cherry fruit molds, and
lemon sherbet. Cases of the king of champagnes, Krug,
sat chilling in barrels of ice. Even Collie, snoozing in

his basket with a bandaged leg, sported a satin bow on his collar.

Elizabeth felt outside herself, as if she were merely an automaton with the right button pushed. Her vital self, the soft bruised inner core, was hiding somewhere, waiting for everything to be over, waiting until it could curl up in a ball and sob, and then later, next week or the week after, pack up the contents of the house on the cliffs and walk away from it.

She had not seen Spencer. His groomsmen, a set of polite, polished Londoners who were staying at his hotel in Folkestone, had come up yesterday to fetch the groom's wedding wardrobe: the Oxford grey cutaway coat, the striped gray worsted trousers, the white waistcoat, ascot tie, silk top hat, and the pleated white shirt with its wing collar that Elizabeth had pressed herself with careful hands and reddened eyes while everyone else had slept.

"Pardon me."

Elizabeth glanced up to see one of the bridesmaids hovering in the doorway of the kitchen demanding attention, her expression flushed and harried. "Miss Worth would like something to eat now. The wedding breakfast won't be served until after the ceremony, which means at least eleven o'clock, and Sara can't possibly endure the long wait on an empty stomach. Tea and toast will be fine, and a poached egg or two."

Elizabeth stirred the oyster sauce Bertha had forgotten and simultaneously sprinkled nutmeg in the pot of soup, speaking over a shoulder. "There are rolls on the sideboard in the dining room. The teapot is in a cozy beside it."

In a huff over the discourteous tone, the girl flew out of the kitchen, sure to complain to Mrs. Maples or Sara, neither of whom would do more than give a distracted but sympathetic nod.

"Look!" Bertha exclaimed suddenly, clattering down the creaky back stairs with her arms full of silk handkerchiefs. "Look out the window, Elizabeth. I saw it from Sara's bedroom. It's a balloon!"

Moving to the window with her wooden spoon in hand, Elizabeth peered out to see the breathtaking sight of a hot air balloon, so graceful it could have descended straight out of a Jules Verne tale instead of simply out of the Folkestone sky. Resembling a white cloud with a basket attached, it was piloted by two bespectacled men who, after landing on the lawn, leapt out and went about mooring it with ropes.

"It's Mr. Spencer's doing," Bertha explained, agog with wonder. "Miss Sara is all in a dither, I can tell you. He suggested the idea last week, doubtless thinking it would be a lark for the two of them, just married, to fly off in a balloon instead of prancing away in a carriage the usual way. She's not enraptured by the notion, a little nervous about it, actually, which one can understand. Dangerous things, balloons, I suppose." She frowned worriedly. "Can we throw slippers and old shoes at it, Elizabeth, as we would do at a wedding carriage?"

"I rather imagine so, Mother." Elizabeth responded absently, her eyes misty. How like Spencer to make an adventure, to think of something novel and just a little perilous in order to break tradition. While he grinned in amusement at their stuffiness, people would shake their heads uncertainly and whisper that a balloon, while admittedly creative, was perhaps not quite the most *delicate* way to carry off one's bride.

"Are the bridesmaids dressed, Mother?" Elizabeth asked, forcing her thoughts away from Spencer's wonderful balloon to the ordeal still to be endured.

"Nearly, dear. They're sharing Miss Talbert's maid, who is a wizard with ringlets and combs."

"Then press those monogrammed handkerchiefs for them, please, Mother, and then carry up their bouquets."

Elizabeth avoided going upstairs herself, having suffered one trip already into Sara's bedroom, which had become a veritable boudoir with its flowery sachets, draped shawls, discarded lace fans, bottles of cologne, and long suede gloves.

Earlier in the day, with her emotions tightly lidded, Elizabeth had finished the hem of the daisy gown, pinning the proper length while Sara preened and tossed her head, unaware that the fabric did not suit her at all. Lace or tulle would have been more fitting for such a rare complexion, or even silk delicately tinted like the petals of an orchid. But not the simple muslin on this special day.

"I hope I'm not to have ill luck," Sara had commented breezily, pivoting before the looking glass with her bridesmaids watching. "Spencer saw the gown yesterday, you know, and went dashing off to get Elizabeth's permission so I could wear it. Such a fuss he made. And dear Elizabeth herself bringing it back to me."

She slanted a glance at the housekeeper's daughter. "You had been making it for a friend, didn't you say, Elizabeth? At any rate, I couldn't help it that Spencer saw me take it out of the bag, and everyone claims it's such bad luck for a bridegroom to see the wedding gown before the wedding . . ."

Her bridesmaids assured her quickly that such a superstition was nothing more than silly nonsense.

Behind them, Elizabeth had smiled with a bitter but aching spite. Yes, Spencer had indeed seen the gown yesterday. He had touched it, too, while it lay pressed to her straining, very willing body. He had kissed her through it until the muslin had grown wet from the ardor of his mouth.

Escaping Sara's room at last, Elizabeth had had scarcely

enough time to drag on her own serviceable black bombazine, crisp and understated with its ruffled white apron, which was appropriate for her station and cool as she moved about checking last minute details, straightening waiters' ties, throwing out a wilting flower here and there.

The day was splendrous, not daring to make the wedding of Miss Sara Worth anything less than perfect, providing just the right amount of sunshine to show off the Gainsborough-style gowns and three-cornered picture hats of the bridesmaids, the sparkling regiment of crystal champagne glasses, the silver service, and—most of all—the ravishing bride.

The Reverend Fiddleton arrived, long faced and very proper, to sit with Mrs. Maples during this most nerve-racking but tender time. Outside on the lawn, after clambering out of three sputtering motor cars, the band began to tune up with a series of toots and whistles. The guests were not far behind, some walking from the village, most riding in old-fashioned coaches or in rented gigs. There was an assortment of people and fashions: new silks on old ladies, old frock coats on retired merchants, overblown bonnets, elegant top hats, and children in stiff petticoats and knickers tensely restrained by gloved parental hands. One hundred guests had been invited to the wedding, and another two hundred would arrive for the reception.

Elizabeth had just hurried into the library to bring Mrs. Maples a glass of sherry for her nerves when one of the groomsmen hesitated on the threshold with his hat in his hand.

"Mrs. Maples?" he inquired tentatively, "May I have a word with you, please?"

"Certainly. Come in. What is it? Oh, shouldn't you be with Reverend Fiddleton? Isn't he assembling you young men in the back parlor somewhere?" She glanced at the stodgy little mantel clock. "Good heavens, it's twenty minutes until the ceremony!"

"Yes, ma'am. However, there's a matter of concern—nothing to get upset about, I'm sure, but—"

"How can we help you?" Elizabeth cut in, noting that Mrs. Maples was blanching, preparing to swoon if a problem were presented to her too ungently on this redletter day.

"Well, you see," the young man continued, taking his cue and softening his tone, perhaps even amending what he had to say, "Spencer is not here. We—the other groomsmen and I—called for him at his hotel room this morning, but he wasn't in. We assumed, of course, that he had already arrived here."

"Well," Mrs. Maples said, going from pale to an alarming shade of pink, the pin curls beneath her enormous hat aquiver, "where is he then? Have you looked outside? Perhaps he's in the coach house or tinkering with that balloon—"

"No, ma'am—"

"Er—Mr. Billings, is it?" Elizabeth smoothly interrupted, smiling reassuringly, touching his sleeve. "Let us go look for him ourselves, shall we?"

With a firm hand she escorted the groomsman out to the deserted corridor where the murmur of guests being ushered to their seats faintly reached their ears. "When did you see Spencer last?" she asked in an urgent undertone.

"Last night, miss. We all met at a club—you know, a gentlemen's club—and drank claret. Quite a deal of it, truth to tell—"

"And Spencer's condition upon leaving the club?"

"Oh, he was quite able to negotiate his way back to the hotel, miss. Steadier on his feet than the rest of us. He might have awakened with a sore head this morning, but it wouldn't have been more than a cup of coffee

could cure. We rapped on his door for ten minutes before
having the manager unlock it. Spencer simply wasn't in
the room, and no note was found."

"And his clothes?"

"He must have dressed in his wedding attire. It was
all gone, right down to the cuff links his father sent—the
old man declined to come, you know—his gout."

"Yes, yes. But have you hunted for Spencer on the
grounds here thoroughly?"

"Of course. Three of us combed the place before
coming to tell Mrs. Maples."

"Can you just go and look down the road again, then?
Perhaps he's been delayed . . ."

"Of course."

The responsibility of informing the nervous flower
garden of women upstairs fell to Elizabeth. She hastened
up the back stairs, intensely aware of the guests leaning
forward in their seats with anticipation, aware of the hors
d'oeuvres warming in the oven, of the bride cake waiting
outside in the marquee with its icing protected from in-
sects by a fan-wielding waiter.

Catching the attention of a bridesmaid tucking a scent
bottle in her bouquet, Elizabeth hissed, "Tell Miss Worth
that the bridegroom has been delayed. The ceremony
may have to proceed a few minutes late."

"Oh, my! How very dreadful for Sara! Her uncle—
who is to give her away, you know—is waiting at the
head of the stairs."

"Then tell him he must wait a little longer."

Elizabeth hurried to the kitchen, shifting the cherry
fruit molds out of a patch of sunlight while peering out
the window to see the groomsman, Mr. Billings, sprint-
ing frantically up and down the road with a hand shading
his eyes. She released an anxious breath.

All day her emotions had been sternly bound up to
allow her both the presence of mind and the endurance

to get through the wedding. Now, when she allowed herself to imagine the possibility of Spencer lying injured somewhere, knocked over by a carriage or an ale wagon, fear gripped her. What had happened?

She heard the old grandfather clock in the vestibule grunt the hour, the *wedding* hour, and through the door glimpsed the seated rows of guests. They stilled, waiting, and when nothing happened, when no procession filed in and no music sounded, they began to turn about in their chairs and murmur.

Fifteen minutes later, Reverend Fiddleton walked in and asked for patience.

But a half hour after his announcement, when there was still no sight of Spencer, no word of his whereabouts, the groomsmen and several male guests hastened for the village on borrowed horses, hoping to find him. At this point, no one dared speculate where he might have gone.

Sara was almost in tears, restraining them as best she could so as not to redden her eyes, but certain her bridegroom had met with a dreadful accident. Elizabeth and Bertha scuttled back and forth carrying trays of punch, serving the bewildered guests, handing out mints to the squirming children, who, a while later, were given lemon sherbet while their parents enjoyed hors d'oeuvres and cordials.

Mrs. Maples, beyond enduring what was fast becoming the most horrific problem of her life, had to be carried upstairs to bed. One of the bridesmaids, spared from consoling Sara, was recruited to fan the poor woman's face and dab her brow with cologne.

"Ladies and gentlemen," Mr. Fiddleton finally announced precisely one hour after the ceremony was to have begun. He cleared his throat with the slightest hint of embarrassment. "I regret to say that Mr. Kenton—ah—still has not been located. We must all go home, it seems, and pray very seriously for his safety. And say a prayer, too, for that poor young woman upstairs, his bride, who is beside herself with anxiety."

Elizabeth turned away, her attention caught by the collective sight of garlands, favors, burdened tables, the marquee on the lawn, the now deflated balloon rippling on the ground like a beautiful, gasping bird.

It was to have been a splendid wedding. No doubt about it. She had done a very good job.

Calmly Elizabeth walked into the kitchen, laid down her serving tray and, creeping into the pantry so no one would hear, began to laugh, very softly at first, then convulsively. She put a hand over her mouth, laughed more deeply, until she was doubled over with mirth, breathless from trying to smother it.

Spencer Kenton had bought his freedom. To be sure, he would pay a high price for it when a complete accounting was done, but he had secured it nonetheless. He had jilted the gloriously beautiful Miss Sara Worth, left her standing—not quite literally but near enough—at the altar in Elizabeth Honeybridge's white daisy gown.

After a moment or two of savoring his audacious triumph, his brazen courage to throw over his fiancée in front of a hundred witnesses, Elizabeth composed herself.

Tightening her mouth so no one would see the traces of laughter around it, she went out armed with trays and brooms to dismantle all the trappings it had taken her nearly two gruelling months to assemble.

She sent the band and the waiters home, dispatched Bertha upstairs with tea for Mrs. Maples, instructing her to remain at the bedside and administer smelling salts or whatever else might be required to keep a nervous fit at bay.

In the meantime, amid a positive deluge of tears, the bridesmaids descended the stairs dressed in traveling clothes and carrying hatboxes and bags, declaring it their intention to return posthaste to London. "Poor Miss Worth," one girl whispered to Elizabeth. "She's so heartbroken she can't bear to stay in the house another minute, especially with so many memories of that despicable, dishonorable, *faithless* man crowding in on her. I hope, we all hope, that when he finally crawls out of his hole and shows his face again, he won't be received in any decent London drawing room, ever. Certainly, *we* will close our doors against him."

The daisy gown, bundled up in Sara's arms as if it were dirty laundry of the most personal variety, was handed to Elizabeth with a kind of contemptuous distaste just before the front door slammed shut.

An abrupt hush fell upon the house then, more complete than ever, so that the surge of the sea could be heard through the open windows framed by their billowing, snapping sheers. For several minutes Elizabeth stood with the gown in her arms, listening to the soft sound, smiling nostalgically.

Then she walked out to the green lawn, past the restless, limp cloud of balloon toward the marquee, where she retrieved each untasted delicacy and stacked it inside. She returned for the grand bride cake circled by its fern and tea roses, struggling to carry it, finally setting it upon the work table in the kitchen, wondering who on earth was going to eat it all.

A moment later, when footsteps sounded in the corridor behind her, Elizabeth held her breath. Then, with her usual self-possession in place, she turned slowly.

A most splendid bridegroom stood in the kitchen doorway, immaculate in a gray cutaway coat and trousers, white waistcoat, gloves, tie, tall silk hat, and the pleated shirt she had ironed herself. He was fine enough, she thought, for a royal bride, for the stained glass and wedding bells of the cathedral of Westminster.

Solemnly, with his head lowered but his eyes level

beneath his brows, he asked, "Do you think I'll be forgiven?"

She considered, then replied with equal solemnity. "No. At least, not for a very, very long time."

A smile spread across his face, that lazy, naughtily slow smile Elizabeth Honeybridge had loved all her life. "Ah, well," he said, hitching an elegantly attired shoulder. "I can wait for forgiveness. But I find myself curiously impatient for a bride."

He walked forward and from behind his back produced a bouquet of daisies, the common sort that brightened the cliffs he liked to wander. The soil still clung to their roots, an indication that, having had no time to find shears, he had simply snatched them from the roadside.

Elizabeth accepted them graciously, watching while he fished a small box from his waistcoat pocket, snapped it open, and removed the gold band inside.

Taking her capable hand in his, he slid the ring steadily over the appropriate finger and, kissing it, said, "I do. Do you?"

And Elizabeth assured him that she did, watching while he took up a kitchen knife, cut the bride-cake, then took a piece to feed her.

She swallowed, and laughed. His aim had been off-center—deliberately she thought—for he did not hesitate to lean and put his lips to her mouth, murmuring that the icing was delicious there. He kissed her thoroughly then, not as a gentleman, but as a lover who by all accounts was just barely restraining himself from doing more.

"Shall we do something very bold?" he breathed against her ear. "Something everyone in Folkestone will be sure to remember. A sort of . . . grand exit?"

Elizabeth nodded, smiled, laughed as he took her hand and pulled her out through the kitchen door. Then with a gasp, she told him to wait while she grabbed the daisy gown.

When she returned, Spencer was standing on the lawn beside the balloon, which the two pilots had reinflated with a blast of the hot-air blower. The silken cloud swelled to life, straining to rise. Putting his hands around her waist, Spencer hoisted her into the wicker basket.

Collie had followed them out, barking wildly at the hissing balloon while circling the bride and groom with a limping exuberance.

When the ropes were released and Spencer jumped in, the magical conveyance ascended eagerly, floating over the striped marquee just as Bertha and Mrs. Maples stuck their heads out of the upper window of the house.

Waving her hands, his grandmother called out to him shrilly. *"Spencer James Kenton!"*

"Don't worry, Granny!" he shouted down, grinning in a way Mrs. Maples knew well. "It was a lovely wedding. Went off perfectly. Elizabeth and I will wire you when we land."

Spencer put an arm around his bride, kissed her in a way that shocked the matronly eyes, his ardency so great that even Elizabeth swayed, losing her hold on the daisy gown.

Like a white sail snapped from the riggings of its mainmast, it took flight, outspread and free, buoyed by the wind.

"Oh!" Elizabeth cried, reaching for it, drawn back to safety by her bridegroom, who laughed and crushed her close.

"You can sew another one," he murmured, growing amorous, exploring the nape of her neck where her hair was properly pinned. "Just as soon as we land."

The balloon leapt suddenly, lifting them high up over the wind-swept cliffs, providing a breathtaking bird's-eye view of glassy blue seas and pale chocolate cliffs.

"And where shall we land, Spencer?" Elizabeth asked, taking his hat off his head so she could run her fingers through his ruffled hair.

"Oh," he mused, having already, she suspected, given it due consideration. "To a place that needs a bridge or two, I should think."

"A place like Folkestone?"

"Elizabeth!" he said with feigned surprise. "What an idea. After today, I'm sure the two of us will be ostracized for months by the townspeople."

"Does that mean they won't bother us for months?" she whispered, putting her lips to his ear.

He tucked a daisy from her bouquet in his buttonhole and gave her waist a squeeze. "A year, if we're lucky."

Their shocking exit, Mrs. Maples informed them later by letter, had caused quite a sensation in the village, filling the newspaper for days, inspiring bawdy songs on the esplanade, causing more than one elderly matron to swoon.

"But, Spencer, dearest," she had written, "how *did* Elizabeth's wedding gown misplace itself? Mr. Whistlebury was so dreadfully angry. He *claimed* he found it in his vegetable garden the day after you left, square atop his new, quite exhausted peas. Bertha and I did not believe a word of it, of course. Despicable old man! But the gown is here, nonetheless, all clean and pressed, should you and Elizabeth require it someday. For a daughter or two, you know. Or a daughter-in-law, if you, dear Spencer, insist upon having a pack of mischievous, thoroughly incorrigible, but quite *forgivable* sons . . ."

The Wrong Man

by
Victoria Thompson

The first time Cassie ever saw Duncan Ferguson, she knew he'd never make it. For a man to last in Texas, he had to be strong. Strong and tough and even a little mean. Duncan Ferguson was none of those things, and Cassie could tell it just by looking at him.

He was standing at the counter of the General Store when she saw him, arguing with the storekeeper, if you could call it that when somebody was talking as polite as Ferguson was.

"Are you telling me my money isn't good in your store, Mr. Harris?" Ferguson asked.

"No, it ain't that," Mr. Harris insisted, a little embarrassed.

"Then it must be the sheep," Ferguson said, his voice as mild as you please, even though he'd just said the word that could've got him beat up or even killed if he weren't careful.

"I'm a businessman," Mr. Harris was saying, kind of like he was apologizing but not backing down either. "I have to consider a man's prospects when I give him credit and—"

"And you don't think my prospects are good," Ferguson guessed.

He was right, that's for darn sure. *Nobody* thought his prospects were good, a stranger bringing sheep into cattle country. A greenhorn stranger, too. Cassie shook her head in disgust.

"Well, let me tell you something, Mr. Harris," Ferguson was saying. "My prospects are probably better than anyone else's around here, and shall I tell you why? Because sheep are much more profitable than cattle. Because you can only sell a cow once, but you can sell a sheep many, many times. You sell its wool every year—and there's always a market for wool, even when times are bad—and when the sheep gets old, you sell it for meat, but only after it's produced half-a-dozen offspring which will also produce wool every year. So when your other customers are broke because cattle prices are down, I'll have cash money, Mr. Harris. I'll be your most reliable customer."

But only if he lasts, Cassie thought, which didn't seem the least bit likely. Not a little fellow like him, skinny and pale except for that shock of red hair. Cassie knew what it took to make it out here. Shoot, even a woman had to be tough. Her own mother hadn't been strong enough, so Cassie recognized the signs of weakness all too easily.

She must've made some kind of noise or something, thinking about it, because all of a sudden Duncan Ferguson looked over at her. She hadn't really seen him good before, not full in the face, but now she did, because he looked straight at her.

She couldn't help thinking how pretty he was, as pretty as a girl. His face looked too perfect to be real, like a china doll she'd seen once in a store in Fort Worth. But she'd never seen eyes like that, so clear and blue they took her breath.

Those blue eyes looked her over from head to foot in the seconds before she got her breath back, and then his perfect mouth stretched out into a smile that might've stopped her heart if somebody hadn't called her name and distracted her.

"Cassie, where are you?" Buck wanted to know. He was outside, loading her order into her father's wagon, or at least he had been. He must be finished now, ready to head on home.

"Coming!" she called back and fled. Yep, she ran for her life, or anyway, she ran. Not because she was afraid Buck would be annoyed at her for keeping him waiting, but because she wanted to get away from Duncan Ferguson and his beautiful smile.

Outside, the sunlight fairly blinded her after the darkness of the store, but she squinted and found Buck waiting by the wagon. Buck, the man she was going to marry.

He was, she understood instinctively, everything a man should be. Big and strong and fearless, he could stand against anything Texas threw against him and never even flinch. If he wasn't pretty, well, men weren't supposed to be pretty. And if he didn't smile when he saw her, well, why should he?

"You ready to go?" he asked.

"Yes," she said, hurrying down the steps of the wooden sidewalk to the dusty street. "Where's Pa?"

"He said we should pick him up at the livery. He's horse trading or something."

Buck waited while Cassie climbed into the wagon, not insulting her by offering to help, then climbed up beside her onto the seat.

"Who was that in the store?" he asked when he'd maneuvered the wagon out into the broad street.

Cassie felt a little stinging in her cheeks, like she might've been embarrassed, even though she knew she didn't have a thing to be embarrassed about. "That sheep fella," she replied with all the disdain she was expected to feel.

Buck made a rude noise. "I bet old man Ferguson is turning over in his grave. Do you reckon he knew his nephew was going to run sheep on his place?"

"I doubt he would've left it to him if he did," Cassie said. But he *should've* known. Rumor had it that Duncan

Ferguson had been raising sheep someplace back East for several years, and now he'd decided to expand his operation using the land his late uncle had bequeathed him. Cassie supposed it was a good idea in theory, if he'd been telling the truth about how profitable sheep were, that is. What Duncan Ferguson hadn't figured on was how other folks would feel about it, and for sure, nobody *else* thought it was a good idea.

They found her father waiting for them outside the livery. Ron Plummer wasn't as big as Buck, but he was big enough so that nobody ever wanted to get on his bad side. He didn't smile when he saw Cassie either, although she knew he was happy enough to see her. She was his daughter, after all.

"Cassie saw that sheep fella in the store just now," Buck reported as her father climbed up to sit on her other side.

"Did he say anything to you?" Ron asked, ready to be mad about it.

"No, Pa, he was talking to Mr. Harris. He didn't even see me," she lied, not wanting to even remember the way Duncan Ferguson's blue eyes had taken her in, and certainly not wanting to tell her father and Buck about it.

"What was they talking about?" Pa asked.

Cassie hesitated, wondering how much to tell. For some reason, she discovered she didn't want to make Duncan Ferguson look any worse than he already did, although how a sheepman could look any worse to cattlemen, she had no idea. "I reckon Mr. Harris didn't want to give him credit."

"Sensible of him," Pa said, and Buck grunted his agreement. Buck never spoke if a grunt would do just as well. Cassie was surprised to realize she'd never noticed this before, and even more surprised to realize she'd noticed it now. None of the men she knew spoke any more than was absolutely necessary. Sometimes whole days went by when her father didn't say a word to her.

But somehow she knew Duncan Ferguson was a talker. Probably from the way he'd been talking to Mr. Harris, like words could somehow change his mind about sheep. Like words could change anything at all.

"He won't last a year," her father predicted. Cassie knew he was right, knew he had to be right, so she didn't understand why the knowledge made her sad.

The next day dawned sunny and warm again, the fickle March weather holding. As Cassie rustled up some breakfast for herself and her father, she happened to notice that she could see the smoke from the Ferguson cabin through her kitchen window. The cabin itself was little more than a bump on the horizon, but the smoke drifted up and away, like a chalk mark across the blue sky, telling her Duncan Ferguson was getting breakfast for himself.

She didn't realize she'd been staring until her father looked up from his plate and said, "You see something out there?"

"What? Oh, no, I was woolgathering, I guess." Then she blushed at the reference to wool, which meant sheep, which meant Duncan Ferguson, but her father didn't notice. He'd gone back to eating. Quickly, Cassie sat herself down and started eating as well.

But after her father had gone, leaving for the range, Cassie once again found herself looking out the window. The smoke had vanished, meaning Duncan Ferguson had banked his fire and gone out to work himself.

The knowledge made her restless, or maybe it was the warmth of the early spring day. Whatever it was, Cassie hurried through her morning chores, put some beans on to simmer for dinner, and left the house. She caught up her mare, Molly, in the corral and saddled her. As she performed the familiar task, she recalled the first time she had performed it successfully. Her father had praised her.

"You gotta be able to do for yourself, Cassie-girl. Can't expect nobody else to do for you."

That had pretty much become her motto. A woman's tasks were different from a man's, of course, but just as hard on her as his were on him and just as important, too. A helpless female would be worthless. No, worse than worthless, because somebody would have to take care of *her*, meaning they wouldn't be able to do the work they were meant to do. Cassie wasn't helpless, not by a long shot, and she'd be more than a match for most men, which was why so many of them had wanted to marry her. Cassie had chosen the right man, too. Buck would do well for himself, and Cassie would help him.

Usually, the thought made her happy, or at least satisfied, but today she felt only a vague sense of unease. Probably spring fever, she reasoned, although she'd never been given to such fancies before. Maybe this disquiet was something girls got along with the monthly curse, a discomfort that would pass if you just set your mind to ignoring it.

But Cassie wasn't exactly ignoring it. No, she was working through it, she decided as she swung up onto the mare's back. Riding side saddle was her only concession to her femininity, one dictated more by custom than personal preference, but she had never let it hamper her riding style. She started out slowly, warming the mare up gradually until she was ready for the run Cassie craved. When she was, the two of them set off, streaking across the prairie until the new grass beneath them was a green blur and the warm air a lash against Cassie's cheeks.

When Cassie finally reined the mare in again, she noticed she was awfully close to the barbed-wire fence that separated her father's land from Duncan Ferguson's. She wasn't really surprised. She'd headed in this direction on purpose, although she hadn't actually thought about her reasons for doing it. She certainly wasn't going to pay Duncan Ferguson a visit or anything like that, not even if he *hadn't* been a sheepman. She wasn't even likely to encounter him, not if she stayed on her own side of the fence, which she had every intention of doing, but she started Molly along that fence just the same. If she saw Duncan Ferguson, she wasn't going to run away, but she sure wasn't looking for him either.

Which was why, after she'd ridden awhile, she was a little surprised to see something was going on up ahead a ways, over on his side of the fence. She kicked Molly into a lope, and as she approached she made out that the activity was building. Somebody'd already thrown up some sheds, and now they were stringing wire to make some sort of enclosures. Pa wouldn't like it, Ferguson building something for those sheep right up next to the fence like that. She'd better take a closer look, maybe even warn Ferguson off before her Pa found out what he was doing. Bad enough having those sheep right next door without him doing his business practically on Plummer land.

By the time she got to where the building was going on, Cassie'd worked herself up into a mad. Not a fighting-mad, but a nice little annoyed-mad, which she figured would be proof against any man's smile, no matter how pretty it was.

There were four men working, but they were all wearing hats, so she didn't pick out Duncan Ferguson until she was close. In fact, not until he stopped what he was doing, took off his hat for a minute, and wiped his brow on his sleeve. Then she would've been able to find him a mile away. That hair was like torch, flaming in the sunlight. Cassie thought of her own dull, brown hair and sighed with what might have been envy if she'd been given to such girlish notions.

He saw her then and came loping over to the fence, waving to her to stop, as if she'd just ride on by without at least saying howdy. She might not like him, but she wasn't rude. Besides, she had business with him.

She couldn't help noticing how he moved, though. Smooth and sure, almost like a panther. Certainly not like the cowboys she knew, who might look like kings when sitting on a horse, but who tended to be bowlegged and awkward on the ground, picking their way gingerly in their high-heeled boots. He stopped at the fence, still waving his hat at her. And smiling, real pleased, like seeing her was the high spot of his day or something.

Cassie had to remind herself she was mad.

"Good morning," he said when she was close enough to see how blue his eyes were again. "You're Cassie Plummer."

"How d'you know?" Cassie demanded, nonplused.

"I asked the storekeeper—Mr. Harris, I think his name is. He told me." His smile got even bigger, although Cassie would have bet it couldn't. He looked real pleased with himself. "My name is—"

"Duncan Ferguson," she supplied, not smiling back one bit. "Everybody knows the sheepman," she added, in case he thought she'd been asking about *him*.

His smile didn't even waver, although Cassie was sure she'd insulted him.

"And why were you asking about me, anyways?" she wanted to know.

"Because," he said without even blinking, "I decided the minute I saw you that you're the girl I'm going to marry. I thought I should at least know your name."

Cassie's cheeks were burning, and she tried to tell herself it was because she was mad, as well she should be. How dare he tease her like this? "I . . . I'm already promised," she stammered inanely.

"I know," he said, not the least bit disturbed by the knowledge. "To Buck Ewing. Mr. Harris told me that, too. The wedding's in a month or so, I understand. Isn't Buck the one built like a grizzly bear?"

"He is not!" Cassie exclaimed loyally, although she'd had the same thought once or twice herself.

But Duncan Ferguson didn't want to discuss Buck. "Now tell me, what is Cassie short for? Cassandra?"

"Don't call me by that name!" Cassie said, too startled not to react.

"Why not?" he asked.

"Because, it . . . it's a sissy name!"

He seemed a little puzzled. "How can a girl's name be a sissy name?"

He had her there. "It's ugly," she tried.

Now he seemed surprised. "No, it's not. It's a beautiful name, almost as beautiful as the girl to whom it belongs."

Cassie's cheeks were scalding now, and she was sure it was because she was mad. "I'm not beautiful and I know it, so don't think you can turn my head with a bunch of lies!"

"Ah, Miss Cassandra," he said, shaking his head in mock despair, "beauty is in the eye of the beholder, so if I think you're beautiful, who can tell me I'm wrong? Surely," he went on before she could even begin to think of a reply, "Buck Ewing must think so, too."

"He . . . he never said," Cassie admitted reluctantly.

Duncan Ferguson shook his head again. "Then he's not the man for you, Cassandra Plummer. You deserve someone who can appreciate you."

Just who did he think he was, anyway? Cassie could have choked on her anger, but she decided to turn it on

Duncan Ferguson instead. "And just what is it you think you're doing here, so close to our fence, Mr. Ferguson?"

He glanced over at where the other men were still working, like he needed to remind himself of what he'd been doing when she rode up. "Oh, we're getting ready for lambing."

Cassie looked at the sheds that were under construction. For *lambing?* Cassie had never heard of an animal that needed a *house* in which to give birth. The very idea was unnatural. "Just how helpless *are* those critters anyway?" she asked acidly.

"Pretty helpless, I'm afraid," Ferguson replied, not the least bit embarrassed to admit it. "They aren't like cattle who just go off by themselves to give birth. We've got to make sure each mother accepts her lamb and feeds it, and we see that orphans are adopted by another ewe. Those little puffballs are worth too much to leave to chance."

"Cows are worth a lot, too, but they manage to tend their own calves without any help," Cassie informed him haughtily.

"And you find that an admirable trait," he guessed, his blue eyes dancing mischievously.

"Of course I do!" Cassie huffed. Being able to do for yourself *was* an admirable trait, whether you were a human or an animal.

He nodded sagely, although Cassie knew he was pressing his lips tight together to keep from grinning. "Well, now," he said after a minute, "there *are* some things in this life that you can leave to chance, but I, myself, am a careful man by nature and I like to take a hand in my own destiny. Which is probably why I like raising sheep so much."

"It's gonna get you in trouble," Cassie warned.

"I'm not afraid of trouble," he said, and this time he

did grin, like he was giving her a challenge or something.

"Then you don't know what Texas trouble is, mister, because if you did, you'd pack up them sheep and head back for wherever you came from."

"Georgia," he said.

"What?"

"I'm from Georgia. You wanted to know where I'm from. You don't need to be embarrassed, Cassandra. If we're going to be married, you've got a right to know everything about me."

"We're *not* getting married!" Cassie cried in frustration. "I told you, I'm marrying Buck!"

"Yes, that's what you said, but a month is a long time. Anything can happen between now and then."

"Yeah, the world might come to an end, but it ain't too likely," Cassie informed him, wishing she wasn't blushing quite as furiously as she knew she was. "And you better be careful. My Pa ain't gonna be too happy when he finds out you're birthing lambs right up next to his fence."

"I'll be glad to talk to him about it," Ferguson offered cheerfully.

"Yeah, well, *he* won't," Cassie sniffed, wishing she knew a good way to make a graceful exit. "And don't let Buck hear you talk about marrying me, either. He won't like it, even if you *are* just teasing."

He smiled for real then, that same beautiful smile she'd seen in the store, and once again it took the wind right out of her. "But I'm not teasing, Cassandra. As I believe I just explained to you, I like to control my own destiny, and you're the woman I want included in it."

"Don't I get any say?" Cassie demanded.

"Only if you say yes," he replied with more confidence than any sheepman had a right to.

"Well, I *don't* say yes, and I never will!" Figuring

that was the best she could do and still leave with some of her dignity intact, Cassie kicked Molly into motion, and the little mare obliged by carrying her away from Duncan Ferguson. Cassie only wished she dared look back to see if he were laughing.

Cassie didn't tell her Pa about Ferguson's plans for birthing his sheep up next to his fence. She didn't examine her motives too closely, mostly because she was afraid of what they might be. For sure, she wasn't protecting no sheepherder. Maybe she kept the news to herself because she didn't want to speak of Ferguson at all, to anyone, for fear of revealing the way he had of unsettling her. All that talk about marrying her. Made her face hot just to remember. Other parts of her, too, although she had no idea why.

But in the end she didn't *have* to tell her Pa, because Buck did it for her. He brought word that night, arriving just in time for supper, as he usually did.

Cassie listened to the two men discussing the situation over the kitchen table as she set out the beans and fatback left over from the noon meal.

"He says he's got to keep the sheep under cover when they foal," Buck explained. Cassie wondered if "foal" were the correct word, then wondered why she was wondering.

"You mean he just sits there all spring and summer waiting for each and every sheep to drop her lamb?" Ron Plummer asked incredulously. Indeed, it was an amazing prospect. Cows mated whenever the urge took them, which meant calves arrived willy-nilly, some even showing up as late as the fall. Keeping track of each and every one would be an impossible task.

"Naw," Buck said, his contempt obvious. "He keeps the males away from the females all year except when he wants them to breed. Then he breeds them all at once, so they all drop their lambs at the same time."

Her father shook his head, his weathered face gaping. "That's a hell of a thing." He shook his head again. "Can you imagine knowing just when every one of your cows was about to give birth and then being there to take a hand in it?"

"Sure would make it easier to keep track of how many you've got and make sure none of 'em got orphaned," Cassie observed, taking her place at the kitchen table.

The two men looked at her with the same astonishment they would have shown if one of the chairs had spoken.

"Well, wouldn't it?" she demanded, more than a little annoyed at their reaction.

Her father blinked. "I reckon it would," he allowed.

"Fat lot of trouble," Buck disagreed. "Who wants to raise stock you've got to play nursemaid to?"

A man who wants to control his own destiny, Cassie thought, but of course, she didn't say it.

"I'll ask the blessing," she said instead. The men bowed their heads, effectively ending all discussion of Duncan Ferguson's queer beasts. No Texan ever wasted time talking when there was eating to be done.

Later, after Cassie had finished the dishes, she headed for the front porch where Buck and her father would be sitting, enjoying a smoke. She stopped just inside the front door to get her shawl which hung on a peg nearby, and when she did, she heard the rumble of the men's voices.

"I say we run him off," Buck was saying. "There's others think so, too."

Cassie froze. Who could they be talking about?

"He ain't done nothing to nobody," her father argued.

"He brung sheep into cattle country," Buck argued back.

Cassie felt a stinging in her cheeks, the same reaction she'd had the first time she'd heard Buck talking about Duncan Ferguson.

"And if that ain't enough," Buck went on, oblivious to Cassie's eavesdropping, "he's gonna ruin that land. You know sheep kill the grass the way they eat it right down to the roots then cut up the ground with them sharp little hooves. That place'll be a dustbowl a year from now, then Ferguson'll move on and leave us with clogged water holes and God only knows what else. Even if the grass ain't ruined, no cows'll ever graze on it after sheep've been there, and that's a fact!"

"I did hear that," her father admitted—reluctantly, Cassie was relieved to note, "but the land is his by law, and he can do whatever he wants with it."

"Not if what he's doing hurts the rest of us. By God, I say we don't give him a chance. He ain't one of us, and—"

The screen door squawked in protest as Cassie shoved it open and stepped out onto the porch. "And just what do you intend to do to him, Buck?" she asked angrily.

Buck had been sitting on the top step, and now he levered his bulk up, lurching like a bear that had just been awakened. "This ain't your concern, Cassie."

"I reckon I'm the best judge of what's my concern and what ain't," she informed him.

"Ron?" Buck appealed to her father.

"Don't get me in the middle," her father protested, lifting both hands in self-defense. "You're gonna have to learn how to handle her sooner or later, Buck. Might as well start now."

Cassie did not feel like being "handled," and she was just about to say so when Buck said, "This is man's business, Cassie. You'd best just leave it be."

"What makes it *man's* business?" Cassie challenged.

"Because it's breaking the law? Because some innocent man is gonna get hurt?"

"He ain't exactly innocent, but nobody said he'd get hurt," Buck tried. "We're just gonna pay him a little visit and warn him off."

But Cassie wasn't having any of it. "You think Ferguson's gonna give up without a fight?"

Cassie didn't miss the look Buck exchanged with her father. They most certain expected him to fight, and she knew Buck would be looking forward to it. "If he knows what's good for him, he will," Buck hedged.

"But *you* know he won't," Cassie snapped, so furious she was trembling. "So what are you going to do? Burn him out? String him up? Or will you just shoot him?"

"Cassie, I told you, this ain't none of your affair. See, now, you've got yourself all riled up and for what? For some lousy sheepherder who ain't even worth your time-a-day. You leave this to me. I know what's best."

Speechless with fury, Cassie could only gape at him. She'd thought she and Buck would be partners, that he would see her as his equal as well as his mate, but now she understood he considered her just a female, useful in her place but not out of it. Silently, she willed her father to say something, to tell him he was wrong, but Ron Plummer held his peace, puffing thoughtfully on his pipe and watching the two of them like they was actors in some play or something.

Finally, Cassie found her tongue. "And what if I don't think you know what's best?"

Buck's face tightened. She'd never challenged him before and she had no idea what he would do, but she realized she didn't really care. Certainly, he was furious. Even in the fading light, she could see the blood flooding his cheeks. "I'm doing this for you, to protect you and all the rest of us."

"From what? From some skinny little sheepherder?" she scoffed.

"From what him and his kind can do to us," Buck insisted. He looked like a small mountain standing there in the evening shadows, solid and immovable. "If we let him in, what's to stop others from bringing in more sheep?"

Cassie had no idea, no more than she understood what harm it would do Buck if they did. "Pa?" she tried, looking for some wisdom.

But she got no help there. "It's getting late," her father said, even though they all knew it wasn't. "Best sleep on this and talk about it tomorrow. Your ma always used to say things look better in the light of day."

It was the first time Cassie could remember ever hearing him quote her long-dead mother. Chilled, she stared at him in amazement and almost didn't hear Buck saying gruffly, "I'll see you tomorrow, Cassie."

"Yeah," she replied absently, still too angry with him to say more.

He strode away to where his horse was tied, mounted up and left. When the sounds of his horse's hooves had died away on the evening air, she turned back to her father and said, "He's gonna do something, ain't he?"

"I reckon so," her father said blandly around the stem of his pipe.

"Tonight?"

Her father shook his head. "I don't reckon he'll be able to round up any help before tomorrow at the soonest."

"Will you go with him?"

Her father glanced up sharply, looking at her with the same dark-brown eyes she saw in her own mirror. "I figure a man's got a right to do what he wants on his own land. I also figure that Ferguson'll go bust all by his lonesome without any help from his neighbors, so I plan to stay out of it."

Her father, she knew, could never approve of raising sheep, so she understood how strongly he must feel about letting a man make his own mistakes, too. She felt her pride in him glowing like an ember in her chest. But still . . .

"Shouldn't somebody warn him? Ferguson, I mean. It don't seem right that he should just be caught out flat-footed with no chance to defend himself."

Her father's dark eyes narrowed through the haze of smoke from his pipe. "If there's somebody thinks he oughta be warned, I reckon they'll warn him. Me, I'm going to bed."

Bed? The sun wasn't hardly down yet and . . . But he winked as he brushed past her and pulled open the protesting screen door. He wasn't really going to bed, just leaving her alone so she could do whatever it was she felt was right to do.

And she felt it was right to warn Duncan Ferguson that somebody he should be scared to death of was planning to turn his destiny upside down.

As Molly carried her across the darkening prairie, Cassie tried not to think how disloyal she was being to everybody and everything she held dear. Nobody would thank her for putting herself out for a sheepman, and certainly Buck would be mad as blazes if he found out she was interfering in what he thought was right. She was going to marry Buck, to live with him for the rest of her life, and this would be a bad way for them to start out, with her defying him.

But if Buck had to do what he thought was right, Cassie did, too. And if Buck found out and got mad, well, he'd just have to get over it because Cassie wasn't going to stand by and let Duncan Ferguson get crushed like a bug. That was just plain wrong.

Which was the reason she gave herself for being so concerned about his welfare. What other reason could she have, after all? She hardly knew the man, so she sure didn't have any feelings for him. In fact, she had good reason not to like him at all, what with the way he'd teased her about getting married. But when she thought about how helpless he was—at least compared to Buck—she just felt sick to her stomach. And when she thought about what Buck could do to him, bare-handed and alone—not to mention with a mob of crazy cowboys backing him, well, she knew she had to give him a chance to get out while all his parts were still in working order. He could make a new start someplace else or go back to Georgia or wherever he was from and take up where he'd left off.

So she guessed she just felt sorry for Ferguson. Yeah, that was it. He'd made a mistake, thinking he could bring sheep into cow country, but he shouldn't have to die for it. And she'd make sure he didn't have to.

His cabin looked different from the way she remembered it when his uncle had lived there. Now it seemed neater somehow, the yard raked smooth and new boards here and there, patching places where the old wood had rotted. There were even new shingles on the roof in spots. Duncan Ferguson must not like getting rain on his head when he was indoors.

The sunset was just a thin crimson streak across the horizon now, and the sky looked like somebody'd smeared charcoal all over it. In a few minutes it would be full dark, but no lights shone in Ferguson's house, although the front door was standing open. She knew a moment's alarm at the thought she might already be too late.

"Hello, the house!" she called giving the traditional greeting.

"Who's that?" a familiar voice called back, and then she saw him, nothing more than a shadow in the darkness, appearing from around the side of the cabin. She sagged in the saddle with relief. "Cassandra, is that you?"

He sounded almighty pleased about it, so pleased Cassie knew instinctively she'd made a mistake in coming. Leave it to Duncan Ferguson to make something more of this than there was.

"I come to warn you. I got some news," she said, keeping her tone curt and businesslike. She swung down from Molly's back, letting the reins drop to the ground so the mare would stand, and strode forward to meet Ferguson halfway.

Which was a big mistake, she saw the instant he was close enough for her to make out clear in the gathering darkness. He was smiling that smile of his which was so bright it actually glowed, even though there was no light anywhere around. And he wasn't wearing a shirt.

Which shouldn't have bothered her in the slightest. She'd seen shirtless men before. Not often, but often enough to know it wasn't too exciting, or at least it never had been before. And as skinny as Duncan Ferguson was, what was there to see? Except he wasn't as skinny as she'd thought, not by a long shot. Oh, he was thin, even wiry, but not skinny. His chest and shoulders were solid with muscles that looked like they'd been carved out of wood or stone or maybe something even harder.

Somebody made a funny little sound, like a gasp, and Ferguson stopped dead and looked down, like he'd just noticed he wasn't wearing all his clothes.

"Oh, sorry, I was washing up. I just got back to the house. Wait right here while I make myself decent. Don't go anywhere, now," he said, as he hurriedly backed away toward the house.

As if she would, Cassie thought, when she hadn't even had a chance to tell him what she'd come to tell him. Only when he ducked into the black square that was his front door did Cassie realize she been holding her breath and let it out in a whoosh. Dear heaven, what was wrong with her? And why on earth did she always forget to breathe whenever she saw Duncan Ferguson?

By the time he got back, which was only a few seconds later, jerking his shirt on and fumbling with the buttons as he came, Cassie was breathing quite normally and had managed even to work up a little irritation at having been put to so much trouble for him.

"Now," he said when he got close, "tell me why you've come to see me, sweet girl."

He had, Cassie suddenly realized, gotten *way too* close, and she took a step backwards. "I'm not your sweet girl! I'm not your sweet anything!"

He pulled up short and his smile vanished. "Oh, is that the way it is, then? All right, what brings you out this way, Miss Plummer?" he asked, pulling himself up stiff and straight.

His voice was as polite as could be, but Cassie had the uneasy feeling he was making fun of her somehow. She shook it off and reminded herself why she had come. "I told you there was gonna be trouble. Buck and some of his friends, they're planning to pay you a visit."

"I'd be more than happy to see them," he replied cheerfully.

Just how stupid was he? Cassie almost groaned in frustration. "Don't you understand? They ain't coming for no tea party! They want you out of here! They're coming to run you off once and for all!"

"Are they?" he asked like he was real surprised. "That's not very neighborly of them."

"They don't figure you're being real neighborly, either, what with you raising sheep and all," she fired back.

"What harm could my sheep do them?" He sounded like he really didn't know.

" 'Cause they'll ruin the grass! Turn this place into a

dust bowl," she explained impatiently, quoting what she'd heard Buck say. "And they'll sour whatever grass is left so no cattle'll ever graze on it again!"

He sighed, like he was real tired, and shook his head. "Is that what Buck told you?"

"It's true, ain't it?" she replied, not doubting it for a minute.

"No, it's not," he said, hurrying on when she yelped in outrage. "All right it is true that sheep will ruin the grass if they're allowed to overgraze, but so will cattle. I'll bet Buck and your father never allow their herds to do that, and I never let my sheep do it either. I want to be here fifty years from now, so I'm going to take as good care of my pastures as I do my flocks. And what I'll bet your Buck doesn't know is that sheep droppings are much better for the grass than cow droppings. Make it grow even better. And as for cattle not grazing after sheep, that's just a lie. If you don't believe me, you can come see for yourself. I've still got cattle on this place left from my uncle's herd, and they haven't been the least bit shy about following the flocks around. In fact, you get much better use of your grass by grazing both kinds of stock, because the cows eat the long, thick grass and the sheep eat the weeds and the short grass the cows can't reach."

Cassie didn't know what to say to that. She didn't like to think Buck hadn't told her the truth, but she would have bet her life Ferguson wouldn't lie, either. Maybe Buck just didn't know the truth. Maybe if she told him, explained how he'd been wrong, he'd understand he didn't have to be afraid of Ferguson and . . .

But then she pictured Buck's broad face in her mind and knew he'd never understand because he'd never want to be wrong. He hated sheep and he hated Ferguson and nobody would ever change his mind.

"It don't matter," she told him. "None of it matters. They're coming for you anyways."

"And you came to warn me," he said. She thought he sounded happy about it, but she must've been mistaken.

"That's right! So you've got some time. Pa said they won't be coming before tomorrow night—"

"Will your father be with them?" he asked, and this time he sounded disappointed.

"No, he don't believe in doing things like that. He thinks—Oh, what difference does it make? It don't matter who's coming or not coming. What matters is you've got time to get away. Maybe you can even save some of your sheep. If they see you're leaving, they might not come at all because they won't need to!"

"Leaving? Why would I be leaving?"

Could he really be that stupid? "To save your life!" she cried, hating to have to say it out like that, hating even more to know it was true.

"Oh, Cassie," he said and took her hands in his. His fingers were strong, his palms rough, she noticed with surprise. Why had she expected his hands to be soft and weak? "And you came to warn me," he was saying, like that was the important thing. "Why? Tell me why."

"I told you, to save your life!" Why did he make her feel so frustrated? Why didn't he understand?

"And why are you so concerned about my poor, miserable life?"

His fingers tightened on hers, and suddenly she felt very warm, like she'd stepped too close to the fire, only there wasn't any fire. "I . . . I don't know . . ." she stammered.

He smiled, showing her his straight, even teeth and lighting up the night with his joy. "I was afraid I was the only one who felt it. I was afraid you wouldn't. . . . But you have. You did, and you came to me."

Cassie didn't know what on God's earth he was talking about, but maybe that was because her heart was hammering so hard she couldn't think very straight. She couldn't seem to move, either, which was why she just stood there when he lowered his face and touched his mouth to hers.

The very lightest of kisses, hardly a touch at all, like the wing of a butterfly brushing her lips, but she felt as stunned as if she'd been hit by lightning. A tiny cry escaped her as he drew away, a cry of surprise and something else, and then his arms were around her and his mouth was covering hers, fierce and demanding.

She clung to him, giving him her lips and her body, abandoning herself to the power of his passion as she reveled in the swirling sensations: her breasts flattened against the solid wall of his chest . . . her hands clutching the straining muscles of his back . . . the steel bands of his arms holding her like he'd never let her go . . . the thundering of her heart and the roar of her own blood in her ears.

She'd never felt like this, not ever, not even when Buck . . . *Buck!* How could she have forgotten? Horrified, she wrenched away from him. He could have held her if he'd wanted, but he released her—too surprised, maybe, to resist until it was too late.

"Cassie?" he said, reaching for her again, but she knew she dared not let him touch her or she would be lost. Desperate now, she turned and ran for her horse.

Molly shied a little at seeing her mistress so distressed, but she stood still enough that Cassie was able to bolt into the saddle.

"Wait, Cassandra!" he was calling, but she didn't look back, terrified of the wanting she would see on his face and even more terrified that she would not be able to resist it.

Molly leaped into a run, carrying her away, and Cassie

clung desperately to the saddle, riding as if her life depended on it, away into the night.

She didn't slow until she reached the fence that separated her land from Ferguson's; and only when she was safely on the other side, certain that he hadn't come after her, certain that she had escaped for sure, did she allow herself even to think about what had happened back there.

He'd kissed her. A pretty shocking thing to be sure, what with her engaged to another man and all. Outrageous. Scandalous even. But more than that, because she'd kissed him back. For a minute there, anyways. She'd kissed him with all her heart and a lot more besides, just like she'd never even heard of Buck Ewing and had never promised to be his wife.

Well, Ferguson had caught her by surprise. She hadn't *gone* there to get kissed, not by a long shot. She'd gone there to do him a favor—to save his life, for heaven's sake!—and that was how he repaid her. By forcing himself on her. By taking advantage. By kissing her and making her feel things she'd never even imagined a woman could feel.

She remembered the way her heart had pounded and how she'd felt hot all over and fluttery and weak and . . . well, Buck had never made her feel like that. Of course, he'd never kissed her quite like that either. He'd hardly kissed her at all, as a matter of fact. *He* wasn't one to take advantage.

All that talk about marrying her, too. Ferguson must be rolling on the ground laughing at how silly she was. One little mention of marriage and she'd let him do anything he liked—even forget about the man she was promised to.

Well, she *hadn't* forgotten about him. She'd remembered, and just in time, too. And as foolish as she felt now, she knew there was no harm done. No real harm, anyway. No one would ever know what had happened back there; and in the morning, Ferguson would pack up and leave. She'd never see him again and neither would Buck or anyone else. Cassie could forget Duncan Ferguson even existed.

She only hoped that was possible.

Buck didn't come for supper the next night. It was Saturday and usually he showed up early in the afternoon, but this time he didn't. Probably, he was still mad at Cassie for daring to argue with him. Cassie wanted that to be the reason. She didn't even let herself think he might be busy rounding up a mob to go after Duncan Ferguson. But so what if he were? They'd find no one to terrorize when they got there. A long ride for nothing.

Cassie should have felt relieved or at least a little proud of herself for having staved off trouble the way she had. She'd even protected Buck in a way, because you never knew what might happen in a fight. Anybody could get hurt, even Buck. So she should have felt good about the whole thing.

Except she didn't. She felt like a drop of water on a hot skillet. All day long she couldn't seem to sit still for more than a minute at a time, and whenever she passed a window, she looked out of it. What she hoped to see, she had no idea. Maybe Duncan Ferguson trailing his sheep down the road or something. Maybe him coming up to the house to tell her goodbye and thanks for her message. Maybe even to tell her he was sorry for stealing that kiss.

But she didn't see hide nor hair of him or his woolybacks. Not that she'd expected to, of course. But just the same, she kept looking out the windows every chance she got.

Her father hadn't said a word to her all day, but she

knew he'd been noticing how restless she was. Finally, when the sun had slunk down below the horizon, he asked, "Do you reckon Ferguson is expecting company tonight?" His way of finding out if she'd warned him without coming right out and asking.

"I expect so," she replied stiffly, not daring to meet his curious gaze.

She half-wished he'd ask her about it, maybe want to know how Ferguson took the news or what he planned to do. Not that Cassie could tell him anything about Ferguson's plans and she certainly had no intention of telling *anyone* how he'd taken it. Still, it would've been nice to talk to somebody about it. Her father didn't say another word about it, though. He didn't say another word at all, as a matter of fact, not until he muttered his good nights before heading off to bed a few hours later.

Cassie sat on the porch for a long time after that, staring off into the distance to where Ferguson's cabin sat, invisible now in the darkness. She thought about him with his red hair and his outrageous ways. She'd never known another like him and likely never would again. Which was just as well, she told herself. A man like that could drive a woman crazy. Everyday life was crazy enough without a man saying and doing things to make it worse.

Which was why Cassie was glad she had Buck. Buck was solid and dependable. She'd always know what he was going to say and do. No unpleasant surprises there.

Or pleasant ones either, a small voice whispered in her head.

Now where on earth had that come from? she wondered with a start. Cassie didn't want surprises of any kind, did she? She wanted a man she understood. A man who'd make a good living and give her a home and never make her worry about what he was up to. Well, maybe Buck had surprised her there, what with wanting to go after

Ferguson and all, but she'd taken care of that. And he'd be more manageable from now on. She'd see to it. And he'd treat her better, too, not look at her funny when she had an idea or spoke her mind. She'd see to that, too.

Yes, her life was going to be just the way she'd always planned it. And if she sometimes remembered the way Duncan Ferguson had kissed her one night in the darkness before he'd disappeared from that life forever, well, what harm could it do?

Cassie woke with a start the next morning, disoriented at first and unable to figure out why she was sitting in a chair in front of her bedroom window. Then she remembered. She'd been sitting up, watching Ferguson's place, expecting at any minute to see it go up in flames.

But the hours had passed and nothing at all had happened, and eventually, Cassie must have drifted off to sleep. Now, stiff and cramped, she stretched and looked out the window again in the light of day.

The Ferguson cabin was still a lump on the horizon, not a smoldering pile of rubble. Her warning had saved it, and had probably saved Duncan Ferguson as well. Which meant he was gone, out of her life for good. The knowledge made her strangely sad, the way she imagined she might have felt waking up on Christmas morning to find her stocking empty. She couldn't imagine why she should be disappointed that her plan had worked, so she shook off the feeling and hurried to dress. She didn't want to be late for church, where she was bound to hear all about the futile raid last night and whatever news there was to hear about what had become of Duncan Ferguson.

As Cassie had expected, the church yard was full of folks talking in groups. She could practically feel the wave of excitement rolling off of them, and suddenly she was anxious and afraid. What if things hadn't gone the way she expected? What if somebody had gotten hurt after all? Or even killed?

But as her father found a place among the other parked vehicles and stopped their wagon, Cassie realized the buzz she heard wasn't the kind that usually accompanied a tragedy. In fact, now that she was closer, she saw a lot of folks was smiling.

Smiling? Whatever for?

Unless they thought a sheepman getting strung up was funny.

The thought turned her breakfast into a hard lump in her stomach, but before she could get really upset, she saw Abigail Wentworth waving at her.

"Did you hear what happened?" Abby called, hurrying over as Cassie jumped down from the wagon. Her little bird face was crinkled into the biggest grin Cassie had ever seen. Her old friend wouldn't be grinning like that if somebody'd gotten killed, even a sheepman.

Cassie took Abby's hands. "No, what's going on?"

"It's that sheep fella. You know, old Mr. Ferguson's nephew?"

Cassie nodded, wanting to shake the news out of her but somehow restraining the urge.

"Well, some fellows went out to his place last night. Pa said they's been some talk about running him off. Nobody wants sheep around here and—"

"What *happened?*" Cassie demanded, ready to scream with impatience.

"Well, they rode into an ambush!"

"An ambush?" This was not at all what Cassie had expected to hear.

"That's right! Seems Ferguson had set up a trap. Near as they could figure it out in the dark, he'd staked out some ropes across the road, like a great big cat's cradle, and the horses stepped right into it. Everybody went down in a great big heap, men and horses alike; and while they was sorting themselves out, Ferguson shouted at them to get going or he'd start shooting."

Cassie could only gape at her old friend. This wasn't what Ferguson was supposed to do. He was supposed to run. Sheepmen were notorious cowards, after all. Or so she'd been led to believe.

"And did he shoot?" Cassie asked when she'd found her tongue.

"Over their heads, just to get 'em started back on their way again. Nobody was hurt or nothing—unless you count their pride, which was beaten to a bloody pulp. And for sure, nobody's claiming to have been one of them *on* the raid. Imagine getting bested by a sheepman!"

"If nobody's admitting to being on the raid, how do you know what happened?" Cassie asked, more confused than ever.

"Because Ferguson hisownself told us," Abby said, pointing toward the church door.

Sure enough, Duncan Ferguson was standing right there, big as you please, holding court for everybody who wanted to hear the story firsthand. Her heart stopped at the sight of him. Somehow he didn't seem little and skinny and helpless anymore. He wasn't any bigger, of course, and he was wearing the same suit she'd seen him wear to church before, but something about him had changed.

Or maybe *he* hadn't changed at all. Maybe it was just the way other folks were looking at him. The way *she* was looking at him, too. With respect. Of course, nobody could respect him for raising sheep; but everybody admired a man who stood up for himself . . . a man who wasn't about to be scared off his own land just because somebody else didn't like what he was doing there.

He glanced up at her then, as if he'd felt her staring at him, and his gaze locked with hers. For a long minute, Cassie didn't move, didn't even breathe. She could almost feel his arms around her and the way his lips had moved over hers, and she definitely felt the heat coming to her face. The heat of embarrassment and the same heat she'd felt when she'd been in his arms and then, quite suddenly, the heat of abject terror.

Had he told? Did everyone know who had warned him of the raid so he would be ready? Would everyone now shun her for betraying her own?

Somehow she tore her gaze from his and turned back to Abby. "How . . . how did he know about the raid?" she asked, her throat thick with fear.

"He won't say," Abby told her, a little disgusted. "He just says, 'A little bird told me.' And I don't guess anybody's gonna admit to that, either, so we'll prob'ly never know. It's a good story just the same, though, don't you think?"

Cassie didn't want to think about it at all, and fortunately, the church bell rang at that moment, summoning everyone inside. Cassie sat with Abby, finding a seat in the back so she wouldn't have to pass Duncan Ferguson or sit through the sermon wondering if he were watching her.

She watched him instead. He sat alone near the front, the way he usually did. Nobody wanted to share a pew with a sheepman, but he didn't seem to mind. And after the service was over—which seemed to take forever—Cassie noticed that a few folks went up and shook his hand. They weren't gonna invite him home to Sunday dinner, of course, but they were talking to him at least. If only he'd give up his fool notions about sheep, he might even be able to make a home here.

Why Cassie should care whether he did or not, she had no idea, but she found herself unaccountably annoyed with him for making himself an outsider. Plainly, he was tougher than she'd thought. Tougher than everyone else had thought, too, which meant he might make it out here after all. But not with sheep. Nobody would ever make it with sheep, not with the whole community against them.

Angry now, she hurried out of church and found her father before Duncan Ferguson could make his way out and encounter her.

"Let's go," she said to him. "I've got the headache."

He gave her a funny look. Cassie never got headaches or the vapors or any of the other maladies to which females were susceptible. She could see now that she hadn't done herself any favors by being so strong, because she didn't have any convenient feminine excuses to fall back on. She was afraid her father was going to ask her a lot of questions, but he just shrugged and followed her to their wagon.

He didn't say a thing until they were halfway home. "That was something what happened out at Ferguson's last night."

Cassie wondered what he expected her to say. "Sure was."

"Could've been real ugly if Ferguson hadn't been expecting trouble," he went on. "I heard about one sheepman got raided, they killed all his sheep. Slit their throats and even set some of 'em on fire. The wool burns pretty easy, I'm told."

Cassie stared at him in horror. "Was that what they was planning to do?"

Ron Plummer shrugged. "I'm just telling you what could've happened."

Cassie knew other things, worse things, could've happened, too. When men rode in a group, they sometimes did things none of them would have dreamed of doing alone. Even a man like Buck who was usually honest and true. Well, she'd have a talk with him about that, about how she expected him never to do such a thing again. And when they reached the house, she realized she'd have the opportunity for that talk very soon. Buck was sitting on the front steps, waiting for them.

Buck usually moved pretty slow, because he was so big, but today he moved even slower than usual; and when he started walking out to where her father had stopped the wagon by the barn, Cassie saw he was limping.

"What's wrong with you?" she asked in alarm when he was closer. She'd heard nobody'd been hurt, but plainly that wasn't quite right.

She saw his gaze dart around, as if checking to see if anybody was nearby to overhear. Which was silly, since he knew perfectly well all their cowboys were still off somewheres sleeping off their Saturday-night drunk.

When he'd satisfied himself that no one was around, he said, "I got roughed up some."

"When you fell off your horse?" she guessed, wishing she could feel more sympathy.

The blood came to his face, but he refused to be embarrassed. "You won't believe what that son of a . . . what he done," Buck snarled.

"I *know* what he done," Cassie informed him, "and so does everybody who went to church this morning: He set a trap and a bunch of polecats walked right into it."

Disgusted, Cassie strode toward the house, leaving Buck sputtering furiously behind her. He came in a few minutes later with her father, who'd unhitched the wagon and put the horses away. The men went out back to wash up while Cassie prepared the noon meal. She could hear the rumble of their voices, probably talking about the raid and maybe even about her, but she didn't want to know what they were saying. She'd already had enough grief from eavesdropping.

When she called them in to eat, they seemed to have

done talking, and for once Cassie was glad no one spoke during a meal. She ate mechanically, not even tasting the food she'd prepared so carefully. Even her apple pie tasted like sawdust today, and all because of Duncan Ferguson. He'd turned her whole world upside-down, made her turn against her own kind and even against the man she was going to marry, and what had she gotten in return? A kiss from a man who had no right to even touch her hand.

Well, she wasn't going to let him ruin her life. In fact, she was going to turn this to something good, because she was going to clear the air with Buck once and for all. The good life she'd planned with him would be even better because Buck was going to see her in a whole new light.

Cassie was planning to talk to him right after she finished the dishes, but Buck didn't leave when her father got up and went outside to smoke his pipe. Instead, he helped her clear the table and carry the dishes to the sink. He even hauled in a bucket of water for her, bad leg and all, without being asked.

All through dinner, Cassie had been trying to figure out what exactly she should say to Buck and whether she should confess to having been the one who warned Ferguson. But as he stood beside her at the sink, before she could even say the words she'd decided she would use to open the conversation, he said, "I know you was the one who warned Ferguson."

She gaped at him, mouth open, but she couldn't seem to speak.

"You was the only one it could be," he went on. "Your pa wouldn't've done it, no matter that he didn't like the idea, and nobody else even had a chance to tell anybody about it. So it had to be you."

She would have expected him to be mad, but he looked sad instead, maybe even disappointed. Cassie felt a twinge of guilt and an odd little urge to comfort him. "I'm sorry Buck, but I had to do it," she said. "I couldn't let you go out there and . . . well, anything could've happened. You might've got shot!"

Buck's eyes widened in surprise. "You was worried about *me?*" he asked incredulously.

"Well, sure," she said. It wasn't exactly a lie. She *had* thought about Buck's safety. She was sure she had. "I was afraid if you caught him by surprise, he'd start shooting; and knowing you, you'd be right up there in front and—"

"Oh, Cass, I never thought! I been imagining all sorts of things, but never that you was worried about *me!*"

"And I figured if Ferguson knew you was coming for him, he'd high-tail it out of the country!" That part was perfectly true, and she had no trouble at all looking Buck straight in the eye as she said it. "I never dreamed for one minute he'd stand and fight. And if I'd known what he was planning for you . . ."

Buck's gaze slid away. Plainly, he was embarrassed, probably even humiliated, about the way Ferguson had run them off. Cassie laid a hand on his arm. It felt like a tree limb, strong and sturdy. "I'm just glad you're all right," she said. "That's the important thing."

Cassie knew perfectly well it wasn't the *really* important thing, and so did Buck, put he seemed willing to pretend it was right along with her. He covered her hand with his own. "Just promise me you won't get mixed up in this again."

"Mixed up in what?" she asked a little suspiciously. "You ain't planning anything else, are you?"

"No more raids, if that's what you're thinking," he said grimly, "but Ferguson still ain't welcome around here. The sooner he finds that out, the better."

"How'll he find out?" Cassie asked, even more suspicious.

"When nobody'll talk to him or do business with him. He ain't one of us, and he'll learn it."

Cassie thought about how some of the folks had spoken to Ferguson after church this morning, but she didn't mention it to Buck. "All right then. And next time I give you some advice, you'd better listen," she said.

He grinned. "Will I have any choice?"

Cassie smiled back. "Not a bit."

"Well, then, we've got a deal."

Buck leaned down and kissed her, a quick little peck on the mouth that seemed to embarrass him because, when he pulled away, his face was red.

"Well, I . . . I reckon I'll leave you to your work then," he stammered, and he limped his way out of the kitchen.

When he was gone, Cassie reached up and touched her lips. They felt dry and cool, just like the rest of her. No tingle, no thrill, no nothing.

But that's the way it *should* be, she told herself sternly. Who could stand kissing if it was like a thunderstorm every time? Hadn't she already decided she didn't need any more excitement in her life? And she wouldn't get any so long as she stayed away from a certain sheepherder. Which shouldn't be too hard, she reasoned, since she had no intention of ever seeing him again.

But then the flowers started coming. Cassie found the first bunch on the back doorstep when she went out the next morning. Somebody had stuck them in some water in a tin can and set them there so she couldn't miss them when she made her first trip out to the privy.

It was just wildflowers, some bluebonnets and Indian paintbrush, but real pretty just the same. At first she thought Buck had left them. How sweet of him to do such a thing, and how unlike him. But then she started thinking about just *how* unlike him it was and remembering how once he'd made fun of her for killing flowers just so she could look at them in the house when all she had to do was go to a window to see them alive outside.

And when he came to supper that night, he made a face when he saw them sitting in the middle of the table. A few days later, just when the flowers were wilted and ready to be thrown out, Cassie again found a fresh bunch waiting for her on the back porch. And when she let herself start wondering just who else besides Buck would be giving her flowers, she only came up with one possibility.

How dare he! Who did he think he was? And exactly what did he think he was accomplishing? Well, the next time he brought her flowers she would be ready for him.

"Just what do you think you're doing?" Cassie demanded of the shadow on her back porch. It was late, about an hour after she'd put out the last light, and she'd guessed he'd be along any minute, figuring she and her Pa would be sound asleep.

"Cassandra!" he said right back, like they were meeting on the street in town instead of in the dark of night with him sneaking around like a thief. She heard the clunk as he set the can of flowers down. "I was hoping these flowers might soften you a little, but I never dreamed they'd work this fast."

She rose from where she'd been sitting at the end of the porch, waiting for him, and planted her hands on her hips. "What makes you think I'm soft?"

"I've felt you," he replied, a big smile in his voice.

Cassie's face went hot, but at least it was too dark for him to see it. "I'm not soft *on you,* if that's what you're thinking. Maybe you figure that just because I warned you—"

"Oh, no, I never presumed for a moment that you warned me because you liked me. But," he added after a second, "I did start to have suspicions after you kissed me."

Cassie stamped her foot in frustration. "I did *not* kiss you! *You* kissed *me!* Before I could stop you, too! And I should've slapped your face!"

"If you hadn't run off so fast, you could have," he reminded her. "What were you running from, Cassie?"

"You!" she told him honestly.

"Why? Did you think I'd do something you didn't like?"

She couldn't answer that question quite so honestly. "I . . . You had no right to kiss me."

"Why? Because you're engaged to Buck?"

"Yes!"

"He must be mad about you warning me. Or doesn't he know it was you?"

"He knows, and he forgave me," Cassie informed him smugly.

He was coming toward her in the dark, and Cassie resisted an urge to run. She wasn't afraid of him, and if he tried to kiss her again, all she had to do was holler and her pa would be here in a second.

"Why should he forgive you?" he was asking. "Did you do something wrong?"

"No!"

"Are you sorry you did it?"

"No!"

"Then why should Buck have to forgive you?"

Cassie didn't like the way he always twisted everything around. "I didn't mean that! He didn't forgive me, not exactly. He just said it didn't matter to him."

"Doesn't it matter that you kissed me?"

"He don't know that!" Cassie exclaimed, forgetting to remind him that he'd got it wrong again, that *she* hadn't kissed *him* at all.

"Why didn't you tell him?"

Why indeed? "To save your miserable life again, Sheepman! You don't know what he'd do to you if he found out you put your hands on me."

"I expect I know what he'd *try* to do," he said, as usual not taking any of this as seriously as he should. He probably still thought the raid was some kind of a joke, especially since he'd got the last laugh. "But that still doesn't explain why you haven't told him . . . why you care so much about what happens to me."

"It's not you! I'm just trying to keep Buck from getting into trouble." There, Buck had believed that story, so he should, too.

But he didn't. In fact, he laughed right out loud.

"Hush! You'll wake my pa!" she hissed.

"I guess you don't want *him* to know about us either."

She started to say she didn't want her Pa to have to beat him up, but then she realized he'd probably want to know why she cared. "Look," she tried, "why can't you just be like other people?"

"What do you mean?"

"I mean get rid of those sheep and raise cattle like a normal man."

"I'm already a normal man. You of all people should know that." He reached for her in the darkness, and Cassie's heart lurched to a dead halt in her chest.

"Don't!" she cried as he took hold of her.

"Don't what?" he asked, his hands warm against her arms. "Don't touch you?"

"Don't kiss me," she pleaded. The heat from his hands seemed to be melting her bones, and she knew she couldn't resist if he did.

"All right, I won't," he said, surprising her, but his hands were still on her, caressing her through the thin fabric of her sleeves. "God, you smell good," he whispered, his breath hot against her face. "Like flowers and sunshine. Why don't you want me to kiss you?"

"Because," she croaked, wondering what on earth could have happened to her voice. She had to clear her throat. "Because I'm going to marry Buck!"

"Do you love him, Cassandra? You always say you're going to marry him, but you never say you love him. Do you?"

"Sure I do!" she insisted. "Why would I marry him if I didn't?"

"I don't know, just like I don't know why you really don't want me to kiss you. A woman in love with another man would say she didn't like me or something. She'd have a *reason,* not an *excuse."*

"I have a reason!" she cried, even though she didn't know what on earth he was talking about.

"Are you afraid of me?"

"No!"

"Then why are you trembling?"

She hadn't known she was, but she was shaking like a leaf. She had to brace her hands against his chest to steady herself, and she could feel his heart thundering against her palms. The heat from his body seemed to envelop her, warming her from head to toe, and her own heart seemed determined to beat its way out of her chest. Maybe she *was* afraid of him.

"Please," she tried, not even knowing what she wanted.

"Please what? Tell me what you want me to do."

What *did* she want him to do? And what right did she have to ask him to do anything at all? "Please give up the sheep," she said, knowing that was the key to everything, because if he wasn't a sheepman and she didn't have to hate him, then everything would be all right somehow.

He sighed, his sweet breath washing over her, and his fingers tightened on her arms. "It's not the sheep, Cassandra. It's you. You're afraid to love me. I don't know why, but you are, and—"

"I'm not afraid!" she cried, wrenching away from him. "I'm not afraid of anything!"

"So you're going to marry a man you don't love so you'll be safe and never have to take a risk!"

"I'm not going to marry a lousy sheepherder and have everybody hate me for the rest of my life!"

"Is that it? Is that what you're afraid of?"

"I'm not afraid at all!"

"Aren't you?"

"Get out of here! I never want to see you again!" she screamed, forgetting that her father was asleep, forgetting everything but how desperately she wanted him gone, out of her life for good.

"All right," he said, his voice hoarse. "But if you change your mind, you know where to find me. I'll be on the other side of your fence, raising my sheep."

Cassie wanted to scream at him again, but he slipped away, into the night and vanished like a ghost. And then all she wanted to do was cry. Which was crazy! She *never* cried. Tears were weak, and Cassie wasn't weak, but she wasn't strong enough to stop these tears. They streamed down her cheeks as she sank down onto the porch and sobbed.

Damn him. Damn him to hell and back. And he hadn't even kissed her!

Cassie threw the flowers away, and even though she opened the back door every morning terrified of finding a new bouquet, none arrived. After a week, Cassie had pretty much decided Duncan Ferguson was out of her life for good. She was glad of it, too. Now everything would be just as it was before. Safe and sure and predictable. If she sometimes caught herself gazing out a window at Ferguson's cabin, well, that was just neighborly concern. Or maybe curiosity. She certainly didn't really care.

Then one night she woke up shivering in her bed. She'd left the window open to the spring breeze, but now that breeze had turned to a stiff north wind. She judged that the temperature had dropped at least thirty degrees, perhaps more, as the wind had shifted in the night, bringing a dreaded blue norther.

Typical March weather, she thought as she hurried across the icy floor to close the window and fetch an extra blanket from the chest at the foot of her bed. When she was tucked back into bed, snuggled down beneath the blankets and curled into a ball while she waited for her feet to thaw out again, she found herself thinking of Duncan Ferguson. She bet he'd never seen a norther before. Maybe he didn't have any idea of how quick they could come and how cold it could get in just a few hours.

Suddenly, Cassie felt cold *inside,* somewhere around her heart. She'd probably never know if the norther had surprised Ferguson because she'd probably never speak with him again. Which should have been a relief to her but just made her feel all funny and restless and kind of sad.

Then she heard the rain on the roof and knew they were in for it. The rain would probably freeze, making icicles on the trees and the eaves and glazing the grass. The cattle would be all right. They'd just turn tail to the storm and ride it out, then paw the ice off the grass tomorrow, if the sun didn't melt it. But she couldn't help wondering how sheep would fare . . . the delicate creatures that had to be watched and taken care of so diligently. With a sniff of disdain, she rolled over in her bed. It would serve Ferguson right if his sheep couldn't weather the storm, if they all died and he had to start over again.

The cold spot in her chest started to melt, and Cassie

felt a tiny warmth there, like an ember springing to life, and she recognized it as hope. If Duncan Ferguson's sheep died, he could raise cattle. He could be like everybody else and no one would hate him and she could . . .

She could what? she asked herself sternly. Love him? Marry him? She already loved somebody else and was going to marry *him,* wasn't she? Well, of course she was. But it wouldn't hurt a thing if Duncan Ferguson changed his ways so people would like him. She wanted that for him. She wanted him to be happy. There was nothing wrong with wanting him to be happy, was there? Cassie couldn't think of a single thing.

So in spite of the cold, Cassie was cheerful when she got up the next morning. She even hummed as she washed and dressed, shivering until she pulled on her longjohns and the woolen dress she'd already packed away for the summer. She could hear her father cursing the weather as she passed his bedroom door on her way to the kitchen, and she smiled to think of Duncan Ferguson waking to a world of ice.

Sure enough, everything shone in the feeble morning sunlight. Long icicles hung down outside her kitchen window, but they didn't obstruct the familiar view of Ferguson's cabin. As she did every morning, Cassie glanced out at it as she made her way to the back door for a trip to the privy, but what she saw stopped her in her tracks.

The cabin sat there on the horizon, just as it always did, but today she saw no smoke coming from the chimney. She always saw smoke as Ferguson cooked his breakfast. He always cooked his breakfast the same time Cassie did, so she knew the smoke should be there.

Oh, well, maybe he had overslept because of the cold. Maybe it had kept him from sleeping last night. Except if it had, he would have built a fire to keep himself warm. Telling herself it was none of her concern whether Duncan Ferguson had a fire or not, Cassie made her hurried trip outside, fetched a bucket of water, and carried it back in. But as she prepared breakfast, she kept glancing out the window, waiting to see the smoke that never appeared.

"What's wrong with you?" her father demanded grouchily halfway through the morning meal. "You keep jumping up and down like you got ants in your pants or something."

"Nothing's wrong with me," Cassie said, fighting the urge to jump up once again and look out the window. "It's just, well, I didn't see any smoke from Ferguson's cabin this morning. I was thinking maybe . . ." She let her voice trail off when she realized she hadn't let herself think about it at all.

"You think he ain't got sense enough to build a fire when it's cold?" her father asked incredulously.

"I was just thinking maybe something happened to him," she admitted, hating herself for even saying the words.

Ron Plummer made a rude noise. "If a man can't take care of himself through a norther, he ain't got no business out here at all."

He was right, of course, so Cassie forced herself to stay in her seat until she was finished eating and not to even look out the window again until she had the dishes in the pan and had started washing them. Then she glanced up, certain that by now Ferguson would be stirring, but still she saw nothing, not the slightest trace of smoke marring the pristine blue of the cold sky.

Cassie knew what she had to do, although she waited until her father and their men had left for the day's work to do it. No use letting everybody else know what a fool she was. Bad enough she knew it herself. She wrapped herself up in her wool coat and her hand-knitted scarf and headed for the barn.

Molly didn't want to go out into the cold, and she fought the saddle, forcing Cassie to take twice as long as she normally would have for the simple operation. By the time Cassie was on her way, she was ready to scream with impatience. Molly didn't want to walk on the icy ground, either, but Cassie coaxed her, and after a while the little mare warmed up and didn't seem to mind anymore.

Still, Cassie felt they moved with agonizing slowness. She watched Ferguson's chimney the whole way, willing the smoke to appear and knowing now that something must be terribly wrong. Nobody would be lying abed this long unless it was. Visions of Ferguson hurt or sick, unable even to get up out of bed, haunted her as she rode. Or maybe it was worse. Maybe . . . but surely, he hadn't frozen to death. It wasn't *that* cold. But death could come in many ways on the prairie to a man who lived alone, and by the time Cassie reached Ferguson's cabin, she had remembered every single one of them.

"Hello the house!" she called, repeating the cry when she got no answer the first time. The place looked deserted, as if Ferguson had picked up and moved on. Could that be it? Could the explanation be so simple? As she swung down from her mare, Cassie didn't know what she feared most: finding Ferguson sick or dead or finding that he'd left without even a word to her.

She didn't bother to wonder why she thought he should tell *her* if he were planning to leave. She just hurried to the cabin and banged on the door. Receiving no response, she threw it open.

"Duncan?" she called, fear tightening her throat as she stepped inside. Quickly, she found the bed in the corner of the room, but it was empty. Empty and neatly made, the colorful quilt pulled snug and tucked in tight.

Some clothes hung on pegs on the wall nearby, which meant he hadn't moved out, but he was nowhere in sight. A table sat in the center of the room, but it was scrubbed clean, the chairs pushed beneath it. The hearth was cold, but a fire had been laid, ready for a match to set it blazing.

He isn't here. He just isn't here, Cassie told herself, feeling the relief wash over her. But the relief gradually gave way to curiosity, and she looked around again. She hadn't seen the inside of his cabin when she'd been here before, and now she began to notice things she'd missed looking around a minute ago when she'd been so sure she'd find his cold, dead body lying on the bed.

The place was spotlessly clean: the floor swept, the bed made, the table cleared, and all the dishes washed and put away. She thought of Buck's cabin, which she'd glimpsed once or twice when she and her father had stopped by his place for something. A pigsty if she'd ever seen one. Which meant Buck needed a wife, and Duncan Ferguson obviously didn't.

There were pictures on the walls, too. Not the kind of pictures the men usually hung in the bunkhouse—drawings of scantily clad women torn from the pages of the *Police Gazette*—but real pictures somebody had painted, pictures of rolling green countryside the likes of which Cassie had never seen. They were in frames, too, fancy frames will all kinds of carving on them.

And then something else caught her eye. Several crates had been set on their sides and stacked against one wall to form crude shelves. On those shelves were books, dozens of books. Cassie had never seen so many all in one place before. As if drawn by an invisible force, she walked over to them. Some of them were old and worn, while others looked new and the gold letters on their spines shone in the morning sunlight.

Could Duncan have read all these books? It seemed

impossible to Cassie, who was unable even to read the titles. Oh, she could write her name, and read it, too, but that was about all. She didn't need to be able to do much more, did she? And neither did anyone else she knew. So what would one man need with so many books? Probably he was educated, she decided. She'd already suspected as much from the way he talked, and now she was sure. He'd gone to school and learned to read books.

And maybe he'd been to the places in the pictures that hung on the wall. She already knew he liked flowers, or at least that he understood women did. She wondered what it would be like to live with a man who didn't mind having pretty things around. A man who read books. A man who liked to talk.

Cassie felt a pang, as if she'd lost something, something very precious, but she couldn't imagine what that something could be. She hadn't lost anything at all, unless you counted Duncan Ferguson, who seemed to be among the missing at the moment.

And then Cassie had a brand new, very horrible thought. She had been so afraid she'd find Duncan here in his cabin, sick or hurt. that she'd forgotten he might just as well be sick or hurt out on the prairie somewhere! From the looks of this place, nobody'd been here all night, which meant Duncan might've been lying out in the dark in the freezing rain, all alone and dying!

She had to go look for him. She had to find him. But where to start? His spread was enormous, just as her father's was, big enough to run hundreds of head of cattle. Then she remembered the place where he and his men had been building those pens for lambing. Maybe they were still at it. Maybe at least somebody would be there who could give her an idea of where to look for Duncan. She ran for Molly.

The world looked like a jewel, glittering in the frigid

sunlight, but Cassie took no time to enjoy the beautiful sight. She leaned into the frigid wind and gave Molly her head as they raced for the only place she could think of where she might find a clue about Duncan Ferguson's whereabouts.

She didn't know exactly when she stopped worrying. Probably sometime after she saw the smoke from the fires the men had built around the lambing pens but before she was close enough to actually see all the activity there or even to hear the bleating of hundreds of sheep. She didn't actually feel good until she spotted Duncan Ferguson's red hair flashing in the sunlight, but then she felt as giddy as if she'd won first prize at the county fair.

He was all right. He was safe and sound and well and whole and working with his damn sheep. Cassie wanted to laugh out loud. What a fool he was. What a crazy fool to mess with animals who couldn't even take care of themselves in a silly little norther. Except when she got closer she saw that in among the big sheep were a lot of little sheep. Oh, dear heaven, the lambing had started!

Cassie left Molly ground-hitched at the edge of the camp and hurried to where she'd last seen Duncan. She found him in one of the sheds, shoving a sheep into one of the numerous stalls he and his men had built.

"Duncan!" she cried.

He looked up in surprise, and she saw his unshaven face was haggard, his eyes bloodshot. He hadn't slept, perhaps for days, and his clothes were damp and dirty. He stared at her for a long moment, as if unable to believe his eyes.

"Cassandra?" he said uncertainly.

"Yes, it's me," she assured him. "Are you all right?"

"If you're really here, I am. I was afraid I was beginning to hallucinate."

Cassie had no idea what that meant, but she figured it must be pretty bad. "What's going on?"

"The lambing started yesterday. Everything was fine until the weather turned bad. The worst thing that can happen to a newborn lamb is to get caught out in freezing rain. It'll chill down and die. We've been working all night, trying to get them under cover, but we can't keep up."

Cassie looked around. She saw the other men herding ewes into stalls and removing others with their newborn lambs. The lambs were so cute, and their bleating tore at her heart. How could anyone stand by and let the poor little things die? "Can I help?" she heard herself ask, completely forgetting how she'd wanted those poor little things to die just this morning.

Duncan blinked and shook his head slightly. "I must be delirious. I thought I heard you ask if you could help."

"I did," she said, blushing furiously. "It's . . . it's considered good manners to help your neighbors out when they're in trouble. Don't you know that?"

His beautiful mouth quirked into a grin. "Even if your neighbor is a sheepman?"

"I expect a sheepman gets in more trouble than most," she informed him tartly. "Now what can I do?"

He set her to work making breakfast, which no one had had time to do. She started with a big pot of coffee which she carried around to the men while the rest of the meal cooked. The herders, she discovered, were mostly Mexican and the rest were foreigners. No respectable white Texan would work sheep, after all. She couldn't understand what all of them were saying, but she had no trouble at all comprehending their gratitude for the coffee. When the food was ready, she called them in, and they took turns bolting down their meal so the sheep wouldn't be left completely unattended. Duncan Ferguson was the last to eat.

"I can't tell you how much it means to me to have you here," he said between bites as he hunkered down by the fire. The heat made steam rise from his wet coat.

"It's nothing," Cassie said, not quite able to meet his eye.

"What brought you out on a day like this, anyway? Did you know we were lambing?"

"No, I . . . no," she stammered, knowing she couldn't possibly tell him what had really brought her.

"Well, don't try to tell me you were just taking a ride on a day like this. Were you coming to pay me a visit?" he asked, his blue eyes sparkling with amusement or hope, she wasn't sure which.

"Certainly not!" she informed him, deciding the truth was probably better than what he was thinking. "I didn't see any smoke from your cabin this morning, and I was afraid something'd happened to you."

"You were worried about me?" He looked even more pleased than when he'd thought she'd just come to see him.

"Neighbors look after each other," she reminded him. "So don't go thinking it's anything else."

"What could I have thought it was?" he asked innocently.

He knew perfectly well what, and so did Cassie, but she wasn't about to remind him. "Better hurry up so you can get back to them sheep," she said, busying herself with cleaning up.

Turning away from him, she went to the chuck wagon, where the tailgate formed a worktable. She poured the water she'd been heating over the dirty dishes that had been stacked there in a pan and began to wash them. She had almost convinced herself she'd forgotten he was there when he laid a hand on her shoulder.

She jumped, almost upsetting the dishpan, but she managed to grab it in time.

"Sorry," he said, slipping his dishes into the water but not removing his hand from her shoulder. It seemed to burn right through the thickness of her coat.

She hazarded a glance up at him. When had he gotten so tall? She hadn't realized he was tall. Not like Buck, of course, but still a lot bigger than she'd remembered. His unshaved beard glinted red against his fair skin, and his blue eyes shone in a way that made her knees feel weak.

"I'm awfully glad you're here, Cassandra. I was afraid you really *didn't* want to ever see me again."

Cassie had no idea what to say to that, even if her mouth hadn't been much too dry for her to say anything at all. But probably he could hear her heart pounding like a sledge, because he smiled that beautiful smile of his and squeezed her shoulder, then he went back to his damn sheep.

Cassie finished cleaning up, not letting herself think about how Duncan Ferguson made her feel every time he came anywhere near her. When she was done, she found some more supplies in the wagon and set some beans on to boil for the noon meal. At least they won't go hungry again, she thought, figuring she'd done what she could here. She'd better get on back home before anybody noticed she was gone.

But of course, she couldn't leave without saying good-bye to Duncan. That would be rude. She found him in one of the sheds. He was hunkered down, doing something, and she couldn't see what until she was standing right over him.

"What kind of man are you?" she demanded in outrage when she saw he was skinning a little dead lamb. She had to shout to make herself heard over the bleating of hundreds of sheep. "Are you so greedy you even want the pelt off that poor little thing?"

He looked up at her, his eyes bleary with fatigue, and she instantly regretted yelling at him. "No, I'm not that greedy," he said wearily, lifting the skin away from the lamb's carcass.

Before she could imagine what he was about, he carried it over to where another lamb, this one very much alive, was bleating pitifully over its dead mother's body. Quickly, he wrapped the skin around the living lamb and tied it in place, then picked up the wailing lamb and carried it to one of the stalls where a ewe was wailing equally loud. She was, Cassie quickly understood, the mother of the dead lamb.

He presented the wrapped lamb to the ewe, tail first. She sniffed it suspiciously, then bleated with joy and stood patiently while the lamb began to root around and finally to nurse.

"They'll only accept their own lambs, and they know their scent," he told Cassie, never taking his eyes off the newly matched pair. "So you have to trick them. After a few days, we can take the skin off the lamb, and they'll get along just fine."

He must have been doing this all night, Cassie thought, matching orphans with new mothers by skinning off the dead babies. How awful for him. Cassie laid a hand on his arm, offering what comfort she could.

He looked down at her hand in surprise, then into her face. His eyes were full of pain that Cassie wanted to share.

"What can I do to help?" she asked again.

"You've already helped enough," he told her. "You don't have to stay any longer."

"But I want to! And don't tell me to cook some more. I already started your dinner, so there's nothing to do for a few more hours. Meanwhile, I can help with the sheep, can't I? Just show me what to do."

"Well, if you really want to . . ." he said doubtfully.

"I do!"

Cassie soon had reason to regret her generosity. Sheep, she quickly decided, were the stupidest animals God had ever made. They didn't have the sense to do anything that was good for them except maybe eat and sleep, but neither of those things was what Cassie was supposed to make them do.

She helped herd the ewes who were obviously in labor into the stalls where they would be sheltered from the weather and in which they could not turn around and thus deny their milk to their newborns, as some of them would if given the choice. The ewe would stay in the stall until she had bonded with her lamb and the baby was nursing well. Then the pair would be moved to a shed where the baby would be warm and dry, protected from the fatal chilling down.

But they didn't always catch the ewes in time, and some gave birth on the cold ground where the lambs, if not found quickly enough, were certain to die. And some of the older ewes succumbed to the weather as well, falling where they stood. Sometimes they could save her lamb and sometimes they couldn't. It was a sad and bloody business. Too often Cassie thought she'd seen a lamb safely delivered, only to find it dead later, its mother bleating over its lifeless body with a cry that sounded all too much like a human mother's.

At some point, Cassie served the men their dinners, carrying the plates to where they worked and pouring cup after cup of coffee for them throughout the day. Time passed in a blur of activity, and when she heard someone calling her name, she had long since been numbed by fatigue and the cold.

"Cassie? Where are you, girl?"

It sounded like her pa, but what would he be doing here? Wearily, Cassie turned from where she'd been getting one more ewe into a stall; and sure enough, there was Pa, looking really mad.

No, she decided when he came a little closer, not mad exactly. Scared was more like it. But why should he be scared?

"What in the hell are you doing here?" he demanded, planting his hands on his hips.

She judged how upset he was by the fact that he'd never sworn at her before. She drew a weary breath and tried to explain. "I came and the lambs were dying. Because of the weather. They chill down and die unless you get them under cover; and nobody'd had any breakfast, so I cooked for them, and then I couldn't leave, not with the babies dying like that, so I stayed to help and—"

"All right, all right," Pa said, holding up his hands in surrender. Cassie knew it wasn't really all right, because she knew she hadn't been making any sense so he couldn't possibly understand, but she was too tired to argue.

"Mr. Plummer," Duncan called, hurrying over. He looked even worse than he had when Cassie had found him this morning. The circles under his eyes were like bruises. "My God, I didn't realize how late it was. I would have made Cassie go on home. I tried to get her to leave right after breakfast, but she wanted to help and—"

"I can see that," he said, glancing at Cassie's coat, which was now just as filthy as Duncan's. "I was just a little worried is all. I came home and Cassie wasn't there, so I sent my men out to look for her. Then I remembered how she was fretting this morning because you didn't have a fire in your cabin, so I figured I'd check to see if she'd been by this way." He turned back to Cassie. "You scared the bejeepers out of me, girl," he told her indignantly.

"I'm sorry, Pa." So that's what he was. Scared. Cassie could hardly believe it. Didn't he know she could take care of herself? "But I couldn't leave. They needed help and—"

"I understand," Pa said, and Cassie could see he did.

"Thanks for everything," Duncan said to her. "I really appreciate it and—"

"I'm not leaving yet!" she informed him. "It's almost nightfall, and it ain't getting any warmer out here. The lambs that come now'll be in more danger than ever." She turned to her father. "Pa, you go on home. I'll be all right."

Ron Plummer looked at his daughter as if she'd lost her mind. "I ain't leaving you here."

Cassie was bracing herself for a fight, but her father turned to Duncan.

"I can see you've got bad trouble. I don't know a damn thing about sheep, but I figure if Cassie can help, I can, too. Just what is it you folks are doing?"

Quickly, Duncan explained. "I really appreciate it, Mr. Plummer. I know how you feel about sheep and—"

"Shut up, boy, and get out of my way. I've just got to send my foreman on home to tell the others to stop looking for Cassie, and then I'll get to work. Cassie, why don't you go make some fresh coffee and drink about a gallon of it yourself? You look like a good stiff wind'll knock you over."

"Yes, sir," Cassie said. Her eyes had gotten so wide with amazement, she was afraid they'd fall out of her head, so she blinked and hurried away to the chuck wagon.

Along about sundown, another rider approached the camp, but Cassie didn't notice him until her father nudged her and pointed. They were standing out in the field, looking for ewes that appeared to be in labor, when she turned and saw Buck Ewing levering his bulk off the back of his long-suffering horse. Cassie had no trouble at all identifying *his* expression. He was just plain furious.

Her father saw it, too. "If you want, I can—" he began, but Cassie cut him off.

"I'll handle it." She glanced around, looking for Duncan. The one thing she didn't want was a confrontation between the two of them since Duncan was bound to come out with the short end of that stick. Not seeing him—he must be in one of the sheds, she decided—she hurried to meet Buck, who was now striding purposefully toward her.

Cassie thought of a dozen things to say to him, but she knew none of them would calm him down any and she wasn't about to say the one thing that would. "Buck, I—" she started, not knowing where she was going, but he didn't give her a chance to go anywhere at all.

"Just what in God's good name do you think you're doing out here, Cassie Plummer?" he demanded. She'd never seen his face that color of purple before. She had to swallow once, before she could reply.

"I'm helping out our neighbor. He's got trouble, as you can plainly see. If we don't get these lambs under cover, they'll chill down and—"

"I don't give a damn about no lambs. In fact, I'd like it just fine if every last one of them died right here, which is why I don't like it at all that you're making sure they don't. Now I don't want no argument from you," he said, raising his hand to silence her sputter of protest. "I just want you to get on your horse and go home with me right now, and I'll forget this ever happened."

Cassie gaped at him. *He'd forget it ever happened?* Like she'd done some sin he had to forgive. Then she remembered what Duncan had said about Buck forgiving her for warning him about the raid. She hadn't done anything then that needed forgiving and she hadn't done anything now that needed it either.

"I ain't going nowhere," she informed him. "There's work to be done, and I'm doing it."

"Did you forget whose woman you are?" he asked, taking hold of her with his big hands. His fingers closed around her arms like vises, and she could practically feel her flesh bruising beneath them. "You're *my* woman, and you'll do as I say, and I say you're leaving here right now!"

His eyes were mean little slits in his broad face, his lips almost white with fury, but for some reason Cassie wasn't the least bit afraid. Instead, she was mad, just plain old ordinary mad. "Take your hands off me, Buck Ewing!" she said right back to him. "I'm not your woman yet, and I won't belong to any man who thinks he can order me around and make me do what he wants just because he's bigger and stronger!"

Buck reared back at that, like he'd been punched right between the eyes, and he released her like she'd suddenly turned red hot beneath his palms. "Jeez, Cassie, what's got into you?"

"What's got into *you?*" she shot back. "I've never known you to turn your back on anybody in trouble before."

"This ain't got nothing to do with that and you know it," he informed her. "You've took to protecting Ferguson like he was something to you. Something important, maybe more important than me. Is he?"

"Don't be a fool!" she said, wishing her face wasn't as red as she knew it was.

"If that's really the way you feel, you'll come with me now."

"Are you saying I've gotta choose between you?" she asked incredulously.

"If that's the way it is, then yes."

But Cassie wasn't going to stand for any such thing. "That's *not* the way it is. The way it is is that I'm helping a neighbor out; and if you don't like it, you don't have to watch. Nobody invited you here, Buck Ewing; so if you're not going to help, you can leave any time."

Buck's eyes were mean little slits again. "If I leave you here, you might not see me again."

The possibility should have frightened her or at least disturbed her. Their wedding was only weeks away, after all; but she just felt angry that he would threaten her. "I'll have to take that chance, won't I? Now I've got work to do, and I'm going to do it."

She turned on her heel and started out to the field where her father was waiting and watching. She half expected Buck to call her back or even to grab her and drag her away. He was certainly capable of it, and she would have been powerless to stop him if he'd tried. But he let her go; and when at last she dared glance over her shoulder at him, he was mounting his horse.

Duncan had just come out of the shed where he'd been working, and he stopped dead in his tracks when he caught sight of Buck. His gaze darted instantly to Cassie, who glared back defiantly. Was he going to get all puffed up now and think she'd sent her fiancé packing over him?

As Buck rode away, Duncan hurried over to where Cassie stood, but his expression was far from triumphant. "What happened? Did you—?"

"He wanted me to leave, and I told him I wouldn't," she said, figuring that was all he needed to know.

"But—"

"I got work to do," she said again and left him gaping after her.

But she still had to face her father, who was waiting for her.

"Well, is the wedding still on?" he asked with deceptive mildness.

"If he tells me he's sorry, it is," Cassie replied, not quite meeting his eye. She thought he gasped in surprise, but she didn't look to make sure. "That one's ready to go," she said, pointing out a ewe in apparent distress, and she went back to work.

The work was a blessing, keeping her too busy to think and too tired to worry. Any other girl would have been nearly hysterical to think her intended had walked out on her just weeks before their wedding, but at the moment Cassie didn't have time to even realize what this might mean to her. She had more important things to worry about, life and death struggles that even distracted her from Duncan Ferguson's speculative glances.

By full dark, Duncan and his men were ready to drop from exhaustion with a second sleepless night stretching before them and the lambs coming even faster now. The night wind had picked up, ready to snatch away the life of any lamb within its grasp. Cassie didn't know how they were going to make it when she saw several men ride up.

For a minute, she was afraid Buck had returned and brought some friends who would undo all the work they'd done to save the lambs, but when they reached the circle of light from the fire, she recognized the riders as some of the Plummers' cowboys. They dismounted, looking around suspiciously and ducking their heads as if they were embarrassed.

"This is all that would come," Ned Yates told Ron Plummer. Ned was the Plummers' foreman.

"Ferguson," Ron called, summoning Duncan from his work. "These here are some of my men. They come to help out."

Duncan looked as if his eyes would bug out in surprise, but he'd learned his lesson about showing too much gratitude. "That's real fine," he said after he'd swallowed once or twice. "I'll show you what to do."

"We ain't never worked sheep before," Ned wanted him to know.

"It ain't hard," Ron offered. "If Cassie got the hang of it, I reckon you boys can, too." He ignored Cassie's black look.

Soon the Plummer cowboys were herding sheep with the best of them; and when they were, Ron suggested that Duncan and his men take a few hours' rest. Duncan was the last to lie down. Cassie didn't know how he found the strength to walk as he made his weary way over to the chuck wagon for his bedroll.

He stopped beside where she sat by the fire, nursing a cup of coffee. "Cassandra," he began, but she cut him off, afraid of what he might say and even more afraid of what he might ask.

"Better get some rest, now. You've got a lot of lambs to take care of tomorrow." She smiled up at him, thinking how handsome he was even if he did look like he'd been rode hard and put away wet.

"Thanks to you," he said. "There are some things I want to say to you, but they can wait until this is over."

She nodded. They'd wait longer than that, if she could help it. "Go on, now."

He stumbled off to find a smooth spot to spread his blankets. Cassie didn't let herself watch him, didn't let herself think about how nice it would be to curl up with him in those blankets and feel his mouth on hers. Such thoughts would've been sinful even if she *wasn't* engaged to another man, which of course she might not be.

Gulping down the last of her coffee, she hurried away to see what needed to be done. The night wore on in the same way the day had. Lambs continued to arrive, and more than once she heard a cowboy muttering about how much he hated sheep. Cassie hated them, too, almost as much as she liked the frisky little lambs that they managed to save from the icy wind. But complaints or not, no one quit. All the cowboys who had come to help were still there when the wind changed.

Cassie didn't notice it at first, at least not consciously. She was too busy herding reluctant sheep to the safety of the birthing pens. But as she entered one of the sheds, a huge drop of water plopped smack down on top of her head.

Muttering a curse, she swatted the water away before it could soak through her scarf; and when she looked up to see if the rain had started again, another drop caught her in the eye.

Scuttling out from under the eaves of the building, she saw the water had come from the icicles, which were beginning to melt. A quick glance around told her the melting was going on everywhere.

"Pa!" she called. "It's warming up!"

"I know!" he called back. "Better tell Ferguson. He'll want to know."

Duncan, like the rest of his men, was still asleep. Duncan had insisted that Ron promise to only let them sleep a couple of hours, but no one had awakened them since they weren't really needed for anything. But Cassie knew Duncan would want to know the good news immediately. Once the temperature rose above freezing, the lambs would no longer be in great danger; and if it got truly warm, they'd be in no danger at all.

She hurried to where he slept outside the circle of light from the fire. When she found him, she almost changed her mind about waking him. He slept flat on his back, probably still in the same position he'd been in when he first lay down, and he looked so peaceful, she didn't want to disturb him. If she'd had bad news, she certainly wouldn't have, either. But he wouldn't want to sleep through this. She knelt down beside him.

"Duncan," she said softly, not wanting to startle him. He didn't move.

"Duncan, wake up," she said a little louder, laying a hand on his shoulder and giving him a gentle shake.

His eyes flew open. They looked black in the shadows. "You're so beautiful, Cassandra," he said, his voice thick with sleep, and Cassie blushed furiously.

"You're dreaming!" she said, shaking him again. "Wake up!"

"I *am* awake," he said. He smiled then, his teeth flashing white in the darkness. "And you're still beautiful. Say my name again. I love the way you say it."

"Duncan," she said obediently, "the wind changed. It's from the south. It's getting warmer already. Can you feel it?"

He scrambled up into a sitting position, throwing his blankets aside. "It *is* warmer," he cried. "Look, the ice is melting."

"It's already off the grass," she told him. "By sunup, it'll be completely gone."

"Thank God," he breathed, struggling to his feet. "Thank God!" He reached down and pulled Cassie up beside him. "Do you know what this means? I'm going to make it! I really am! Oh, Cassandra, I love you!"

Before she could even think, he threw his arms around her and swung her around, laughing like a crazy man. Then he set her on her feet and kissed her square on the mouth. Caught up in his happiness, she kissed him back, wrapping her arms around his neck and holding him like she'd never let him go.

The kiss went on and on, until Cassie thought she'd faint from the shear joy of it, but finally, he tore his mouth from hers. "Oh, darling," he whispered breathlessly.

Oh, Lord! she thought. Is this what it's like? Is this how love feels? She felt helpless and invincible, silly and wise, happy and terrified. And oh, so wonderful in Duncan's arms.

"Ferguson?" her father's voice called. "Did Cassie tell you?"

They broke guiltily apart just as her father reached them, but not soon enough because he must've seen something. "Oh, sorry," he mumbled, his sharp gaze moving from Cassie to Duncan and back again. "I reckon you know."

"Yes, sir, I do. I can't thank you enough for what you did. The lambs you saved might make the difference between me going bust or making a profit." He shook her father's hand, although Ron's gaze kept slipping back to Cassie questioningly. She only hoped he couldn't hear the way her heart was pounding or see how red her face must be.

"Yeah, well, I just hope you won't go telling folks I helped save sheep. It might ruin my reputation," Ron said, only half in jest.

"I won't tell a soul," Duncan promised.

For a long moment, no one spoke, even though Cassie could see her father wanted to know just what had been going on before he walked up. Neither she nor Duncan offered any explanation, though, and of course Ron was too embarrassed to ask outright.

After the silence had become awkward, Duncan finally found his tongue. "Well, now, look how late it is. You should've woken me up. I never intended to sleep so long. I better go check on the sheep, see how they're doing."

He strode away, leaving Cassie to face her father alone.

"Cassie?" he asked, the word a whole slew of questions, none of which Cassie had any intention of answering.

"I better make some coffee," she said and scurried away like the coward she was. Maybe by the time she had to face him again, she would have thought of something to say that would make sense to him.

Meanwhile, she had to think of something that made sense to *her*. If she truly did love Buck and want to marry him, how come she'd deliberately picked a fight with him over a bunch of sheep? And how come she found herself kissing Duncan Ferguson practically every time he came near her? And had he really meant he loved her just now or was that just something he'd said because he was so happy that his sheep were saved? And what if she did decide not to marry Buck? Did Duncan Ferguson really want to marry her or had he just been teasing as she'd firmly believed up until now? And if he *was* serious, did *she* want to marry *him?* Good heavens, she hardly even knew him!

The more she tried to find the answers, the more confused she became. By dawn her head was aching as much from the puzzle of Duncan Ferguson as from the sleepless night she'd had. When she'd gotten breakfast started, she sank down beside one of the wheels of the chuck wagon and closed her eyes against the pounding of her temples.

When she opened them again, Duncan Ferguson was just inches away, his beautiful smile shining out from his unshaven whiskers. His eyes were so blue and clear she wanted to cry, although she had no idea why such a thing should move her to tears.

"It's time for you to go home, sweetheart," he said softly so that only she could hear. "But don't worry, I'll come for you just as soon as I can."

Cassie was sure she must be dreaming, but then her father was there, helping her to her feet. "Do you think you can ride?" he asked gently. He hadn't spoken to her in that tone of voice since she'd been a little girl.

"Of course I can ride," she told him, although she was dismayed by how faint her voice sounded.

"Maybe I should . . ." Duncan began, but Ron cut him off.

"She'll be fine, won't you, Cassie-girl?"

"Sure I will." She even managed a smile for Duncan. "Take care of those sheep now."

His answering smile was so sweet it made her ache. "I will," he promised.

Their cowboys were leaving as well, she saw when she reached her mare, who had been waiting patiently for almost twenty-four hours for her mistress to return. The boys were already mounted and ready to go. Pa helped her up into her saddle, something he hadn't done in years, and Cassie thought she should probably protest. She would have, too, if she'd had the slightest hope she could have gotten up by herself. As it was, she barely made it. Then they were riding away.

She looked back and saw Duncan waving, his red hair bright in the morning sun. Already her coat felt too hot, so she knew it would be a beautiful day. A beautiful day for the lambs, who wouldn't die. Duncan would be all right now. She'd seen to it. If she could never give him anything else, she'd given him that.

Cassie fell into bed as soon as she'd stripped off her filthy clothes, and she slept until nearly sundown. She woke starving and sore. Somehow she staggered out of bed, then splashed cold water on her face from the pitcher in her room. She needed a hot bath and a square meal. The meal would have to come first. And after that . . . well, after that Cassie would have to figure out what she was going to do with the rest of her life.

She brushed out her hair and threw a robe on over her nightdress. Pleased to see the warm weather had held—the breeze coming in her window was heavenly, which meant Duncan's lambs would be just fine—she made her way to the kitchen. There she found her father sitting at the table nursing a cup of coffee. He looked as if he'd just gotten up, too.

"There's some bacon in the pan," he said.

Cassie sliced herself some bread and drizzled the bacon grease over it, then carried her makeshift meal to the table.

You look some better," her father remarked as she sat down across from him.

She just nodded, not knowing what to say, and started eating. He let her finish before he said, "That boy Ferguson, he's got sand."

The ultimate compliment. Her father liked Ferguson and thought he was a real man. Well, he was. She'd been wrong about him, too, but she knew the truth now.

She was just about to say so when her father added, "Too bad he runs sheep."

She swallowed her own words. Nothing she could say would change that, and the sheep were the important thing, the thing that kept him from being one of them and always would. No matter how much respect he might earn, no matter how tough he might be, he'd still be a sheepherder.

"That was real nice, what you done for him," she ventured, wondering if there were some way around it. After all, her father and his men had helped save Duncan's sheep. Maybe . . .

Her father shook his head. "If you ride up and see your neighbor's barn is on fire, you help put out the fire even if you don't like your neighbor. You hope he'd do the same for you, too, but that don't make you friends. Some of our men, the ones who didn't help, are real mad that the rest of us did. They might even quit over it. And for sure other folks won't like it. One in particular I'm thinking about is already pretty mad that his girl was over there."

Cassie nodded, dropping her gaze. In the light of day,

she felt the heavy lump of sadness she should have felt yesterday after her fight with Buck.

"Cass, is there something you need to tell me?" her pa asked.

"What do you mean?" she asked uneasily.

"I mean, it looked to me like you was kissing Ferguson when I walked up to tell him the weather had broke."

Cassie's face caught fire, but she shook her head. "Oh, no, he just . . . well, I reckon he was so happy about the news, he picked me up and hugged me; but it wasn't nothing romantic or anything."

"Maybe not for you, but that boy's sweet on you, as anybody with eyes can see; and if you don't feel the same way, you'd best not give him reason to think you do."

"How could I?" Cassie asked, appalled. "I'm going to marry Buck!"

"Are you?"

Cassie realized she could no longer be sure of that. After the way she'd defied him, he probably wouldn't have her at all. Of course, if he really loved her . . . "He's still got a chance, like I said. If he says he's sorry . . ."

Her father frowned. "And maybe you're hoping he won't because maybe you've changed your mind about him. You wouldn't be the first girl who did, you know. Have you?"

"I . . . no! Of course not!" But had she? She simply didn't know.

And she could see her father wasn't convinced, either. "Shoot," he said shaking his head. "I wish your mother was here. She'd know what to tell you."

This was the second time her father had mentioned her mother, and again it unnerved Cassie. "Nobody needs to tell me nothing!"

"I think they do. I think you're wondering if Duncan Ferguson would be a better husband than Buck Ewing."

"How could he? He's a sheepman!" There, she'd said it, and she could see from her father's face that he understood completely.

"That's right, he is," he said, proving it, but then he surprised her. "What you've got to decide is whether that matters more than what you feel in your heart."

Cassie could only gape at him. What did he know about her heart? What did *anyone* know?

This was the longest conversation Cassie could ever remember having with her father; and it was so disturbing, she could only be glad she'd never had any others.

"I . . . I need a bath," she said, knowing she was being a coward but not caring. She needed some privacy now more than anything.

He nodded, understanding her need perhaps more than she did, and left her alone in the kitchen. But privacy didn't help much, and long after Cassie had bathed and gone back to bed, she still hadn't made any sense of her feelings. With Duncan, she felt things she'd never felt before, but those things frightened her almost as much as his being different frightened her. Buck wasn't very exciting, but he offered stability and security and all the things she'd always thought she wanted. But did she even have a choice? Buck wasn't speaking to her, and Duncan Ferguson hadn't even really proposed to her, had he?

And then she remembered what Duncan had said just as she was leaving his place. "I'll come for you." Had he really meant that? And what would she do if he did?

Two days passed without any word from Buck. With the wedding less than two weeks away, his silence should have upset Cassie; but she only felt numb, as if the fatigue of tending the sheep had never quite lifted. If Buck didn't come to make up with her soon, she would have to let people know that the wedding was off. She would be embarrassed, even humiliated, but would she mind? Did she even still want to marry Buck at all? Cassie found herself hoping he wouldn't come just so she wouldn't have to decide.

And then a suitor did show up, but it was the wrong one. The evening of the second day, while Cassie and her father were sitting on the front porch, she saw a lone rider approaching the ranch. She knew him instantly, long before she could make out his features or even the glint of his red hair beneath his hat. Duncan Ferguson had come for her.

"Looks like we got company," her father observed around the stem of his pipe.

Cassie rushed inside, not bothering to ask herself why she was suddenly so concerned about her appearance. She never primped when Buck was coming, but this was different. She didn't bother to ask herself why.

By the time Duncan Ferguson had ridden up to the porch, Cassie was back in her chair again, sitting primly with her hair carefully tucked and combed into place and her cheeks pinched to pinkness. She only wished she could put the inside of herself into order so easily.

"Good evening, folks," Duncan said, stopping his horse at the hitching post but making no move to get down until he was invited. He was wearing his Sunday-go-to-meeting suit and a crisp, white shirt with a brand new collar.

" 'Evening," her father said. "Get down and set a spell. How about some coffee?"

"Not right now, thanks," Duncan said. He swung down from his horse and tied the reins, carefully not looking at Cassie through the whole procedure. Which was fine with her, since she was finding it more and more difficult to breathe with each passing second.

Then, just when she was expecting him to turn to her, he started rummaging in his saddlebag for something. He brought out a small square package wrapped in brown paper and tied up with string. It looked like a present. Cassie couldn't imagine whom it was for.

He was smiling when he finally came up the porch steps, and now he was looking at her, although he spoke to her pa.

"I'm sorry I couldn't get over sooner, but I've been pretty busy with the lambing. Things have settled down some though, and I figured my men could handle it for a while so I could come over and thank you folks for what you did."

"That's what neighbors are for," Ron Plummer said, and Cassie felt his gaze on her, too. He knew as well as she did that this wasn't just a social call.

"Mr. Plummer, I know you're a smart man, and you do what you have to, so I know you won't take offense at what I'm going to say," Duncan went on, and now he was looking at her father, much to Cassie's relief. She found it so awful hard to breathe when he was looking at her. "A lot of cattlemen in other parts of the state have started running a few sheep along with their cows because they've discovered they like the extra income the sheep bring in. It helps them out when beef prices are low."

"Is that a fact?" her father said. He sounded interested.

"Yes, sir," Duncan assured him. "I've got some information on it back at my house, if you're interested. Anyway, I won't insult you by offering to pay you for your help the other day; but I want you to know that if you ever decide you're interested in sheep, I'd be proud to give you the start of a flock."

Well, now, if that wasn't the most outlandish offer Cassie had ever heard! She half expected her father to come flying out of his chair and punch Duncan Ferguson in his smart mouth, but she should've known her pa was too much of a gentleman to do any such thing. Instead he just puffed on his pipe for a minute like he was really thinking it over.

"That's a mighty interesting offer, young fella," he said at last. "I'd like to think on it some." Pa was even too polite to refuse it outright.

"Certainly, sir. Take as long as you like." He grinned. "Thanks to you, I'll be around for a good while."

Cassie had just started to breathe normally, figuring he'd forgotten all about her, when he turned those sparkly blue eyes on her again.

"I've taken the liberty of expressing my gratitude to your daughter in a more immediate way," he said. "This is for you."

He handed her the package. Cassie took it automatically, even though she knew that was a mistake. She shouldn't be taking presents from other men. If Buck was mad now, just wait till he heard about this!

"What is it?" she asked suspiciously.

"Open it and see," Duncan suggested.

She shouldn't do it. She knew that, but her fingers untied the string all the same, and the paper fell away to reveal a book.

A book! Cassie had never owned a book. Oh, the family had a Bible and her pa read to her out of it sometimes, but she'd never owned a book all her own. It was pretty, too . . . red leather cover with shiny gold letters stamped on the spine.

"What is it?" she asked.

"It's a book," he told her, plainly amused.

"I know that," she informed him. "I mean, what kind of book?"

"It's a book of poetry, one of my favorites. I marked a few I thought you'd like," he said, pointing to some scraps of paper sticking out of the top. "I wrote something in the front, too."

Cassie stared at the book lying in her lap. A book of poetry that he'd thought she'd enjoy because he didn't know she couldn't read, a book he'd written something in that she couldn't read either. She laid her hand on it. The leather was smooth and cool beneath her fingers. She felt a stinging in her cheeks, and the book seemed to blur before her.

As if from a distance, she heard her father say, "I reckon I'll go inside for a spell."

Coward, she thought as the screen door closed behind him, wishing she could run away, too. Well, she supposed this was for the best. If Buck had eliminated one of her choices, she might as well eliminate the other one, too.

"I can't read," she said.

"What?"

She cleared her constricted throat and tried again. "I don't know how to read."

She hadn't dared look at him while she said it; but when he didn't respond, didn't gasp or anything, she had to glance up. At least he wasn't glaring at her with contempt. He was only surprised.

"I had no idea. You're so smart that naturally I thought—"

"I'm not smart! I'm stupid! I just told you, I can't even read!"

"Not being able to read doesn't have anything to do with whether you're smart or not. And you're not stupid; you're just ignorant. Nobody ever taught you how, but I could teach you, Cassandra. In fact, I can only think of one or two things I'd enjoy more."

His grin was so wicked, she had to ask, "What things?"

"Oh, that'll have to wait until we're married."

Cassie felt a funny little flutter in the pit of her stomach, but she ignored it. "I never said I'd marry you. I'm already promised to—"

"To Buck Ewing, I know," he finished for her, but he didn't seem too concerned. Probably, he figured that after their fight, Buck wasn't a consideration anymore. "I realize I'm asking a lot of you, Cassandra. We haven't known each other very long, but I think we know each other pretty well. After the other day, when we worked side by side for all those hours, well, I've never known another woman who could do what you did. You worked around the clock and never complained once, and you weren't even getting anything out of it. It was all for me. Let me pay you back. Let me make you happy every day for the rest of your life."

"How could you do that?" Cassie had no idea.

"By teaching you to read. By teaching you all the things you don't know about. And by loving you. I do love you, sweetheart. I fell in love with you that very first day in the store when you turned up your pretty little nose at me for being a sheepman; and everything I've seen of you since has only made me love you more. Let me show you. Let me prove it to you."

It was tempting, so tempting. And there was more, things he didn't even suspect. She thought of the pictures in his cabin that proved his love of beauty, and his way with words that could fill the silence of the long evenings that would make up their life together. She ached with longing for the future she saw and had never dreamed she could have. Only one thing stood in her way.

"Would you . . . would you do something for me?" she asked, hardly daring to breathe for fear that he would refuse.

"Anything, my darling girl, anything in the world!" he promised recklessly.

"Would you give up your sheep?"

His beautiful smile vanished. "What?"

"You could raise cattle!" she hurried on, desperate now to convince him. "You already do! All you'd have to do is get rid of the sheep! Then everybody would like you. They already know what kind of man you are; and if you'd give up the sheep, you'd be one of us for sure! Nobody'd ever refuse to speak to you on the street or sit with you in church or—"

"I don't care about any of that! I don't care what people think of me or say about me behind my back, and neither should you! What matters is doing what you think is right so you're not ashamed to look yourself in the mirror every morning. I respect myself, and that's the only opinion that matters to me!"

"Doesn't *my* opinion matter?" Cassie cried.

He looked down at her solemnly, his blue eyes glowing like the center of a flame. "Only if you can love me for what I am."

"A sheepman," she spat, suddenly on her feet, the book sliding to the porch with a clunk.

"That's right, a sheepman who can make you feel like this!"

He hauled her into his arms and plundered her mouth with his, taking everything she wanted to give him and more while she clung to him, lost in the onslaught of emotion. Her body responded instinctively, heart thundering and blood roaring while her bones seemed to melt from the heat that blazed between them. Just when she thought she was completely lost, he thrust her away and held her at arm's length.

"Does Buck make you feel like that? Think about it, Cassie. You'll be married for the rest of your life. That's a long time to sleep beside the wrong man!"

Why couldn't he understand? "I just can't!" she cried helplessly.

His handsome face twisted with the same kind of pain

that tore at her heart, and then he was gone. Without his hands to hold her up, she sank back down into her chair and watched him ride away, out of her life forever.

Duncan was right. The rest of her life *was* too long to spend with the wrong man. Who could stand fifty years of being stirred up the way she'd been ever since she'd met him? Who could stand fifty years of having everybody hate you for raising sheep? And who could stand fifty years of living with a man who didn't even love you enough to give them up? Not Cassie, that was for sure. Everything had been so simple before he'd come along, and it could be again, too. All she had to do was forget all about Duncan Ferguson and everything could be like it was before. Which was just what she wanted. She was sure of it now. After a while, she probably wouldn't even miss him. She was sure of that, too.

Of course, for *everything* to be back the way it was before, she'd have to get Buck over his mad so they could get married like they'd planned. *That* would show Duncan Ferguson just how important he was to her! Cassie spent most of the next day trying to figure out how to do it, but she still hadn't come up with anything when her pa called out to her that Buck was riding up. Pa hadn't said a word about what had happened between her and Duncan, but he'd been looking at her funny ever since, like he expected her to tell him something. Well, she didn't have anything to tell, or at least she wouldn't until she'd seen Buck.

Nervously, she smoothed her dress and fluffed her hair and tried a smile on for size. It felt wooden. She let it slide away as she went out onto the porch to meet him. She heard her father saying, "Did you get tired of eating your own cooking?"

"I'd like to speak to Cassie," Buck replied stiffly. Apparently, he wasn't in the mood for joking around. Well, neither was Cassie.

"Why don't you come inside, Buck," she suggested, holding the screen door open for him. No use letting all the cowboys watch what was going to happen.

Buck stepped past her into the front room. Pa said, "I reckon there's something in the barn I better see about."

Well, she couldn't blame him for not wanting to be around to hear this either.

Buck didn't sit down, but he did take his hat off. He held it awkwardly in front of his chest, like he was a visiting preacher come to ask for a donation and a little embarrassed about having to ask. Suddenly, Cassie noticed how dressed up he was. He wore his best shirt and stiff new jeans and he'd polished his boots to a shine. Even his battered hat had been brushed. She blinked in surprise.

"Buck, I—" she began nervously, but he cut her off.

"Everybody's talking about how you helped out that sheepman. They're saying you're sweet on him."

"That ain't true!" she cried. She might have been once, but she wasn't anymore. She couldn't love a man who raised sheep, could she?

"It ain't?" Buck asked. He looked suspicious, but she thought he also looked hopeful. Was it possible? Could Buck have come here wanting to make up with her, too?

"Of course it ain't! How could I be sweet on him if I'm marrying you?"

"Are you? Marrying me, I mean," he asked uncertainly, and suddenly everything made sense—the good clothes and him taking off his hat to talk to her. He *had* come to make up with her.

"Well," she said sweetly, "I never said I wasn't. You was the one who walked away the other day." Which was perfectly true.

"That's because you made me so mad, Cassie," he informed her indignantly. "You shamed me by helping that sheepman; and when I told you to come away with me, you shamed me again."

"I didn't mean to!" she said quite truthfully. She hadn't been thinking of Buck at all when she'd decided to help Duncan. "I mean, I never thought of it that way."

"You should've; and if we're getting married, you better never do it again."

"Oh, I won't!" she promised. Why would she want to shame her husband, after all?

"And you'll have to do what I tell you from now on. No more sneaking around behind my back, like when you warned Ferguson about the raid."

"I only did that to protect *you!*" she insisted, almost believing it herself.

Buck frowned. "I never knowed you was so headstrong, Cassie. I can't have no wife of mine going off and doing things I don't approve."

"I wouldn't!" she promised rashly.

"Or disagreeing with me, either. If we're married, we gotta think alike. You gotta stand by me, like the Bible says."

"I would!" Cassie promised even more rashly. Everything was going to be all right. She could see it in his broad face, which had lightened with relief.

"I'll take care of you, Cassie. You'll see. And you won't never have to worry about what to think or what to do, because I'll tell you everything you need to know. We'll be a team, you and me."

Cassie nodded vigorously. Yes, yes, this was what she wanted, a life with no surprises and nothing to be ashamed of. As Buck's wife, she'd have the respect of the entire county. No one would ever look at her with pity or disdain, the way they would if she married a sheepherder.

"Oh, Cassie," Buck said, smiling real big and scooping her up into a bear hug. For a second she remembered how Duncan had hugged her just like this the night she'd awakened him to tell him the weather had changed, but she ruthlessly blotted out the memory. She'd never think of Duncan Ferguson again. Her life was with Buck now.

And she'd be happy, too. She'd be happy if it killed her.

The days passed quickly in a flurry of activity. Cassie had to clean and cook and sew to get ready for the wedding. She'd been caught short since she'd wasted a lot of time worrying about whether there would even *be* a wedding or not, and now she had to work extra hard. Some of the ladies came to help, her friend Abby among them, and Abby spent the night with her that last night.

Abby sat on the bed while Cassie packed up her belongings. Tomorrow she would be moving out of the only home she had ever known and into Buck's house. She would be his wife for the rest of her life. Cassie tried to scare up a quiver of excitement at the prospect, but couldn't quite manage it. Which was fine, she decided. She wasn't marrying Buck because she wanted excitement. She was marrying him because she *didn't* want it!

Abby was chattering away, something about the cake and how pretty it was, when Cassie opened her bottom drawer and found the book Duncan had given her. Her heart stopped at the sight of the pretty red leather nestled down there where she'd hidden it away among the things she seldom used. She hadn't looked at it since, hadn't let herself even think about it and all the things he'd promised her that day. Things she'd never even dreamed about before.

Things that could never, ever be.

She slammed the drawer shut. "I'll finish this up tomorrow. I'm too tired now," she told Abby, picking up the lamp and carrying it to the bedside table. She hoped Abby couldn't see that her hands were shaking.

Abby snuggled down under the covers as Cassie took off her robe and blew out the lamp.

"Just think," Abby was saying as Cassie climbed into the bed beside her. "Tomorrow night you'll be getting into bed with Buck!"

Cassie's heart froze in her chest as Abby dissolved into girlish giggles. Cassie hadn't thought about that, hadn't let herself think about it; but now Duncan's warning came back to her: The rest of her life *was* a long time to sleep beside the wrong man.

But Buck wasn't the wrong man; Duncan was! She'd already decided that, hadn't she?

"What do you think it'll be like?" Abby whispered when Cassie was beside her in the bed.

Cassie didn't want to think about it at all. "I don't know."

"Is Buck romantic? When he kisses you, I mean. Does he make you feel all tingly inside?"

"Don't be a goose!" Cassie snapped. She'd felt that way once and decided she didn't like it.

"That's how Gus makes me feel," Abby confided. Gus was Abby's sweetheart. "Once he even put his hand inside my bodice. I slapped him, of course, but it felt so *good!* He said when we're married, we'll do all sorts of things that feel even better!"

"Abby, I'm tired," Cassie said through a throat that felt awfully tight. "I need to get some sleep."

"You'll need it 'cause you'll probably be up most of the night tomorrow!" Abby teased, dissolving into giggles again.

But long after Abby had rolled over and gone to sleep

herself, Cassie lay awake, staring up into the darkness and wondering if she weren't making a terrible mistake.

When she woke at dawn the next morning, she was sure of it. Today was her wedding day, and she should have been happy. Instead her stomach felt like it was filled with lead and her head ached and her muscles were sore, as if she'd been beaten.

But no one gave her any time to think. The ladies who had come to help took charge of getting everything ready and making sure she was bathed and dressed and primped and curled.

"It's natural to be nervous," one of the women told her gently as she was pinning on her veil.

"Good heavens," Abby observed. "She's almost as white as her dress."

"If you feel like you're going to faint, just take deep breaths," another woman advised.

But Cassie wasn't afraid of fainting. In fact, she would have welcomed the oblivion. But she stayed all too conscious as the preparations reached a climax and suddenly it was time for her to walk down the aisle.

It wasn't really an aisle, of course, since they were being married in her front yard because the church was too small to hold all the friends and neighbors who had come. But it was time nonetheless. She met her father in the front room of the house. They were supposed to go out the front door and march down the steps and out between the groups of guests to where Buck and the preacher were waiting. Abby was her maid of honor, and she was fluttering around the door, looking out to see if they should go yet.

Her father looked handsome in his suit, although Cassie could see the stiff collar was uncomfortable. "Oh, Pa," she said, wishing she knew the words to use to tell him of her fears.

"It ain't too late to change your mind, Cassie-girl," he said softly, for her ears alone.

"What?"

"I said it ain't too late to change your mind. You just ain't acting like a bride should act. Haven't been, as a matter of fact. I been thinking maybe you're sorry and would like to back out."

"I couldn't!" she protested. "What would people think?"

Her father gave her a pitying look. "I thought I raised you better'n that! What do you care what people think? You've only got to worry about yourself, and you've got to do what will make *you* happy. Sure, you're worried about embarrassing Buck, and that's a bad thing, but just think how much worse it'd be for him to be married to a woman who don't love him."

"But everybody's waiting!" she cried.

"It ain't too late until the preacher pronounces you man and wife."

"It's time!" Abby called excitedly.

And when Cassie saw Abby's face, she knew that's how *she* should feel. Happy and singing inside, not terrified. But then she thought of what would happen if she refused to go out. How everyone would start whispering and murmuring. They'd start talking about her and they'd be talking about her for the rest of her life. And she'd shame Buck. Hadn't she promised never to do that again?

"Cassie?" her father said.

Cassie pulled herself up straight. "Let's go, Pa."

"Are you sure?"

"I'm sure."

She didn't look at him, though, because she was afraid he'd see the lie in her eyes and call her on it. She'd go through with this because she'd promised and because it was what she wanted, what she'd always wanted.

She didn't need to tingle inside or feel joy just because her husband walked into the room, did she? It was more important to be able to hold her head up, wasn't it?

But as she walked down the aisle dividing the two groups of people she had known her entire life and she saw the familiar faces gazing at her, she began to doubt. How important was it to have them look at her with respect if she didn't respect herself? If she were living a lie? If she were married to a man she didn't love? If she had turned away the man she did love because she was ashamed of him?

And then she saw Buck waiting for her, his broad shoulders straining against the fabric of his new suit, his familiar face set with determination. He was going to think for her. He was going to tell her what to do. She would have a safe, boring life with a man she didn't love.

And that was when she knew she couldn't do it. She couldn't do it to herself, and she certainly couldn't do it to Buck. Pa was right. Better to shame him now than make him miserable forever.

The preacher was saying something, words that had no meaning to her now. Cassie would have to break in, would have to stop him. She didn't like to be rude, but she had no choice. And then she heard him say, "If anybody can give a reason why these two here shouldn't be joined together, let him speak now or forever hold his peace."

Of course! She'd forgotten! This was the time, the very last chance for someone to change their mind.

Cassie turned to Buck. "I'm sorry," she began, but another voice cut her off.

"Wait!"

Cassie and everyone else turned to where Duncan Ferguson had stepped out of the crowd into the aisle. Cassie gaped at him, and she heard Buck swear under his breath.

"Young fella," the preacher tried, but Duncan cut him off, too.

"Cassandra, I'll do what you asked me. I'll do whatever you want if you'll marry me."

Cassie couldn't even remember what she'd asked him to do, nor did she care. All she cared about was that he was here and he was even more handsome than she remembered and she loved him with all her heart. But before she could say so, Buck took off after him, lumbering down the aisle and roaring like a turpentined bear.

Cassie screamed at him to stop, but everybody else was yelling, too, so nobody heard; and then it was too late. He was going to tear Duncan Ferguson apart.

Cassie threw down her flowers and snatched up her skirts, ready to race after him; but before she'd taken two steps, Duncan reared back and slugged Buck smack in the stomach.

The air went out of him with a whoosh and his eyes bugged out with surprise, and then Duncan brought up his other fist and slammed it square into Buck's jaw. The big man went down like a pole-axed steer and never even twitched.

For a long second, nobody moved or even breathed. Cassie just stared, her jaw hanging open, her heart stopped dead in her chest.

Then somebody asked, "Where'n hell did you learn to fight like that?"

Duncan, who was flexing his fingers gingerly, grinned and said, "I did a little boxing in college."

Then he looked up and saw Cassie staring at him. He stiffened defensively, still not quite sure he'd done the right thing. "I'm sorry I ruined your wedding, but I couldn't let you . . . I mean it, Cassandra. I'll give up the sheep. I'll do whatever it takes to—"

He never got to finish because Cassie had thrown her arms around him and stopped him with a kiss. A whoop went up from the crowd. They were loving this. This was better than a circus. Better even than a two-week revival. They'd be talking about Cassie Plummer's wedding for the next hundred years.

And Cassie wouldn't care. She knew now that it didn't matter *what* people said about her as long as she was happy. As long as she wasn't married to the wrong man.

By the time she broke the kiss, the whoops had turned to cheers. Duncan looked almost as surprised as Buck had when Duncan punched the wind out of him, but Cassie had one more shocker up her sleeve.

"I don't care about the sheep," she told him. "You can raise all the sheep you want. I was a fool. Can you forgive me?"

He smiled that beautiful smile. "Well, now, I might need one more kiss to persuade me," he allowed. Cassie was only too happy to pay the penalty.

"Ron, are you gonna let your daughter marry a sheep-herder?" Cassie heard someone ask.

"Shoot, I might even take up raising sheep myself," her father replied jovially. "Lots of ranchers have started running sheep and cattle together to make out in hard times."

"You don't say!"

"Are we gonna have a wedding here or not?" someone else wanted to know.

Cassie reluctantly pulled her mouth from Duncan's and asked the question with her eyes.

His smile was almost blinding. "We better get it done before you change your mind again."

"I won't change my mind, not ever," she promised.

"What about Buck?" someone in the crowd asked, reminding them all that they had an unconscious former-groom lying at their feet.

Buck groaned.

"He'll be awful mad when he wakes up," Cassie said in alarm.

"We'll take him home," one of his men said, and several of them came forward. They were grinning but trying not to. Plainly, they'd enjoyed the show but knew they shouldn't let on they had. "We'll put him in the wagon. Just give us a minute to get away before you start."

It took three of them to drag Buck off.

Cassie turned back to Duncan. "I was going to stop the wedding myself. I couldn't go through with it."

"I know, I heard you," Duncan said, his eyes as bright as the Texas sky. "That's what gave me the courage to speak up. I wanted to; that's why I came, but I'd already decided I couldn't embarrass you like that, even though it was going to kill me to see you marry somebody else. But when you—"

"You two'll have a lot of years to hash this out," Cassie's father said. "Meanwhile, all these folks are standing out in the hot sun. Let's get this over with so they can get themselves a drink."

The crowd cheered, and this time Cassie walked down the aisle with her groom. Some might think he was the wrong man, but Cassie knew better. And she was going to spend the next fifty years proving it to them.

Taylor—made Romance From Zebra Books

WHISPERED KISSES   (3830, $4.99/5.99)
Beautiful Texas heiress Laura Leigh Webster never imagined that her biggest worry on her African safari would be the handsome Jace Elliot, her tour guide. Laura's guardian, Lord Chadwick Hamilton, warns her of Jace's dangerous past; she simply cannot resist the lure of his strong arms and the passion of his *Whispered Kisses*.

KISS OF THE NIGHT WIND   (3831, $4.99/$5.99)
Carrie Sue Strover thought she was leaving trouble behind her when she deserted her brother's outlaw gang to live her life as schoolmarm Carolyn Starns. On her journey, her stagecoach was attacked and she was rescued by handsome T.J. Rogue. T.J. plots to have Carrie lead him to her brother's cohorts who murdered his family. T.J., however, soon succumbs to the beautiful runaway's charms and loving caresses.

FORTUNE'S FLAMES   (3825, $4.99/$5.99)
Impatient to begin her journey back home to New Orleans, beautiful Maren James was furious when Captain Hawk delayed the voyage by searching for stowaways. Impatience gave way to uncontrollable desire once the handsome captain searched *her* cabin. He was looking for illegal passengers; what he found was wild passion with a woman he knew was unlike all those he had known before!

PASSIONS WILD AND FREE   (3828, $4.99/$5.99)
After seeing her family and home destroyed by the cruel and hateful Epson gang, Randee Hollis swore revenge. She knew she found the perfect man to help her—gunslinger Marsh Logan. Not only strong and brave, Marsh had the ebony hair and light blue eyes to make Randee forget her hate and seek the love and passion that only he could give her.

Available wherever paperbacks are sold, or order direct from the Publisher. Send cover price plus 50¢ per copy for mailing and handling to Penguin USA, P.O. Box 999, c/o Dept. 17109, Bergenfield, NJ 07621. Residents of New York and Tennessee must include sales tax. DO NOT SEND CASH.